Give My EVERYTHING

Hermosa Beach Series 3

JILLIAN LIOTA

This book is a work of fiction. While reference might be made to actual historical events or existing locations, the names, characters, places and incidents are either the product of the author's imagination or are used fictitiously, and any resemblance to any actual persons, living or dead, business establishments, events, or locales is entirely coincidental.

Copyright © 2020 by Jillian Liota

All rights reserved. In accordance with the U.S. Copyright Act of 1976, the scanning, uploading, and electronic sharing of any part of this book without the permission from the author is unlawful piracy and theft of the author's intellectual property. Thank you for your support of the author's rights.

Love Is A Verb Books

Book Cover Design and Layout by Jillian Liota

Editing by C. Marie

Formatting by Jillian Liota

Cover Photo © iStockPhoto.com/Portfolio/g-stockstudio

ISBN 978-1-952549-02-1
ISBN 978-1-952549-00-7 (eBook)
ISBN 978-1-952549-01-4 (kindle)

For the survivors:

You are strong and brave and resilient

Don't let anyone *ever* make you
believe any different

<3

Trigger Warning

Give My Everything contains content associated with the very difficult topic of rape and sexual assault.

Please proceed with caution.

Chapter One
BEN

"I'm sorry, I don't think I heard you correctly," she says, letting out a huff of laughter that belies the confusion I can hear in her voice. "Can you say that just...one more time? Because it sounded for a second there like you said..."

"I think we should get married."

She freezes, her confusion morphing into completely puzzled curiosity.

It's kind of like the look you see on a teenager's face when they sit through sex ed for the first time: slight discomfort, mostly bewilderment—but definitely a thread of interest.

Remmy's reaction isn't surprising to me. Not at all.

To her, my statement comes out of nowhere. Completely unbidden. Without any kind of depth of thought as to what it would mean for her. For me.

For us.

She doesn't know the careful planning that's occurred before this moment, the deliberation I've gone through in determining what should be my next steps in moving toward my ultimate goal.

Remmy may not have been my first choice—or even a true consideration—until just moments ago when I first sat down with her on the rooftop bar at my restaurant, but that's because I didn't know she *could* be a consideration.

And the longer she sits there just staring at me, the more I am convinced Remmy is without a doubt the most perfect person to play this game with me, the ultimate companion in a game of retribution that has been a long time coming.

I relax back in my chair, my body tilted just slightly to the side as my fingers brush over my five-day beard growth.

The facial hair was Ivy's idea. My baby sister told me I look too scary with my face cleanly shaven every day and said I should soften myself with a beard.

Like our brother's.

Though why she thinks Wyatt's vagabond-esque appearance makes him look any amount of affable is beyond me.

She doesn't seem to mind Lucas' hair-free face, although he is nothing but soft and silly and playful, that special kind of charming only boy bands can pull off, the kind that enthralls young girls. I can see why she doesn't find him...what were her exact words about me?

Too severe.

Quite the opinion from a thirteen-year-old, but that's Ivy.

She might come across to many as a dainty little wallflower hoping to fade into the crowd, but I've been watching her bloom over the past year or so, her voice getting louder and stronger without even speaking a word.

So I'm trying out the facial hair, even if it is itchy as shit.

Remmy remains silent across from me, though her posture has relaxed just slightly. She doesn't look ready to bolt out of her seat, which I consider a definite positive when taking into account her shocked reaction to my proposal.

"Nothing to say?" I taunt playfully as I reach out and take hold of a coaster that sits on the table between us. Tapping it twice, I continue. "I would have assumed you'd have quite a strong opinion. That *is* your style, after all."

Her eyes narrow slightly before she relaxes her face just as quickly.

Learning to put on a mask comes from years of conditioning, though hers isn't as good as most of the women in Hermosa Beach.

Any other woman who was irritated at me wouldn't have allowed that tiny wrinkle between her brow. Her face would have stayed pleasantly neutral, regardless of how much anger was brewing beneath her skin.

That's women for you—master manipulators who hide their true intentions with a smile and a hand down your pants.

Not Remmy, though.

She's never been able to conceal how she really feels. Sure, she's quick to shift her facial expressions into what she thinks should be shown, but she's *never* fast enough.

Ever.

She and I don't know each other well, but I *do* know she's got a rebellious streak in her that has driven her mother mad. I also know she dated Lucas for the better part of a decade even though she never planned to be with him forever, and that she carries more secrets behind those hazel eyes of hers than anyone else would ever be able to guess.

And that's just from my casual observations. That comes without even trying to know her or understand her or her motivations.

Because that's who I am: a quiet observer, a man on the sidelines who holds the playbook. I'm not the battle-weary military man on the front lines covered in dirt and blood, but the general dictating war games with only a few words.

And right now, Remmy is a wildcard. She's something I didn't see coming, without a doubt, but a true gamesman knows how to use a wildcard at the exact right time in the exact right way.

If she'll let me.

So now it's my job to convince her to let me use her.

"Come on, Remmy. Say something to me. Your silence is unnerving," I say, giving her a charming smile.

She rolls her eyes and shifts in her chair, crossing her arms.

"I don't know what world you live in, *Bennie*," she says, using the nickname that has become the namesake of my restaurant, "but in my world, two people don't just randomly decide to get married without knowing each other at all. As ancient as our parents can be at times, even *they* don't force arranged marriages."

My smile remains in place as I pick up my glass of scotch and take a sip. She has so many tells, and she doesn't even realize it.

"So my answer is no," she continues. "Definitely...definitely not."

Everything about her right now tells me she wants to ask more, get more information, possibly consider the idea.

I know because I took the few moments when she was speaking to me earlier—about breaking up with Lucas, about her pregnancy, about her parents—to rationalize things for her from every angle. The positives from her vantage point are substantial.

"You know, you said no, but I don't think that's what you really mean," I reply, enjoying the way her jaw clenches in irritation. "And I'll be honest, I don't know that you've truly thought this opportunity through."

Her eyebrows lift. "Opportunity?" she huffs out, incredulity tinging her tone.

"Because if you had—if you'd *really* thought it through—you'd see how many ways this would make your life so much easier and simpler."

She shifts again in her seat, uncrosses her arms, and leans forward. "Fine. Tell me, oh wise Mr. Calloway, tell me all the ways this will save my desperate, damsel self. Because from where *I'm* sitting, you sound like an absolute lunatic."

I smirk.

All I needed was her approval to share my reasonings and I know she'll see it from my perspective. Because Remmy is one of those fake-rebel types.

Shove something in her face and she'll push back, her desire not to go with someone else's flow overpowering her actual interests and aspirations. She's the woman who would never be willing to go along with something if she didn't want to do it in the first place, regardless of whether her perspective has changed on whether or not that particular thing could help her in any way.

She's a fighter. A constant, relentless fighter.

And the only way to reason with a fighter is to make them feel like they're in control.

Hence my need for her to agree to hear me out.

It means she's in charge. That it was her choice to consider what I have to say.

Even if I've orchestrated every step so far.

"Correct me if I'm wrong, but you've pretty much just told me your parents will be kicking you out of the family if you come to them as an unwed pregnant mom, correct?"

She watches me but doesn't say anything.

"Not only that, I know for a fact your mother loved Lucas since I've heard her talk about her 'future son-in-law' on multiple occasions. So, I'll paint a picture of her perspective for you. You went to a subpar collegiate institution, rarely came home, and graduated late without any announcement or fanfare. Then, once you *do* come home, you're pregnant, have broken up with the man your mom thinks you're going to marry, and have no other father as a potential support for you, a young, unemployed woman who is about to be a single mother."

I drag my tie through my fingers as I watch her sitting in front of me, her irritation bristling and bubbling for anyone to see.

She looks like she wants to glare daggers at me, but there is disappointment hiding in the depths of her eyes, maybe directed herself.

"Remind me to never have you paint a portrait of my life ever again," she chides as her gaze slips off into the distance.

I ignore her irritation and focus on convincing her that this is the right move—the *best* move. Because if she agrees to this, all my patience will not be for nothing.

"If you marry me," I continue, "*all* of that goes away. Every single bit. No offense to Lucas, but a Calloway is a much bigger fish in our humble little sea…"

Remmy scoffs and rolls her eyes but doesn't protest or interrupt me.

"…not to mention the fact that a marriage and a baby could be tied up nicely without any significant complications. Marry me, and I take full responsibility—for you, and for the baby."

I pause, giving her a moment to digest it. Then I go in for the kill.

"You're no longer the unwanted single mother. You're a fiancée with a future as Mrs. Calloway and a child who will be taken care of for the rest of its life."

Her eyes reconnect with mine.

"And what do you get out of this?" she asks.

If I'm honest, I wasn't certain she would think to ask this of me. When someone is drowning and somebody else reaches out to save them, the person gasping for breath doesn't often pause to ask why.

Because you're drowning, of course.

But Remmy is much more shrewd than many others. It's likely one of the reasons she has problems disguising her facial expressions. She's too busy examining others to worry about whether her lip is curling or her eyebrows are arched.

Her attentiveness is actually a point of caution for me. As perfect a candidate as Remmy is for the role of future Mrs. Calloway, there is some value to marrying someone with a mind that stays a little blurrier on a regular basis. The sharper you are, the faster you can cut through the bullshit, and I'm not sure I need those kinds of eyes watching my every move.

Not when I'd rather handle my business undetected.

"Me?" I repeat back to her. "My motives are my own."

Her eyes narrow, and I see my mistake instantly. Her focus shifts, no longer having asked a flippant question to abate her own curiosity, but having inquired about something I don't want to address.

Shit.

I pause, let out a lingering sigh. "Although, I guess...you knowing wouldn't be so bad," I tack on, tapping my fingers along the tabletop while trying to douse the fire of interest I see flickering inside of her. "I'm at a point where my parents are both vocalizing their desire for me to get married."

A lie.

My parents don't give one shit about who I'm in a relationship with as long as I don't cause any more problems for the Calloway name.

I've caused enough of those in the past.

Too bad for them, I'm not even close to being done.

"I'm regularly accosted by women they deem appropriate to marry and settle down with, and I'd like them to kindly back off as I have no interest in any of the people they've brought forward."

That last part is true, at least it was on my mother's part back before...'the scandal'.

That's what she calls it: *the scandal.*

It makes me want to laugh and roll my eyes and continue right on without a worry.

Ever since then, she hasn't pushed anyone toward me, hasn't tried to get me to settle down. She hasn't given me any attention at all, if I'm honest.

Both of my parents ignore me now, though my mother is the one who called me an embarrassment and uninvited me indefinitely from all functions where she would be attending with 'family', aka my sister and brother. My father still demands appearances from me on occasion to represent the Calloway name, especially while Wyatt was in college at the other end of the state.

I go along with his expectations while I lie in wait, allowing him to believe he has *any* control over my life. He won't know the reality of the situation until I deem it necessary.

Remmy watches me, taking in my explanation with that perceptive mind of hers. Apparently, what I've said has satiated her desire to know more.

"I don't know that you've thought everything through," she finally says, "as wonderfully logical as your reasons might be. This isn't just marrying some dimwitted socialite." She leans forward and drops her voice. "I'm pregnant."

"I know that."

"Do you?" She grits her teeth. "Do you really? Because this is a real baby, one who will cry and scream and shit all over your house and your perfect, fancy fucking life. And I doubt it's much of a secret that I'm a handful, too. So I just...don't know. I don't know if you're really prepared for what this would mean. For you, for me—for either of us. I can't jump on board when I feel like you have no idea what you're getting yourself into. I've made that mistake before."

Silence settles between us as her words wash over me.

As foolish as I think she is to shoot me down, there's a part of me that's impressed as well.

I've never thought of Remmy as anything other than one of those dimwitted socialites she so clearly detests, and in the past thirty minutes, she's demonstrated herself to be quite the inquisitive, curious, and thoughtful sparring partner.

I allow myself to consider her points for a moment—just a brief one. I try to see things from where she sees them, because you can't control a chessboard if you don't understand the purpose and perspective of each piece in play.

"Is that your only concern?" I ask, folding my hands together. "You think I haven't thought the baby part through?"

She sits in silence, assessing me, before she nods.

Interesting. That means I definitely have her on the hook, means she's finding enough value in what I'm saying to actually mull it over in that very busy mind of hers.

"I've gotta go," she says, cutting off my thoughts before I can identify the best way to convince her that a baby is actually—in my mind—the best part about this deal, the least worrisome. It is for me, at least.

Wyatt and I took care of my sister when she was a baby. We changed diapers and fed her bottles when my mother was out on the town and too self-absorbed to be worried about breastfeeding.

Being a father is actually something I'm truly looking forward to in life, something I've wanted for quite some time.

It's finding the right mother that concerns me. The idea of finding a wife. Kids are innocent and perfect until we corrupt them.

I can manage a baby.

What I *can't* manage is a woman who plans to use me without my knowledge, betray me when it suits her, stab me in the back and leave me behind, bleeding on the ground.

Which is why this arrangement would be perfect with Remmy. We would both go into it knowing exactly what it is.

A chance for us both to use each other for what we need. A solution to both of our problems.

Even if I don't plan on sharing with Remmy *just* how perfectly she fits into my plans.

But before I can vocalize any of that, she stands abruptly, her chair grinding across the concrete floor of the rooftop where we sit overlooking the pier and promenade.

"Where are you going?" I ask, confused about her sudden desire to flee. "There's still a lot to talk about."

But she just shakes her head. "I don't think so. I think...I think you're insane for even suggesting this idea, and I don't want any part of it."

My shoulders drop when I realize my plan has failed. It doesn't happen often, so when I actually do get pushed down, it tends to knock the wind out of me for a bit longer than I'd like.

Perhaps another woman would be a better fit.

"I'll see you around, Bennie," she says, her voice taking on a soft quality I doubt she shows very often. "And thanks for considering how you might be able to save me," she adds, "even if it isn't going to work out."

Then she steps over and places a kiss on my cheek before maneuvering through the other tables and down the stairs to get back to ground level.

I stay in my seat for a while longer, my eyes shifting down to the beach where the Pier-to-Pier Swim is still finishing up, the weakest of the swimmers dragging their exhausted bodies out of the water and making for the finish line.

They look drained to the last drop, like they could pass out there in the sand as they crawl toward their end goal.

Watching them spikes my pulse with a hint of inspiration.

A reminder that you rarely get what you want on the first try, with the first attempt, on that first plunge into the ocean.

I know marrying Remmy Wallace is a decision that would benefit both of us in more ways than she can possibly imagine, even if I wasn't prepared to share my true reasonings with her just moments ago.

And if I'm planning on getting what I want, I just need to work a little harder, do a better job of convincing her, find the right method to show her exactly what we could be.

Because she really is the perfect woman.

To help me with my ultimate revenge, that is.

With that thought, I finish my drink in one long swallow and head back to work.

"Ingrid, you can't tell a customer to get up and get their own drink just because you're irritated with them."

My newest waitress gives me a smile that falls somewhere between plastic and nauseated.

"I'm so sorry, Mr. Calloway. It won't happen again."

It will happen again.

I know it.

She knows it.

The only thing I *don't* know in this moment is if I'm willing to let her go during her probationary period because of this, or if I'm going to hold on to her because I'm shorthanded.

That's the thing about owning a beachside restaurant, no

matter how successful it is: there is always a summer rush and a need for more staff. Once August rolls around, though, employees start putting in their notice as they make plans for the off season.

Two of my regular servers are heading back to college in September.

Another is leaving to work as a manager at her mother's store.

I have a handful of bartenders who were hired to deal with the influx of summer tourists, who will be leaving soon for whatever else is on the horizon.

A sous chef is moving a few hours away to start a job as a head chef at a new restaurant.

And even though all my temporary workers have end dates on September 1st, that's never what ends up happening. They start dropping like flies weeks before then, and my manager and I are left scrambling to hire additional people to cover the load.

We are just creeping into August, and I'm already starting to feel the effects of it.

Which brings me to Ingrid.

I hired her because she had waitressing experience on her resume, four years of working at a beachside hot spot in San Diego.

Too bad it was apparent on her first day that she hadn't been completely honest. Most of her waitressing knowledge is probably from YouTube or TikTok or whatever young people are using these days.

"Good," I finally say, accepting the fact that I need Ingrid, at least for a little bit longer. "If it does, you'll likely find yourself out of a job, got it?"

Ingrid nods, smiles, and then spins on her heels, heading out of my office and through the kitchen, back out to the main floor to continue terrorizing customers.

I rest my head in my hands, wishing I'd done something different with my life. Never in my wildest dreams did I anticipate that owning a business would be like this.

Scratch that—owning a *restaurant.*

Customer service jobs are all the same. You bend over backward to give someone what they want or need so they return to you. I knew that going into this industry.

The problem is that I never pictured myself in a role like this one.

I was never supposed to stay here. I was supposed to hire a

manager, get things settled, and then move on to build my next restaurant. I planned to take the subsequent steps toward creating the culinary empire I've been planning and plotting for the past decade.

There's some famous quote about making plans, right? Woody Allen or something. If you want to make God laugh, tell him your plans.

That's why my life is a joke right now.

I had plans—strong ones, a thought-out and well-designed vision for my future.

Until my father decided to stab me in the back.

Now, I've committed to staying here until I can finish the war he started, even if it means delaying my professional goals longer than I intended.

Which is why this wildcard with Remmy is so essential.

It has the potential to turn things around and get them back on course.

Get me moving in the direction I want to go instead of where I currently sit, floundering and waiting for what's next.

"Got a second?"

The sweet voice has me lifting my head and turning to the door, where my younger brother Wyatt's girlfriend stands with a big smile on her face.

"Hey, Hannah," I say, letting out a sigh and waving her in to take a seat. "What do you need?"

She maintains the smile, and I instantly know this is a request I'll probably grant for her, even though I would tell anyone else to take a hike.

"Well, I wanted to ask you a favor, and I totally understand if you say no."

I wave her concern away. "What is it?"

She bites her bottom lip. "I'm wondering if I can be taken off the schedule for the last week of the month."

My eyebrows rise. "The entire week?"

Hannah nods. "Wyatt said he has a surprise and he won't tell me what it is, but he wants me to take a week off."

I let out a low chuckle. Leave it to my younger brother to be a closet romantic who whisks his girlfriend off on a week-long vacation.

"I know it's last minute, and if you can't make it work, I totally understand. I can always trade some shifts and we can do something shorter," she says, her words coming out in a rush.

I have to bite back a smile at her nervous rambling.

I love my brother, but I never would have pictured him with a girl like Hannah. She's all soft and sweet and caring, always willing to go the extra mile and accommodate others. I've only had her on staff for three months, but I can already tell she's going to be the best employee I'll ever have—hardworking, thoughtful, positive.

Wyatt always seemed like the kind of guy who would live his bachelor life for as long as he could, so his commitment to her and how much he loves her...it was definitely a surprise.

A happy one, of course, but a surprise nonetheless.

I'm not usually a fan of surprises. It means I'm not adequately prepared or haven't thought through all the possibilities.

With Hannah, though, I'll make an exception.

Because they really do seem happy together.

"Hannah, it's fine," I say, resigning myself to keeping Ingrid on for a few more weeks at minimum, regardless of whatever other shenanigans she might pull in the future. "I'll make it work. Go on your trip with Wyatt."

She beams at me. "Oh my gosh, really? Thanks so much, Ben. Seriously. You're the best."

I shake my head and give her a grin. "Just don't tell any of the others. I don't want them to think I'm getting soft."

Hannah giggles. "Oh come on. I've seen you with Ivy—I know you're a big softy in there."

Her mention of my baby sister—*her* sister, too—has me rolling my eyes. "You don't get to pull the Ivy card, okay? Not fair."

She stands from her chair and picks up her purse off the ground.

"Your shift over?"

Hannah nods. "Yeah. I'm just the early rotation today. Eleanor and I are going to the movies tonight."

I've noticed Hannah and Eleanor have gotten close, but I didn't realize they hung out outside of work. "Well, have fun."

"Thanks again, Ben."

With that, Hannah heads out the door, and I turn back to look at my computer screen, at the financials from this quarter and the purchase orders for ingredients and alcohol.

What a tangled web our lives are. How strange this summer

has been.

And now, with this potential tangent with Remmy, it's just going to continue to become much more convoluted.

Chapter Two
REMMY

Julia stares at me from the doorway to my bedroom as I slowly fold my laundry. She's had this same expression on her face ever since I moved home a few weeks ago, the first true time I've been back under her watchful gaze since I left for college.

"I promise I'm not trying to take your job from you," I joke. "I just...started to enjoy doing it, alright?"

She lets out a huff and continues down the hall, mumbling in Spanish—something that sounds suspiciously like "*Crazy girl, I'll never understand you.*"

I grin to myself and finish sorting through my underwear, folding them neatly into little squares and stacking them one on top of the next.

When I went away to college, everything changed.

Everything.

So many of the people I went to school with growing up allowed everything in their lives to stay the same when they left home.

They went to Ivy League schools that provided them with suite-style rooms and maids, with door service for laundry and healthy meal prep and a thousand other things.

I kind of went off the beaten path, I guess.

What Ben said last weekend about me moving away to go to 'a subpar collegiate institution'—I roll my eyes just thinking about it—was actually true. At least it's true according to most of the people I know.

Including my parents.

I didn't pick an Ivy League. I didn't go to an institute of higher education with some sort of reputation within the community of elite, wealthy families my parents socialize with.

But I went anyway. I ignored their rules, ignored their expectations, ignored their anger at my willingness to break tradition and cultural expectation and did exactly what I wanted.

I chose for myself.

And I fell so hard and so far that I'm astounded I didn't shatter into pieces so irreparable nobody could save me.

Thankfully, I figured out a way to pick myself up and dust myself off, to allow the pain of my mistakes—and the brutal lash of others' envy—to fade into the background as I refocused my energy and attention on something meaningful. I centered my attention on something purposeful, something that gave me hope.

I feel like I'm losing that part of me again, though.

With every day that I'm home, it feels like a little bit of the new version of me fades away, being replaced by the old me that was afraid and angry and didn't truly know herself.

The amount of work that goes into fighting for your own life is staggering. I'm not sure I have the mental fortitude to do it again.

After finishing with my undergarments and tucking them into the top drawer of my dresser, I begin sorting through my pants. Jeans, leggings, skirts. Once that's done, I hang up the few dresses I've worn since I've been back.

I love dresses.

The shorter the better.

They provide easy access when you're feeling high strung and need a guy to help you find the release you need.

Knowing those days are behind me, I let out a sigh as I lift up the deep burgundy Armani dress I wore to The Wave last week. It was a mistake to go in the first place, but for some reason, I love to torture myself.

So I went.

I went and I sat in the corner and watched Lucas and Lennon together. The two of them with our group of friends, all of them smiling and laughing and enjoying themselves like nothing has changed.

There wasn't a single nerve ending in my body that wasn't on high alert. I was equal parts angry and irritated and sad and just...pissed the fuck off.

Until I realized something.

For them, nothing *has* changed.

Not really.

The only thing that's different is that Lucas and Lennon don't have to try to hide how they feel about each other in public. They're free to smile and laugh and enjoy themselves.

And when I realized that—when it finally shifted in my mind that the only thing changed, the only thing different is *me*—I finished my drink and left as quickly as I could, not wanting anyone to see me sitting in the corner like an absolute fucking creep.

I mean, our decision to break up was mutual. Entirely and completely. It just happens to be a reality that he has someone to move on to and I...don't.

Well, if I want to make jokes, I guess I could say I *do* have someone to move on to.

This little parasite that's growing inside of me.

I wince.

I've thought it a few times and always mean it facetiously—kind of—but it still sounds horrible.

Shaking my head, I head into my massive walk-in to hang up the Armani. Then on a whim, I take my favorite black Gucci dress off the hanger and slip it on, posing for myself in the full-length framed mirror that sits at an angle in the corner.

The stretchy fabric fits me like a glove, the hem fitting tightly around my upper thighs. The neck is high and the sleeves are three-quarter length, but the back dips low, low, low, showing off the tattoo that runs down the entire length of my spine.

Probably the most painful thing I've ever done, though I've

heard childbirth will far surpass that.

My favorite part of this dress is the fact that the fabric shimmers. It looks black, but when it catches the light, the underlayer almost glows, undulates. It's so sexy.

And now, looking at myself in the mirror in my favorite dress, I turn to the side and look at my body's profile, at the tiny pooch of a stomach that's *just* beginning to show.

If I focus on sucking in, I can probably hide it for a few more weeks, but I know the inevitable is nearing.

I don't know how much longer I'll be able to fit into my clothes, don't know how long until my body will announce the secret I've been keeping inside of me.

I'm not ready for all the changes coming my way.

Sure, there's the clothing and the body aches and pains I'm learning about as I slowly read through the baby book Lucas gave me.

But I'm also not ready for all the information, for the opinions—about the baby, about my body, about the pregnancy. I'm not ready for anything at all, really.

I'm just...not ready.

"I've always loved that dress on you, *mija*."

I spin at my mother's voice, finding her at the edge of my closet, watching me as I watch myself.

I flush, worrying she saw me with my hands on my lower belly and wondering if she may have figured it out.

That's the thing about holding on to a secret—it doesn't feel like a secret. It feels like a stamp on your forehead that screams the worst part for the world to see. *Slut. Trash. Bitch.*

"You have the body I always wanted when I was younger," she continues, and I let out a quiet sigh of relief. "Long and curvy, like Sofia."

I huff out a laugh and roll my eyes. My mom likes to reference the Colombian celebrity as if they know each other.

She waves a hand at me. "Oh, you know what I mean, Remington. Don't give me that face. I'm talking about real bodies. People aren't skin and bone like the majority of models in the magazines," she says, her voice pitching at the word 'models' like she would discuss a dog's 'wedding'—like the word itself is a complete joke.

"You know 'models' are real people too, right?" I reply,

stepping past her to get out of my closet, returning to my bedroom.

"All I'm saying is that you've got the length and the curves men love," she says on a smile. "You know the Colombian genetics give us a split chance at being the hostess or the help. Thankfully, you're the former."

I roll my eyes again.

My mother, born and raised in Medellín, has this idea that all Colombian women fall into one of two categories. If you're lucky, you get the long legs and the big rack and the throaty voice. Those are the women the strong, sexy Colombian men want to marry, the alpha males who keep your genetics robust and your family lineage on the right path.

Everyone else is 'the help': shorter stature, rounder features, and apparently significantly less likely to find a strong male to procreate with.

She believes she was born into the latter category, but she was lucky enough to find a man to marry her who saw past it, a young American representing his father's business in Medellín for two months. She always tells me she 'snatched him up' before he realized she was 'the help'.

It makes me sad, hearing her talk about it—as if she had to manipulate my dad into wanting her.

But I also know part of what she's saying is true.

You have to work hard to keep a man interested, especially when there are so many other beautiful women in the world—other women who can make them laugh harder, who can keep their asses tighter, have bigger boobs, or know how to give better blowjobs.

It was always my fear with Lucas, though I tried not to think about it too often.

I knew the open relationship was what I wanted, knew it served me and *my* needs.

But I was always worried about how it was serving Lucas, too, whether or not the next person would be the reason I lost him.

And I was right.

I did lose him to someone who makes him laugh more, who fits him better.

Maybe it makes me selfish to think about it this way. Shouldn't I want someone I love to be with the person who fits them the best?

But if I did that, I would end up alone, because the type of broken I am doesn't fit with anyone.

So I had to be selfish. I had to try to keep him, even though I knew deep down it would never work.

I mean, how could I ever see it working with Lucas when I wasn't willing to put on the chastity belt for him, no matter how much I wanted us to make it?

No, I wanted to allow myself the freedom to enjoy my body when and where I wanted to, with Lucas or without.

I'm the only one who gets to control my body.

"You're not planning to wear that *tonight* are you?" my mother asks, almost like she's just considering this for the first time even though I've been moving around my room in it for the past few minutes.

I sigh, knowing I don't have the energy to get into an argument with her today, especially not over something so useless.

"No. I was just trying it on. I was thinking about wearing the green Valentino, the floral one I got in—"

"Rome, yes, I remember. I love that dress on you. Good," she says, giving me a nod of approval. "Your father and I are leaving straight from the club to go to LAX," she tacks on, "so you and Dominic will need to ride separately."

I cross my arms. "What about Mati?" I ask, referring to the younger of my two brothers. Dom and Mati are both a few years older than me.

"Mathias already had plans tonight," she replies, her form sashaying across the room, heading for the door. "We're leaving at seven on the dot. Don't be late."

And then she's gone, taking with her the swirl of motherly overbearingness she brought in when she came into my room.

I love my mom—I truly do—but she's the most controlling person I've ever met, and she bases all her opinions on how 'the family' is supposed to behave.

It's why she was so vocal when I decided what college I was going to and told them I was going to move out. Thankfully, my dad was my supporter, reminding my mom that the younger generations see things differently than her, that we want more freedom and independence.

"Too much freedom and she'll forget where she came from," my mom said, but she relented eventually, allowing me to move away to college even though I know she took it as a personal offense.

I hate how controlling she is, how she wants to dictate everything in my life. It drives me insane.

And it makes me want to show up to dinner tonight in the black Gucci instead of the green Valentino.

But I won't.

Not because I wouldn't dare do it, but because I know this isn't the time.

Sure, I may be the rebellious one of the three of us. Dominic is the one who toes the family line without complaint. Mathias— Mati—is the one who has a job with the family company but only shows up when he has to. A playboy without question, but at least he plays by my parents' rules.

I'm the one who fought her way out of the stifling straightjacket of a life they'd planned for me, and I did so kicking and screaming. I'd rather be on my own and fail spectacularly than follow quietly in their carefully crafted wake.

And look at me now.

I'm exactly what Ben said I am: an unwanted single mother who came home with a broken relationship, an unnamed father, a worthless degree—though my parents don't know that just yet— and no true goals for my future.

God, I sound like some destitute maiden in *Pride and Prejudice* or something.

No, now is not the time to ruffle feathers. That will come soon enough—though in what way, I'm not sure.

Besides, I've been working to calm the angry part of me, to keep her muzzled as I lay my head down each night in my parents' home.

Because I do love them. Immensely. And I know they love me, too. The problem is just how we each see the world.

I think I should have freedom.

They think I should have a husband who chooses to give me freedom.

Okay, maybe not *they*. It's very clearly my mother who pushes for that old-country, old-world, Catholic kind of mentality that women submit to their husbands.

And I know no matter what I do or say, whether I go along with them or fight, whether I bend the rules or break them, my mother just is who she is.

So I have to decide whether I want to swim upstream or quit fighting so hard and just go with the flow.

Which is why a part of me is still strongly considering this…absolutely ridiculous proposition Ben has put in front of me. It's a potential solution to my problems without me having to give in or give up, not really.

It's been nearly a week since our conversation on the rooftop at Bennie's at the Pier, and when I'm not hunched over the toilet, stricken with horrible morning sickness, I'm thinking about what he said to me.

Stripping off the Gucci, I hang it back up in the closet, pulling out the Valentino to breathe while I shower and get ready for my parents' business function.

I may not have been willing to work for the company, but I'm still expected to show up when they tell me to. Because I've been away at college for so long and filled with excuses for not coming home, they're going to expect even more from me now.

More visibility. More attendance. More involvement.

Even though it's one of the things I've tried to avoid like the damn plague.

I crank on the shower and stand under the frigid spray, allowing the cold water to pummel my body while waiting for it to get warmer.

I don't want to go along with the family expectation that I get involved with Wallace Media. I don't want the attention, whether it's on screen, in publication, or behind the scenes.

No matter what kind of pitch they throw my way, there isn't a single job they could give me that would make me happy.

Because that's exactly what it would be: given to me.

They give me *everything*, and now I'm at a point where I don't want shit just handed to me anymore.

My best friend from college, Josslyn, liked to tease me. She poked fun at the poor little rich girl and how hard it is to have everything handed to you in life.

But the only reality I know is my own.

I can try to empathize with people who have a worse lot in life than I do. And I try to, but my reality is still complicated. My world is still filled with uncertainties and fears and nerves and expectations.

Should I not be allowed to have feelings just because my life isn't as hard as someone else's?

Should I be forced to smile every fucking day just because I'm not facing the same inequities others do?

No.

I should be allowed to cry when I'm hurting. I should be allowed to get angry when someone expects me to be something I'm not. I should be given the freedom to rage when someone steals my ability to control my own life, my own self, my own body.

I turn and push my face under the now warm water, allowing myself just a single moment to feel the emotions I've been experiencing in waves since I was fifteen years old, since the day the world as I knew it shifted and morphed into something much darker than I ever would have realized.

I let that younger me take a deep breath for just a moment before I swallow back the tears.

I had an amazing therapist when I was in college who helped me work through a lot of things. She helped me see that once I've sorted through the hardest part of the work, I get to choose who I want to be every day.

So that's what I do.

I choose who I want to be today.

The strong version of me.

The one who is in control of herself and her life.

I wash my hair, a long billowing wave of thick brunette locks I've allowed to grow and grow and grow.

Like a weed.

I love when it's dry and big and full, love how it hangs and swings and wraps around me.

I glance through the glass at the small clock that rests on my counter, cursing when I realize I've wasted too much time in the shower.

Finishing up quickly, I turn off the water, towel-dry my body, and step out, rushing over to my phone to check and make sure...

Perfect. Klinton and Marcus are finishing up with my mother and will be over to do my hair in a few minutes.

I put on a pair of shorts and a loose shirt I can change out of once I'm ready to go, and then I go back to the bathroom, taking a seat at my vanity while I rub lotion on my legs.

Having someone else handle my hair is probably one of my

favorite things in the world. Having it brushed, cared for with products, dried and styled...it makes me feel like a princess even on the shittiest of days.

My makeup, though, is another story. I don't like having someone else put it on. I like doing it myself, because every time I put on my makeup, I feel like I'm putting on my war paint, like I'm preparing myself for whatever shit is going to come my way that day. And if someone else does it, I just don't feel as strong or capable, even if they do it *exactly* like I would.

I sigh, grabbing my phone and looking at the text I got earlier this morning.

Ben: Have you thought any more about my proposal?

I snort. From anyone else, it would sound like he's talking about some sort of deal or agreement for business. Which, I guess, he kind of *is*.

But he's referencing a literal proposal, a proposal of *marriage*, and I'm still having a hard time getting my mind around it.

There is a part of me that thinks I can manage everything on my own, that thinks I don't need him—or any man—to help me through whatever is coming next.

But there is another part of me...a part that is truly scared about the next chapter of my life. I can't help but think about how much easier it would be to have someone else by my side, taking care of things, making sure I don't crumble and fall like I did when I went to college.

Sure, it makes me sound weak as shit. Like I'm useless. Can't handle things on my own.

As much as I want to be strong, though, the part of me that doesn't want to be alone feels bigger.

So I let my fingers fly across the screen, punching out a message just as Klinton and Marcus come barging into my bedroom.

Me: Let's talk

Chapter Three
REMMY

    The dinner my parents host every year for the board members of Wallace Media is always a spectacle.
    They rent out the main hall at the Hermosa Beach Country Club, a large space with three-story ceilings, floor-to-ceiling windows along one side, and an entire wall that can be moved to create an indoor-outdoor event that looks out onto a large courtyard with the golfing green in the background.
    Every year there's a live band, dinner catered by a celebrity chef—a regular occurrence the wealthy residents of Hermosa Beach like to repeat—a presentation about the state of the company, fancy desserts, and a fireworks show to end the night.
    It's been a few years since I've attended, but my dad still knows how to make the board members happy.
    It really is spectacular.
    I just wish I could actually enjoy it.
    I used to, when I was younger. Mati and I would abandon

Dominic—who preferred to stand at my father's side—and run off to the dessert table. We'd sneak champagne and dance and take turns practicing our flirting technique with the older guys. I was always much more successful than Mati, though he did learn his best moves at these functions.

This time, there's no Mati.

And there's *definitely* no champagne or flirting.

Instead, my mother is glued to my side, intent on walking me around from man to man.

Clearly she's been made aware that I'm no longer dating Lucas, even though I haven't actually talked to her about it. I planned to sit her down and share the news at the same time I told her about the pregnancy, a rip-off-the-Band-Aid kind of moment.

But I still haven't gotten around to it.

And honestly, it looks like I missed my chance to talk to mom about Lucas. That's the Hermosa Beach gossip machine at work.

Nothing stays a secret for long.

"Bronson spent the last year working for his father's company in Spain," my mom says, gesturing to the cookie-cutter man standing in front of me. "How was it working in Seville?"

Bronson—what a chode of a name—starts sharing about his experiences working for his dad, Bronson Tinsley Sr., in Europe.

I can only feign interest for a few minutes before my mind starts to wander, along with my eyes.

The members of the board are almost all geriatric white men with white hair and white collars. I mean, I guess I shouldn't judge too harshly. My dad is one of those men, though he's the president because he's the owner of the company.

Everyone present this evening is following the semi-formal dress code: cocktail dresses, high heels, dark suits.

My dress stands out, even though that wasn't my intention. I honestly might have fit in better if I'd worn the black Gucci.

I smirk to myself.

My mother is quite the crafty one. She probably knew the Gucci dress would cause me to be lost in the sea of dressy women this evening. The green, floral, floor-length dress I'm currently wearing makes it impossible for me to be a wallflower—and I appear less like a harlot, sure—which fits perfectly into her plans to introduce me to every available or semi-available man here this evening.

"Isn't that interesting, Remmy?"

My mother's voice tugs my attention back to where she's standing with a perfectly posed smile, looking at me with darts in her eyes that only I can see.

"So interesting," I reply, having no idea what I missed in their conversation and deciding to respond with something vague enough to make it seem like I was paying attention. "Sounds like you've had quite the experience."

Bronson smiles at me, and something curdles in my stomach. Though it would be fun to blame the nauseatingly charming bachelor in front of me, I have a feeling the little swimmie inside me is at fault.

"Excuse me," I say, dashing away without a care that my mother is probably fuming inside at my incredibly rude departure.

I don't make it to the restroom in time, instead only managing to heave my insides into a trash bin situated by the main entrance.

Thankfully, only the event coordinator is there to witness my debilitating moment, and she rushes over to help.

"Can I do anything? Is everything alright?" she asks, handing me a napkin, her voice aflutter with nerves.

I accept the napkin but wave her away, taking a deep breath and carefully dabbing my mouth.

"Just the end of a stomach bug," I say. "Nothing for you to worry about."

Her shoulders fall and she nods. "Absolutely. Well if you need anything, I'm happy to—"

"*Remington.*"

I spin at the sound of my mother's voice hissing at me from a few feet away.

"Mom, I'm sorry, I—"

"How *dare* you run away like that? I can't imagine anything more rude than cutting someone off midsentence to dash out of the room," she continues, completely ignoring anything I might have to say.

The event coordinator takes that moment to tiptoe away.

Lucky lady.

"Thankfully I was able to smooth things over with poor Bronson before he moved on to talk to that Callandra or whatever her name is. You know, Peter's daughter."

I dab my face again. "Mom, I'm sorry I ran off, but I'm not

interested in Bronson and I don't care if he talks to Callandra."

"Is that *really* her name? God, how ridiculous. It sounds like something you'd name your horse."

"Mom!" I say, incredulous. "You named me *Remington*. I don't think you get to be the judge of whether or not someone else was given a ridiculous name."

She scoffs. "Remington is regal and comes from a long line of incredibly strong Wallace women. It was your grandmother's middle name and her mother's first name and..."

I roll my eyes.

Well, *emotionally* roll my eyes, not physically. My body is feeling a bit too tired at the moment, having just heaved up the only thing I managed to consume today—half of a piece of banana nut bread and a glass of water.

So instead of actually rolling my eyes, I just stand there, allowing my mother to continue telling me why my name isn't ridiculous.

When she pauses, I interject.

"Look, that's great, really—but I'm not interested in being shown off tonight. Okay? I don't feel very good, and these guys are just..." I trail off, not knowing how to explain to my mom that the last thing I need is someone like these men.

What I really need is a break.

"Really, Remington, don't you want to date one of these incredibly fine young men? I mean, sure, Bronson might be a bit of a stretch. He's only an inch taller than you, and that wouldn't look very good in family pictures..."

I can't help but let out a titter at that.

Everything is about appearances.

"...but surely someone else here would be a wonderful gentleman to take you out and get to know."

"Who's taking you out?"

The sound of the voice to my left has my entire body freezing up. When I finally manage to turn my head to see who has approached us, I wonder if I might have slipped on my way to the bathroom and bonked my head, because I *have* to be hallucinating.

"Benjamin Calloway! How are you, sweetheart?" my mother enthuses, stepping toward Ben and kissing him on the cheek.

He gives her a smile.

"Wonderful to see you, Mariana," he says, all smooth

gracefulness and charm as he takes my mother's hand between both of his. "I'm here representing the Calloway Corporation. I know we're not currently on the board, but I've always told my father how important it is to show up in support of our old friends. Plus, you know I never miss an opportunity to break out my favorite suit."

My mother blushes, clearly smitten.

"And what a fine suit it is," she replies.

I take a brief moment to admire Ben as well. I might find him incredibly exasperating for showing up here tonight, but that doesn't mean I can't appreciate how he looks in a suit that was custom tailored to fit his physique.

Ben Calloway isn't a shabby man, that's for damn sure.

I'm a tall girl. A lot of girls I knew growing up always used to say how lucky I was to be tall and have long legs, but it's hard sometimes when you're long and gangly and dating.

Lucas is only a few inches taller than me, though it wasn't ever an issue unless I was trying to wear the five-inch Louboutins I bought for senior prom.

Ben, though—that man towers over me. Tall, lean, and toned with long legs and broad shoulders, he looks like he could be a swimmer, or a runner.

"Well, we're happy to have you, of course," my mother continues. "Come with me so I can let Robert know you're here. I'm sure he'd love for you to sit at the head table."

I have to hold back a chuckle. The head table. Even *I'm* not invited to sit at the head table.

A minute ago, she couldn't bear to have me anywhere but at her side. Now she's ready to run off and leave me behind so she can spend time with *Benjamin Calloway*.

"As much as I'd love that, Mariana, I want to make sure my girl is doing okay first," he says, turning his body to face me. He steps closer, his hands coming up to each of my biceps to give them a light squeeze. "You look like you're not feeling a hundred percent, sweetheart. Should we get you some water?"

There's an extended pause, and I can feel my mother radiating next to me, her emotions bubbling up and ready to burst out of her at any moment.

"I'm *fine*," I reply, my voice low, my jaw locked in both irritation and disbelief, wondering just what the fuck he thinks he's doing.

"*Your* girl?" The surprise in my mother's voice would be laughable if she didn't also sound so damn delighted. She turns to look at me. "Remington, why didn't you tell me you're seeing Benjamin? I would have stopped walking you around from man to man in an instant."

"You've been taking Remington around to find an eligible bachelor?" His voice sounds wounded. "See," he says to me, his voice dropping so as to pretend the words are *only* for me, though I know that's absolutely not the case. "This is why I told you we should just tell your family about us. We don't have anything to hide, sweetheart."

"Ben," I say, interrupting him before he can say anything else, that same vein of nausea beginning to push its way through my body again.

I glance at my mother and see she also has a slightly wounded expression, like the fact that I'd keep my relationship with Ben a secret physically pains her.

There isn't a relationship, though I can't say that now. How would I explain it?

I take a deep breath and look to Ben, realizing I don't have room to make this decision anymore. He's effectively just made it for me.

My nostrils flare and I feel a wave of emotion well up inside of me.

"I didn't want... I felt like..." I start my sentence twice, trying to figure out the right thing to say but failing.

"She was worried about how it might look to other people," Ben interjects, his eyes radiating sympathy as he watches me struggle with my words. Then he looks to my mother. "She and Lucas had been ending for quite some time, but things weren't over officially until just a few weeks ago. She didn't want anyone to get the wrong idea about the timeline and how things are between us. You understand."

As irritating as he is, he's also *very* good at this—something I'm not sure if I should admire or despise.

My mother's smile returns. "Oh I *completely* understand."

"Mom," I say, wanting to end this conversation as quickly as possible before there are more questions to answer and more lies to tell. "Would you mind giving us a minute? We'll be back in there soon."

She beams. "Absolutely. Take your time. Lovely to see you, Benjamin."

"You too, Mariana."

And then she glides out of the foyer and back into the main hall, probably feeling thankful that she no longer has to play wingwoman to her single daughter and can just go enjoy herself at my father's side.

I spin to look at Ben, glaring at him with every bit of anger and irritation I can muster.

He just smirks at me.

"*What the hell were you thinking!?*" I hiss, realizing I sound just like my mother.

"I was thinking you were going to say yes to a marriage proposal, and what better place to be seen together than your father's business event. It implies parental acceptance."

My eyes stay wide and I throw my hands out.

"I can think of at least a *million* places that would be a better place for things to begin. Not here, in front of my family before they even know we're together or—"

"See? I told you—you were planning to accept."

I lift my hands and place the heels over my eyes, frustration barreling through me with swiftness.

"That's *not* the *point*," I reply. "I wanted us to talk things out and…and decide on a few things first."

"Remington—"

"And don't call me Remington," I bark, unable to help it. "I hate my name, and my parents won't listen to me when I tell them I don't like it. But you sure as hell will listen to me when I say my name is *Remmy*."

I turn and walk away, not planning to go far, just needing a moment to myself where I don't have his infuriating face in mine.

I pace the foyer a few times, taking some deep breaths and shaking out my hands.

Fuck.

I'm so irritated right now. So frustrated. I hate when people stomp all over me, like my voice doesn't matter, like how I feel is meaningless.

I keep promising myself I won't ever let that happen again, promising I'll take a stand when someone tries to push past me or walk around me and I'll *make* them listen to me.

But I'm unpracticed.

I don't know how to speak in a way that means my voice will be heard. I don't know how to implore a man to see me as someone to listen to, someone of value.

Right now, I feel like I'm talking to a brick wall. Like every word I say to Ben doesn't actually have any significance. Like I'm speaking a foreign language.

"You act like I didn't give you a choice," he says, his voice close enough that I turn to look at him. "You had a choice. You could have told me I was insane and then left."

I scoff. "Are you kidding? That's not a choice."

"It is. It just isn't one you preferred."

Gritting my teeth, I step closer, sticking a finger in his chest.

"You don't get to back me into a corner and then tell me I had a choice. My only safe option was giving in to you, and I don't care what world you live in, *that is not a choice.*"

My words come out low but strong—stronger than I thought they would and very much laced with my feelings about men who strong-arm women into decisions they wouldn't make on their own.

I can see on his face that my words have startled him.

He takes a step back and watches as I continue to pace.

"I refuse to be in a relationship with someone who handles me like that, real or otherwise."

There's a long pause, drawn out as I head to the large window overlooking the circle drive at the entrance to the club.

"Remmy."

His voice is softer, which surprises me enough that I turn to look at him.

He stands with his hands tucked into the pockets of his pants, and his eyes are focused on my face with an expression of...contrition? Is that what that is? I can't tell.

All I know is he looks a lot less like an asshole when he isn't trying to be charming.

"What?" I breathe out, my voice failing to hide just how frustrated I feel.

His head tilts to the side and his eyes rake me up and down, almost like he's searching for something. Then he shakes his head and crosses his arms, one hand rising to rub at the beard on his face.

"You look beautiful tonight," he says. "I should have led with that instead of...anything else."

He pauses again, drops his arms, and steps closer to me.

"I've only been responsible for my own emotions for a long time," he says, then shakes his head a little bit. "Other than my sister, of course. I'm used to going after the things I want, cart blanche. I didn't realize it would upset you so much."

My lips part in surprise. Was that...some form of an apology?

"I can't promise I won't ever do it again," he adds, his lips quirking up at one side. "Habits are a hard thing to create and even harder to break. But...I'll try not to make choices for you again."

My shoulders fall.

I wasn't expecting him to feel remorse or regret, let alone put it on display for me to see.

Part of me would prefer he just stay the arrogant asshole I assumed he was. It's easier to be angry at someone when they're a total douchebag.

But the other part of me is thankful that I've gotten to see this part of him, this somewhat soft and feeling part of Ben Calloway that I didn't know existed.

Especially if I'm going to be...marrying him.

Because I am.

I step forward, bridging the gap between us and coming up to his side.

The power he radiates is intoxicating. How have I never noticed it before?

Maybe because my memories of Ben are from high school, seeing him on occasion when he was home from college and dressed down in something casual. He always seemed a bit, I don't know, nerdier? Is that the right word? He seemed nerdier when I was younger.

Any recent interactions with Ben have been few and far between—an afternoon grabbing lunch with my brothers at Bennie's, an evening when I might notice him at a society function.

Come to think of it, I can only really think of a few instances when I've seen or talked to Ben over the past five years, most recently being when Lucas had a group of us over for the 4th of July.

It makes sense that he'd be somewhat different now, that I would be aware of him in a different way.

And I am definitely aware of him.

Even now, my brain feels like it's short-circuiting as I stand inches away, smelling his cologne and looking up into those beautiful blue eyes.

"How long have you had the beard?" I ask, hoping to lighten the tone and shift the conversation away from something so mentally taxing.

Ben scrubs at the carefully manicured beard growing on his face, something he never used to have, always opting for that stern, clean-shaven look.

"About two weeks," he replies. "You like it?"

I nod, lifting my hand touch it, my fingers stroking lightly through the coarse hair on his cheek and chin.

"You seem less..."

"Severe?" he offers, his lips curved in something resembling a smile.

I grin in return. "I was going to say intense, or maybe intimidating. But severe works."

"I'm not intimidating."

I shrug, not wanting to press it any further. How do you explain to a man how intimidation feels when you're a woman who's been through what I have?

"So...we're doing this, then?" he prompts, breaking the silence.

I blink, my eyes searching his face for some kind of confirmation that I can trust him, that I can trust who he is and what he wants and how he's going to treat me.

But that isn't something you can necessarily see in someone's face, in their eyes, in the way they're dressed or how they speak.

You have to wait and allow them to prove it to you, with their actions. That's the intimidating part—that I have to choose to trust him even though I'm not certain he deserves it.

"Yeah," I finally say. "Yes, let's get married."

I expect him to smile. He's won, after all. He's gotten what he wanted.

But instead, he reaches over and slips his hand into mine.

For just a second, I think I catch something uncertain within his gaze, but it's gone too quickly for me to know for sure.

Instead, he turns his head and looks toward the entrance to the main hall.

"Ready?" he asks, giving my hand a squeeze.

I let out a long breath, knowing I have no real idea what I'm getting myself into, but also knowing I don't have any better options.

"Ready," I reply, squeezing his hand back.

And then the two of us walk into the party together.

We spend the rest of the evening side by side, our hands together.

Ben truly is a great actor. He knows just how to look at me, how to keep me next to him, how to lift my hand and kiss the inside of my wrist in way that makes it seem like he thinks nobody is watching.

But we both know everyone is watching.

A Calloway and a Wallace? Together?

If you ask my mother, a truer match couldn't be found, not even in the movies.

We both come from new money families, strong backgrounds, good education, and the right upbringing.

To be honest, it hadn't ever occurred to me before. In all the things Ben talked to me about when trying to convince me this marriage idea of his wasn't completely insane, never once did he mention the way it would feel for me to stand at his side.

The only person I've ever had a true relationship with is Lucas. As amazing as he was, the expectation weighing on his shoulders is a fraction of what rests on mine.

His mother is barely a part of his life and he lives a very free, very independent kind of existence. There isn't any pressure to conform, to be a family representative, to carry yourself a certain way because you're in the public eye.

Sure, he has to be careful because he's a surfer and needs to manage his sponsorships, but that's his own choice, a life of his own making. At any point, he could shuck all of it off and move away, never having to deal with it again.

The expectations I face are...grand, and often suffocating.

It's one of the reasons I stayed away for so long, one of the reasons I fled from here as soon as I was able to and tried to create a life for myself somewhere else.

Away from the watchful eyes.

But I always knew I would eventually have to come back to this, would have to come back home to the family that expects me to be a certain way. To say certain things. To follow certain rules.

Feeling completely directionless doesn't fit into that.

A pregnancy *definitely* doesn't fit into that.

Standing at Ben's side, though? Hearing him talk business and socialize while I smile and laugh beside him?

I'm almost shocked at how easily it fits.

When Ben proposed marriage to me, I assumed it would feel like shoving a square peg into a round hole.

I never expected for it to immediately feel like slipping into a shoe tailor made for me.

I let out a small huff of laughter through my nose at my own reference. Leave it to me to assume my role in life is to be the wicked stepsister and not the fucking princess.

Ben looks at me, a question in his eyes.

"Nothing you said," I say in response to his unspoken inquiry. "Just laughing at something stupid inside my own head."

His lips tilt up.

"Anything you want to share with the class?"

I shake my head, my lips pursed in faux irritation. "Not a chance, mister. What goes on up here is strictly for me and me alone."

He nods, but his eyes are floating around the room. "Is there anyone in particular here you want to see us together?" he asks.

"Not tonight," I say, knowing I should take Ben over to talk to my dad but not ready to do so. "Besides, I think the fireworks are going to start soon."

"Well then," he replies, slipping his hand back into mine, "let's head outside and make sure we get the best view."

I chuckle but allow him to lead me out to the courtyard that overlooks the green, my long dress flowing out behind me as he moves us quickly.

"Where are we going?" I ask, giving in to my desire to laugh as we maneuver through people and over behind a manicured bush.

"You'll see."

We aren't moving for much longer before Ben stops abruptly and spins around, the two of us colliding just enough that he has to lift his hands, bracing me so I don't fall over.

I straighten, suddenly realizing how close we are. How tall he is. How good he smells.

Apparently that's a thing in pregnancy; I read about it the other day. Heightened hormones increase your sense of smell, and holy shit does Ben smell good right now.

"So where are we?" I ask, my breaths coming out in pants as if I've been on a run or walking up a steep hill.

"The place with the best view," he says, his eyes focused on mine.

I shake my head. "You can see fireworks from anywhere in the courtyard," I reply. "We didn't have to move. We could have watched with the crowd."

If it's possible, I feel Ben shift even slightly more forward, the length of him pressed along the length of me.

What was it I told myself? That he was nerdier when we were younger?

That may have been true, but whether he's nerdy or not, someone has been spending time in the gym. I can feel his strong body, toned muscle, and sinewy figure as it presses against me, our faces only inches apart.

His eyes drop to my mouth.

"You know, Remmy, I try to be a fairly calculated person in life, and you are…incredibly unexpected."

My breath hitches.

My body hums.

I don't know where this is coming from.

This sudden physical connection, the heightened awareness of him.

I've always known Ben is handsome. In my opinion, he's much more handsome than his brother, Wyatt. I've never been into the bad boy look, preferring the kind of soft charm and easy smile that come along with the cleaner style.

Ben isn't a bad boy like Wyatt or clean-cut like Lucas.

He falls somewhere in the middle.

Leave it to a Calloway to create his own category.

He's not soft, that's for sure, and his smiles don't necessarily come easy. There is a flexibility to him, though, a way he bends and moves that makes me feel like he's slow-rolling thunder as opposed to a violent storm.

Something comforting with just a hint of danger.

"I thought someone calculated would learn to expect the unexpected," I whisper back, our faces even closer, our lips hovering.

But our eyes are open, still watching each other.

"Clearly I have a lot to learn," he answers, smiling. "Why don't you teach me?"

And then he presses his lips to mine.

It's a chaste kiss, much more chaste than I'm accustomed to, that's for sure.

But I still feel it in my toes.

Still feel where my nerves and synapses are firing all along my body.

My hands reach out and rest on his hips, and I pull him even closer to me, loving the feeling of his hardness against my softness.

I can feel him through his fancy suit.

And he is *definitely* hard.

But at my pressure against him, he rips his mouth off of mine, breathing hard, his brow furrowed.

A distant whistling sound is the only warning I get before a firework explodes in the sky.

I turn my head, looking off in the distance.

"I thought you said this was the best view. I can't see the fireworks over these bushes," I say, knowing the explosions of light are happening just on the other side of the shrub, over the green.

"It *is* the best view," he replies, taking my chin in his hand and tilting my head so I'm looking back toward the courtyard where everyone stands, watching the fireworks in the distance.

And where they have the perfect vantage point to see me and Ben kissing in the alcove of the bushes.

I swallow loudly, something thick and unwelcome falling into my stomach and settling in a way that makes me feel uncomfortable.

He put us here so everyone would see us.

Which makes every word out of his mouth just now a completely calculated plan.

If I were walking, I would trip.

It was only a few moments ago that I was talking about what a great actor Ben is. And yet, when he puts us up on a stage for everyone to see, it feels like he's yanking a rug out from under me.

I stretch my neck from left to right, trying to loosen up the muscles that seem to have suddenly tightened up.

The last thing I need to do is forget—even for a second—that what we're doing is something to solve our problems.

I can't allow myself to slip into that well-fitting shoe, no matter how comfortable it might be.

Chapter Four
BEN

The whirring sound of the bicycle finally begins to slow as I tap a few buttons on the screen so I'm in cooldown mode.

Today is a cardio day, and it felt good to punish my body with a twenty-mile ride through the Italian Alps—not that I was really looking at the screen while I was going, my mind too full from last night to really give myself a moment to zone out.

All growing up, we had a private gym inside our house. Then when I went to college, I realized it was a lot more fun to work out with other people, so I got really into cycling classes and group rides.

The thing I like about cycling is that I get to be around other people, but I don't have to talk to them. I just put in some headphones and people leave me alone.

Maybe it makes me weird that I want to be around people but not engage with them.

Regardless, it's what I like.

Which is why I got a membership at Jim's Gym.

It started as a joke back in the seventies, a small-time club for a group of friends who wanted a private place to get together to work out without having to deal with interruptions. The man who opened it was James Tillman, hence the name.

It didn't take long for Jim's Gym to become an exclusive, invitation-only kind of establishment everyone wanted access to since Hermosa Beach is what it is—a place completely consumed with status.

I might not put a lot of stock in that exclusivity shit, but I *do* value select services that help me manage what little time I have free for exercise.

Which is why I find myself at Jim's five or six days a week. Three days of cycling, two days of muscle toning, and Saturdays I allow myself to just enjoy my own time on a bike outside of any expectation.

I'm usually able to crank up my music and turn off the outside world. My mind goes blank and I can just enjoy the noisy solitude of my workout.

Today, though, all I can think about is last night with Remmy. That kiss.

And the way she looked at me afterward.

I stretch my arms over my head, my legs moving slowly as I finish the cooldown and allow myself a chance to look around the gym.

It's early for a Saturday—only a few minutes after six—so there aren't many people around. The other members are scattered here and there, jogging on treadmills, lifting weights. The first group class of the morning just started, a yoga class in a room with a huge glass wall.

I'll admit, I generally avoid working out at this time because I know I'll be watching a group of women stretch and flex through that wall, which the bikes face, and I don't have time to be distracted by women or their bodies.

I have too much on my mind, and time in the gym is supposed to be the single hour each day when I can focus on exercise, enjoying the exertion and thinking about nothing else.

Too bad Remington Wallace and her delicious fucking lips were on my mind the entire ride.

I kept that kiss chaste for a reason. The last thing I need is for there to be messy emotions between us. Even emotions that arise solely from something physical need to stay firmly tucked away.

But that kiss…

Shit.

Her lips tasted like the grapes she spent the entire evening nibbling on. Grapes and sparkling water.

When we were texting earlier in the evening, she made it sound like she was pretty much on board.

Let's talk. That's all she sent to me.

Are you accepting?

She responded an hour later. *Heading to the club for an event with my family. I still need some convincing.*

It sounded kind of flirtatious, like she was into it but just wanted me to jump all in.

So, I tracked her down and convinced her.

Clearly I went about it the wrong way if I'm to take at face value her emotional response to me showing up at the annual Wallace Media function and telling her mother we're dating.

I'm just…not used to people not agreeing with me, especially when I know for an absolute fact that something is the right choice.

Which this is. For both of us.

I knew I'd need to apologize if I wanted to turn things around and get us back on a level playing field, but when I prepared to give her the apology—the one-off *Sorry, it won't happen again*—the very basic words evaporated.

Looking at her as she paced the foyer, emotion brimming from her every nerve and vein and pore…I knew it wasn't enough.

Whatever was going on inside her mind was…I don't know. Something bigger. Her response was more filled with feeling than I had ever anticipated, and a bullshit response wasn't going to cut it.

So I *didn't* apologize. I didn't promise to never do it again, because that would be a lie. I know myself. I know I can't make an assurance like that and expect anyone to actually believe it.

Instead, I said exactly what I was thinking. I tried to make sure she believed me when I said I regretted how I approached the start to that evening and assured her I'd try not to do it again without talking to her.

Because those are words I mean.

Those are words that are true.

And if Remmy and I are going to be in a relationship like this one—where almost everything is a lie—the truth has to be something we cling to, for our own sanity.

The beeping from the bike brings my focus back to the screen, and I allow my legs to spin to a stop.

Twenty miles isn't far for me, but I really worked up a sweat this time, setting the incline to a higher intensity than I normally hit. I just wanted that burn. I wanted that empty mind, and mile after mile passed without me achieving it.

I sigh, knowing I'll have to wait until tomorrow morning to try again. A full day at work is ahead, and unfortunately, I won't be able to turn my brain off at any point.

Slipping off the machine, I grab my towel and water and begin walking to the locker room.

"Hey Ben."

I turn at the sound of my name, smiling when I see who it is.

"Wow, Logan," I say, stepping forward and shaking his extended hand. "Good to see you."

He returns my grin. Logan Becker was my mentor when I was a senior at Roth Prep, a part of the 'Prep the Prep' program during college application season.

He graduated quite a while before me but was instrumental in my application to Yale as an undergraduate, and then he came back around to talk things through with me again when I applied to Stanford to get my MBA a few years later.

"Good to see you, too," he replies.

I tilt my head to the side, assessing what's different.

"Have you...changed something? You look...I don't know. Happy? Am I allowed to ask that?"

Logan laughs, something I'm pretty sure I've never seen before. He's always been a friendly guy, but he seems more relaxed.

"Yeah, a lot is different, actually. A few big changes in my life, but most importantly, I'm back in town."

My eyebrows lift. "On holiday, or are you talking permanently?"

"Permanently." He pauses. "Well, that's the plan if everything goes smoothly. I'm the new pediatric attending at Roth Memorial."

I snort and roll my eyes. "Oh you mean you're in the top position for your specialty?" I say sarcastically. "I'm so surprised."

He grins but doesn't address my comment. He's always been a humble guy about his accomplishments, even considering everything he's been through in life.

A scholarship student at Roth when he was in middle and high school, he got by on hard work and the assistance of others—the people who saw his value, even if his last name didn't mean anything.

"So how long have you been back?" I ask, leaning against an open bike to my right and taking a swig from my water.

"Just a few weeks. I've only been at work for a few days. I've mostly been...getting settled."

I nod, getting the feeling he's not sharing everything. "Well, I'm glad you're back. We should get together soon. I'd love to hear about life."

He grins, but there's a pinched quality to it, like I fed him something sour but he doesn't want me to know he doesn't like it.

"Definitely. A few beers would be great. Just let me know when." He takes a step. "But, I'll let you get back to it."

I give him a wave as he heads down the path between the bikes, walking toward the juice bar in the corner.

Something inside me pulses, tells me I shouldn't let too much time pass. Logan is a good guy, and he's clearly going through something.

I rub a hand over my chest, not liking the tight feeling in my muscles.

Touchy-feely isn't my thing. I try not to get too involved with emotions. It isn't how I process, so I struggle to empathize with anyone else when that's how *they* process.

I sigh, resigning myself to the idea that today is definitely not going to be a day I get a lot done. Then I follow in Logan's wake, catching up to where he's stopped and is staring up at the juice menu.

"The chocolate banana protein thing is pretty good," I say, grabbing his attention. "It's a blended one."

He bobs his head, considering. "Okay. Thanks."

"Look, Logan, I was thinking it over, and I'm actually free tonight if you wanna grab that beer."

He doesn't look at me, but I see him grin.

"I never thought I'd see the day Benjamin Calloway intentionally attempted to make a friend."

I narrow my eyes at him, but he chuckles.

"It's my own fault," he continues. "Clearly, I'm not good at hiding the fact that life is shit right now."

I cross my arms, my earlier suspicions confirmed. Something is up in Logan Becker's life.

"Grab a beer with me and you can talk about it. I'm shit at advice—you know that—but I'm a good wall to throw your pasta at."

At that, he laughs—a real one.

"Where did you get that?" he asks.

I shrug. "You know how people throw pasta at the wall to see if it's ready?"

"No, I've honestly never heard that."

"Well then you won't get the joke."

He laughs again.

"So, beer tonight?"

Logan nods. "That would be great actually. You know a good spot?"

The only thing I can do is smile.

"I know the perfect place."

"This is quite the view," Logan says, whistling when we make it to the rooftop after we've finished the tour of Bennie's. "I'm surprised you brew your own beer."

"It's the hip thing right now. When I bought the property, the neighboring business approached me about purchasing the back lot of *their* property, saying they didn't have use for it." I lift a shoulder and take a seat at the bar, which is bustling with the Saturday evening crowd. "The restaurant is booming, but the brewery part is still building."

"Still, very impressive for a guy who didn't ever think he could pass calculus."

I groan, motioning to the bartender. "Don't remind me. That class nearly killed me. Two Bennie Blues, chilled mugs, please."

Sonia, one of the bartenders who is leaving in the coming weeks as the summer wraps up, gives me a nod and spins around to get our drinks.

"So tell me about life now," he says, turning on his stool to face me, one elbow on the bar. "We haven't talked since you graduated from Stanford. I knew you wanted to open a restaurant and build a—what did you call it? Culinary...kingdom?"

"Culinary empire, actually, but I do like culinary kingdom," I say, chuckling as I accept the beer from Sonia. "Has a nice ring to it."

Logan takes a sip. "That's actually really good. Okay, tell me about your empire."

"It's not an empire yet, just the one restaurant, and...I've gotten kind of stalled out."

"Oh really? Anything I can help with?"

I pause, wondering if Logan's the type of guy I can talk to about this...about everything that happened, about the reason I'm still here, managing this restaurant instead of moving on to the next one.

I'm not the guy who asks for help. Not often, at least. And as much as I can appreciate Logan's place in my life, I don't need to get him wrapped up in my mess.

So I only wonder for a moment before I let the thought pass. Even if I thought Logan *could* help, I wouldn't ask for it.

"Nah, it's just something I...need to handle by myself. But thank you. I appreciate it."

I take a moment to sip my beer before redirecting to Logan.

"What's your deal, though? I thought you were going to relish life in Washington. The Seattle weather not agree with you?"

He lets out a laugh, though it isn't really filled with any kind of humor.

"Something like that."

There's a long pause, and I start to wonder if I should say something in response.

"I moved because I got divorced."

I let out a quiet sigh of relief.

It's not that I want him to be going through something difficult, but divorce is something I'm familiar with since my parents went through it when I was in high school. At the very least, it's something I'm comfortable talking about.

"That sucks, man. I'm sorry."

Logan shakes his head. "I'm not."

I laugh.

"Really, I'm not. It was the best decision, for both of us, but it feels like shit. It feels like a failure. Moving away felt right at the time, but now that I'm here, it feels like..." He trails off.

"Like running away," I finish for him.

He doesn't answer, and I know I hit the nail on the head.

"You know, there was a day not too long ago when I might have thought that was true," I say, twisting my glass so it rotates within its own ring of condensation. "But that version of me was a lot younger and, truthfully, hadn't experienced much of life yet." I lift a shoulder. "Now, I'm a firm believer that you have to choose what you want and go after it, regardless of how it looks to other people."

"Is that what you've done?" he asks.

I think it over, trying to figure out a way to give him an honest answer without telling him too much.

I settle on: "It's what I'm trying to do. I know when I finally get where I want to be, when I get to that end goal I believe will make me happy, it won't sit right with everyone. But I can't allow my life to be dictated by what other people think."

He bobs his head as if he understands. Part of me hopes he does understand, but another part hopes he doesn't.

Because if he truly understood what I'm saying, I'm not so sure he'd want to accept my advice.

We shoot the shit for another hour, enjoying the sunset in the distance before Logan finally heads off back to his short-term rental unit. It's a back house only a few blocks from me, though he declines a ride, saying the walk back will do him good.

The rest of my evening is spent plotting out the next quarter's financials, setting up purchase orders, reviewing schedule processes, and organizing a new training to comply with upcoming changes to OSHA standards.

It's the kind of shit I should be paying someone else to do but have hoarded all to myself, a way to pass the time as I try to get closer to the day when I can wrap all of this up and move on.

"You're still here?"

I glance up at the doorway, my eyes bleary from staring at my computer screen for what feels like hours.

"Just finishing up," I reply to Hamish, my floor and hiring manager.

"There's a woman out front looking for you," he says. "Looks familiar. Remmy?"

My brow furrows.

Why would Remmy come to visit me at work?

"I'll come out," I say, and Hamish leaves me behind.

I glance around my office, knowing I should head home. The work can wait until tomorrow. I'm already ahead of schedule on a handful of things, and besides, maybe it will do *me* good to leave on time for once.

I head out to the front, pushing through the doorway that divides the offices and kitchen from the dining room, and come to a stop when I see Remmy at the unmanned hostess table, her eyes scanning the room.

Passing me briefly before returning.

And then she smiles at me.

Something friendly and genuine.

Jesus, how long has it been since I've had a smile like that aimed at me from anyone other than my younger sister?

I return her smile and walk in her direction.

"Hey Remmy. What can I do for you?"

Her mouth opens but no words come out, and I know she's regretting her choice to stop by.

"Do you want to go back to my office and talk or...?"

"No, no. Not that. I'm..." She clears her throat. "I'm just here to see if we can set up a time to talk. You know, lay everything out."

I tuck my hands in my pockets, nodding my head. "Yeah. We can set that up."

She grins, her shoulders dropping. "Good. Because I just want to make sure..."

But she doesn't finish her sentence as her eyes track someone across the room.

I turn to look behind me, realizing her eyes are focused on Hannah as she walks out a tray of food.

"Hannah works here?" she asks, her brow furrowed.

"Yeah. Has for a few months."

"How did I not realize that?"

I lift my shoulders, unsure how to respond.

Her eyes look back to mine. "Do all of them come here a lot?"

It takes me a second to understand what she's asking, but when I do, I finally get why Remmy suddenly looks so apprehensive.

Wyatt, Lucas, Lennon, Paige…that group was her group. If Hannah works here and she's dating my brother, *and* she's Lucas' sister, it would make sense that the crowd Remmy is now avoiding would be at Bennie's often.

"Is that something you're concerned about?" I reply, answering her question with a question, trying to feel this out.

She takes a minute to respond, but when she does, I can see her answer before she gives it to me. I can see it in how she pulls her shoulders back just slightly, in how she lifts her chin.

"Not at all. Just wondering if I'm going to be seeing them, is all. So are you free tonight or should we get together another day this week?"

Tilting my head to the side, I wish—not for the first time—that I could understand what is going on inside of Remmy's head. Sometimes, she seems so sure and strong and resilient, rebellious and determined with a wicked sense of humor to boot.

Other times, she seems like a shell of that person. Fearful and nervous, a house of cards that could blow over at any moment with just a tiny puff of nothing.

What happened to make you so inconsistently fragile?

I push the thought away, reminding myself that it doesn't matter if I know how Remmy's mind works. It doesn't matter if I understand what has made her who she is today.

All that matters is that Remmy serves as a means to an end.

"I can do tonight," I reply, knowing the sooner we get moving on this, the better. "Do you want to come to mine?"

She nods, her eyes still on something behind me. Probably Hannah again. "Yeah, just text me the address and I'll meet you there."

And then, without another word, she spins and heads back out the front door.

I shake my head and let out a long sigh, rubbing at the back of my neck.

If all that matters is the means to an end, why do I get the feeling this is going to be a lot more complicated than I intended.

Chapter Five
BEN

She reaches out to accept the glass of ginger ale from me, a soft "Thanks" coming from her mouth before she takes a sip.

When I pulled up to my house twenty minutes ago, I found Remmy throwing up into the bushes that border my property, my next-door neighbor's window shades closing when I looked that way.

Alice has always been a bit of a snoop, though I've kept my life boring enough that she doesn't have anything to share with her book club about me.

So instead of paying her any attention, I focused on Remmy. She looked miserable. I got her inside and into one of the bathrooms with a new toothbrush and some mouthwash, followed by some saltines and a can of ginger ale left over from a horrible stomach flu I had earlier this year.

Hopefully she'll start to feel better soon, because I'm exhausted just looking at her.

"Sorry about the bushes," she says.

I laugh. "Remmy, I'm not worried about the bushes, okay? You're growing a human. You're allowed to be sick and sad and tired and anything else you feel."

She gives me a gentle smile.

"How'd you get to be such a softy when it comes to pregnant ladies?" she asks, setting her glass down on the coffee table and adjusting herself so she's more comfortable under the throw blanket.

I scoff. "I have a thirteen-year-old sister—I was in my teens when my mom was pregnant. Wyatt and I took on a very active role with Ivy and all the stuff that comes along with pregnancy and newborns, so I know all about how crazy it can get."

Her eyes narrow, her mouth curving a bit. "First rule: Don't use the word crazy."

I grin at her. "I'll only use it when it's well deserved."

"That is not a thing."

"It absolutely is."

"No it's not! Men think women are crazy all the time. That's like...that's like...just...completely unfair."

I lift a shoulder, completely aware that I'm baiting her and, surprisingly, enjoying every second of it.

There's something about seeing Remmy a little bit flustered that makes me smile.

"Oh we are absolutely coming back to this later, because I will *not* marry someone who will call me crazy at the drop of a hat."

Chuckling, I settle back into my own corner of the couch, feeling oddly comfortable with Remmy sitting across from me.

"Well, let's not spend too much time on that tonight since we're supposed to be talking about our relationship timeline."

Remmy perks up, suddenly becoming all business. "Yes. That's what we need to talk about. I feel like it would be a good idea for us to get on the same page about...everything. What we are doing when and who we should tell about it." She pauses, worrying her bottom lip between her teeth. "I don't like to feel ambushed, and that's how I felt at the country club. If we lay things out, we won't have confusion like that again."

I nod, seeing her logic and, not for the first time, wishing I hadn't been such a pushy bastard. "That makes sense," I say, making sure she can see the sincerity in my eyes.

There's a momentary pause where we just look at each other before I continue.

"So, I spent some time earlier putting together a list of things we need to take into consideration," I say, opening the notebook I have on the coffee table. "We've already gotten through the biggest hump, our first time being seen in public together. That should be enough to get the tongues wagging around town."

Remmy giggles.

"Now we just have to make sure the information spreads at a normal pace. We should schedule out some date nights, decide when you'll be moving in, set an actual engagement date, and then talk about when we would get married because—"

"Wait, wait, wait. You're moving too fast," she interrupts. "Back up. Did you say...a date for me to move in?"

I let a beat of time pass before answering, feeling like this is going to be a big conversation. "Well, it would only be natural for my beloved fiancée to move in with me."

"No. It would not be natural—not in my family."

I'm sure my confusion is evident on my face.

"How are we supposed to be married and not live together?" I ask, quite unnecessarily, I think.

"I'm not suggesting we *never* move in together. I just think you have the order of events wrong. First of all, I know you zero percent. I'm not moving in with you yet. We need to give it some time before we even start talking about something like that."

I bite back the urge to roll my eyes. "Obviously we wouldn't move you in today. That would look suspicious to your family."

"But most importantly," she continues, "there's no way my family would let me just up and move in with you without putting you through your paces."

I don't like the way she looks so pleased with herself at that statement, like she's going to enjoy whatever 'putting you through your paces' means.

"And that involves...what exactly?"

"I might be the rebel of the family, but my *very* traditional parents would drag me home by my hair if I tried to move in with you before you've even asked them to marry me."

I bark out a laugh, sure she must be joking. "Say what now?"

She does that thing again, pushing her shoulders back and raising her chin. "It might be fine that my family knows we're 'dating'," she says, giving the word air quotes, "but my dad will want you to go talk to him about getting engaged, get his permission before you ask me."

My mouth opens wide and my eyebrows about fly off my face at her statement.

It takes a minute for me to form a response—any kind of response. I don't know why, but I'm having a visceral reaction to this idea, my whole body revolting at the notion.

Eventually, I manage to get my thoughts together and sit forward on the couch cushion, resting my elbows on my knees.

"Remmy, it's archaic. I'm not asking for your dad's *permission*."

She twists her lips. "Ben, it's just a tradition in Colombian families."

"I'm not asking any man for permission. The only permission I need is *yours*. The only thing that matters is that *you* say it's okay."

Something shuts off in Remmy's face when I say that. I'm not sure exactly what happens, but it looks like she short-circuits. She blinks a bunch and her lips purse, her eyes darting all over the room.

"What's wrong?" I ask, wondering what's going on.

It takes a second for her to respond, but when she does, something tightens in my chest.

"Thank you," she whispers, whatever flash of irritation she felt a moment ago passing by.

I sit silent, wondering what I'm missing. Does she want me to ask her dad or doesn't she?

She clears her throat, her eyes still tracking around the room as she avoids my gaze.

"I've always thought my eventual husband would ask my dad for his permission," she says. "But maybe that's the wrong word. You're right, I should be the only person you ask. I know our marriage isn't going to be real, but it would mean a lot to me if you could ask him...for his blessing."

That thing that tightened in my chest eases when she puts it that way, and I can't put a finger on why.

I find myself nodding in agreement, wanting to do this for her if it means something.

To her, not to her dad.

"That's fine, but we still need to set up a timeline, right? For all of that?" I need to shift this conversation away from whatever emotional stuff we're mucking through and back toward logistics. "I created a list of all the different components of a relationship from start to finish, and we should probably start by picking a wedding date and working backward."

I hand Remmy my notebook so she can scan through everything.

Be seen in public. First date. Refer to each other as boyfriend and girlfriend. Kiss in public. Introduction to family. Update relationship status on social media. Move in together. Engagement. Out-of-town trip together. Wedding. Baby announcement.

"How did you come up with a list like this?" she asks, a hint of amusement in her voice.

"I searched online. There are a lot of relationship progression charts with healthy evolutions, like how long to wait before introducing each other to our families. But obviously, our timeline is going to look a little different."

Remmy's just watching me with a smile on her face.

"Obviously," she says, handing the notebook back.

"Some of this stuff is more time-sensitive than others," I continue. "You have to decide how much of our relationship you want to happen before you start showing. How far along are you?"

Remmy's smile falls away and she tilts her head back, letting out a long sigh as she stares at the ceiling. "Around three months."

I nod. "So you'll start showing in the next month or two, right?"

Remmy doesn't answer me. Her shoulders rise and fall as she takes deep breaths, her eyes closed, her entire body looking uncomfortably tense.

"Are you okay?" I ask. "You look..."

Suddenly, Remmy bursts into tears, her hands rising to her face to cover her eyes as she cries.

I feel frozen. Literally incapacitated.

The only woman's tears I've ever had to deal with were Ivy's, and she's a kid who can usually be calmed with ice cream or a new toy or *something.*

I don't know what kind of something I can give Remmy to help with these kinds of tears, or even what caused them in the first place.

"I didn't ever think I'd be pregnant," she finally says, her voice wobbling as she chokes through her tears. "I didn't think I'd ever have a…a family, any kids. I just…I don't understand why I'm crying right now, but all I can think about is the fact that I'm three months pregnant and I never thought this would happen to me."

I sit quietly by her side as she cries, equal parts wishing I could be anywhere else but here and wanting to do something to help her feel better.

"I know I can't fix how you feel," I say, my voice soft, my eyes fixed on my own hands. "And I'm sure some of how you feel is just hormonal."

Her head turns in my direction and she glares, her eyes morphing from overwhelmed to deadly in a split second.

I raise my hands.

"But I'm also sure you're scared and unsure and nervous. I just want to take a second to remind you that…" I lick my lips, knowing the next words I say are deeper than I planned to get with Remmy but knowing still that it's the right thing to say. "You're not going to be alone."

Her face scrunches up as more tears assault her.

"You'll worry and feel anxious sometimes, and other times you'll cry and not understand why because your body will be filled to the brim with more than you can handle or understand. But you won't be alone when you feel those things. I'll be there, too."

Remmy continues to cry, her body racked with sobs I'm not sure she understands. But she tilts to the side and leans toward me, and I take the invitation for what it is, scooting forward and bringing her in to lean against me.

As she shakes and cries in my arms, I have a sudden and very stark realization that I may need to rethink this whole thing.

Ever since that first day when I suggested this idea to Remmy, I've had a vision in my head of what our marriage would look like if I planned it out perfectly, but maybe I'll have to let that idea go. Maybe my grand plan isn't going to fall into place as neatly or seamlessly as I thought it would.

But that's okay. I have a mind that can adjust under pressure. I can take Remmy, snuggled into my arms right now, and figure out a way to make all of this work. For both of us.

So I continue to hold her. I lift my hand and stroke my fingers through her hair, telling her it will be okay and she can cry as much as she wants to.

Eventually, her shaking subsides. Her tears begin to dry, and she leans back, pulling away from me.

Part of me wants to laugh at how her makeup has streaked down her face, the mascara and eyeliner she wears in excess streaming down her cheeks.

I reach out and take her face in my hands, my thumbs brushing lightly underneath her eyes to clear away the marks I know she would probably hate to see in the mirror.

Remmy is beautiful. All the time. She doesn't need all this shit on her face, but she's worn her makeup like this for as long as I can remember knowing her, even back when she was a little high school sophomore just starting to date Lucas.

"My makeup is probably a streaky mess," she says, laughing in that post-crying way that sounds stopped up because you still need to blow your nose.

"It is," I reply truthfully, "but you're still beautiful."

Her eyes soften and she leans forward, pressing a kiss against my lips. It's a chaste one, similar to the kiss I gave her yesterday at the country club under the fireworks.

The difference between my kiss yesterday and her kiss now is I planned for that kiss to be in front of the crowd. I wanted people to see us. There was a purpose.

This kiss...this is just Remmy wanting to kiss me, filled with emotion and gratitude.

Two reasons I *don't* want to be kissed.

I don't want her to confuse things between us. I don't want her to get wrapped up in the emotional aspect of her pregnancy and see me as anything other than a means to an end. I don't want her to feel thankful that I'm saving her from a shitty conversation with her family and want to thank me with her mouth and her hands and her body.

As tempting as it might be.

Because Remmy really is beautiful.

Curvy and wonderful and sexual.

A different man would have fallen into Remmy's eyes and lips at the drop of a hat. He wouldn't know how to separate the emotional and the physical from his true intentions and focus on his future, on his plan.

But I'm not a different man.

I'm me.

I don't fall into the webs women weave.

I don't want the complications and emotions that come along with relationships.

I don't need to give anything to this thing between us other than my commitment to see it through and the dedication to give Remmy and the baby the best life I can.

The relationship we're going to have doesn't mean I can get emotionally distracted.

My focus has to stay on one thing and one thing only, and that doesn't include Remmy's feelings.

Sure, I might need to shift my original perspective, perhaps provide more emotional support than I've been planning. She's dealing with the pregnancy. I can be a man who helps to take care of her financially and ensures she isn't kicked out of her family because of some bullshit ideas about what is or isn't morally acceptable. And I can also be a man who listens when she's emotional.

But there has to be a dividing line somewhere, and this kiss feels like Remmy is interested in crossing it.

What she doesn't know is that I'm incapable of giving her anything more than what we've already agreed to.

And that even if I were capable, she wouldn't want to get it from me.

"So we'll go to dinner Wednesday and sort things out then?" she asks me, her face looking soft, a bit of embarrassment coloring her cheeks.

"I think that sounds perfect," I say, reconfirming the conversation we had after she finally stopped crying.

She was embarrassed about a lot of things, even though she wasn't vocalizing all of them.

She was embarrassed about getting sick in my bushes. About bursting into tears. About kissing me.

Something inside of me wanted her to say she meant the kiss, to tell me it wasn't just her emotions running wild.

But I'm glad she didn't.

That would have opened up a can of worms inside of me that I have no interest in attempting to manage.

"Are you sure you're okay to get home on your own? I don't mind taking you and figuring out your car later."

Remmy shakes her head. "I'll be fine. Promise."

She slips her shoes on at the door as I pull it open and we both walk outside, the damp beachside air dusting our skin with moisture.

"You know, I'm still trying to figure out why you have any interest in this marriage thing," she says, abruptly shifting the direction of the conversation. "I mean, from everything we've talked about—though I know we haven't talked *a lot*—it seems like I'm the only one who benefits."

My lips twist as we continue the short journey to her car, a blue BMW I would guess belongs to one of her brothers if the racing kit is anything to go by.

Remmy doesn't seem like the type.

"I've already told you," I reply, tucking my hands into my pockets as she unlocks the doors. "I'm interested in finding a way to get my—"

"Parents off your back...yeah, you did tell me that."

She pauses, her eyes searching for something in my face that I'm worried she'll find.

"I guess I just...don't entirely believe you."

I don't say anything at her statement, not liking the way her head tilts to the side as she examines me.

"You're a great listener, Ben, and you seem like a pretty decent guy if your willingness to deal with my sobbing and throwing up is any kind of indicator." She steps forward, her body close to mine, her hand reaching out and taking the tail of my tie between her fingers.

The move doesn't feel sexual, although it might from someone else.

It does feel intimate.

Too intimate.

Closer than I want or need.

"You're not very good at letting *me* be a good listener, though," she continues, seemingly oblivious to my discomfort. "You seem like a guy who doesn't want to let anyone get too close. Even now, just this right here...I can see how you're bristling at what I'm doing."

My nostrils flare.

Not oblivious then—just uncaring.

Another thing I don't need.

"Are you one of those guys who's full of secrets, Ben?" she asks, continuing to ignore that I don't want her standing so near, watching me so meticulously.

I tug my tie out from between her fingers and step back.

"If I had secrets to share with anyone, Remington, it definitely wouldn't be with someone like you."

My words are blunt and carved in a way meant to strike and wound.

It's something I'm good at. Always have been.

Though I've never cared about the outcome.

Stick Wyatt in front of me, or one of my parents, maybe a business colleague, and I say exactly what I mean in a way that's meant to hit you where you'll feel it.

So then why does my stomach pitch over at the look that falls over Remmy's face?

It's like a mixture of sadness and disbelief and…something else.

Dejection, maybe.

A kind of gloom I wasn't expecting.

Most of the time, people brush my words off. They fling them aside with the wave of a hand, as if I wasn't intentionally trying to cut them off at the knees for whatever reason.

I'm quickly realizing, though, that Remmy doesn't seem to be the same. Her reflexes at handling my irritability aren't as well honed.

We watch each other for a beat, my own pride not allowing me to apologize for a comment that clearly hurt her feelings.

I can't apologize because I meant to say it. It wasn't said in ignorance. It wasn't said without care.

It was a targeted remark meant to do exactly what it has done: get her to stop talking.

"I'll see you Wednesday," she finally says, her voice a whisper of what it was a moment ago.

She opens her car door, which I catch at the top and keep open for her, and then she yanks it shut with enough force to echo down the street.

It's so...Remmy.
A whisper and a slam.
Melancholy mixed with anger.
She's equal parts soft and dark.
I don't like it. It hints at something I don't understand, at something deeper that I'm not meant to know.

And the last thing I need to do is start to truly care.

So I take a step back and let Remmy pull out of my driveway then speed down the block.

I chuckle to myself. Maybe that car isn't her brother's after all.

Chapter Six
BEN

It's rare for me to feel speechless.

I'm usually full of shit to say and very opinionated, which is why my inability to say anything feels so out of character.

I should just blame the pregnancy hormones. It seems like everything is this little swimmie's fault anyway. What's another thing to lump into the mix?

I feel like an emotional pendulum, swinging back and forth at the drop of a hat, at every little word or comment. Overwhelmingly happy and then bursting into tears. Laughing hysterically and then getting incredibly angry. Talking someone's ear off and then having nothing to say.

Like now.

I thought I'd take some 'me time' this morning, get out of the house and grab some new paint supplies, maybe find a way to deal with everything going on inside of my mind in a way that's more constructive than moping around my parents' massive estate.

Not once did it occur to me that I'd bump into anyone I know as I'm stepping away from the checkout counter with a big bag of new canvases and acrylics.

Especially not Paige Andrews.

Lucas' best friend.

Standing across the room from her makes me feel like my tongue has been removed.

When I met her for the first time, it was right after my family moved to Hermosa Beach. Paige, Lucas, Lennon, and Wyatt were this little quad of friends who had known each other for what felt like forever. It was long enough that letting in a new friend to their group took a while. It was mostly Paige, actually, who pushed to invite me to things and tried to make me feel like a part of the group.

Then we moved away, to my family's property in Colombia for a summer while my dad stayed in California. I didn't know it back then, but my parents were considering a divorce, which is like, the *least* Colombian thing you can do.

I loved the expanse of land on my grandfather's *finca,* the farmland that stretched as far as my eyes could see, especially the rows and rows of avocado trees on the southeast corner, near the small homes that the staff lived in.

I spent weeks lounging by the pool and riding horses, wandering the property trying to practice my horribly rusty Spanish with anyone who would appease me. I took the car into the city a few times a week and went shopping, exploring the plazas and museums. I even hiked a few times, enjoying nature in a way that just isn't encouraged in America.

Most of that summer was wonderful, and I fell in love with Medellín in a way I hadn't been expecting when my mom first whisked me out of the country.

But by the time we finally moved back and my parents had decided to give their marriage another chance, a lot had changed.

I had changed.

In painful and immeasurable ways.

But also in ways that gained Lucas' attention, which is exactly what I'd wanted when we were younger.

Paige wasn't as friendly the second time around, and I always assumed it was because she had a thing for Lucas that was unrequited and she resented me for it.

Maybe now that things between Lucas and me are over, she can move on to hating Lennon instead of me.

"Oh my god. Remmy?"

Paige's voice breaks through my trip down memory lane, and I do what I'm supposed to do.

I smile and pretend nothing is wrong.

"Wow. Paige. What a small world. What are you doing in this neck of the woods?"

We cross the shop toward each other, embracing in what we both know is an entirely plastic and disingenuous way.

"What do you mean what am *I* doing here? I'm here all the time. This is my store," she says on a laugh. "What are *you* doing here?"

I shrug a shoulder, trying to shove down the irritation I can feel bubbling up at Paige's response.

She's been this way as long as I can remember.

Everything belongs to her.

My friends.

My school.

My store.

She sees herself as a gatekeeper.

And for some reason, I've never had the password.

"Just grabbing a few supplies for something I'm working on," I finally reply, not wanting to share any further.

Paige's mouth stays open but her eyebrows furrow. "Huh," she says. "I guess I just wouldn't picture you ever coming here."

I can feel the hairs on the back of my neck stand to attention. "Oh? How come?"

She runs a hand through her short hair, fluffing it up a bit.

"Well, I guess I just picture you shopping more on State Street, you know?"

I can't tell if she's trying to be rude or nice, which is weird. Normally Paige is an open book, often to her significant detriment.

"You mean the shopping district by my school?" I ask, though I didn't really need to clarify anything. "Why's that?"

"Because it seemed like you were so desperate to never leave that area. I'm just surprised you managed to find the time to come down here when you could never find time to come to Hermosa and spend time with Lucas."

There are the claws I was waiting for.

I'm not surprised it only took a few sentences for her to lash out. Paige doesn't like playing the society game. She wants to be who she is and say what she wants.

And the truth is that after my weird conversation with Ben this weekend and how my mom has been acting and the emotions that always seem to pulse through me at just the wrong moment, I welcome her anger.

I've been *spoiling* for a fight.

So if Paige wants to get down like that, maybe it's time for the gloves to come off.

"Well come on, Paige. Now that Lucas and I have broken up, why don't you tell me how you *really* feel?" I say, surprising even myself a little bit. "Lay it all out there, because I know you've been pretending to try to bottle everything up since the minute Lucas and I got together. Half-ass sucking it up for seven years has to be exhausting."

Her eyes narrow, and it literally feels like she's taking a moment to mentally roll up her sleeves.

"Okay, you wanna know what my problem is? What my problem has *always* been?"

I nod, though she likely didn't need the encouragement.

"My problem, Remmy, is that from day one, you've had your sights set on Lucas. In and of itself, that isn't an issue. But what *is* an issue is when your sights lock so tightly on someone, when your grip is so strong on another human being, you don't realize when you're drowning them."

My stomach clenches at how she's worded that, so closely matching the sentiment I expressed to Lucas as we sat in the car together several weeks ago and ended things between us.

"You latched on to him and would not let go. Not when you cheated on him in high school and he started to move on with Lennon, the girl he'd had a crush on for years. Not when you moved away to college and cheated on him *again,* instead keeping him locked into some bullshit open relationship you *knew* he would never take advantage of. Not even when you slept your way around and came back to find him happy with someone else."

I grit my jaw, willing myself to stay quiet.

To take it.

Because I deserve it.

"You have continued, over and over, to fight the inevitable.

And in the grand scheme of things, two of my best friends lost years they could have had with each other. Thank fuck they're finally figuring shit out together, because if they hadn't, I would have considered you personally responsible. My only hope is that you don't sink those same fucking fangs into someone else I know and care about, and maybe you'll realize moving on is what's best for everyone."

She looks like she's just finished running up a flight of stairs when she's done. Her face is flushed and her eyes are wide, her nostrils flared.

Even though I was hoping to get into an argument, something that would help me expel some of this energy I haven't been able to get out of my system in weeks, my shoulders fall when I realize this isn't going to be the moment I've been searching for.

Paige isn't the person I want to fight with.

I deserve every single word she just said.

"You're right."

My words take a moment to penetrate, probably because she's exhausted and her brain isn't currently functioning at full capacity. I can tell when she does comprehend what I've said.

Partially because her shoulders drop and the flush on her face begins to fade, but also because she says, "Excuse me?"

I shake my head. "Everything you just said...well, *most* of what you just said is completely true. You're right."

She crosses her arms and glances around like she's confused.

It actually makes me laugh a little bit, which makes Paige look angry again, which makes me laugh even harder because she's super adorable when she's angry because she's so short. Paige has always been the cutest one in our little group of friends, no matter what her mood.

"I'm sorry, I shouldn't be laughing. Really. I just...I was planning to let you shout at me and then I was going to shout back because normally, I like to argue and fight when I'm emotional and upset, which is why I went shopping in the first place today. But after listening to you, I just can't shout back, because I'm exhausted. Totally exhausted."

I chuckle again, because I can't help it, but my eyes well with tears at the same time.

"And you're right," I add, my voice hitching when I think about it. "I did fuck up with Lucas. I knew I was holding on to him by a thread and that our days were numbered and instead of cutting him loose and moving on, I gripped on tighter because I was scared to let go of the only thing I've ever known."

I shake my head, some of my tears falling free and streaking down my face. The last thing I planned on doing this morning was breaking down in front of Paige freaking Andrews, of all people.

But I can't help it.

"My life is a mess right now and I feel so *fucking* lost, which is like, the *last* thing I ever thought I'd be telling *you*. I mean, you *hate* me. And I get it, I really do…because I hate me, too," I say, my voice choking and cutting off at the end. "But God, I'm so glad he's happy with Lennon. As much as you might not think it, I really do care about Lucas, and I would feel horrible if my shit caused him to drown. So I get it, Paige, I really do. I promise."

There's a long pause as she just stares at me.

"Well." It's all she says before shifting back and forth in her little tennis shoes. "This is not at all what I expected today to be like," she adds, giving me a somewhat chagrined smile.

My returning smile is watery. "Me neither."

We both stand in silence for a moment longer before I decide it's time to get out of here, to find some other way to deal with the feelings coursing through me, because this chat with Paige is definitely not it.

"I'm gonna go," I say, my voice soft, softer than I expected. "I'll see you around, Paige."

We give each other these really awkward waves, something that makes me feel like a kid, and then I turn away, exiting the store as quickly as possible.

When I get home, I take a long, hot shower even though I already took one this morning. I'm just hoping for a moment of calm before I push myself to have one final emotionally draining conversation.

Because today, I need to do the thing you're not supposed to do.

I need to call my ex.

"Hey, Remmy."

Lucas' voice feels like something smooth and warm caressing my cold, hard heart. Lucas has always been that for me: the place of refuge, the one space I felt safe and secure.

"Hey, Lucas. Sorry to bother you, I just—"

"You're not bothering me," he interjects. "I told you I'm still here for you, no matter what."

I nod as I take a seat on one of the oversized armchairs in my room, wrapped only in my towel.

For just a moment, I allow myself to feel that pang of wistful youth as I remember what it's like to love Lucas.

I'm not sure I was ever in love with him, not in the traditional way. Not in the way that meant I couldn't breathe without him. Not in the way true love in a relationship is supposed to look.

How I felt about Lucas was always this desperate scramble, this ache of need for his love that was rooted in a dark place. I felt like his love could heal my wounds, make me whole, fix the broken parts of me that were destroyed by someone else.

But that's not how life works, and instead of him lifting me up, I began to drag him down.

"I'm just calling to let you know I ran into Paige today," I say, feeling like this is the right thing to do. "I was shopping and she was there and she said all these things that I know are true and I just...I don't know. I wanted to make sure you know—not because Paige did anything wrong, but because I don't want the truth to get misconstrued."

There's a pause. "Yeah, she called me right after you left the store, actually."

I laugh, though the humor in it would be hard to find, even with a microscope.

"She said you apologized to her about us, and I just want you to know, Remmy...you never have to apologize, okay? Ever. We loved each other for a long time, and it's okay for that to have not been enough to keep us together."

"I know," I whisper, my emotions feeling raw and exposed.

Lucas was the one person I thought might have been my way to have something normal.

To *be* something normal.

But I was wrong.

Because even when I had him, I was still broken. I still did things that hurt him, things I thought would protect me but only ended up costing me his love in the end.

I clench my jaw, not wanting to stew in those memories. So I cut things off as soon as I can.

"Look, I gotta go, okay? But I hope you're doing well."

Lucas pauses again, and I think I hear a female voice in the background.

"Call me any time," he says. "And I hope you're doing okay, too, Rem."

I hang up without responding, wanting to get off the phone as quickly as possible, dropping it onto my bed like it's burned me.

And it has.

I wasn't holding out hope for anything between the two of us to repair itself—not even a little bit—but there's something about calling Lucas and knowing he's with Lennon that twists sharply inside of me.

It's not because I want *him*, but because I know he's happy without me...because I can assume he's happ*ier* without me.

And if that isn't enough to wrench apart something inside of me, I don't know what is.

My brush streaks across the white.

Blues. Grays. Blacks.

It isn't until my canvas is over halfway covered that I realize what I'm painting.

A storm over the water. Out in the distance, approaching the shore.

It's such a representation for how I feel right now even if I didn't paint it intentionally.

I never paint intentionally.

That's never the goal.

Instead, I allow how I'm feeling to explode in front of me, to take on a life outside my mind. It's a chance to purge out whatever feeling or fear or rush of joy is running through me.

Though mostly, my emotions tend to cover the canvas in darker colors, gloomier images, scenes that reflect the pains from my past, the worries of my present, my fears for the future.

There is so much on the way, scary things that are bigger than I can understand, things I don't know if I can handle on my own.

I sigh, mixing two colors together and smearing them into a corner, hoping to replicate the movement of the ocean. But it doesn't look right. Something's missing.

Setting down my palette and brush, I stretch my arms high above my head then twist slowly left to right, hoping to get the kinks out of my back.

Painting has been...a little less comfortable since the pregnancy.

I mean, technically *everything* has been a little less comfortable, but sitting for long periods of time in front of a canvas has been particularly bad.

Maybe I need to get a new chair or some kind of support?

I don't know.

I never seem to know.

Instead of going back to the unfinished canvas, I decide it's time for a break, maybe a walk down to the water or a solo lunch at Mary's, if my stomach decides not to be difficult.

I leave the canvas sitting on the easel in front of the window in my dad's mostly unused study and head in search of my keys.

Once they're tucked into my front pocket, my phone and credit card slipped into the back, I leave the house, wandering along the alley to the right of our estate that I know will take me all the way down to The Strand and open up to the water.

Being back in Hermosa Beach feels like...a bad trip.

Not that I have much experience with drugs. I have been given enough to know when it doesn't feel good, though.

That's what being here feels like.

What being *home* feels like.

Nothing feels right, or safe, or warm.

It's all cold, emotional, upset.

And then I wonder, not for the first time, if I should have just stayed in Santa Barbara, kept my small apartment and my shitty car and the life I was living that was *so* different than the way things are here.

When Paige told me she could see me shopping on State Street, I wanted to laugh.

I haven't bought anything on State Street in years. I didn't have the money.

Sure, I had *access* to it.

But I didn't use it.

Mostly because I didn't feel like lying to my parents any more than I already was.

I was only enrolled at the college they agreed to for a single semester.

Just one.

One was enough.

Enough for me to realize that no matter where you go, people are the same.

Selfish.

Manipulative.

Angry.

One semester was enough to break me until I didn't know if the pieces would ever be put back together.

So I left.

Took a semester off and used the tuition check from my parents to party and lose myself in the faceless, nameless men I thought could make me feel better.

The ones who liked to use me, too.

Slip inside of me and distract me from my disaster of a life.

Make me feel good again when I couldn't find a way to get there myself.

And then Josslyn about kicked down my door.

My old roommate first semester, before I fled our hall like a thief in the night. She was the only true friend I ever had at that school, and she wasn't going to let me shit my life down the drain.

She helped me apply to Alta Mesa Academy, a small art college in the foothills of Santa Barbara.

I had to lie to my parents about where I was going to school. My parents, my brothers, the friends I had at home—it just felt like everything was a lie. Everything was a lie, all the time.

So I stayed away.

Called rarely.

Kept things to myself.

Hid who I was.

Who I *was* and who I was *becoming*.

And my life changed.

I thought it would be enough, but apparently it's not.

It never is.

When I finally make it down to the beach, I let the breaking water rush up and cover my toes, the salty coolness sending a chill racing through my body and dampening the hem of my jeans.

I might regret that later, but for now it feels right.

The gravelly discomfort of the sand getting lodged between my skin and the fabric is a reminder that I'm alive.

A reminder that I *enjoy* being alive, even if things are hard and unsure and uncomfortable.

Because there was a time when I didn't.

When I wondered if being alive wasn't for me anymore, if I could quiet the memories and the pain forever.

It was my darkest time, something I've only ever shared with the therapist I saw during my senior year.

And Josslyn.

She was the only one who went to bat for me when everything happened at the end of that first semester. The only person to care when I just…disappeared from school.

The only person who has ever truly been there and known exactly what lurks in the recesses of my mind.

God, I miss her.

A shriek from a nearby child pulls me from my thoughts and I watch as a woman chases a young boy across the sand and toward the water.

"Jones, come back!" she shouts, though there's laughter in her voice.

The little boy giggles, getting closer and closer to the ocean before suddenly he's swooped into the air, his little voice bursting into full-out laughter.

The woman kisses him rapidly on his cheeks. "You can't run off like that, you little goofball," she says, spinning the child in her arms.

When she comes to a stop, she sees me, flashing me a somewhat embarrassed grin. "Oh, hey. Don't mind us," she says, her voice still filled with laughter.

I grin but say nothing, just taking in the comfortable way she interacts with her son.

I wonder if I'll ever look at my child like that.

If I'll love it.

If I'll mean it.

"Annie!"

My head turns to the side and I see a man in the distance, holding a toddler. He waves the woman over.

Annie, I assume, sets the little boy on the ground and then lifts her hand in the air. "Coming!" She glances back at me. "Have a great day."

She smiles, her happiness radiating through her, and then she slips her hand into the hand of the boy and the two walk off in the direction they were called.

Something about that interaction lances through me and I wince, my eyes brimming with tears.

I try to remember a single day in my life when I've looked as happy as that woman, even on the good days.

I can't find it. I can't find the memory that reassures me I haven't always been this dark thing, a mess, a waste.

I spin on my toes and march up the beach, my emotions feeling ragged and torn and suffocating.

For my entire life, I've only been worth what I can provide to men. I've only been used and enjoyed and discarded, by nearly every person around me.

I don't know how to do anything. I don't know how to be anything other than what I've been.

How am I supposed to give any kind of future to this swimmie thing if all I have to provide is toxic sludge and self-hatred?

When I make it back to the house, I don't even wash my feet off. I just storm through and up to the study, gripping a nearly full tube of black paint and squeezing it straight onto the canvas.

Lifting a brush into my hands, I smear it across the unfinished image I was working on. I swipe it back and forth, over and over and over.

Until it's covered in solid black.

And when I'm done, the entire canvas filled from edge to edge, I step back and take a deep breath.

I paint what I feel. It's what I know, and right now? This is a better reflection of my insides.

It isn't a storm in the distance, brewing and building.

The storm is already here.

And it will be a miracle if I make it through.

Chapter Seven
REMMY

"Correct me if I'm wrong," Dominic says, his voice low as we both lean against a wall in the entryway, "but isn't your boyfriend's name *Lucas*?"

I grin at my brother, though I'm sure it looks slightly disingenuous. "We broke up."

At that little bit of information, Dominic gives me a rare, legitimate, small smile. "When?"

"Oh, things with Lucas have been fizzling out for a long time," I respond, sticking with the part of the story that's the actual truth.

Ben and I agreed that vagueness about the length of our relationship is better than saying exactly how long we've been 'together'.

I don't usually lie to my brother, but with my mother a few feet away, I can't risk being honest.

"Besides, didn't you hear he's dating Lennon Day?"

At *that* bit of news, Dominic's posture shifts where he stands, his eyes narrowing.

"Lucas dumped you for a Roth?"

My own shoulders straighten, not liking that my brother's immediate reaction is to assume *I* was the dumpee, not the dumper. "It was a mutual decision. Besides, Ben and I are much better suited."

Dom grumbles something that sounds a lot like, "*Preppy fucking asshole,*" and I look toward the front door to hide my smile.

I don't think Lucas is a *preppy asshole*, but it's definitely easier to make fun of your ex than remind yourself of all their wonderful qualities.

"I don't know how I feel about this. For you to jump right into dating some guy—"

"He's not *some guy*. It's Ben Calloway. You were in the same year together at school. Stop being dumb."

"Dating some guy," he stresses again, his jaw like granite, "so soon after ending things with the *pelota*—it doesn't sit right."

I roll my eyes. Dom loves to call Lucas a *pelota*, has been doing it since we were younger. In Spanish, it literally means ball, so Lucas always assumed Dom was saying he was a ball to hang out with, or the life of the party.

Yeah, in Colombia, *pelota* is slang for idiot.

I never had the heart to tell Lucas my brother had been shitting on him for years and he was taking it as a compliment.

"Something smells off about this whole thing," he continues. "But if you want to play this little game and pretend you're not making a mistake, I'll go along with it."

Even though he pokes at me and might go overboard with the protective older brother routine on occasion, I love Dom. So much.

I glance at my phone, noting that it's been ten minutes since Ben sent me a text to let me know he was outside.

So why am I standing inside my house waiting for him to come up and knock?

My mother.

And I guess my brother, too, although he isn't really the one calling the ridiculous shots right now.

My mom is hovering, waiting at the door for Ben to walk up and 'collect me appropriately' for our date.

It's a scene straight out of fucking *Gilmore Girls*. All we're missing is the witty banter.

"Can I at least text him to let him know he needs to come to the door?" I say, gritting my teeth. "It's unfair for him to sit out there and wait when we agreed I'd just come outside."

"He'll figure it out."

I glare at my mom.

Another minute goes by.

"This. Is. *Ridiculous.*" My voice is ripe with irritation, and I even stomp my foot, just to really demonstrate how I feel. "I'm twenty-three years old. I'll go on a date with whoever I want, and I don't have to introduce them to my family first, especially when you already *know* him."

My mother's eyebrows pinch together.

"As long as you're staying in this house, you'll be treated right by a gentleman. You, *mija*, will be treated with respect, and he can come to the door and greet your family. You won't be *summoned* out to a car like a lady of the night."

Dominic's laughter is a quiet rumble that he cuts off quickly when he catches my glare, but I can't help the tiny smile that creeps onto my face.

My brother doesn't laugh often. The product of being around my parents so much, in my opinion.

"Lady of the night, mom?" he says. "I was on your team until you went there."

"Oh come on," she replies. "We can't expect—"

But whatever she wasn't expecting gets cut off by a knock at the door.

She lifts her eyebrow. "See? I knew he'd figure out what to do eventually."

I heave a sigh and wait as she opens the door, her body poised as if she's royalty about to greet an honored guest.

If I'm completely honest, she probably sees herself that way.

I giggle at the image of my mother in a crown.

But the giggle cuts off when I hear Ben's voice in the doorway.

"Good evening, Mariana. Always a pleasure."

I roll my eyes. Such a charmer.

"Benjamin, lovely to see you. What can I help you with?"

There's a pause, and I shake my head as my brother gives me a small grin.

They're evil.

Both of them.

"I'm picking Remmy up for our date this evening. I apologize. Did she not tell you?"

"Oh yes, she told us about your date. But I'm just feeling a little...confused, perhaps? Yes, that's the right word. I'm confused as to why you would beckon my daughter out to the car like—"

"Don't say it!" I shriek, eliminating my mother's chance to use *lady of the night* again.

She puts a hand to her chest and looks over at me, shock covering her face.

"*Remington!*"

Dominic laughs again, and I shoot him another irritated glare as I stride toward the door.

"This whole thing is a farcical mess. You made me wait in here until he walked to the door because of some old-school belief about dating and parental respect and whatever, but *guess what*—I don't care about it, and what I think is the only thing that matters."

My mother still stands at the doorway with wide eyes, clearly taken aback at my attitude. It's rare for me to get irritable with her, so I bet she has no idea how to respond.

"You already know and like Ben. We're going to dinner. I'll be back when I want, *if* I want, though I might spend the night at his place. *Bye.*"

And then I take Ben by the hand and drag him behind me as I walk down the pathway and out toward where his car is waiting in the circle drive.

When we get to his car, a sleek black Lexus that looks brand spankin' new, he opens the door and helps me inside.

Then he bends down and leans toward me, a smile spread wide on his face. "That was amazing."

I don't smile, but I know my eyes are sparkling. "It *felt* amazing."

He chuckles and closes the door, rounding the back and hopping in next to me.

"I thought your primary issue was that you didn't know how to stand up to your parents," he says as he pulls away. "Clearly, that's not entirely true."

I glance in the side view mirror at our massive house as we exit the drive and turn onto the street.

"It's not about whether or not I can stand up to them," I clarify. "*That* I'm capable of. I'm the black sheep, remember?"

Ben chuckles.

"I know how to stand up to them. The reason I agreed to the marriage is because..." I pause, realizing I'm admitting this out loud for the first time.

"Because?" he prompts, his eyes turning to me briefly before returning to the road.

"Because...they'll have a million questions about the father and I don't think they'll be able to handle the answers."

Ben's quiet for a moment, but when he does finally respond, I'm shocked at how well he gets me.

"Sometimes, it's easier for people to believe the lies we've crafted about ourselves for protection than it is to get them to accept the truth."

Neither of us says anything else as we continue down the road, on our way to a fancy dinner at The Royal as our first big outing together.

I guess it could be considered our coming out party, like those old cotillion things people used to do.

Scratch that—I don't like that idea. The last thing I want is another weird pointless tradition to dictate or define what we're doing tonight.

We have enough bullshit guiding us as it is.

"It's been a long time since I've gone on a date," Ben says, his voice warm. "Even longer since I've been to The Royal. This should be an experience."

The Royal is an old hotel in Hermosa that faces a large beach-front park. It's actually on the very edge of town, right near the Manhattan Beach Pier.

Which is probably why Ben picked it.

That end of town is filled with locals and money, and the people who frequent The Royal are the types to get our presence together into the grapevine faster than anything.

It really is perfect.

"I haven't been on a first date in seven years," I reply. "So just keep that in mind if I do something stupid."

Ben laughs. "Don't worry. We'll be doggy-paddling through this thing together." He pauses. "That will definitely make it seem more believable, I think."

My eyes drop from his face and fall to my hands.

Is it wrong of me to hate when he brings up the fact that what we're doing is for show?

I mean, logically I completely understand. But at the same time, how am I supposed to really commit myself to this...part? Yeah, part. How am I supposed to commit myself to it if he's always yanking me out of the scene?

We pull into the drive of The Royal and my door is opened, a valet worker assisting me out of the car, his eyes on my legs.

It might not be much longer that I'm able to fit into dresses like this one, so I wink at him, enjoying the attention.

"Remmy."

Ben's voice is curt, and when I look at him, I see his eyes narrowed in my direction.

I look back at the valet. "Thanks." And then I walk to where Ben is standing, looping my arm through his.

It feels natural and not at all for show.

"You know, it would be easier to convince people we're together if you weren't encouraging the high school boys to give you lusty eyes," he says, his voice low and only for me to hear as we walk through the front.

I snort. "Trust me, I don't have to encourage it."

His eyes narrow, but I can see something dancing behind them. Sometimes I wonder if he likes when I'm sassy.

"Ben?"

Both our heads turn at the female voice, and my heart sinks when I catch sight of the woman in front of us.

Hannah.

Lucas' sister.

"Hey, Hannah," Ben says, stepping forward to kiss her cheek, a smile on his face. "You here with Wyatt?"

She nods, her eyes tracking from Ben to me and then back to Ben. I can see on her face that she's a little confused; she's very bad at hiding it, having not been raised with the expectation that she constantly monitor her facial expressions.

I know what that feels like, when your every emotion is broadcasted on your face.

It sucks.

So I pretend not to notice.

"Yeah. It's so fancy, though. You think I'm dressed okay?"

Something inside me softens at Hannah's hushed question to Ben.

I don't know her whole story, even though I know the gossip machine was churning like mad when she showed up earlier this summer. It had to have been if I heard about it all the way up in Santa Barbara.

What I do remember is that she's a girl with a dark past, too.

Maybe I shouldn't be so wary of her.

Ben reaches out and gives her hand a squeeze. "You look great."

"Promise?"

He nods just as we hear another person say his name, this one male and a whole lot more familiar to me than Hannah.

"Never in my life would I have expected to see you here," Wyatt says, grinning at his brother and giving him one of those manly hug, back-tap, handshake things.

Then his eyes hit me and his expression shifts, almost like he's actively choosing to keep his face neutral.

"Remmy. I wouldn't expect to see you here, either."

He might be keeping his face free of any kind of displeasure, but the tone of his voice is filled with it.

"Wyatt. Good to see you, too."

His eyes return to Ben, a question in them that I'm unsure if Ben will answer honestly.

"Are you two on a date?" he asks, almost like he's just now realizing we're here together.

Ben steps to the side and slips his fingers in between mine, lacing them together.

I'm not sure if it's meant as a sign of solidarity to me or a message to his brother, but I'm taking all the strength from it that I can regardless.

"Just because I don't share my private life with you doesn't mean it's nonexistent," Ben replies, his face turning to mine, his expression morphing into something that has warmth pooling in my belly. "Things with Remmy are pretty serious, though, so it's good you've bumped into us."

I could get lost in his eyes, but he looks back to Wyatt when there's a beat of silence that goes on a little too long.

When I look, I have to bite the inside of my cheek to keep from laughing. The look on Wyatt's face is...one of a kind.

"Calloway, party of two."

The hostess' voice brings us back to the fact that we're

standing in the middle of the entry for The Royal, surrounded by a handful of others milling about and waiting to be seated.

"Looks like our table's ready," Ben says, squeezing my hand.

"Or our table," Wyatt murmurs.

At that, Hannah laughs.

When nobody else follows suit, she pauses. "Does nobody else feel like this is funny? This is like a sitcom. I bet they don't have two reservations. They probably thought you were the same person and only booked you for one table."

Ben and Wyatt look at each other for only a minute before they both walk off to talk to the hostess, leaving Hannah and me behind.

"I thought it was funny," I mumble, earning me a grin.

We stand in silence, waiting for the guys to come back, and I spend the free moment assessing Hannah. The girl who popped up in Hermosa Beach without any warning. Lucas' surprise and very secret sister.

But hardly any time passes before the men return, both striding towards us looking every bit the strong, handsome, rich men that they are.

My stomach dips a little bit when Ben gives me a satisfied looking smile, though it falls away when I see Wyatt looking tense and uncomfortable.

"They're going to seat us together," Ben says. "They would have made it work, but I figure this is a great chance for Wyatt and Hannah to get to know you a little better."

I feel like I'm listening to him underwater with subtitles. Like, I hear the words he's saying and I can understand them, but it sounds murky.

He can't be...seriously suggesting this, can he?

We *just* had a conversation about making sure we're on the same page. Was that just lip service?

I look to Wyatt and see that he doesn't look as happy as Ben about the decision, only confirming that it's true.

"Calloway, party of four."

The hostess re-calling us as a group has us all moving awkwardly in the direction of the front.

Well.

A dinner with my fake fiancé, ex-boyfriend's sister and his best friend.

This will definitely be a first date to remember.
Or one to forget.
I guess I'll just have to wait and see.

We're thirty minutes into dinner when I start to feel sick, but I try to push it aside since we're actually having a decent conversation and I don't want to look like I'm faking something in order to get out of having dinner with my date's brother and employee.

Or perhaps I should say my ex's best friend and sister.

Either way.

"So you're enjoying Hermosa Beach so far?" I ask Hannah, trying to make sure I'm participating.

She nods. "I love it. It's been an adjustment. It's very different from Phoenix." Then she looks to her left, at her man. "But Wyatt's been really great."

He reaches over and I can see him put his hand on her knee, his expression warm.

"And Lucas has been just...so instrumental in me feeling at home. You know? We've been doing family dinners—me, him, Wyatt, Ben, and Ivy."

There's a long pause as I consider what she just said.

"Wait...what?"

Hannah's eyes go wide and she turns to look at Ben and Wyatt, unease coloring her skin.

"It's good to know the word hasn't gotten around, then," Wyatt says, his eyes locked on Ben.

Ben lets out a long sigh and shifts his weight in his seat, turning slightly so he's looking at me.

"Ivy isn't just *our* sister. She's our legal sister, not blood, since we were adopted, which is all public knowledge. But what *isn't* is that she's also related to Lucas and Hannah. The three of them have the same father."

My mouth drops open as I search their faces for any kind of hint that this is some sort of joke, but all of them are looking at me with serious expressions.

"Who...who else knows?" I finally choke out once the first bang of shock has worn off.

"Lennon, Paige, my parents, and Ivy. That's it."

"And now you," Wyatt adds, his eyes narrowing, something unkind slithering through his expression. "We're not keeping it a secret out of shame. We're doing it to protect Ivy while she's young. The world isn't very kind to young girls these days."

I nod, completely agreeing with him, the surprise difficult to suppress.

"I would...*never* do something to hurt Ivy. Ever."

We may never have been close, but I grew up with Ivy running around, a little toddler with so much hair and lots of laughter. I'd never want to do anything that would negatively impact her life.

"It's actually a good thing Remmy knows now," Ben says, his voice strong.

Wyatt and Hannah turn their attention to him as he reaches over and places his arm around my shoulders.

"Especially since she's going to be a part of the family, too."

I grit my teeth, trying to hide my irritation.

This is the second time tonight he's done exactly what I made him promise not to do—make a decision without me.

And this one I *very much* disagree with.

"Ben," I say, my voice a whisper, though I'm not sure what I could say now. It's not like he can take a statement like that back.

"I'm sorry...what?"

Wyatt's question is marked with something that sounds like indignation.

"Remmy and I aren't announcing it just yet, but...we're engaged."

My eyes flit between the two sitting across from us, watching as that information ripples through their bodies. First their eyes, then their mouths, then their shoulders and postures.

Hannah just looks shocked, but Wyatt? There's no hiding the unhappiness, the sheer look of discontent etched in every feature.

"Congratulations," Hannah says, putting a smile on her face that—I'll give her credit—looks mostly genuine. "When you said things were serious, I didn't realize you meant *this* serious. I'm so happy for you, Ben."

He smiles at Hannah.

"Especially since you've always made it seem like you never

thought you'd settle down. Remember that chat we had? It couldn't have been more than a few weeks ago, right, Wyatt?" she continues, elbowing him gently in the side. "He said he didn't believe in *the one.*"

She laughs, like she's so glad he's finally come around.

"He did say that." This from Wyatt. His voice is cold and distant, his gaze locked on his brother.

"Alright, I've got a Waldorf salad."

A large plate is set in front of me, and suddenly, the idea of a salad with tuna and eggs and olives has my stomach turning over.

"Excuse me," I say in a rush as I push back from the table.

I move quickly through the restaurant, thankfully making it through the restroom doors and into a stall before I vomit up the tiny remnants from the avocado toast I had for breakfast.

Luckily, the morning sickness seems to be edging away, only happening every few days and only coming on for a short period, but it still seems to pop up here and there.

It's funny what you think is acceptable when you've experienced worse.

I flush the toilet and grab some toilet paper, dabbing my mouth and blowing my nose, then turn to wash my hands.

That's when I see Hannah leaning up against the sinks, concern in her eyes.

"Are you okay?" she asks.

I nod. "I've just had this weird stomach flu," I reply, maintaining the same story I've been using at home. Stepping up to the sink, I look at myself in the mirror, making sure I don't look like I was just throwing up. "It's at the very end, but it keeps hitting me at weird times."

She doesn't respond, so I don't look at her, not wanting to see whatever is on her mind, because I'm sure it will be easy to tell just by glancing at her.

Can she tell just by looking at me that I'm lying?

Because it feels like everyone can tell. Like it's stamped on my forehead.

"I know how it feels to be overwhelmed by change," she says.

"You don't know enough about my life to try to give me advice."

I can feel her recoil at my snappish attitude, and I instantly regret it. But I stay silent, wishing she would leave.

Clearly she belongs out there with them. She's more like family than I'll ever be. It doesn't matter whether or not Ben tells them we're getting married.

I'm just...not.

"I also know what it feels like to want to push away people who are nice to you because you don't feel like you deserve it."

My eyes fly up to hers, my nostrils flaring.

"I'll be honest, I'm in a tough spot. Your ex is my brother. I'm dating one of his closest friends." She pauses. "But something tells me not a lot of people have been nice to you in life, Remmy. I've been there. I *know* how it feels to be...the unwanted one."

My eyes close and I pray to any god who will listen that my eyes don't brim with tears.

They do anyway.

"Nobody deserves it. *Nobody.*"

The ferocity in her voice has me opening my eyes to finally look at her.

"I'd like to try to be your friend...if you'll let me."

When I continue to stay silent, she steps forward and squeezes my bicep in some sort of...I don't know, attempt to show care?

"Think about it."

And then she leaves the bathroom.

Leaves me standing there alone to think over everything she just said.

I brace myself on the counter and look at my reflection in the mirror, wondering what it is about me that screams *unwanted*.

Because if Hannah can see it—someone I've just met for the first time tonight—surely everyone else can see it, too.

Chapter Eight
BEN

"Okay, what the fuck is going on?"

Wyatt asks his question in a rush the second Hannah leaves the table, following Remmy to the bathroom.

Instead of responding, I reach across my untouched plate and grab my glass of whiskey.

"You're engaged to fucking Remmy *Wallace*? Are you serious right now? Because the last time I checked, you're not supposed to marry someone like that."

My eyes narrow at Wyatt, and I swear I'd grab him by the throat if we weren't sitting in this dining room right now, surrounded by people who make this town run and work with our parents.

"Don't you *ever* say something like that again. Do you hear me?"

His head jerks back at my tone.

Understandable.

I don't get angry at my brother. I doubt I've ever even used that aggressive tone with him before.

But whether I love Remmy or not, I will *not* allow someone else to talk about my future wife like that.

Or any woman, for that matter.

"You're right," he says, his gaze dropping. "That was too far."

I nod, taking another sip from my glass.

"But come on, Ben. Remmy? After everything we've heard about her and Lucas? Really?"

Sighing, I set my drink down on the table, perhaps with a little more force than I should, the loud thud of the thick glass bottom enough to draw at least a few eyes our way.

"Wyatt," I say, lowering my voice to make sure we aren't overheard. "What's going on between me and Remmy is between us, okay? We're getting married—soon. And I don't want to hear any negativity or advice from you on the subject."

He settles back in his chair and just observes me.

It's this new thing he does, and I'm not a big fan. Mostly because he looks like he's trying to read my mind.

His eyes widen and he leans forward. "Oh my god, is she pregnant?" he asks, his voice low.

My eyes close in irritation. *How the fuck...?*

"Oh my god. Ben."

I look back at him and crack my neck, trying to alleviate the overwhelming stress that has just come into my shoulders.

Count on my completely oblivious brother to figure something like that out as quickly as he did.

"Jesus." He rubs his hands on his face. "Does anyone else know?"

I pause, wondering how honest I should be. I'm not the only one who knows, and I don't like hiding things from my brother.

"Lucas knows," I finally answer, watching the color drain from his face.

"Fuck. Is he...?"

"No, he's not the father."

Wyatt falls back in his chair, his hand to his chest.

"I'm too young to have a heart attack, Ben. Seriously. This shit is ridiculous."

I shake my head. "You can't talk about this. Got it?"

He nods, rubbing his hands across his face again.

Behind him, I see Hannah returning from the bathroom.

"Not even to Hannah."

His nostrils flare, but he doesn't have a chance to respond as she sits down next to him at the table.

"She's okay, just a little stomach bug or something," she says, her voice sweet and clearly concerned as she sets her napkin back on her lap. "That must be the worst. I've never had a stomach bug, but it seems completely unfair. I hate getting sick."

I look at Wyatt.

He glares back.

"Let's dig in, huh?" I say, lifting my fork and knife, preparing to cut into my ribeye.

I take a big bite, watching Wyatt as he continues to stare at me. Clearly, me telling him he can't talk about this with Hannah is a bigger deal to him than everything else we've talked about this evening.

Good. It's important for him to be in a relationship with someone he trusts, someone he wants to be honest with.

Hannah doesn't seem the manipulative type, so I don't feel like I have to worry about them.

But if that's truly the case, she's one in a million.

I'd bet good money every woman in a relationship has an ulterior motive.

Money.

Power.

Sex.

Fear.

Sheer, unadulterated craziness.

There are probably a million other reasons, too.

It's why I don't do relationships anymore.

If you're going to be in a healthy relationship, you have to trust that person, and I know I'm incapable of trusting someone I'm in a relationship with.

So that means I should just steer clear of them entirely.

Enjoy the good times for what they are—good times.

I see Remmy making her way back to the table from the bathroom and something slices through me.

Everything tonight has happened so quickly, this is the first time I'm really seeing her.

Her short black dress shimmers as the light hits it, her long hair down and wavy, her lips slicked with something that looks like a delicious cabernet.

In another life, I could get lost in her.

Those long legs and curves are built to be gripped and held and chucked onto a bed, tangled in sheets and sweat.

I take a deep breath and try to shove that thought aside.

Good times, not forever.

It's important that I remember that.

"That was…interesting," Remmy says as we pull away from The Royal, leaving Hannah and Wyatt behind as they wait for their own car to be pulled up by the valet.

I chuckle. "It's always interesting when my brother's around."

"That's not what I mean," she replies, and when I glance at her, I see a hardened look in her eyes that I'm not expecting. "I'll be honest, Ben, I'm having an issue with how you keep pulling the rug out from under me, first with dinner at the same table and then with announcing our 'engagement' without asking me how I felt about it."

She puts quotations around the word *engagement* and then crosses her arms, her irritation visible in every muscle in her body.

I rub the side of my jaw with one hand and steer with the other as I try to decide what to say in response.

Because she's right.

I do keep making decisions without her, even though I told her I would try not to.

"It's hard for me," I reply, the words coming out of my mouth before I can think to stop them. "It's hard for me to allow someone else to influence my decisions."

When I glance over, I see Remmy sitting quietly, but her eyes are focused on me.

"But as my future wife, you aren't just *someone*. I'm sorry for not considering you. I'm just still…adjusting to that expectation, to the idea that my actions impact you and we need to do things *together*."

Remmy nods but continues to stare at the front of the car, the lights from the dash brightening the otherwise dark interior.

"We have to be on the same page about what we tell people, Ben, and *when* we tell them. My parents know nothing except for what my mother saw at the dinner you crashed last week. You might think they're super old fashioned—hell, even *I* think that—but they're still my parents. I don't always keep things from them because I'm afraid of them knowing. Sometimes it's because I don't want them to be hurt, and I don't want to risk something about us getting back to them before I'm ready to talk to them about it."

"That's fair," I reply.

We drive a little longer in silence before Remmy pipes up.

"So, what next?"

"What do you mean?"

"Well, we didn't really get a true date," she answers. "We spent time with your brother and his girlfriend. I was hoping for a little solitary us time, you know? I'm committing to marry you and I don't even know your favorite color."

"Orange."

She snorts. "Come on."

"I'm serious."

"Ben, nobody's favorite color is orange. That's like saying your favorite flavor of ice cream is...like, watermelon or something."

I shrug. "There's nothing wrong with orange."

She laughs, the sound filling the space with something much lighter than the mood was a few moments ago.

It reminds me that it's not so bad having Remmy around.

I might even say it's nice. For the most part.

Sometimes, I still wonder if I'm making a mistake, but generally, she's really...fun. And funny, like the comment about my favorite color and ice cream.

Speaking of which...

"Wanna get some ice cream?"

She giggles. "Actually, yeah, that sounds awesome."

I plop down next to Remmy twenty minutes later, the two of us seated on a bench outside Frosé, a new dessert and wine bar that opened up on the promenade at the pier, only five or six businesses down from my own.

Part of me wishes we'd just come here and enjoyed ourselves instead of going to The Royal. It's a gorgeous restaurant, but it is definitely a see-and-be-seen kind of establishment.

This place is so much more casual, much more conducive to a first date.

"What flavor did you get?" she asks, mixing her chocolate ice cream with her triple helping of Oreo crumble topping.

I take a bite of the pink goodness I've loved since I was a kid, lick my lips, and then respond. "Watermelon."

Her mouth stops moving, though it's still full of a way-too-big bite of ice cream.

"Shut up," she says, looking at me like I'm insane.

Laughing, I take another bite and shake my head before giving her my real answer. "It's strawberry."

She giggles, trying to finish off her mouthful and failing spectacularly.

"How did you get that much chocolate on your face?" I ask, unable to hide my grin. "You've taken *one* bite."

She keeps laughing, shaking her head and trying to wipe off the excess with her hand but only managing to smear it more.

"Did I get it all?" she asks, grinning at me, the look almost childlike in its ridiculousness.

"Not even close."

I set my cup down and tilt Remmy's face up so I can wipe the brown marks away. There are only a few, but she won't be able to get them without a mirror.

Once I get it all, I finally look into her eyes—those caramel beauties that have likely hypnotized stronger men than me—and for a moment, I'm lost in them.

They're so bright right now, so full of hope and happiness. I would never claim to be someone who knows Remmy well, but I *can* say it's rare for me to see her like this, especially up close.

Maybe too close.

Because for a brief moment, my eyes drop to her lips. They're plump and stained with a wine color that makes them look perfect for kissing.

When I manage to look away, back up to her eyes, I see they have grown hooded, that they're zeroed in on my own mouth, her mind likely contemplating the same things I am.

Wondering if kissing now is a good idea.

Remembering the kissing before, both at the country club and on my couch through the dampness of her tears.

"Thanks for taking me out," she says, turning her head away and extricating her chin from my hand. "Even if it wasn't exactly what I thought it would be. I still enjoyed it."

I clear my throat, reaching for my momentarily forgotten cup of strawberry ice cream.

"We should plan the next date," I finally reply, twirling my spoon into the pink dairy that is slowly starting to resemble soup. "It feels like we keep trying to schedule things and it never works out."

Like on Monday when she could barely stop crying and then kissed me with something so sweet I had to shut her down, or tonight when I got distracted by my brother.

"I work a lot, but I'll make time for this. I just need to know days, so text me what your schedule looks like for this weekend."

Remmy smiles. "Well I don't have a job, so I'm open whenever."

I puff a soundless laugh out of my nose. "Friday, then? I'll make another plan once I get home and take a look at the calendar?"

"That works."

We finish our ice cream in silence, sneaking glances at each other every now and then.

"You know, for my first date in seven years, this wasn't bad," Remmy says as we meander through the sparse weekday evening crowd to where my car is parked behind Bennie's.

The summer is coming to a close in a few weeks, but in a town that stays warm year-round, we're lucky to be able to enjoy the outdoors most days. The humidity is thick tonight, almost like rain is in the air.

"So glad to hear your rave review," I reply, sarcasm heavy in my voice.

Remmy smiles at me as I open her door and wait for her to climb into the passenger seat.

"But I agree. This date definitely wasn't as bad as I thought it was going to be."

I shut her door, round the back, and climb in the driver's side.

"Just how bad did you think it was going to be?" she asks.

I laugh. "Well, when you tout yourself as the black sheep of the family, I can't help but wonder if we're going to get accosted by a motorcycle gang or something."

She shakes her head. "You're ridiculous."

Just as I'm starting the car, the sky opens up, rain pouring down as the humidity breaks through the clouds and dumps all over the handful of people still on the promenade. Many of them start squealing and running for cover.

"Perfect timing," I say, backing out and heading toward Remmy's house.

"Not for me when we get home."

I lift a shoulder. "It's California rain—it could pass in minutes."

But it's still raining when we pull up in front of her house, the almost melodic sound of water falling onto the roof and windows filling the space with noise.

Instead of getting out and running to the door, Remmy turns to the side, her back against the door of the car, the movement highlighting her long legs as they stretch out before her.

I can't help but allow my eyes to run the length of them...all smooth, tan, sexy skin.

"Mr. Calloway," she teases, her voice lightening, "are you looking at my legs?"

My tongue runs along my lips without my permission, but I shake my head.

Remmy's head falls back against the headrest and her hand reaches up, her fingers twirling the strands of her hair.

She looks like every fantasy I've ever had rolled into one package, right there for the taking.

"What's on your mind?" she asks.

I can't tell her—not honestly.

How do you tell someone you're imagining what it would be like for them to hike up their dress and straddle you in the front seat of your car?

I've never been particularly forward. As confident as I come across, I know I'm a completely different person in business and friendships than in relationships.

And honestly, Remmy makes me a bit nervous.

Sure, I struggle with trusting her in general, with trusting any woman.

But I also know she's much more experienced than I am. If the rumors are true, her sexual history reads like a Kama Sutra book mixed with the cliché shit you see in porn.

Sex in public places.

Threesomes.

Letting people watch.

So, no, I can't tell Remmy what's on my mind because the last thing I want her to see is just how insecure the idea of sex with her makes me.

I lean forward, wanting to say this with sincerity and—

But Remmy leans forward, too.

"Oh thank God," she says, pressing her lips against mine.

Kissing Remmy wasn't my intention when I leaned in. I wanted to tell her... What did I want to tell her? I can't think through this fog as her mouth opens up and her tongue peeks out, tracing my lips until I let her in, eager to taste her.

She tastes like chocolate ice cream and sin.

She moans into my mouth as the kiss goes deeper, her hands rising to move into my hair.

Remmy gives my short strands a little tug, her fingernails scraping my scalp in a way that sends a shiver down my spine and along my arms, into my fingers.

God, I can feel her everywhere.

Her hands drop and rub along my chest, but when she gets to my belt buckle and starts to undo it, the metallic clanging noise has me pulling back.

Remmy, lost in a fog of lust, takes my retreat as an invitation and begins to climb over the console, slipping across with ease before I can say anything.

And then she's sitting in my lap, straddling me, her hips pressing into where I'm aching and hard, exactly like I envisioned just a moment ago and...

"God, it's been so long," she whispers as her hips begin to move and twist on top of me.

"Remmy," I say, momentarily giving in to the part of me that wishes I could get lost in her.

But my rational side knows this is a mistake, knows this isn't the right thing for us.

"What do you want me to do?" she asks, her voice breathy, her eyes closed as she kisses my neck and continues to rock against me.

My hands flex where they rest on her thighs, her tan skin warm and smooth in my grip.

"I'll do anything."

She sucks on the skin at the base of my jaw and her hands grip me tightly.

I wince, knowing I'm going to regret this later when I'm at home with blue balls.

"Remmy—stop."

It doesn't feel like I say the words that loud, but they echo in the car like a whip, the sound blasting the rain away and leaving the car completely silent for a second.

She stops moving.

Remmy pulls back and looks at me, her eyes wide as she takes in my expression.

"Remmy, we can't...we shouldn't be..."

I don't know why, but I can't get the words out. Maybe because what we *should* be doing doesn't really matter to me when I know what we *could* be doing, something slick and wet and... I nearly groan just thinking about what almost happened.

"Oh my god," she says.

I can see the mortification creeping through her body, the red flush that edges along her neck and up into her cheeks.

She shoves the driver-side door open and climbs off of me, much less gracefully than she climbed *onto* me.

"Remmy, you don't have to scramble," I say, trying to reassure her that she didn't do anything wrong.

But she can't get away from me fast enough.

Her ass hits the horn and her high heel slips off her foot, falling into the well beneath my feet. Her arm somehow gets stuck in my seatbelt and she actually trips as she finally makes it onto the concrete drive in front of her house, falling onto her ass on the wet pavement.

God.

I'm mortified *for* her.

Not because she's done anything wrong or stupid or worth laughing at, but because I've been in that position—so caught up in your own emotional reaction that you'll do anything to get away.

"Remmy," I try again. "You—"

"Save it, okay? I get it. You aren't interested." Her jaw is tight, her shoulders back and her chin high—that same defensive posture I've already seen from her multiple times. "I won't make that mistake again."

And then she storms off, hobbling up her driveway, leaving her shoe behind like a regular princess.

But the last thing I feel like right now is her knight in shining armor.

Instead of going home, I go to the gym. It's been a long time since I've gone at night, though the facility is open around the clock for the high-paying clientele.

The last time I was here this late was back when everything happened with...

I wince just thinking about it as I strip out of my dinner clothes and change into the workout shorts, shirt, and shoes I have in my locker. It's one of the things that convinced me Jim's was the way to go—I leave my clothes here and they launder them for me, making sure I have exactly what I need every time I want to work out.

Once I've changed, I head out to the long stretch where the bikes are lined up. I pick my favorite—the one at the very end—hop on, set it to a random scenic ride, and get moving.

Two miles. Four miles. Eight. Fifteen.

It's around mile twenty that I realize my mind isn't going to be distracted. I won't be finding that blissful nothing that comes when I choose to get on and ride. It's been happening more and more recently, my inability to truly calm myself with physical exertion.

No.

Instead of fading to black, my mind zeroes in on exactly what I don't want to think about.

Krissa Bilson.

I increase the incline and the resistance, standing up and pushing hard.

In the technical sense, she could be considered 'the one that got away'. She was a girl I was willing to do just about anything for, change my entire life for, give my everything for.

And it was all a lie.

Instead, she used me—used me to better her own life, even though it required the ultimate betrayal.

We met just after she graduated from high school. She was celebrating her eighteenth birthday, which should have been my first clue that the age difference between us—five years—was too much.

Maybe just a few years later in life, five years isn't that big of a difference, but for us it was. I just couldn't see it at the time.

Because I was blinded.

I wasn't the coolest of guys growing up. I wasn't into the things that make kids popular—kids like Wyatt.

No sports. No partying. No girls.

I liked school. I liked learning. I liked being planned and organized and thinking about the future.

Guys like who I was then don't get the girl. The hot chicks don't set their sights on them.

I spent my three years at Yale breezing through my undergraduate degree then another year at Stanford getting my MBA. All of my time was spent surrounded by books and computers, with other amazing minds and successful businessmen.

Which is why my return to Hermosa Beach to refurbish a restaurant and begin the next stage of my career as a culinary entrepreneur felt like a logical, calculated choice.

And why I never would have seen someone like Krissa coming.

Sure, she was a little young, and looking back, there were some red flags—some big ones.

But it's hard to see a red flag when you're wearing rose-colored glasses.

She seemed enamored with me, like she couldn't believe *I* would give her any attention.

Which was ridiculous, because I felt exactly the same. How could a young woman as beautiful and as charming as her see anything in me that would make her want...anything?

That arms-wide-open vulnerability—because I'd never been taught to close myself off—was what ended up being my downfall.

I thought I was falling in love with her. I bought a house, started making plans.

And then walked in on her and my dad fucking on his desk.

What absolutely kills me is that *he* set the appointment with me, told me I should come in to go over a few things.

He had the audacity to *smile* at me when I walked through his office door as he fucked her. *He smiled at me.* Like he'd been waiting for the day when he could screw me over by screwing my girlfriend.

And Krissa...I can't even fathom her perspective. She came to me with a fake-ass apology that wasn't even an apology, spouting bullshit about love happening when you least expect it and how she hadn't wanted to hurt me but thought me finding out was for the best.

Hell yes finding out was for the best.

The last thing I wanted to do was continue to dip into the same well as my father.

Disgusting.

I know the truth, though. Krissa wanted my dad because he was better leverage for the life she wanted, a life of pampering and spoiling. She wanted to be a trophy wife in a mansion, and my aim was a bit too low for her with my white picket fence.

So now, my goal is to bring him down. Cut him off at the knees. Cripple and debilitate him in a way he will never see coming.

It's why I need Remmy, though not in the physical sense, even if my body is trying to convince me otherwise.

Fuck, just thinking about her lips on mine, her body pressed against me, her hips rolling...

I feel something raw pulse through me, something that starts in my chest and trickles through my body, making me feel wobbly on the bike.

There's some kind of connection between us that I've never had with anyone else. It's almost enough to convince me I should give something real a try.

Almost.

But not enough.

I don't think anything will be enough to convince me I should put myself on the line again.

Krissa took what I thought was love and twisted it into something that made me wonder if I ever truly understood it in the first place.

Remmy could surely do the same.

A woman like Remmy is the type to bring you to your knees.

The type to take any kind of wall you build around yourself and blast through it without even trying.

Clearly I need to construct a stronger barrier.

When I hit thirty miles, I drop everything on the screen to a cooldown setting, my heart pumping hard and wild in my chest. It's been a long time since I've done riding with resistance like that, especially not for that long.

And I'm absolutely exhausted.

Hopefully this is just what I need to shower, go home, and pass out on my bed without thinking about anything too complicated.

Without my mind drifting to Krissa.

Or Remmy.

Chapter Nine
REMMY

Ben doesn't bring up the kiss in the car when we go out again on Friday.

I can't tell if I'm relieved or resentful.

We go more casual, grabbing some burgers at Beachside Brewing. Thankfully, we don't have any more run-ins with other people we know who might want to eat with us.

That doesn't mean there aren't eyes on us, though. I notice a few people take pictures out of the corner of my eye.

"Don't look at them," Ben murmured to me when the first flash went off.

I simply narrowed my eyes at him and took another bite.

Thankfully, we've been able to stay in the comfortable groove we momentarily found in front of Frosé, our conversations feeling full of both information and laughter.

It seems like as long as I focus on things between Ben and me staying strictly in the friend zone, we'll be fine.

So we'll be friends without bennies. Until we're engaged without bennies and then married without bennies.

Sounds *so* awesome.

Not.

I hadn't considered sex as a part of our deal, but now that I know it's off the table, it's all I can think about. I wonder if no sex is what normal marriages are like, which is why people find mistresses and misters. Will I end up having one of those?

I don't like that idea, but I can't imagine being in a sexless relationship. Mostly because I *love* sex. I love the control and the pleasure and the emotional high.

Too bad Ben feels differently—about sex or about me, I can't tell, but my guess is that it's me.

He was super hard in his car after he drove me home from our first date. I could feel him through his slacks, that rigid length was perfection as I rocked against him.

But he pushed me off.

So it's probably not the sex. It's probably me.

Which is definitely *not* a confidence killer or anything.

Who knows, maybe he's planning to have a mistress. Or he already has one, someone to sate his sexual appetite while he marries the girl his family will approve of.

I'm not a fan of that idea at all.

Although, I'm not sure what I dislike more: the idea of him meeting his sexual needs with someone else, or the fact that I'm feeling jealous.

Now it's Sunday and we're going to a movie hosted by the city council at the pier. *Jaws*—so unique.

It's been a long time since I've been to one of the summer showings, an August staple in the community I grew up in. I think everyone loves it so much because it's a way to distract from what's coming.

A new school year, for many. Change, for some. A shift in the weather, though not as drastically here as other places.

I wish a movie at the beach was enough to distract me from the change on the horizon.

Too bad there isn't anything that can really accomplish that.

"Remmy."

My brother Mathias—younger than Dominic, older than me—grabs my attention from where he stands at the door.

"Your *boyfriend* is here."

I roll my eyes. "Don't say boyfriend like that. You sound like an idiot."

Mati snickers but then continues down the hallway back to his room.

The three of us are all in our twenties—twenty-three, twenty-five, and twenty-nine—and we all live at home. I know it's normal in Colombian families for children to live at home until they get married, *and* that I really upset my mother when I chose to break from that tradition and move away.

I love my heritage, and feel proud of the traditions that have been passed down to me by my mother. But as high school started wrapping up and college got closer and closer, I resented my parents for putting pressure on me to go to a nearby school that would allow me to live at home.

That's what Dominic did, commuting to UCLA three times a week then getting his master's online.

Mati didn't go to college, was never interested. Instead he just started working for my dad straight out of high school. Staying close to his family like he's *supposed* to, even though he didn't go to college, means that he's still in my mother's good graces.

Me, though, I couldn't imagine staying at home.

I felt smothered.

Now, part of me wishes I'd stayed, wishes I'd never left.

Maybe things in my life would have turned out differently.

Or maybe they would have been just the same.

All I know is that I love my parents. I hate disappointing them, and I want to make sure anything between myself and Ben doesn't fly in the face of what our family values.

I wrap up the little doodle I've been messing with in my sketchbook and chuck it to the side, crawling off my bed and heading downstairs.

I've been ready and waiting for a while. I told Ben I could just meet him at the pier since his work is literally a football field away, but he insisted on picking me up.

He left work, went home to get ready, and then drove over here—as far as I know. So, I don't understand why he's showing up thirty minutes late.

"Sorry I'm late," he calls up to me as I round the top of the bannister and head down the stairs. "I got caught up with my distributor."

"I could have just met you there," I reply, my irritation at feeling forgotten simmering beneath my skin. "It would have solved all of this."

"But then we wouldn't be arriving together," he replies.

That's always his focus.

Who's seeing us? Who's watching? Is there any point if we aren't in the public eye?

I get it. I really do.

But we're only going on our third official date and it's already starting to get irritating.

"Do me a favor," I say, grabbing my towel and purse from where I set them near the door an hour ago. "Stop talking about who's watching us, okay?" I know my voice is holding more irritation than I should let on, but I'm feeling particularly bristly today. Then I say the words I wanted to say to him last time, and the time before that. "If you want me to act the part, stop yanking me out of the scene."

And then I breeze past him and out to where his shiny black car is waiting for us.

I hear him sigh behind me and pull the front door closed, his feet eating up the walkway as he catches up in time to open the passenger door for me.

Before I can climb into the car, he grabs my hand.

"I just...don't want to confuse anything," he says, his eyes searching mine.

I huff out a humorless laugh. "Trust me, Ben, after how you responded the other night, I know *exactly* how you see things between us."

And then I drop myself into the seat.

He hovers at the door like he wants to say something else, but after a beat, he steps back, letting out another sigh before closing it.

We spend the ride to the pier in silence, a calming station playing on low on the stereo.

When we park in his space behind Bennie's, he leaves the car running, the silence between us filling the space like it's a living thing.

He looks...wounded. Maybe a little unsure. And for a moment, I worry that what I said made him feel guilty, like I was expecting him to feel more for me, to feel anything for me.

"I didn't say that earlier to make you feel bad. I just..." My words trail off, my mind scrambling to try to make sense of how I feel.

How *he* makes me feel.

"You said you know exactly how I see things between us," he interrupts, his eyes focused straight ahead, the tail end of the setting sun blazing a light straight in his eyes. He shakes his head. "I actually think you *don't* know how I see things, because if you did, you'd run far away from me."

My stomach dips at his words, at what they mean.

"There is a part of me—a big part—that would love nothing more than to take you home and throw you on my bed."

My lips part in surprise.

"But I can't give you what you want, and going that route would do nothing but hurt us both."

"What do I want?" I ask, my voice a whisper.

I honestly want to know what he thinks I want from him and how it can possibly be any different than what he wants from me. It has been at least two months since I've been with anyone, and all I want is for him to slip between my thighs and pull me away from the worries on my mind.

I want him to distract me.

And I think he could use a little distracting, too.

Instead of answering, he laughs—but it reeks of something sour. Something tainted. Something twisted and dark.

"What all women want."

It's all he says before he turns off the car and steps out, the door closing with a soft thud.

I don't understand what he means by that. What do all women want? I could assure him that whatever *I* want is probably vastly different than what someone like Hannah wants. Or Paige. Or Lennon. Or Josslyn.

And honestly, I don't know what I want, so how could I even answer that for myself?

The passenger door opens and Ben's hand appears. I take it as he helps me out of the car.

Then he surprises me by leaning in and pressing his lips against mine, his hand coming up to cup the side of my face.

"We'll figure it out, okay? Whatever it is, we'll figure it out."

My heart softens, because whatever is going on between us…it freaks him out, too.

Maybe I don't have to be so uncomfortable or nervous, because like Ben told me as I sat crying on his couch like a total mess, I don't have to feel those things alone.

It feels like the entire city has come out tonight. There's a market going on in the promenade with live music and food stands. I can see a crew setting up the massive screen and speakers over near the base of the pier.

We wander through the crowd, hand in hand.

It might not be our first date, but it is definitely our first true night out on the town, surrounded by crowds of people who are likely seeing us together for the first time.

And we play our parts to perfection.

We laugh and point things out to each other. We chitchat with locals and people who frequent Bennie's.

He gets a thing of popcorn and tries to feed me pieces by chucking them into my mouth, then blames me for missing because I can't stop giggling.

He smiles a lot.

I smile a lot.

It's that same fun connection Ben and I always seem to share when we're just trying to enjoy ourselves, when we aren't putting so much pressure on things.

It's a good night. A good time.

Even though I know Ben is adamant that nothing happens between us, I can't help but take advantage of the situation before me.

Lingering touches. Long glances. Flirtation on high.

It's enough to twist me up inside in the best ways.

Maybe nothing will come from it, but I know how to make a man beg for my attention. I've been capable of doing it my entire life, even before it should have been something on my radar.

And if I were ever going to try to use that power of mine? Ben is the perfect candidate.

When an announcement comes over the speakers that the movie is going to start soon, we wander over to where I laid out Ben's massive picnic blanket a little while ago.

"Take a seat. I'll be back in a few minutes," he says. "I just have to grab something from the car."

I plop down, using my towel to wipe as much sand off my feet as possible so I can keep my blanket space as sand-free as I can.

Glancing around, I can't help but let my mind wander to what Ben told me earlier in the car, that he'd love nothing more than to throw me down on his bed.

I close my eyes, allowing myself just a moment to play out that fantasy in my mind.

A night after we've moved in together and he comes home from work to find me wearing nothing but a semi-sheer tank top and some lace panties, eating chocolate ice cream in the kitchen.

No. Too cliché.

Eating Nutella straight from the jar.

Yeah. Long licks on the spoon as he walks in to find me.

He loves the hazelnut spread as much as I do and decides to taste it from my lips. We don't even leave the kitchen as he begins to build my desire, to fan the flames that want to burn straight through my body.

A shiver races through me.

"Getting cold?"

My eyes fly open and I look up to where Ben is standing before me, his head tilted to the side as he assesses me.

I shake my head, both in response to his question and as a way to shove off the daydream I momentarily lost myself in.

Nutella and kitchen sex.

That's new.

"I brought us a little something," Ben says, placing a small cooler down next to me before he also takes a seat and brushes off his own sandy feet.

My eyebrows rise in surprise at the charming gesture.

"Mr. Calloway—you packed a picnic?"

He grins.

"I couldn't let us come all the way out here and not experience a true beach picnic, could I?"

I lift the lid, peering in. "I wish you'd told me. I would have saved my appetite for this instead of wasting it on popcorn."

He packed some cheese, a little loaf of bread, and a bottle of Martinelli's.

I pull the cider out first.

"And you even went alcohol-free," I tease. "So thoughtful."

We settle in and start nibbling on the snacks just as the movie starts playing, the sounds echoing across the beach.

"I've never seen this movie."

My mouth drops and I whip my head around to look at him.

"You've never seen *Jaws*!?"

He laughs a little bit and then shushes me. "Not so loud. You don't want to disturb the other moviegoers."

I roll my eyes and place a slice of aged cheddar onto a piece of bread. "More like you don't want me to embarrass the shit out of you by announcing to the crowd that you haven't ever seen one of the most amazing movies ever created. I cannot *believe* you haven't seen this. It's like...a childhood staple to get super freaked out by the score." When he just keeps watching me without reaction, I set my snack down and rise up onto my knees. "Duuuhhhhh dun."

He shakes his head at my childishness.

I creep even closer to him.

"Duuuhhhhh dun."

"Remmy."

But I can hear the laughter in his voice, my hands tapping along the blanket between us as I continue to creep closer to him.

"Duh dun, duh dun, duh dun, duh dun—"

"Okay, okay!" He laughs. "I get it."

I fall onto my back and laugh too, appreciating the levity of the moment.

It's been a while since I've been able to laugh like...a kid.

Not that I *am* a kid—that ship sailed a long time ago—but it feels good to let loose a little bit in a way that just allows for silliness and ridiculousness without a need to impress anybody.

Ben lies back on the blanket next to me, neither of us at all interested in paying attention to the movie.

"You know, you're a lot different than I thought you'd be."

He turns to his side, propping himself up on his elbow.

"How so?"

I shrug, though the movement is awkward since I'm lying on the blanket.

"I don't know. I guess I'm just figuring you out a little bit."

He's quiet for a moment, and I turn my head to watch him where he hovers above me.

With any other man, I'd consider how we're positioned an invitation to do something more, something inappropriate for where we are.

In public.

But I can't read his expressions like I can with other men.

He guards how he feels like it's something he wants to hide away from me.

"I'm still trying to figure you out, too," he whispers.

And then I see it.

His eyes drop to my lips.

Just for a moment.

A brief second before he looks away, his jaw tight.

"You should call in sick tomorrow," I say, the idea popping into my mind out of nowhere. "We can do something fun, maybe go up to Santa Monica for the day."

It takes him a minute to respond, and when he does, whatever tension gripped him a moment ago is gone.

"I don't take days off."

He says it so matter-of-factly that I actually laugh, assuming he's joking. But when he doesn't join me, my own laugh cuts off abruptly.

"Are you serious?"

He nods.

"You never take a day off?"

"Not unless I'm actually sick."

My face contorts. I don't think I've ever known someone to just...work *every day.*

"But *why?* Like, why would you ever choose to work like that?"

He just lifts a shoulder in a half-shrug. "I like being busy."

My chuckle is full of disbelief. "So get a hobby. Take up fencing or make those little airplane models or whatever. You don't need to just live at your job. That's not healthy."

He snorts. "What makes you think I would *ever* make airplane models?"

"Oh come on." I give him a shit-eating grin. "I might still be figuring you out, but you know you're a big nerd. Always have been."

"That is..." he scoffs. "That is absolutely false."

I level him with a look that screams *I call bullshit.* "You created the Young Entrepreneur Club when you were at Roth—nerdy," I say, referencing a student organization that is still thriving.

"Because I wanted to go into business for myself—not nerdy."

"You were voted Worst Social Skills for your senior year superlative—nerdy."

"Excuse me, how do you remember that? That was definitely before your time, and it got taken down almost immediately after being posted because someone reported it."

"Was it you who reported it?" I ask.

Ben pauses, and I can see a flush of red on his neck where his polo shirt parts at the collar. Polo shirt—also nerdy.

"So you're a narc—nerdy," I say.

His eyes narrow, and he leans forward again.

"You know, I don't appreciate this little game you're playing right now, Miss Wallace."

I chuckle. "Well I'm *loving* it."

"Oh really? Would you love it if we flipped it around on you?"

My smile drops a fraction.

"I didn't think so. Besides, if I remember correctly, I'm not the only one who's had a shitty superlative in life. Didn't I hear about you getting voted something your freshman year of college?"

My smile completely disappears, the shock that Ben has heard anything about this rippling through my body and leaving me immobile. I don't want to play this game anymore.

"What was it again?" he says, his eyes facing toward the movie screen, lost in thought, a grin on his face.

"Ben, stop. It's not funny."

"Oh yeah," he says, snapping his fingers, his eyes coming back to mine. "The Bicycle Award."

The pain lances through me swiftly, and I know I can't hide the wince on my face. I swallow awkwardly, my face feeling flushed, and I can see the moment when Ben realizes what he said.

His eyes widen, a sudden expression of bewilderment filling his features.

I turn my head away from him, looking off to my right, to the large crowd surrounding us, everyone completely unaware that I'm dying inside.

"Remmy," he says, and I can feel his hand taking mine into his. "Remmy, I'm sorry. I didn't..."

I look up at the sky above us, only able to see a few twinkling stars because of all the light pollution. It's mostly just a vast open mass of blackness, and I wish it would swallow me whole.

That fucking award.

Given to me at the Christmas party in my freshman hall by my RA who hated me.

I'd already known she didn't like me, but giving me that award in front of everyone was...it was like swallowing a piece of hot metal. It scalded me on the inside and left me sick for a long time.

The Bicycle Award...given to the most ridden girl.

I was completely mortified.

It wasn't until later that I found out I'd slept with her boyfriend. It didn't matter to her that the guy didn't tell me he was dating someone. He sure hadn't had to deal with the brunt of her rage after fucking me in a gazebo behind his fraternity a few weeks before.

So why the hell had it been *my* fault?

"I didn't think about it all the way through before I said it, okay? I'm sorry."

Ben's still apologizing, and I can tell he feels bad. Like, really bad. But that's the thing about wounds, right? You can say all the nice things you want after the cut has been made, after the scab has been ripped off, after the infection has grown.

But that doesn't mean the resulting scar will just go away.

That doesn't mean it doesn't still hurt.

I had a teacher in my mass communications class give us an example of apologies by bringing someone to the front of the room and handing him a plate.

"Throw it on the ground," he said, so the student grinned and smashed the plate into bits on the carpeted flooring.

"Now tell it you're sorry."

The student laughed uncomfortably. "Um...sorry."

The class giggled, myself included.

"Did your apology fix the fact that the plate is broken?" the teacher asked.

Everyone remained silent, probably the most silent we'd ever been.

"That's the thing about words—once you say them, they can't be taken back. Sure, you can use glue to try to put the plate back together, but it will always carry the mark from having been broken in the first place."

I'd never felt so fucking seen in my entire life.

Because that plate was me.

Smashed up and broken into little bits on the floor.

And no amount of pretty words or niceties will ever be enough to fix me.

Chapter Ten

REMMY

I told him I'd be back, said I just needed a minute to myself.
It's been an hour and I can see him from where I'm cloaked in darkness underneath the pier.
Where I'm hiding.
He's sitting there, his knees bent, his arms resting casually, his hands clasped together.
Not watching the movie. Not looking at anything in particular. Just…staring off in the distance.
He looks miserable.
Logically, I know Ben's comment to me was not an intentionally inflicted wound. I know he was just messing around.
But that particular gash in my side—the memory of a time when I worried for my safety and my sanity in equal measure—isn't something that has healed over neatly.
I don't know how long it will take me to regrow my skin.
It's a hard thing to admit to myself, for sure, especially when I

like to believe the armor I wear makes me virtually impervious to attacks from others, intentional or not.

I look away from Ben, settling back against the rocks that form the wall surrounding the base of where the pier meets land. My long legs stretch out in front of me, my jean shorts growing more and more damp the longer I sit in the wet sand, allowing the waves to reach up and touch my toes.

Living a few hours away clearly wasn't enough distance to keep the gossip from churning right down the coast and hitting my hometown. I thought I left that bit of life behind when I dropped out of college.

Clearly I was wrong.

I don't know how Ben knows about what happened my freshman year, but I hate that he does. Truthfully, I hate that *anybody* would know about what happened, but for some reason, Ben seeing what people really think about me cuts far deeper than I was expecting.

I know what I am.

I know how men see me.

What they want me for.

For most of my life, I made the choice to lean into it.

You want me to be your whore? I'm going to be the best goddamn whore you're ever gonna have. You're going to remember your nights with me.

I saw a therapist during my first few months at Alta Mesa, although it was only for a few sessions.

Apparently artistic folks have a lot of emotional problems, so the school has therapists and psychologists on hand to deal with the drama and trauma we've all decided to ignore or work through.

His name was Dr. George, and I loved saying his name. It made me laugh. He helped me realize that we often use what the world considers a weakness or a negative—for me, sex; for others, it could be addiction, anger, or a million other things—to cut people out of our lives.

You think you want to know me? Well here are all of my worst qualities. Here are my most negative facets, my shittiest pieces. I'm going to show you my everything to see if you're really willing to stick around.

I honestly think he's right.

Because that's what I do. It's what I've done with everyone I know.

It's easier to show them my worst and watch them scramble to get away from me than to hold it in and have them abandon me later when I show them my soft spots.

I would have liked to continue seeing Dr. George, but he referred me to another therapist after I fucked him during one of my sessions. He claimed it would be a conflict of interest for him to keep seeing me.

See? Just another example.

I showed him my weakness, my broken parts, the part of me that craves the physical like I can't breathe without it.

And he couldn't handle it, so he pushed me away.

I heard he got a new job at a different school later that year, went as far as leaving Alta Mesa to get away from me.

Because he knew it then just like I know it now.

I'm only good for one thing.

"Remmy."

My head jerks up when I hear my name, my eyes colliding with Ben's.

But I look away just as quickly. The last thing I want to see is whatever that look is on his face.

Pity.

Sympathy.

Compassion.

I don't deserve those things.

And I don't want them either.

"Remmy, I'm sorry."

He drops down to my right, his knees in the sand, a single hand coming out to rest on my thigh.

"I'm *so* sorry. I've been sitting over there trying to put words together, but I realized...there isn't anything I can say to fix this. All I can do is tell you I spoke out of turn, and even though I don't know the whole story, I know for a *fact* that you don't deserve whatever that...award was for."

I laugh, feeling the toxic sludge inside my soul begin to bubble over.

"You think I didn't deserve it?" I reply, my voice barely loud enough for him to hear with the waves rushing to shore so close to where we sit.

I look off into the distance, toward the moon that hangs low in the sky, the reflection glowing in the water.

"Do you know what a Bicycle Award is, Ben?" I don't look at him when I ask, because I don't want to see his response in his face if he does. And if he doesn't, I don't want to see his reaction when he realizes what it means about me. "It goes to the whore, the most *ridden* woman, the one who fucks everyone because that's all she's good for."

"Remmy..."

But I continue, not letting him correct me or lessen it. "That first semester, I slept with new guys every week, sometimes with more than one at a time." I close my eyes, trying to push away the sticky tar that makes me feel like trash, instead focusing on remembering the pleasure that muted the world, if only for a little while. "It made me feel good to know they wanted me, to know I held that power and *I* was the one who got to control it."

When I open my eyes, I see Ben just staring at me, his lips parted, not even trying to hold back his surprise.

"An award like that makes it sound like *I'm* the one being used. Because I'm the bicycle, right? The one everyone wants to ride?"

I let out a long moan, the sound quiet but loud enough for Ben to hear.

"Being that woman is intoxicating, though, and you know why?" I ask, rising up on my knees and moving closer to Ben. I place my hands on his shoulders and lean close to whisper in his ear. "Because what they want is something only *I* can give them, something warm and tight and wet."

I press my hand beneath Ben's legs, feeling the manhood between his thighs and rubbing my palm against it through his jeans.

"God, Ben, don't you want that?" I croon in his ear, feeling his dick thicken and lengthen in my hand. "Don't you want to get lost on a ride so long and good you can't remember where you are?"

He pants out a breath in my ear, a small groan rumbling from his throat, and I do what I know he wants.

I press my lips to his neck and start to suck and nibble at his warm skin. My hands undo the button and zipper of his jeans and I reach inside his pants to take hold of him in my hand.

God, he's big.

"Fuck, Remmy," he says, his head back and eyes closed, his

breathing coming out fast.

"Does that feel good?" I ask him, my teeth nipping at his ear as I jerk him in his jeans. "Do you want me to ride you right here where anyone can see us?"

He groans again, louder this time.

And then I whisper into his ear. "Do you want me to be your whore?"

I barely have the words out when a firm hand grips my wrist and yanks me away from where I'm holding him.

When I jerk my head back to look at Ben, I see he's looking at me with wide eyes, his lips parted, his chest rising up and down with his panting breaths.

"Remmy," he whispers, and then his head shakes from side to side in slow movements.

Not even addressing his still-hard dick, he yanks me to him, wrapping his arms around me and tucking me in against his firm body, his hands squeezing me tight.

I'm so confused... I don't... What is he doing?

"You're not a whore, Remmy. You're *not*."

He strokes my hair, the wavy mass tangling and untangling between his fingers.

"It doesn't matter what you've done, or what you've been called, or what has happened in your life to make you believe that," he says, his voice firm and warm and sure. "You are strong and resilient and wonderful. Do you hear me?"

And then he pulls back, his hand rising to my face, cupping my cheek, his thumb stroking away wetness I didn't realize was falling from my eyes.

His eyes search mine for a moment longer, and then he pulls me back against him so we're lounging against the wall underneath the pier. We're in the darkness, hidden away.

His hand keeps stroking my hair, and his other arm continues to hold me tight to him.

I've never felt so confused and unsure, so lost and yet...not.

I don't understand Benjamin Calloway. I don't know where his mind goes, what he dwells on, how he thinks about what he should say or do in any given moment.

I meant it earlier when I said he was different than I originally thought he would be.

My assumptions were that he would use my body as much as

he wanted to.

And that I would use him right back.

To make myself feel good.

To make myself feel better.

But that isn't the case, and now...now I feel like I'm flailing.

A fish out of water.

The only thing I've ever understood about men is that they want what I have to offer, and now even *that* doesn't seem to be true.

Now it seems like Ben thinks there's something else I have to give.

Something different.

His words fill the hollow place in my chest instead of wreaking havoc on what I thought were the foundations of my life.

So where does that leave me in the grand scheme of things?

How does this change the way I see the world?

Should it change the way I see the world?

Or is Ben just an anomaly?

Is Ben a different kind of man? Or is he just a man who doesn't yet fully understand what he's capable of taking from me?

All I know for sure is that the way he makes me feel inside is overwhelming. It's too much at times, and I don't understand how he does it—how he's managed to weasel his way into a space beneath my ribs in such a short period of time.

He makes me want to ignore everything I've learned about men and just lean hard into his side, allow him to continue treating me the way he has been.

Like I matter.

But I don't know for sure if that's a risk I'm willing to take.

I guess only time will tell.

It's four days before I finally send Ben a text.

I'm not sure if he's been avoiding me or if he's giving me space he thinks I want.

But the shame I feel after the epic clusterfuck that was the Sunday movie at the pier has finally started to dissipate enough that I'm willing to interact with him again. Although I'm not entirely sure what I hope to gain from reaching out.

Me: Hi

I stare at my screen, wondering if I'm an idiot for sending something so damn basic, then slip my phone into my pocket before heading down to the front patio for breakfast.

My brother Dominic is sitting in the same place he always is. Back rigid, face clean-shaven, wearing a three-piece suit, he sips a cup of coffee and reads the paper as I approach the table.

"Morning," I say, plopping down in a seat opposite him and lifting my feet to place them on the chair next to mine. "Is Julia making breakfast?"

My brother observes me over the top of his newspaper for only a moment before his eyes return to whatever is on the page.

"She is."

"Perfect. I'm *starving*," I say, reaching over and plucking a strawberry from the bowl in front of Dom.

"Interesting."

I expect him to say more, but he doesn't. So I do the stupid thing and ask.

"What's interesting?"

"That you're starving, considering you've been so sick every morning for the past few weeks."

I freeze mid-chew, my eyes flying back to my brother, who is now looking at me again over the top of his newspaper, his expression far more neutral than would be natural for anyone.

"I'm glad to see you're getting over that...*stomach flu*...or whatever it was," he continues.

Just like that, whatever appetite I'd managed to drum up for myself dissolves, my throat growing dry.

Unfortunately, that's the moment Julia decides to walk outside, a smile on her face. Always a smile, this one. The ultimate optimist in the face of anything and everything.

As present as my parents were throughout the course of my life and as much as I love them, it was Julia who was around for much of my childhood. She was the person I told my secrets to when I was younger.

If I were going to pick anyone in this house to talk to about the pregnancy first, it would be Julia, even though I wish it could be my mother.

Although, if Dominic is implying what I assume he's implying, I may not get a choice in deciding who knows what and when.

"Morning, sweetie. What can I get you for breakfast, hmmm?"

I smile at her, but my face feels brittle.

"Just some scrambled eggs and orange juice. Do we have any muffins?"

"No, but I just made some croissants this morning."

"Perfect."

She heads back inside, and it takes all of my energy to look back at my brother, who is no longer watching me.

I let out a quiet sigh of relief.

Maybe I was assuming something. Right? Like the guilty person who thinks everyone is looking at them. It's all in my own mind.

I pull out my phone and start flicking through my social media accounts. I'm not very active, rarely posting or sharing anything. I use it more as a way to watch the world than to share.

I don't like to share.

Josslyn sent me a picture of the art store where I used to work and a message saying she hates walking by knowing I'm not there.

A text confirmation for a hair appointment at H2O this week.

I sit up straighter when I see what else.

An email from my advisor at Alta Mesa encouraging me to apply for a graduate program.

At that, I can't help but grin.

I've been feeling a little discombobulated about the future recently, and this feels like a reminder that not everything in life is so chaotic.

Not that I *have* to go to grad school. Or have a job, for that matter. But I can't imagine not doing anything and just continuing to live at home here with no true care about the future. Some of my friends do that—just live off their inheritance and their parents.

I guess I don't have any room to judge. I spent my whole life being taken care of, having everything I wanted given to me, within reason. And then when my world felt like it was falling apart, I used money from my parents to fund a life of the most vapid, self-indulgent, unhealthy bullshit any girl could ever wrap herself in.

But I don't do that anymore.

And I don't *want* that for myself.

Which is why this email is such a welcome surprise in all the muck and sludge I feel like I've been trudging through for the past few weeks.

"So tell me..."

My brother's voice has the smile slipping from my face.

"...this...*stomach flu*..."

I swallow awkwardly, my tummy pitching over as I wait for the rest of his sentence.

"Is Lucas the one who got you...*sick?*"

It takes longer than I'd like it to for me to admit I understand exactly what he's asking.

His eyes narrow, and I can tell.

He knows.

He knows I'm pregnant.

And he thinks Lucas is at fault.

Part of me wants to laugh.

If you only knew, brother. If you only knew what really happened, you wouldn't look like that.

Slowly, I shake my head.

As much as I want to resist this faux conversation about 'the stomach flu', there is also a part of me that wants *someone* in my family to know what's going on.

I might not see eye to eye with them on everything, but they're my family, my rock, the center of all that I know.

I've been hiding myself away from them for so long for a million different reasons.

Having Dominic on the inside of what's going on with me feels like a different kind of relief than I've felt in a long time.

"Is Ben?"

At that, I pause.

If I'm honest with Dominic, there's no taking it back. If he knows Ben isn't the baby's father, there's always a chance someone will come along and figure out who the father really is. And that would be...

I blink, pushing that thought away.

I want to lie to Dominic. I want to tell him what makes all of this easy.

But I can't.

So I shake my head again.

Dom's nostrils flare, but he doesn't say anything else.

"Alright, sweetheart. Scrambled eggs and juice and a few little croissants. I cooked up some bacon for you, too."

Julia's voice breaks through the moment, and a tray appears in front of me as she places two plates and a cup on the table.

"Let me know if you need anything else, okay?"

I nod, though I don't look up to meet her eyes.

"Thanks, Julia."

She disappears back into the house and I pick up one of the croissants, tearing apart the flaky dough and shoving some of it into my mouth.

Hungry or not, I'm growing a human. Hopefully the bready goodness will help keep my stomach feeling a little more balanced.

"Have you considered…taking any medication to…get rid of the flu?"

At Dom's question, my face twists, and the faux nature of the conversation goes out the window.

I sit up straighter, my face twisting.

"Are you suggesting I consider an abortion?"

His entire neck flushes red, but his facial expression never changes. That pale skin of his—definitely thanks to our dad's Irish background—is his one area of weakness, the one thing he's never been able to get control of.

It almost makes me want to smile.

But I don't.

"Not suggesting," he finally replies after a long moment where he looks slightly constipated. "Merely…asking if it was ever a consideration."

I grit my teeth. "I thought about it, okay?" I admit it to my brother, the shame of that consideration leeching through my veins. "I did. But I just…can't."

The last thing I want to do is get into a conversation like this with Dominic. I love my brother, and I appreciate that he cares enough to talk to me. But at the same time, the nitty-gritty of this should not belong to him.

It belongs to me and me alone.

Which is why I don't tell him *just* how closely I considered and examined and weighed my options.

That information is between me and God and is something we can talk about someday when I'm at the pearly gates waiting for

Him to decide whether all my shitty behavior outweighs forgiveness.

Being raised in a strictly Catholic family grooms you to believe certain things, some of which are wonderful and amazing—and some of which are not.

I'm still on the fence in regards to how I feel about my faith, but some of the tenants I've learned at mass over the years are hard to escape.

Forgiveness being one of them.

I can only hope the forgiveness I've been promised is enough to wipe clean the depth and breadth of my sins.

Though I won't hold my breath.

Dominic and I sit in silence as I finish breakfast and he pretends to continue reading the paper.

I can tell he's pretending because he's turning the pages too quickly. He's never been a fast reader. Mati used to tease him about it when we were younger. I know his eyes are just skimming the text and not really taking anything in as he moves from page to page.

"You can't tell mom and dad," I say sometime later, realizing Dominic is the one who doesn't keep secrets from our parents.

"You don't think they should know what's going on?" he asks. "Don't you think they'd be of some kind of help to you?"

"Absolutely not!" I cry out. "Helpful is the *last* thing they would be in this situation."

My brother actually looks lost for words.

"What they'll be is judgmental and harassing. They'll take every opportunity to dig into me for the *choices I've made* or the *lifestyle I've lived*," I say, shifting the pitch in my voice to mimic my mother. "We live in completely different worlds, Dom. You can do no wrong. You can do whatever you want and they'll say you're a man just sowing his oats or that you're so strong and independent. You want to know what I am?"

I know my voice is too loud. I know I'm being too emotional, but I can't help it. These feelings have been building up for months as I've sat with them and thought about how my parents will respond to me being a single, unattached, pregnant woman in her early twenties without a job.

"To them, I'm not strong—I'm *strong-willed*. I'm not independent—I'm *irrational*. I'm not a man sowing my oats—I'm a woman who has *low self-worth* and a *propensity to spread my legs.*" I shake my head. "According to mom, I allow men to treat me like a *lady of the night.* I don't get to just be myself and enjoy life, Dom. When I'm myself, I get their disappointment. So I am begging you, *please*, do not tell them. Because if they know I'm pregnant, I will never, *ever* hear the end of it."

"Holy shit, you're fucking pregnant?"

My head whips to the side and my face pales when I see Mati standing at the doorway, his eyes wide.

I can feel what I managed to eat start to work its way back up from my stomach, my body's nerves rejecting anything that might make me unable to flee from my current position.

And then something crazy happens.

Mati's smile spreads wide across his face, his arms following suit as they stretch out to his sides.

"Holy fucking shit, Rem!" he cries, the happiness on his face the most shocking thing I've ever seen or experienced in my life.

He rushes at me, yanking me out of my chair into a hug I didn't realize I desperately needed until right now as my brother crushes me to his chest.

I cling to him, the emotions pulsing through me until they leak out of my eyes and onto his wrinkled, cigarette-smelling blue shirt. I don't even care that he smells like an ashtray.

"Hey, hey, hey," he says, his voice soothing and kind and loving. "Remmy girl, you okay?"

He pulls back slightly and looks at my face, his brow pinching when he sees my tears.

"What's the crying for?"

I just shake my head and wrap my arms around him again.

How long has it been since I've been hugged like this by someone in my family?

God.

I can't even say.

Months, at least.

Probably longer.

It feels like an incredible weight is falling from my shoulders at this embrace.

"I'm just scared," I whisper, my words just for Mati, just for my younger older brother who might normally be a tornado but right now is the calm in the storm.

"Oh sweet girl, no need to be scared."

I know his words are meant to be reassuring. I try desperately to cling to them as much as I'm clinging to Mati himself, but they ring hollow.

Because he doesn't know why I'm scared. Not really.

Neither of them do.

Nobody will.

I hold tight to Mati for a few moments longer as I try to gather myself, rein in my emotions, suck back the tears.

Then I step back and dry my eyes, laughing off my display of emotion.

"Pregnancy hormones, you know?"

Mati laughs.

Dom watches me with assessing eyes.

I try to smile, try to play things off and relax.

My brothers know now. I should feel relieved.

I *did* feel relieved.

For a moment.

But now there's a pressure sitting on my chest.

A clock that lets me know there isn't long until everyone knows. Until I can't keep things secret. Until there are more questions than I'm willing to answer.

But that clock is ticking, ticking, ticking without any hands on the face. I don't know when my time will be up.

I don't know when I'll have to face the things I'm trying so desperately hard to avoid.

Chapter Eleven
BEN

It isn't often that I reach out to my brother to meet up and talk, mostly because we've never been particularly close—even though we've been growing closer recently—and partially because our family is a fucked-up mess.

But a few days after my absolute disaster of a conversation with Remmy and that absolutely crazy shit that happened under the pier, I find myself on the rooftop of Bennie's in the cool, damp air of a Hermosa Beach morning, waiting for my brother to join me.

Maybe it was cowardly of me, but I decided not to reach out to Remmy the day after what happened. I don't know if I should have, don't know if it would have made her feel better or worse.

God, that conversation was just…ugh. It never occurred to me that Remmy might get upset at the mention of the stupid award she got in college. I mean, yeah, I know what a Bicycle Award is. Some of the fraternities gave those out when I was in college.

I guess I've just never thought a lot about it, about what

means to the person who receives it.

And Remmy...well, I might not know her that well, but the rumors have been plenty. My assumption was that she didn't care or was maybe proud or...

Yeah, it all just sounds gross now.

The most ridden girl.

A buddy of mine was in a fraternity that gave out that award to his girlfriend at the time. We went out for beers afterward and he bitched and moaned about how embarrassing it was for *him* to be dating the girl who had slept with so many of the chapter members. I hadn't given it much thought then, though I remember finding the whole situation to be something that made me uncomfortable.

Now, years later, seeing the reaction on Remmy's face...I'm finally able to pinpoint why that feeling of discomfort stayed with me for days, why I—maybe subconsciously—avoided fraternities and 'frat bros' from then on.

That girl was a person, someone who was enjoying herself and making choices based on what she wanted, and someone else decided to call her a whore for it.

By bringing that shit up with Remmy, I basically did the same thing.

I take a sip of my whiskey, knowing it wasn't necessarily a good idea to start drinking this early, especially when I have work to do. But I need *something* to wash this nasty taste out of my mouth.

The thing that kills me is that I could tell things were moving in a good direction, too. We were laughing and joking, teasing each other. Almost like we were...I don't know, friends or something.

Not that Remmy and I need to be best friends for this to work. We're definitely both in this for what we can get out of it, but we might as well make it as positive an experience as we can, right? The last thing either of us needs is to be stuck in a shitty marriage.

Having witnessed the absolute disaster of relationship my parents had, I can aggressively state that I have no desire to follow in their footsteps.

So then why did I open my big mouth?

I let out a sigh and continue to watch the morning runners getting in their workouts along The Strand three floors below me.

And then there was what happened *after* my idiotic mention

of the assholes she knew at college. What happened under the pier...

I can't stop thinking about it.

Her hand on my dick, stroking me and asking me in that throaty voice if I wanted her to fuck me where someone might see us.

Jesus.

I can't remember ever getting that hard that fast before.

Even now, I have to shift in my seat at the thought, remind myself that Remmy has a lot going on in her mind and that I shouldn't take advantage of her body, even if she's throwing it at me.

That's why I need to talk to Wyatt.

Remmy has been wobbling through these interactions with me. Sometimes she's the bold, brazen, sassy woman I always assumed her to be, but other times she's this emotional wreck that shuts down and closes off.

I don't know how to handle it.

And Wyatt...I don't know how close he ever was with Remmy, but I assume they were friends at one point, assume he knew her on a different level than I did.

Realistically, he's the only person I know who I can talk to about what's going on with Remmy right now. I have a few friends from college, but they all live out of state, and my friends from high school aren't really 'friends' anymore.

Besides, even if I wanted to talk to them, none of them know Remmy, or her history.

What I want is just to chat with my brother—probably the only other person on this earth I actually trust—and get his perspective based on his own past with Remmy, on the years he and Lucas were best friends while Lucas and Remmy dated. He's got some information somewhere inside his brain that I know will be beneficial to me. I just have to figure out what it is.

"You know it's creepy to wake up to a text that says I need to meet you on a rooftop, right?"

My brother's voice makes me smile.

Okay, maybe not smile. I rarely do that.

But I can feel the corners of my mouth tip up at his stupidity.

"It makes me feel like I'm going to get chucked off a building or something," he adds as I turn my head to look in his direction.

"When have I ever given you the impression that I murder people?" I ask.

Wyatt smirks and drops into one of the chairs facing me. "Ever since I was eight years old and you said to me, 'Wyatt, if you tell mom I broke the TV, I'll murder you,'" he says, his tone light. "You literally said those *exact* words."

At that memory, I do end up smiling slightly.

"Holy shit, I forgot about the TV."

Wyatt crosses his arms, his eyes narrowing at me in mock displeasure as he likely *also* recalls exactly what happened back then.

We'd been playing around in the house, something we were normally forbidden from doing—you can't risk damaging the art, of course—but dad was somewhere and mom was out of town and Vicki had been left in charge of us.

She was already our nanny and house manager and maid and a million other things, but she had usually only been left in charge of us for a few days at a time. This particular time was for two entire weeks, a whole fourteen days without our parents.

So of course, we brought out our toy light sabers and had quite a time running through the house and making *wohm* noises as if the glowing sabers were actually real.

It was all fun and games until Wyatt hit me a little too hard. So then I hit him back a little too hard.

As brothers do, we started wrestling and rolling all over the floor of the living room.

Until I shoved him way, way, *way* too aggressively.

Which resulted in him pitching backward, his eyes wide, his arms flailing. Wyatt fell right into the entertainment center, the force of his body causing the brand-new plasma TV, which had been delivered the day before but not yet installed properly, to wobble and wobble and fall to the ground with a clatter.

We just stared at it for a second, both of us wide-eyed with shock, before we scrambled to lift it up to survey the wreckage.

The screen itself was a shattered mess, but all the broken pieces were still inside the TV—one of those weird plasma things—so there wasn't really a mess to clean up.

Even so, there was definitely no way to hide what had happened. This wasn't a vase we could throw in the trash. This was the brand-new TV.

Looking back, what I actually said to Wyatt in the wake of us looking at the broken TV was just slightly different.

"Wyatt, if you tell mom I broke the TV, I'll murder you. We both know it was actually *your* fault."

"No way!" he shouted, his face contorted with anger. "You pushed me—it's *your* fault."

I crossed my arms, glaring down at him even though he couldn't have been more than an inch shorter than me.

"*Everything* is your fault."

Wyatt's face pinched in pain, his sudden emotion startling me, and he sprinted off through the house.

We never talked about that. I mean, we were kids. Kids say stupid shit, and I don't even know if Wyatt remembers the whole conversation.

But I've remembered it.

Now and then that specific memory will come to me and splinter something inside me, will remind me why I don't deserve a brother like Wyatt, or a sister like Ivy.

"Alright, so hit me. I'm assuming this is about Remmy, right?" he says, leaning back in his chair and watching me with curious eyes.

I nod just once. "Yeah. I'm hoping for some advice."

The words come out stilted, mostly because it's a difficult thing to verbalize out loud. I've never asked Wyatt for advice before, especially not about something this important.

And the guy doesn't let it pass.

Wyatt's face breaks out into a shit-eating grin like I've never seen before.

"Seriously? *That's* why you called me? Because you want *my* advice?"

My expression flattens into a hard line as I wait for him to finish gloating.

"Alright, alright," he says, waving his hand around and then leaning to the side, his face resting in his palm as he settles in. "Hit me with it."

So I launch in. I go through the entire evening on Sunday, from picking her up to our conversation in the car, how great things were going at the promenade market, then as we settled into the movie…and ending with…

"Fuck, man. That is…" Wyatt pauses, like his words are getting stuck in his throat. "I can't *believe* assholes give out awards like that. And I didn't know it happened to Remmy." He stops and his head tilts to the side as he considers something. "How did *you* know about it?"

I roll my eyes. "I saw a post on Facebook when it happened. It was complete chance, actually. Mark Jessup's younger sister was Remmy's roommate."

"Josslyn Jessup and Rem were roomies?" Wyatt asks, wrinkling his nose. "How'd that work out?"

I shrug. "I wasn't friends with Josslyn, but I think she had a crush on me at one point and friended me or something. Honestly I don't even remember adding her. Anyway, she posted about what happened and it popped up. Seriously, though, this was years ago. I don't even remember why I saw it."

"Think the info is still online somewhere?" he asks, drawing his phone out of his pocket. "Because now I'm curious what happened."

I take a sip of my drink and watch Wyatt as he fucks around looking at who knows what. I'm not personally a fan of technology that isn't directly related to managing my business.

I hire people to deal with things like social media and marketing, and if I want to know something, I just hire someone and get *them* to spend the time collecting the information. I don't waste my time trying to dig around and find it myself.

"Alright, here we go," he says, surprising me with how quickly he was able to find what he was looking for. "It probably popped up because Josslyn shared a link to the university's newspaper."

My eyebrows rise. "It was in the newspaper?"

He nods, his thumb tapping around on his phone. "I think this is it. It's short. Looks like it's on their community safety page."

The confusion I feel grows. "Are you sure you're looking at the right thing?"

Wyatt holds his hand up then starts reading.

"*Campus security reports indicate that a female student called and asked for an escort to provide safety as she packed her belongings during winter finals. The student, a freshman at Caldin Hall, indicated she had been the target of harassment and threats from fellow residents and her Resident Advisor, and that she was withdrawing from the university and moving out of the hall but was hoping for assistance. Two campus security officers were a visible presence in Caldin Hall as the student removed her belongings and loaded them into her vehicle. All names have been removed to protect personal privacy."*

"How do you know that has anything to do with Remmy?"

"What I found was in the comments section," he continues. "*Well it's about time the trash got the fuck out of Caldin. Maybe don't fuck your RA's boyfriend and half the guys in the building if you don't want people to call you a whore. The Bicycle Award was well deserved for a trashy-ass slut like Remmy Wallace.*"

My mouth drops open.

"There are more comments, a few people calling that first poster an asshole and then people saying you should be able to have sex with whoever you want without fearing for your physical safety on campus." He shrugs and keeps scrolling. "This shit's crazy. I can't believe this happened and we didn't know about it."

Wyatt's attention stays on his phone as he continues to dive into what happened, but I'm still so surprised by all of this that I can't seem to form a fully functional thought.

Remmy was so uncomfortable about things after that happened that she moved off campus. No wonder her face went ghost-white when I referenced it. It's probably something she's been trying to move past, and I brought it up as a joke.

There's a voice inside of me that's refusing to be quiet, that's saying I have to right this. I have to tell her I'm sorry in a way that convinces her, that absolves her of any fear or embarrassment that comes her way when she thinks about what happened.

I rub my hand against my beard, scratching it slightly.

"So what do I do now?"

Wyatt's eyes connect with mine. "Huh?"

I shake my head. "What do I do? I mean, I barely know her. You know her much better than I do. You're the one who knows what a relationship looks like. And if you and Hannah were able to come back from your shit...just...I need some help on this."

Wyatt chuckles. "What is it with everyone thinking I'm some relationship expert now?" he mutters. "Honestly? If you're hoping for advice, you shouldn't ask me. You should ask Hannah."

"How's that?"

He lifts a shoulder. "Dude, I lucked out that Hannah chose to forgive me based on the effort I put into it, but I had no idea if it was going to work." He points a finger off in the distance, down

The Strand, in the direction of where Hannah lives. "If you want to figure out what's going to convince a girl to forgive you for being an idiot, go ask a girl. Not me."

I let out an irritated sigh and lift my glass, taking another sip and finishing off the last of it.

It's a hard thing to explain. I don't necessarily need Remmy to *forgive* me. I didn't really do anything wrong; I was just teasing. But at the same time, I know what I said hurt her, or took her back to an unhappy time in her life, and I don't know how to move us forward, move us beyond that.

Maybe my brother has a point. I only wish I knew what girl to ask, because I'm definitely not going to ask Hannah. She's my employee, and our relationship is already crossing enough boundaries with her dating my brother.

"Speaking of Hannah," I say, realizing this is the perfect chance to find out what's going on, "she came to me the other day and asked to have the last week of the month off for some surprise you're planning. What's the deal?"

He chews on the inside of his mouth, a clear indicator that he's either hiding something or doesn't want to be talking about this. That's the thing about brothers—a lot of your tells are the same, so it's harder to get away with things.

"Honestly?" he says, and I nod, surprised he might be willing to tell me what's up. "I'm taking her to London for a week."

My head flies back. "Why London?"

"Well...I'm supposed to be moving there soon. For work."

When I realize what's going on, I can't hide my surprise, not in my expression or my body language.

"Are you...taking her to London to try to convince her to move there with you?" I ask.

Wyatt doesn't answer. He just taps his fingers against the table between us, the methodic thud slightly soothing and slightly irritating at the same time.

"Didn't she like...*just* move here to try to develop a relationship with her brother?"

Wyatt looks off into the distance, his emotions showing clearly on his face even though he's trying to hide it.

"I love her, okay? And if there is even a small chance we can stay together instead of being apart for who knows how long, I have to go after it."

I sit in silence, watching my brother from across the table, wondering when he grew into this...man. It feels like only months ago he was getting wasted and trolling the clubs, begging out of family stuff, moving away because he was the king of avoidance.

Now? It's like finding something he knows he wants has given him a way to measure everything else in life.

It's not something I ever thought I'd see in him, not considering the way we were raised. How our dad demonstrated 'love' and 'commitment' and 'marriage' to us. The ways he has manipulated and bullied and betrayed us over and over again.

But seeing that in his face...the certainty, the desire, the loyalty—the exact opposites of everything we knew growing up...

I'm happy for him.

And, if I'm willing to listen to that tiny little voice inside of me that seems to be getting a bit more vocal...maybe just a little bit jealous.

As confident as I am in myself, in my strength, there's something about standing in front of Dominic Wallace that leaves just a sliver of unease running through me.

Give him a scar under his eye and a gun and he'd be a nameless bodyguard serving any 90s movie villain.

"Dominic."

I give him a nod and stick my hand out.

Unfortunately, he lets it hang there. It's the universal sign for *you're not welcome here and I plan to put you in your place.*

The great thing is that I'm not at all concerned about getting Dominic to like me. We went to high school together, and we didn't exactly run in the same circles.

Unsurprisingly, this big guy was on the wrestling team, while I tried to avoid school stuff as much as possible.

I need to remind myself of that and tell Remmy since she seems to think—erroneously—that I was a nerd. I wasn't. I was just...not as sociable as the other kids were. I spent a lot of time on my own, studying, working for my dad, volunteering for...okay maybe I was a little bit of a nerd.

"Look, I get that you're being a protective brother—I have a younger sister, too—but Remmy and I need to talk."

His eyes narrow, but he steps to the side just enough to let me walk through the entry and into their foyer.

"Look who it is!"

A shout from a nearby room has me looking to the right just in time to get barreled into by Remmy's other brother, Mathias.

With his arms wrapped around me, he gives me a strong pat on the back. "It's the man who is making me an uncle!"

My eyes widen when I process his words, and over his shoulder, I catch another sneer from Dominic as he spins and leaves the room.

Well, I guess I can understand why he looks like he wants to kill me.

Mathias pulls back and looks at me, a big grin on his face, his hands on my upper arms. "Congratulations, man. Welcome to the family."

The smile I give him must not be enough because he looks at me with a hint of embarrassment. "Don't be mad at Rem for spilling the beans, okay? She didn't mean to. And our parents still don't know."

I shake my head. "Well, glad to know someone else is excited for us," I say, giving him a grin.

He claps me on both arms again and then waves for me to follow him.

"Yeah, it might end up just being me, if I'm completely honest. Dominic is always a little emotionally stunted, and our parents are going to *shit a brick* without a doubt," he says, leading me through a courtyard at the center of the house that has an open roof. "But don't worry—I will always have your back."

I'm not certain anything he just told me is reassuring, but I still manage to give him a smile when he stops in front of a wet bar and pulls down a bottle of whiskey.

"Thank you so much, but I'm gonna pass on a drink," I say. "I'm just here to see Remmy, so would you be able to point me in the direction of her room?"

Mathias's easy smile returns. "Sure, man, but I don't think she's in her room. Try checking my dad's study. Just back to the front and up the stairs, third room on the right."

I nod and give him some sort of weird salute then spin around and head in that direction.

Even though it would be simple to just stand there and wait with Mathias, have a drink or two, and find something to shoot the shit about, I'd much rather go see what the deal is with Remmy.

She sent me a text this morning that I didn't see until this afternoon. With all the busyness at work, sometimes I'll put down my phone and not see it until hours later.

Ivy tells me it means I'm a workaholic. I say it just means I'm dedicated to my job.

I glance back at my phone, seeing her one-word message again.

Remmy: Hi

I can't help but want to laugh at how short it is, almost like she's just reaching out and dipping her toe into the water to make sure things aren't too hot or too cold or too...something.

When I finally make it up the stairs and to the door, the Wallace Estate feeling more and more like a labyrinth with every step, I give a light knock on the door, which is cracked open.

"Yeah?"

I push the door farther open, smiling when I see her sitting on a chair facing an easel, a large canvas in front of her.

She's facing a massive window overlooking the courtyard, a sliver of ocean off in the distance.

I've never seen Remmy paint before. I didn't even realize it was something she was interested in—or good at, which is definitely the case if the artwork on her canvas is anything to base things off of.

But I only catch a glimpse before she turns her head over her shoulder, her eyes widening when she sees me standing here, leaning against the door frame.

"I got your text," I say, giving her a small smile.

Her eyes fall away, dropping to the floor, and I can see how uncomfortable she is just in the way her body is angled and how she's sitting.

"Yeah," she says, the word coming out in the scratchy voice of someone who hasn't spoken in a while.

She clears her throat.

"Yeah, I just...wanted to extend the olive branch after

my…after Sunday," she says, her words choppy and uncertain.

This is the Remmy I'm still trying to figure out—this kind of shy, very awkward, unsure woman who tries to fade into the background.

The other version of her? The balls-to-the-wall, fun, over-the-top Remmy? I get her. I know that form of her is her fun side wrapped in protective armor.

We all have shields, ways to deflect.

And Remmy seems like she's strong one moment, ready to take on anything you can throw her way…and then the next, she wilts like she's been sprayed with poison.

I've never thought about it this way, but maybe that's protection, too?

Maybe she pulls back when she's too tired, retreats when she needs some time to lick her wounds.

I don't want her to have to do that around me.

"I didn't know you paint," I say, pushing off the doorway and wandering into the room, closer to her and the easel. "Have you been doing it long?"

My eyes focus on the canvas, but I can see her in my peripheral vision as she turns to take a look at what she's been working on.

It's an open doorway with light shining through, the rays from the hall outside cascading into a blank space on the canvas that hasn't been painted yet.

"I started painting in high school," she says. "But I didn't realize I was any good until I went to college."

I nod.

"I don't know anything about art," I say, my voice heavy, "but it feels…dark." Then I point to the empty space. "What's gonna go there?"

There's a long silence from Remmy. So long I turn away from the art and look at her.

And I'm startled at the look in her eyes.

Vacant. Empty.

"Nothing," she answers, her voice still a wobbly whisper. "Nothing goes there."

Something sits uncomfortably in my stomach as she gets up out of her seat and begins to collect her supplies, but I don't know how to vocalize how I feel, or whether I should.

Maybe I'm reading into it.
Maybe I'm seeing things or totally misunderstanding.
All I know for sure is that I've never seen a look like that on Remmy's face before.
Even on Sunday.
And I never want to see it again.

Chapter Twelve
REMMY

Nothing.

That's what he called me.

I knew what I was painting when I started. I know because I've tried to paint it what feels like a million times.

I can never paint the blank space, though.

Instead, I normally just sit there and stare at it, lost in thought. The blue doorway that haunts my nightmares.

Sometimes I wonder what I could have done differently.

Other times I imagine what life could have been like if things had turned out a different way.

Neither of those things do me any good.

"We should talk," Ben says, reminding me that he's still in the room with me as I tuck all my dirty brushes into my holder, rolling it up so I can carry them to the sink in the kitchen.

Mom hates for me to wash them in the kitchen sink, but I do it anyway.

"About?" I ask, trying to focus on picking up my materials.

"About...everything," he replies. "We've been having all these...half-conversations that get us nowhere, and I don't want it to be like that anymore."

I know he's right, but that doesn't mean it sounds like something I want to do.

Ben seems like the kind of guy who likes to address things head-on.

No thanks.

I'm very good at avoiding things.

But I doubt he's going to let that happen with this.

I take a deep breath and then let it all out in a long sigh.

"Sure," I reply. "Let me just get this shit off my hands." I lift them up to show him my dirty fingers. "I'll meet you in my room. It's just down the hall on the left."

He nods but continues to watch me as I finish packing up my brushes and pick up my canvas.

I leave the easel, though. My dad rarely comes in here, and it's just easier to leave it behind for when I'm back in here tomorrow and the next day and the next.

"I'll be back in a minute."

I leave the study and head down the stairs, first setting my canvas down with some of the others in one of the spare rooms on the ground floor, then heading into the kitchen to clean my brushes.

"You know, I think the thing I'm most interested in is that he's willing to pretend to be the father."

Dominic's voice has me turning to look at him as he walks into the room.

He makes his way over to the basket of fruit that sits on the corner of the island, plucking out a banana and beginning to remove the peel.

I return my focus to where I'm scrubbing my brushes.

"Isn't that interesting to you?" he continues. "Why would he do that?"

I stay silent.

My brother doesn't goad me. Not usually, anyway. So this feels...different.

"What does he have to *gain* from something like that?"

I sigh. "Why does it have to be about something he gains,

Dom? Why can't it just be because we're helping each other out?"

The last thing I want to say is that I've had the same question on repeat in my mind for the past two and a half weeks, that I've wondered what his motives are.

His explanations have always been too vague.

But I keep that to myself.

"I can see how *he's* helping *you*," Dom says. "I just don't get how *you're* helping *him*."

There's a long silence.

I refuse to let him lure me into focusing on this.

"This is a wise use of your time?" I ask. "Sitting in the kitchen and trying to make me feel like shit?"

Dominic steps up next to me just as I open some turpentine to clean the paint off my fingers.

"That safe?" he asks. "With the pregnancy?"

I pause, looking at the small clear bottle in my hands, then set it off to the side and resign myself to cleaning up with good old soap and water.

"I'm not trying to make you feel like shit," he continues. "I just want to make sure you're being smart about this."

He stands next to me as I scrub the remnants of the blue door off the heel of my right hand, but he doesn't say anything else.

I finish rubbing that one particularly difficult spot over and over, only turning to look up into my brother's eyes when I'm done, making certain that he understands me.

"I'm capable of handling this myself," I say, my jaw tight. "I've had to handle a lot of shit in my life on my own. I don't need you to start meddling *now*."

And then I leave Dominic and my paint brushes behind.

When I get up to my room, I find Ben standing in the corner, looking at a bookshelf filled with yearbooks and pictures and mementos from my high school years.

He picks one up to examine it closer, and I wince.

It's a picture of me and Lucas at one of his earlier surfing competitions. He's sitting on the sand, his legs bent, one arm wrapped around me, pulling me in close.

After we broke up, I came home and boxed up almost all the things that represent our relationship. Pictures from prom. Old stuffed animals and bullshit he gave me when we were dating. Just junk, and now it's all shoved into a box I placed with the other things my mother has boxed up and kept over the years.

I didn't get rid of that picture, though.

That picture—that was us *before* we started dating. That's us at fourteen, just being friends. A whole group of us were there to support him that day as he took some of his first steps toward becoming a professional surfer.

We were at our best when we were just friends, and I wanted to keep something that would help me remember that.

I'm sure it doesn't look that way to Ben, though.

Not that he has any reason to be bothered by a picture of Lucas. It's not like he wants me to love *him*.

But I know any attempt to explain myself right now will just make me look like I'm trying to...well, *explain* myself.

Also, we have other things to talk about at the moment.

"Alright, let's talk."

At the sound of my voice, Ben turns his head to look at me. For some reason, I thought maybe he'd be startled, like I was catching him looking at my pictures, but of course he looks as cool as a cucumber.

He's always that way.

I walk over to the corner near my closet where I have two oversized chairs that are perfect for curling up and chatting with a friend.

Or with the guy you're fake-engaged to, slash actually marrying.

Ben replaces the picture he was holding and follows me over, dropping into the chair across from me with a plop.

"The past two weeks have been kind of...a lot," I say, interrupting before he starts talking. "My whole world has been a lot to deal with recently."

I gather up all my hair and bring it over my left shoulder, my fingers beginning the slow work of partitioning off the pieces so I can bundle it into a long braid.

"So the only thing I'd really like for us to do is start completely over, like today is the day you approach me at Bennie's and say we should get married. And instead of waffling, I just agree with you. Instead of weird interactions where we're kissing in front of people and having dinner with my ex's sister and your brother, we just have normal dates, normal interactions—as friends." I pause, though my fingers continue the methodical work of braiding my hair. "Friends who are getting married."

When I finally look up at Ben, I see him watching my hands, though his eyes rise to mine as soon as he realizes I'm looking at him.

"I think…that's probably a great idea," he finally says, settling more comfortably into his chair, one leg rising to rest on the other. "We should go on a few more dates, absolutely, but we also need to spend more time getting to know each other better."

I nod. "Yes. That will be a great way for us to be friends."

Maybe I sound like an idiot, but I'm also hoping if I say the word 'friends' enough, maybe I won't get a little flutter in my belly every time his eyes are focused on me.

I'm not in love with Ben, but my body definitely loves his, and I need to do everything I can to remind myself that it is off limits for forever.

As sad as that is.

"I think we should limit any PDA outside of holding hands," he adds. "Just to make sure we're…keeping good boundaries. Since we're going to be friends."

My face flushes.

I know what he's really saying. I know he's using these neutral words to tell me I need to keep my hands and my mouth and my vagina to myself.

Unable to respond verbally because I'm dying of embarrassment, I give him a nod.

"I also think we should begin making arrangements for you to move in with me in the next week or two."

I purse my lips and glare at him.

"Ben, I've already told you how I feel about this. I'd be fine with it, but my parents will not be. I hide enough from them. I don't want to also cause them…" I wave my hand around. "…whatever added stress this might cause."

When we originally spoke about me moving in with him, I hadn't known him very well and used my parents as an excuse. Now, I may still not know a lot about him, but I feel like I've gotten a good picture of the kind of man he is, so I have no concerns about it happening eventually.

"Alright. Then at least keep it in the back of your mind as something I would like to happen sooner rather than later."

I nod, though I don't repeat myself. I just know my parents, and there's no way in hell they're going to agree to something like that.

"Back to the dates," he says. "A friend of my family's has an exhibit tomorrow night at Sheldon House. I'd like for us to go together."

"Yeah, I can do that."

He shifts in his seat. "It will also be a chance for you to meet my parents."

"I've met them before."

"Not as my fiancée."

My eyebrows lift. "You want to introduce me as your fiancée? Already?"

He nods.

"But you haven't even actually proposed."

His head tilts to the side, and I realize what a stupid thing that was to say.

"Never mind. Whatever. You don't think they'll wonder what's really going—"

"I don't actually care what they think," he says, waving my interrupted question away before I'm done asking it. "Besides, this shouldn't be a big deal."

But he doesn't meet my eyes, instead picking at some imaginary lint on his shirt.

"I'm not sure I'm ready for your parents to know I'm your fiancée when I haven't talked to my own family about it yet," I say. "I'm worried they'll find out somehow."

Ben shakes his head. "We can't put it off forever, Remmy. If you want to move forward with this, we have to move forward. If you want to tell your parents first, we can."

I sigh, realizing he's right. All I'm doing is delaying the inevitable. It's not that I'm ashamed of being engaged to Ben. I just…hate the idea of telling my parents. There's no telling how they'll react.

"Alright. We'll tell your parents, but I still need to think about mine, okay?"

Ben nods and stands, extending his hand to help me out of my chair. Then he walks to my door.

I follow, realizing he's ready to leave.

Secretly, I'm bummed. I don't know if I thought we'd *hang out* or something, but I didn't expect him to leave so soon after he got here.

Suddenly, I realize I don't want him to leave.

"Do you want to stay and watch a movie or something?" I ask as we head down the hallway. "We're trying to be friends, right? We should hang out."

I want to slap my palm against my face.

We should hang out.

How stupid do I sound?

Ben gives me a smile, but I know his response before he even says anything based on the tilt of his head.

"I have some work I still need to get done tonight, so I'll have to pass," he says as we continue down the stairs toward the front door. "But thanks for the invite. Maybe some other time."

When we get to the door, I open it for him, leaning my body against the wood as he steps outside.

"I'll see you tomorrow. Ready by seven, okay?"

My head bobs robotically. Now that I've made a fool of myself—again—I'm actually glad to see him go.

"See you tomorrow."

I wave as he heads down the path toward his car in the circle drive, then close the door. When I turn, I see Dominic watching us.

I glare, saying nothing, and head back up the stairs to my room, to the space I can close everyone out of and just...be.

My brother's sudden fascination with my relationship with Ben strikes me as odd, even if my mind isn't currently in the right state to try to piece together why.

Plopping back into my comfy armchair, I click on Netflix and scroll through the movies until I find one I think will sufficiently distract me from life.

Then I settle in and try to keep my mind from thinking about Ben.

I fail.

I run my hands down my dress, smoothing out the fabric for what feels like the millionth time tonight.

I swear I can feel people watching me, like they know I'm

hiding a baby inside of my body and they're just trying to catch me at the right angle so they can leap forward and point it out.

Ben takes my nervous hands in his.

"You look beautiful," he says, his voice low and meant only for me. "The more you fidget, the more people will think you're uncomfortable being here with me, and we don't want that."

I grip his hand. "Don't I look super fucking massive in this, though? I should have picked a different dress or—"

"Remmy," he says, spinning me so I'm looking up at him, our faces close enough that I can smell the faint hint of whiskey on his breath from his earlier cocktail when we first arrived. "Take a deep breath in."

I do.

"And let it out long and slow."

I do.

"You're fine. You're perfect." He shakes his head. "Don't overthink it. We're here together and we're friends."

I nod. "Okay. I'm ready."

He grins, something like affection crossing his face. "You sure?"

I nod again. "Let's do it."

He squeezes my hand and then turns his head, looking for his family. Then he gives me an easy tug and leads me off to the right.

I didn't realize how nervous I would be about seeing Ben's parents, and I can't figure out exactly *why*. I've been racking my brain trying to identify what the fear is rooted in.

At first I thought it might be something left over from the few times I interacted with Lucas' mom. Brenda was always nice to me, but I don't know if she ever really liked me. She wasn't very warm, although Lucas always tried to assure me his mom just wasn't very maternal.

Then I wondered if maybe it's more about my fear that I'll be meeting Ivy as well. Ben didn't say she'd be here, but I know she's often with her mom. Maybe I'm just worried about being rude in some way I don't understand since I haven't seen her since she was around eight years old and have no idea how to do sign language.

But I don't think it's that either.

I'm not worried his family will talk him out of marrying me or some other stupid normal worry a girlfriend or fiancée would have about meeting future in-laws.

So I don't get why I'm such a fidgety mess.

I'm a Wallace. I know I'm a catch in a world that's fascinated by leveling up and names that matter.

But still. Something feels off.

"Benjamin!" The soft, feminine voice sounds surprised to see him as we approach Vivian Calloway.

She either has an *amazing* plastic surgeon or a magician on her household staff, because she looks like she hasn't aged a single day since the last time I saw her.

"What are you doing here?"

Now that we're closer and I can see her face, I note a hint of worry in her tone that instantly puts me on edge.

Her eyes dart to the side, as if she's watching the people around us or looking for someone.

"I knew Rowan had an exhibit tonight, thought I'd do my duty as a Calloway and come support her."

I blink, realizing for the first time that Rowan Geffries is the artist on display. We went to high school together, and I think she's...related? Somehow she's close with the Calloway family; that's all I know.

My eyes turn to scan the artwork, seeing the dark, murky colors of the mixed media canvases on the walls.

I remember her being talented when we were younger, but these are stunning. I'm surprised I didn't actually look at any of the art pieces when we first walked in.

Another reason I'm irritated by my fidgeting.

When I turn to look back at Mrs. Calloway, I see she's looking directly at me, confusion in her eyes.

"And," Ben continues, "I wanted to officially introduce you to my fiancée. Mom, you remember Remmy Wallace, right?"

There's a long pause...a stretch of time that feels far too long before she responds. I brace myself, wondering what she might do or say. Maybe I *was* just worried about how his parents would react.

But she smiles at me, something warm and genuine in it.

"Fiancée?" she whispers, and I see her eyes well up as she looks from me to Ben and then back again.

I give her a big smile, feeling my insides sag with relief that she isn't pissed or angry or preparing to storm out of the room.

"It's so good to see you again, Mrs. Calloway," I say, finally finding my voice.

She waves her hand in front of her face. "Oh, please. Call me Vivian. We're going to be family."

And then she steps forward and gives me a hug.

To say I'm surprised is an understatement, and when I catch Ben's eyes over his mother's shoulder, I realize he's just as surprised as I am, the shock on his face standing out starkly.

But he wipes it away as quickly as it appeared.

Vivian pulls back, her hands still holding me by my shoulders.

I expect her to say something, but she doesn't. She just squeezes my arms and then steps backward, grabbing a flute of champagne off a passing tray without even looking at it.

Her eyes find Ben's. "Does anyone else know?"

There's an extended pause before Ben responds. "Just Wyatt."

Vivian nods, taking a sip of her drink, her eyes shifting to watch the room once more.

"I am truly happy for both of you," she finally says. "Truly." Then she leans forward just a little bit and looks me right in the face. "Good luck with everything coming your way. In this family, you're going to need it."

Her words make something curdle inside my stomach. Whatever happiness and buoyancy I was feeling a moment ago at the emotion she allowed me to see is now gone.

I look to Ben for direction and see that his face doesn't look any different.

He isn't concerned, I realize.

This isn't a weird or strange or crazy interaction.

I slip my hand back into his, giving it a squeeze, hoping to tug him away and talk to him for a minute so I can get my bearings.

What does that mean? *In this family, you're going to need it.*

But before I can give him any indication that I'd like a moment just the two of us, I feel his entire body tense and shift even though his expression fades into something jovial and easygoing.

I turn slightly and find Ben's father approaching, a young woman with plumped lips and a bitchy expression glued to his side.

When he's finally in front of us, his deep voice raises every hair on my neck and shoulders.

"Well, if it isn't the prodigal son."

Chapter Thirteen
BEN

I knew he'd be here.
I was banking on it.
Hoping for it.
For this opportunity to finally begin.
I can feel Remmy shift uncomfortably next to me, but I'm not as aware of her as I was a few minutes ago.
That's how things normally feel when she's around, almost like I have a direct connection to her emotions and feelings and moods.
My father's presence, though, changes all of that.
Now, all I can focus on is him. Standing in front of me.
With Krissa Bilson on his arm.
I don't know why I'm surprised to see her here with him.
Logically, I know they're married, know she goes with him to society events and public spaces.
But I've been meticulously avoiding any place where she might

be, so her presence is a surprise.

A shock to my system that I wasn't prepared for.

I used to always be prepared, but recently, I've been off my game. Distracted by the things happening in my own life. By Remmy.

Time to refocus my efforts.

I do have a plan, after all.

A plan she's a part of.

And now it's time to actually follow through.

"A prodigal son chooses to leave," I say, keeping one hand tucked in Remmy's and slipping the other in my pocket. "I don't remember ever being given that choice."

One side of his mouth tilts up.

"You make choices every day, Benjamin," he replies, "just like I do. You make choices with your actions. Your actions caused a lot of problems for this family, which was your decision."

I shrug. "Semantics. Looks like we just see it differently. We see a *lot* of things differently."

There's a pause, and my eyes drift to Krissa for just a second.

If people were curious about the innerworkings of my mind, they might assume I'm still upset with her for what she did.

I'm not.

She taught me that trust is something we give away too freely and honor too rarely.

I'll never let someone teach me a lesson like that again.

"Krissa," I say, nodding my head in acknowledgment.

She smiles, but it's tight, the exact same expression she's given me the handful of other times I've seen her since everything happened.

"Good to see you, Bennie."

She winces, and that's when my eyes zero in on the hand gripping her side.

My eyes flit back to his, and the level of anger aimed my way is almost startling.

What he doesn't seem to get is that he doesn't have a right to be angry with me.

So these little spouts of rage that always laser in on me? I rarely worry about them.

When you fuck your son's girlfriend, rub it in his face, and then marry her, *you* have to deal with the consequences.

Like the fact that I had her first.

And the way she says my name, in that soft voice she used to breathe out when I'd make her come saying the exact same thing...

Bennie.

Those are things *he* has to deal with.

Not me.

Though I enjoy his bristling more when he doesn't take it out on Krissa.

She might not be my favorite person—one of my least favorites would be more accurate—but nobody deserves to be grabbed like that, with aggressive, possessive hands that can leave bruises.

Unless they want it.

"Good to see you, Calvin."

The sound of my mother's voice shatters the little box of discomfort I've been standing in.

I shift my body slightly and my mother steps forward.

How she can greet my father with a smile and kind words after everything he put her through over the years is *beyond* me.

Though I'm assuming she might interact with him differently if they were ever together away from the watchful eyes of the public, which they're not.

"Vivian," he says.

That's the only acknowledgment he gives her, turning his focus back to me.

No.

He's not focused on me.

His eyes breeze past me and to my left, where Remmy stands at my side, her hand in mine.

"Remmy, this is my father, Calvin Calloway," I say, looking at her face and noting the stiff smile and attempt to appear friendly. Then I look back to my dad and continue with my plan, even though there's a little voice in the back of my mind telling me I'm making a mistake. "This is Remmy Wallace, my fiancée."

I see the shift in my father's posture, the reaction vibrating in his entire body, his eyes boring into mine like he would light me on fire if he could get away with it.

Knowing the things my father has done, he probably could.

"Fiancée," he says, his eyes returning to her. "How...interesting."

"We've met before, Mr. Calloway," Remmy says, detangling her hand from mine as she gives him a smile and reaches out to shake his. "Back when I was in high school."

He smiles at her, that shark-like grin he thinks is charming but I know is full of manipulation and self-interest, before slipping his hand into hers.

"That's right, that's right. Remmy *Wallace*. My, you've grown up quite a bit, haven't you?"

She steps back, taking her place back at my side and returning her hand to mine.

"What have you been up to recently?" he continues. "You left town a while back, right?"

Remmy nods. "I went to college up in Santa Barbara," she answers. "But now I'm back."

"And engaged to my son it seems."

I see her smile wobble but then she looks up at me, and whatever nerves or fears she was allowing to fuck with her mind just a second ago clear like clouds as they part for the sun.

"I am." She goes up on tiptoe and presses a soft kiss to my cheek. When she drops back down, her expression is just as soft. "And I couldn't be happier."

Something inside me warms at her words, acting or not. Maybe because I do truly want Remmy to be happy, maybe because I never envisioned a life for myself where I'd make *anyone* happy, least of all a wife.

Regardless of the reason, I can't help the easy smile I give back to her as I take in her eyes and tan skin and the deep wine color on her lips.

"Congratulations are in order."

My father's voice feels like a bucket of ice water down my back, severing the connection I have with Remmy, my focus returning to where he stands next to us.

"We should do a...family dinner, perhaps?"

The calculated part of my mind can already guess what his next words are going to be.

"That way we have a chance to celebrate with your family as well."

And there it is.

My father's mind moves incredibly fast. It doesn't surprise me that it only took a minute or two for him to identify the true threat

Remmy represents.

"We already have a dinner planned," I interject. "Just a small engagement party, though, mostly just close friends."

My words hang there between us, crystalizing in the air.

He looks displeased, though I doubt many other than me would be able to identify it through that charming smile of his.

After all, I *am* the one who has displeased him the most.

"Keep us in mind should there be any changes," he says, then his eyes return to Remmy's. "Congratulations again."

And then the two of them turn and disappear into the crowd, like two pieces of ice in hot water, like they were never standing in front of us at all.

I stare at the space they used to occupy, my mind finding it difficult to refocus, to return to what's happening around me.

But all it takes is a soft squeeze from Remmy's hand for me to reattach to this moment.

She looks confused.

I'm not surprised.

It's got to be confusing when you don't realize you're a pawn in someone else's game.

I crack my neck, side to side, the thought not sitting well with me, but I try not to dwell on it.

It has begun, whether Remmy realizes it today or on another.

"Let's get another drink, huh?" I say to her, and then I look to my mother. "We'll see you around tonight, I'm sure."

She nods, but I can see worry in her eyes.

It's almost startling to see since she so rarely allows her true emotions to come out to play when she's in public.

Wyatt says she's plastic, thinks she's unfeeling and selfish.

I don't agree with him, and I never have.

She's not plastic.

She's like Remmy.

Vivian Calloway spent decades building up her armor for protection, and it's very rare that you get a peek of what's truly behind it.

My mind races at that thought.

My mom built up her armor in the face of a villain like my father. It was the way she stayed safe when she felt like she didn't know how to protect herself.

As I watch the beautiful woman next to me, holding my hand

as we move through the crowd, I can't help but remember that she's built up her own defense, her own kind of protection.

So who is Remmy's villain?

Who is the dragon that made her feel so scared she started building her armor at such a young age?

And are they still close enough to wound her?

"I know what you're doing."

She corners me when I'm alone, when I'm in the side hallway that leads to the restrooms and the staff-only area.

Out of the view of my father.

Krissa sidles up next to me, leaning against the wall that's at my back, and situates herself to make sure I can see the deep V of her cleavage.

It's so obvious now, how she used her assets to try to manipulate me. I think a lot of men find it sexy because they don't see the manipulation part. They can't identify that they're being pressured into things because they're blinded by the big titties in their face.

Or, they're willing to go along with whatever because they *want* those big titties in their face. The lips wrapped around their dick. A warm piece of property to slide into whenever they snap their fingers.

I was definitely the former.

I'm assuming my father is the latter.

Though I'm also assuming he wouldn't be so happy finding out his *property* is sticking those tits in someone else's face.

Especially mine.

"Oh, and what is that?" I ask.

I shouldn't care what she has to say. I *don't* care, actually, but I can't miss an opportunity to best her at her own game, and I have a pretty good feeling I know what's coming my way.

Krissa bats her eyelashes and looks at me with eyes that say she knows I want her.

She couldn't be more wrong.

"You're trying to replace me."

I laugh.

"You're laughing at me, but it's true. I know it is because I know how you looked at me, and that's not how you look at her. *Remmy Wallace.*"

She says Remmy's name like it's dirty, drawing out the S sound at the end like it's gum she's trying to wipe off her shoe against the pavement.

"Krissa, I know it's hard for you to grasp, but the world does *not* revolve around you."

Her eyes narrow.

"My dad may have decided you were worth ruining his life for, but I could not be more thankful that he showed me your true colors."

She gasps. "Mine!? You act like I was working alone. Your dad came after *me*, not the other way around."

"I know, but I already knew my dad was a selfish asshole. You, on the other hand...*you* I didn't see coming. And that was my own fault."

I lean close to Krissa, reaching down and tugging lightly on some of the hair extensions she wears now, my face inches from hers.

She's a cheap imitation of what I know I truly want, even if I doubt I'll ever allow myself to have it.

"I don't forgive people who try to manipulate me for their own gain," I whisper, giving her a smile that's nothing but shark teeth.

She looks furious.

I shouldn't want to waste my energy on her. Usually I don't, but there is something so wonderful about thinking of exactly the right thing to say at exactly the right time, especially when it's directed at someone who sent an earthquake through the foundation of your life.

Krissa was that person in mine.

Not my father.

Like I said, I've always known who he was.

I just never realized his sons were fair game.

Leaning back, I give her a smug grin, appreciating the moment for exactly what it is.

Until the door next to where we're standing opens and Remmy appears, seemingly startled by our presence in the hallway.

"Oh, hey," she says. Then her eyes flit back and forth between us, taking in our close stance, assessing.

"Just wishing my Bennie here some additional congratulations," Krissa says, her voice dropping into something sultry and sensual.

My nostrils flare and I turn to face Remmy fully, hoping I can convince her with my eyes that she doesn't have anything—*anything*—to worry about when it comes to Krissa.

"You know, that is *so* sweet of you," she says, a smile crawling onto her face.

I lift an eyebrow as she steps toward me, the gorgeous length of her body on display in a way only a confident woman knows how to manage.

Fully clothed in a deep burgundy dress that matches her lipstick, and all I can do is picture her naked.

"We've been hoping to share the news for a while, but..." Remmy pauses and lifts a shoulder, her eyes staying on me as a slightly devious expression takes over. "Sometimes you're just so happy, you don't waste time on anyone but each other."

Then she looks over at Krissa, who is watching Remmy with just as much awe as I am, but with slightly more distaste.

"You must remember what that was like back when you and your husband were our age, right?"

Krissa's mouth drops open, and she looks like someone just spat in her face.

I feel like my brain is short-circuiting and I want to burst into laughter, but Remmy keeps talking.

"God, that feeling when you just..."

She lets out a long sigh and allows her eyes to slip closed as she takes another step forward, our fronts pressed together.

"...can't get enough of each other. When you live your life for that next moment when you can be pressed together."

Her hand takes mine and places it on her hip then slides up my arm and down my chest, one finger scratching across my nipple through my shirt, sending a quick zing through my body.

Fuck, everything she's doing is setting off shoots of lightning in my muscles.

Then I feel it. Her hand pressed between my legs as she leans forward and places a kiss on my neck.

My hand on her hip squeezes and I have to fight not to close my eyes.

"God, I'm so horny all the time," Remmy whispers, "and Ben knows how to hold me down and give it to me just like I need it."

I swallow, my entire body ready to take Remmy into a back room and give her *exactly* what she needs.

"I can't believe you act like this in public," Krissa's voice says from my left, sounding tinny, like she's talking at me underwater.

But I don't allow my attention to be truly divided. I don't even look at her.

I can't.

Instead, I focus on Remmy pressed against me, her hand between my thighs, and I feel my resolve slipping.

Then suddenly, the heat from her body is gone and I refocus my eyes.

Remmy stands in front of me with a weird expression on her face.

"She left. God, Ben, I'm so sorry. I know you said no more stuff in public and we're trying to draw the line at friendship, but I just…shit, I could just feel the bitchiness radiating off of her and I couldn't…"

I grab Remmy by the hand and drag her behind me, toward the door that says *Staff Only*. I don't even stop, just walk right in, pull Remmy in as well, and slam the door shut, turning the lock.

"Are you really that mad? I said—"

But she doesn't get out any more words because I shove her back against the door we just came through and silence her with my lips.

She makes a surprised noise but instantly responds, her mouth opening to mine, our tongues twisting together in a dance that's all our own.

I don't allow myself to focus on all the reasons I shouldn't be doing this with her. Instead I focus on what I should have been thinking about the other times she's tried to get something physical going.

How good she tastes.

How her ass feels in my hands.

How hard my dick gets when she presses against me.

The question is no longer whether something physical is a good idea. Instead, it's whether or not we can fuck on the couch back here and be quick enough and quiet enough that nobody will notice.

Our hands are everywhere, and I can feel Remmy's desperate need to continue whatever this is between us as surely as I can feel my own heart beating.

"On the couch," I whisper as we pull back from each other and start peeling our clothes off.

I take my pants and lay them out on the couch so I'm not resting my naked ass on it, then I strip down my boxers, leaving my shirt and tie on.

Once I'm sitting, I realize Remmy is completely naked and I missed the show.

"Do you have something?"

I hear her ask the question, but my eyes are too focused on everything I see in front of me, too busy drinking in the absolute magnificence of her body, all five feet eight inches of her.

Long legs, thick thighs, beautiful breasts with nipples that match her lips.

I won't be able to get it out of my head every time I look at her mouth from now until the day I die.

I stroke my dick absentmindedly, part of me forgetting that we're in a rush and unable to do anything but think about sucking those nipples into my mouth.

"Ben, do you have something?"

My eyes connect with hers and I snap out of the haze, reaching into the pocket of my pants that are underneath me and digging out my wallet.

I actually don't know if I have something. I don't have random trysts in art galleries with sexy women. That's more Wyatt's old style than anything I've ever done.

But there was one period of time when I was hoping to find someone to take home after things ended with Krissa and I kept a condom in my wallet.

I open it up and look, my shoulders falling when I realize what I pretty much already knew: empty.

Looking up at her, seeing her standing in front of me looking so beautiful and sensual and everything I've ever wanted, I make a decision.

A calculated risk.

"I'm clean."

Her eyebrows rise.

"I was tested a few months ago and haven't had sex with

anyone since I found out about the baby," she replies. Then she smiles. "I'm not on the pill, but I promise I'm as pregnant as I'm gonna get."

I laugh, and so does she, the small bit of humor cooling the heat of the moment just enough that I don't feel like I'm on some sort of lusty autopilot.

It allows me to really take her in as she steps forward. The desire on her face causes my heart to race as she straddles my hips, lowering her body so we're pressed together.

Her lips return to mine, and our kiss breathes something into my chest. Something warm and cozy, like a fire on a brutally cold day at the beach.

My hands rest on her soft hips then stroke down over her naked skin, onto her thighs.

I reach one hand between her legs, slipping a finger against her core and she moans, panting out a breath that sounds just as good as it feels.

She's slick, so wet I'm able to slide two fingers inside of her, loving the sound she makes when I pump them in and out.

Remmy presses her face against my neck and starts sucking on my skin.

"You're so wet," I say.

"I'm so *ready*," she replies, her voice a lusty whisper in my ear.

"Yeah?"

She nods and I pull my fingers out, adjusting her hips so that warm wetness is pressed against my dick, and then she groans and pulls her head back, her mouth open as she grinds on me.

Her hips move steadily, back and forth as she works against me, her lower lips a welcome respite from the years of stroking my own dick.

And then suddenly, without warning, she crooks her pelvis just slightly and I realize I'm inside of her.

I shout out but Remmy presses her open mouth against mine, our tongues resuming their earlier dance.

The pressure and heat of her pussy gripping me like this is unreal as she rotates and moves above me. The slapping sound of our bodies connecting over and over again gets louder as she rides me, her breasts bouncing in my face.

I wish I could transport us to my bed, to her bed—to *anywhere* I'd be able to focus on her and give her body the stimulation and pleasure I want to. I want to spend time on her breasts, on her clit, on her ass, make sure she feels all the pleasure coursing through her body that I'm capable of giving her.

But instead, I know we have to hurry.

And if I'm honest, my own sexual inexperience is making it known that I might have a hard time lasting.

So I place my hands on her hips and start to take over, fucking myself up into her with aggressive pounds that have her fingernails digging into my skin where they grip my shoulders.

I might come fast, but I'll be damned if I leave her unsatisfied.

"Fuck, Ben," she whispers, her voice breathy and exhausted. "Stroke my clit."

I drop my hand and rub her, groaning when I feel her inner muscles clench me.

"I'm almost there," she says, her voice strained, her eyes closed. "Right...right—oh my god."

And then she clenches me over and over and over as her body hits the peak.

I'm right behind her, giving a few more firm strokes into her before I feel that warm heat grip my spine and race through the center of my body, tingling into my fingers and my toes.

I bite my tongue, trying to keep myself from making any noise that might attract attention from outside.

It feels so good to hold her against me like this, both of our bodies naked and sweaty, my dick still snug inside her, though it's becoming more sensitive by the second.

I leave my arms wrapped around her waist as I catch my breath, allowing my head to fall backward, my eyes looking up at the ceiling above us.

"That was awesome," I say, letting out a short chuckle. "Clearly we should have been doing that from the beginning."

But Remmy doesn't say anything.

"Remmy?" I say, tapping her lightly on the spine.

She pulls back, and I'm almost startled at the look on her face.

Her makeup is fine, her lipstick a little smudged, a few beads of sweat at her brow. She looks like normal Remmy.

Except for her eyes.

The normally beautiful brown looks muddy and dark, her face neutral and dull.

"You okay?"

She nods and begins to crawl off my body, but her eyes don't connect with mine. If I'm honest, she looks like she can't see me, like she doesn't want to look at me.

I stay quiet, unsure what to do as she slips her bra back on and her dress over her head. She looks completely put back together in a matter of seconds.

Then she walks to the break room-style kitchen in the corner and rinses her hands in the sink.

I scramble to get my boxers back up to my hips and shake out my pants. By the time I've gotten them on, Remmy is walking to the door like a fucking zombie.

"I'll see you out there," she says, still not looking at me as she unlocks the door and exits the room.

What the fuck just happened?

Chapter Fourteen
REMMY

"I'm telling you, Remmy—if you don't apply for spring admission, I will drive down to Hermosa Beach and strangle you myself."

I laugh at Melody's words, feeling thankful once again that I was lucky enough to be assigned to her when I enrolled at Alta Mesa.

Melody Cohen's focus as an academic advisor and part-time instructor is to assimilate transfer students to campus culture. As a person who was going through a lot when I started there, it made all the difference in making me feel like I belonged.

She has also been the most vocal advocate for me continuing my studies, encouraging me to look into graduate school when I was only a junior.

It was also *because* of her that I was first introduced to art therapy, a type of counseling graduate degree I've considered applying for over the past year and a half.

"I appreciate the vote of confidence, but I'm just not ready," I say, smiling at her face on the screen of my phone. "But when I am, you'll be the first person I call. I promise."

My freshman year of college was mostly a wash, though I was able to transfer a few credits from that first semester over to Alta Mesa. When I started my program, a bachelor's in art education, it was like someone had taken my body and hooked me up to a battery, to a life source that pumped my blood through my veins and made me believe I could have a purpose.

I never really planned to become a teacher. I just wanted a chance to explore art in a way that would take me back to a place my mind rarely had a chance to go.

I was seriously considering her suggestion that I apply to a graduate program, though I knew I wanted to take at least a semester, maybe a year off from school before going back.

I never realized I would find that chance to go back a dwindling option with a pregnancy looming.

Now, I'm wishing I had made different choices, wishing I'd continued to follow my heart instead of going with my family on a trip to Colombia in May when I finished my final semester. I wish I'd been brave enough to tell them about my graduation from Alta Mesa instead of pretending I finally decided to drop out of college without a degree and move home.

My life would be so different if I'd just decided to do what felt right to me instead of going along with what my parents wanted.

But fighting against expectations is a hard thing to do.

"You know I'm here for you, whatever you need!"

I grin at her, feeling truly thankful that there is a woman in my life who wants the best for me for no other reason than because she thinks I deserve it.

Even if she doesn't know the real me.

Even if she might be wrong.

"Thanks, Melody. I've gotta get going, but I'll call you again once I've decided."

Once I'm finally off the phone, I stretch out on my bed, my hand falling to rest on my stomach.

It's hard to believe there's a living thing in there.

Apart from the morning sickness, I don't really feel any different at all. Maybe a bit like I'm on my period all the time, minus the tampons. Weird cramps, sore boobs, tired body.

No, that part is different.

I'm tired all the time.

All. The. Time.

Logically, I realize my body is like, creating an eyeball right now or something magical like that, so it makes sense that I'm always exhausted, but it still sucks.

I reach out and open the drawer of my nightstand, fishing around until I find what I'm looking for.

And then I just stare at it, my nerves a constant, steady strum through my body.

The grainy picture doesn't look like much.

I found out I was pregnant after my missed period. I've always been irregular, so I didn't think much about it until I thought I had a stomach flu that never felt like it was going away.

So when a doctor at a small private practice unaffiliated with my parents' insurance confirmed what an at-home test had already told me, I threw up on the floor of the exam room I was in.

She scheduled my first ultrasound for just a few days later, and I went alone, having the conversation with myself about whether or not I wanted to terminate the pregnancy or give it up for adoption or…I don't know. I never imagined I would want to keep it.

Especially when I think about how it happened.

But they showed me on a little screen what was growing inside of me, a little baby that was almost exactly eight weeks along.

I spent several days waffling between what I wanted to do and what I thought I *should* do and what I was expected to do. I went to a clinic. Signed in. Sat at the front, but then left before they called my name.

I moved home just a few days later, preparing to talk to Lucas about it, thinking I would be honest and tell him the truth.

I wasn't honest.

He didn't get the whole truth from me.

And I don't know that anyone ever will.

I need to schedule my next appointment, though I have to be careful because I don't want anyone seeing me. When I told the doctor in Santa Barbara I was moving, she said I'd need to find an OB right away.

I've been here for over a month and haven't even started looking.

Does that make me a bad person?

Does that make me a bad mom?

I've thought about it a handful of times, even picked up the phone and tried to find a place I might like.

But the idea of going in for a prenatal visit, scheduling an ultrasound to possibly hear the heartbeat...it feels like too much—too much to do alone.

I snuggle into my body pillow, holding the ultrasound picture in my hand and wondering if I should reach out to Ben.

He might not be the *actual* father, but he's clearly still up for the job, and he's told me I don't have to do this stuff alone.

The idea of calling him today makes my nose wrinkle, though, especially in light of how I acted last night after our tête-à-tête in the staff room at Sheldon House.

I have a hard time understanding what happened to me at the end. All I know is we were having sex and it was amazing and I couldn't get enough of fucking him.

And then I felt it.

I felt him come, felt the pulse of him inside me.

Only one person has ever done that before in my entire life.

And he's the reason I'm pregnant right now.

I've never let someone do it before, and I didn't realize I would have such a...strong reaction to it, to how it feels, to how *dirty* it makes *me* feel.

So I shut down. I tuned him out.

After some mind-blowing sex that made me feel like I was walking on sunshine, riding a cloud, tasting the rainbow, or any of those other clichés.

I look at Ben's number in my phone and wonder if I can summon up the courage to talk to him.

A moment passes.

Two.

Nope.

Text it is.

Me: I need your help with something. Can we not talk about last night?

There's a delay in his response, but eventually I see the little bubbles on my screen pop up, then disappear, then pop up again. It happens a few times before he finally sends a message.

Ben: What can I help with? I'm here for whatever you need.

Something tense settles in my chest at his answer. As firm as Ben likes to be, as much as he considers himself to be a man with a plan or whatever, he really is just a solid guy.

Me: I need to make an OBGYN appointment to get a prenatal visit, but I have to keep this shit secret and not go through my insurance or my parents will find out since I'm still on their plan. Any ideas?

It only takes a second for him to respond this time.

Ben: I can absolutely help. I know a guy.

My head jerks back at his response, and part of me wants to laugh.
He knows a guy?
Who *knows a guy* when it comes to pregnancy doctors? Is that a standard thing I haven't known about, or is this just Ben-specific?

Me: That's a...weird answer.

Me: Who is this guy that you know?

He sends back a laughing face and I roll my eyes. Of course he thinks this is funny.

Ben: Just trust me and give me twenty minutes.

And then it's radio silence.
I pass the time by watching the end of that shitty movie on Netflix I fell asleep to the other night.
When my phone rings, I wince, realizing Ben wants to talk as opposed to text.
Don't you realize texting is the preferred method of communication!?
I sigh and click accept then hold the phone up to my ear.

"Who is this back-alley friend of yours?" I say before he can utter a word.

Ben laughs, and even though his laughing face over text was irritating, the sound of his real laugh has my heart skipping a beat. He sounds the way my body pillow makes me feel.

"My friend Logan is the head of pediatrics at Roth Memorial," he says, "and I called him for his recommendation on how to handle it. He's going to schedule you for a walk-in appointment with an OB under a pseudonym. Typically only walk-ins can request emergency appointments, but he'll go down and talk to someone later today for us, and we can just pay in cash at reception."

My mind trips over the word 'we' but focuses on the more pressing part.

"But I don't want to sit in a waiting room and possibly run into someone I know. Literally everyone I know is posting pregnancy or baby pictures on Facebook. It's bound to happen."

He chuckles again.

"You won't have to. Logan said we can wait in his office and that you can request the clinic text you with your room number when it's time for your appointment."

I feel stopped up, no words coming to mind as to what I should say in response.

"Does that work for you?" he asks when I don't say anything.

I nod, then realize he can't see me.

"Yes. Yeah, that works. That's...great actually. Thank you for doing that."

"No problem. He told me to text him when you're available in the next week since walk-ins are usually quick turnaround appointments as opposed to ones they schedule weeks out."

"Every day, all day," I reply. "My social life sucks right now."

I can hear Ben grinning on the other end of the line. "Ah, come on now. I seem to recall you being out and about quite a few times over the past two weeks. Always eating, though—clearly eating for two."

I burst into laughter. "Hey, rude. I don't look like I'm eating for two...yet." Then I look down at my tummy, where I rested my hand earlier. "But you'll be able to tell soon, that's for sure."

There's a pause before Ben speaks again.

"Have you been able to feel it all? Like any kicks or anything? Or is it too early?"

"I think it's too early, but I need to finish reading the stupid pregnancy book Lucas got me on our breakup date."

Ben snorts. "That guy *would* give you a pregnancy book after you break up. I swear, I've never met someone as genuinely nice as he is in my entire life, even if he *is* a little bit self-absorbed."

I let my eyes stray up to the picture that still sits on my bookshelf, to the image of the two of us, so young and happy.

And then I think about Ben. About how much he loves his sister and brother. About how kind and caring he has been to me, even in the wake of our weird conversations and interactions.

I can't help but hum a noise of disagreement.

"I can think of someone else who is genuinely nice, *and* selfless," I say. "And he just found a way to make my life a whole lot less difficult."

Ben's silent on the other end of the line.

"Thanks, Remmy," he finally says. "Someday, you'll realize I don't deserve that, but for now, I'll take it."

We talk for a few more minutes. He asks if Dominic still hates him—yes—and I ask when I will get to see Ivy—he isn't sure.

Then we get off the phone with Ben promising to let me know what Logan says about scheduling an appointment.

I feel oddly sad when we hang up. I've never been a phone person, someone who enjoys sitting on one end and listening to someone on the other. It's honestly probably one of the reasons why Lucas was always so bothered about our time apart.

We dated long distance for five years, and I called him on average once every one to two months.

That's not a relationship.

Now, I'm talking to Ben for ten minutes and wishing I could schedule a time to talk to him again. It's crazy how things change.

But who knows? Maybe I can blame this on pregnancy hormones, too.

I don't know what I was expecting, but a text from Ben an hour later saying we're scheduled for an OB appointment on Monday was *not* it.

Now, as I walk into the hospital, Ben at my side, I realize it was probably better to have a 48-hour turnaround as opposed to something where I had to wait for weeks and build up the anxiety of wondering if someone was going to see me.

This way, we just rip off the Band-Aid.

After scanning the room and letting out a sigh of relief that I don't recognize anyone, I walk up to reception and sign in, snorting as I write my fake name on the sheet.

Allie McLovin.

This guy has seen *Super Bad* too many times.

Once we've checked in and I've provided the receptionist with my phone number so she can text me when it's time for our appointment, Ben and I take a walk out of OB and into pediatrics, down a long hallway, stopping at room 483.

Ben knocks twice, then verbalizes it as he opens the door.

"Knock, knock."

No answer.

"Perfect. He told me he'd probably be in a meeting but that we could take a seat and relax. Sometimes it can take an hour or so before a walk-in can be seen."

I nod, following him in and then closing the door behind me.

"How do you know this guy again?" I ask, my eyes roving around the sparsely furnished office.

Ben takes a seat behind Logan's desk.

"He was my mentor when I was at school."

"He was your Prep-the-Prepster?" I ask, grinning a little bit. "You actually did that program?"

"Of course I did it."

"Such a nerd."

He lets his head fall back and releases a laugh. "Ah, you're never gonna let that go, are you?"

I shake my head. "Not a chance in hell, mister."

The door behind me opens and I turn to step out of the way.

"Woah, sorry about that," the man says, a charming smile on his face. He reaches out to give me his hand "You must be Remmy. I'm Dr. Logan Becker."

I smile, clutching his hand with mine and giving it a good shake. "Hi, Dr. Becker. Thank you so much for sorting things out for us today."

He nods. "Anything I can do to help, especially for this

asshole," he says, thumbing in the direction of where Ben is still sitting at his desk.

"Good to see you, too, *Dr. Becker*," Ben says, a good natured smile on his face as he teases his old mentor.

Logan chuckles as he closes his office door.

"Congratulations to you both," he says, walking over to where Ben has vacated the desk chair. "I didn't realize you were expecting."

He sits down and looks at me expectantly, and I realize I'm supposed to say something about the baby.

"Well, actually—"

"We're very excited about it," Ben says, interrupting me. His eyes don't look my way, but he does walk over and wrap an arm around my shoulders. "It wasn't expected, but sometimes the best things in life come in the form of surprises."

I grin at the way Ben says that, and so does Logan.

"Oh gross. You're one of those super-in-love couples, aren't you?"

I laugh, finding his observation really funny.

"Absolutely," Ben says.

"I'm actually really obsessed with him in a creepy way," I add on, wrapping my arms around his waist and snuggling in close. "I love to watch him when he's sleeping."

Ben rolls his eyes and Logan laughs.

"You know, I've *never* been in this hospital before."

"It's new," Logan and Ben say at the same time.

Ben waves a hand out in front of himself and Logan takes the invitation to continue.

"I just got the tour when I started, so forgive me if I sound like a brochure," Logan jokes. "Roth Memorial has only been here in its current state for three years. The old hospital was due for some serious renovations. The Roth family completely overhauled everything. They're the reason I have a job, actually. Apparently a big part of their plan was to expand pediatrics."

I barely hide my eyeroll as I think about Lennon's family and their philanthropic mission. Noble? Yes. Irritating as all hell to have my ex's new girlfriend's name everywhere I sit? Absolutely.

But I quickly push that thought aside.

"Even before all of that," I say. "I've just...never been seriously injured or had any reason to come to the hospital before."

"Well, if you're gonna have to go to the hospital for anything, at least it's something you're looking forward to, right?"

I nod, but I zone out when he looks to Ben and keeps talking.

Do I look like I'm looking forward to it?

Sometimes I wonder if people would know how terrified I am if they knew I was pregnant.

Lucas might be the only one to truly know how scared I am, and that's not even because I really told him. It's just because he knows me.

Ben kind of has an idea, but I doubt he really gets it to the true level.

When I joke about the baby being a parasite, when I wonder if I made the right decision, when I think back to how this shit all started...

It makes me sick to my stomach.

And not because of morning sickness.

It's because I'm worried about the decisions I'm making.

It's because I'm afraid I'll be a shitty mom.

It's because I'm scared I won't be able to love it.

Because as much as I'm trying to do the right thing, I can't help but allow myself to wonder...

How do you love a baby when it belongs to a man who raped you?

Chapter Fifteen
REMMY

Eventually, Dr. Becker has to leave to go back to work. He wishes us luck and then heads out.

Ben wastes no time returning to sit in his desk chair.

"Did you not have to work today?" I ask, the thought having just occurred to me.

He shrugs, looking a little bit like a kid. "I'm using a personal day."

I press a hand to my chest, unable to contain my smile.

"Ex*cuse* me?" I say, my voice pitched high. "Mr. I Never Take Days Off took a day to accompany me to my prenatal appointment?"

He lifts his shoulder again, reaching over and grabbing one of those squeezy stress balls off the desk and squishing it in his hand.

"Priorities, Remmy."

My shoulders drop and something in my chest swells, making

me feel full.

Sometimes, Ben says stuff that just hits me in my gut in a weird way that I don't know how to handle.

It takes nearly two hours for us to get a call to see the doctor, but the text does eventually come through.

We hustle out of the office and make the long trek back to the reception area, breezing through and right into OB toward the room that's reserved for us.

A nurse greets us as we walk in.

"So, we're doing an ultrasound today, right?" she says, giving me a smile.

I lift my eyebrows. "Oh. I thought we were just doing a prenatal."

The nurse nods as she goes around the room, pulling out a paper dress for me to wear and setting up the little bed with stirrups.

"Dr. Quinn wants to do both today since you're a new patient and you're further along. It's just to be safe and get our own good picture of how baby is doing, okay?"

I giggle. "Dr. Quinn?"

I look back and forth between Ben and the nurse. Neither of them look like they know what I'm talking about.

"Like *Dr. Quinn, Medicine Woman*?"

No reaction.

"It was a show with...never mind." I wave my hands to brush the moment away.

Clearly I'll have to enjoy that little tidbit alone.

We go through the appointment at a steady pace. The meeting with Dr. Quinn begins well, even if she gives me a slight reprimand for letting so much time go by between my first appointment and seeing her.

We talk about my body, the morning sickness, my sore breasts, and what feels like a bucketload of topics about the birth.

The longer we speak, the more overwhelmed I get, the more I realize I don't know anything. I started reading that book Lucas got me, but I've really only been reading about how the baby has been growing as it happens.

I haven't read about what's happening to my body, thought about what kind of birthing environment I'll want, paid attention to what I should be eating.

I don't even realize it, but at one point, I feel a hand on my back, rubbing in slow circles.

Looking to my right, I see Ben standing next to me, his eyes warm but filled with concern.

"Are you okay?"

Dr. Quinn's question has me wanting to shrink into myself.

I don't want her to see that I'm an emotional wreck.

"It's okay if you're not, you know. Lots of women come in here and cry their big beautiful hearts out because they're feeling a little maxed out, a little overwhelmed by how big and scary this experience is. It's totally normal."

A single tear drops and I bat it away.

"It is?"

She nods.

"But...what if I do everything wrong?" I ask, not caring that I have an incredibly intelligent doctor and a probably very stunned man watching me begin to blubber. The dam breaks and tears pour forth at will. "I wasn't ready for this. I...I don't...know what I'm doing."

Ben's hand stays warm on my back, a silent sign of support, as his other reaches up and massages my shoulder.

Dr. Quinn leans forward and takes my hand between both of hers.

"I promise you...one hundred percent promise you...that every first-time mother feels this way. Even the ones who have been working hard to get pregnant, who have always known it was what they wanted—they're scared, too."

I wipe my eyes with my free hand.

"Why do people put themselves through this if it's so terrifying?" I say, letting out a half-cry, half-laugh that brings a smile to Dr. Quinn's face.

"It's a good thing that you're nervous, Remmy. It means you care. If you came in the door smoking a cigarette and not caring about anything I have to say, *that's* when I would be worried—for you *and* the baby."

I take a deep breath, her words helping me feel a little more stable, even if I do still feel like I'm balancing precariously.

Getting up, I walk over to the box of tissues on a shelf in the corner. Dry my eyes. Blow my nose. Check my face in the mirror above the sink and make sure my makeup isn't a disaster.

"Alright," I say, feeling a lot calmer when I turn around to face them both. "Let's see the little swimmie."

Dr. Quinn smiles. "I'll grab Jessica and we can get started on your ultrasound, alright?" She pats her hand on the seat I just vacated. "Because you're still in the first trimester, we're going to do a transvaginal ultrasound today, so get undressed from the waist down and hop up here. Jessica will help you get your feet into the stirrups and will talk you through the process."

I nod, remembering how uncomfortable it was the first time.

"I'll be back in a few minutes."

She leaves the room, closing the door with a soft snick.

I glance at Ben, wondering what he thinks about me and my breakdown. I know he's seen me cry before. I could argue that he's already seen me at my worst.

But there's something about being the one growing this baby inside of me that has me on the defensive. I don't want him to question my capabilities as a mother, even though I question them myself every day.

He can think I'm crazy all he wants, but I want him to think I'll be a good mom.

I don't know why it's so important to me, but it is.

"I'm sorry about that," I say.

But before I can even say anything else, Ben gives me a look that tells me to cut it out.

"You have nothing to be sorry for," he replies. "I'll step out while you change, okay?"

I nod, waiting until the door closes to strip off my jeans and underwear and get settled on the seat with the paper dress hanging over my lap.

Dr. Quinn and Jessica walk in a few minutes later, Ben following in their wake.

He hovers awkwardly near the door as Dr. Quinn reviews my chart and Jessica prepares the machine and lubes up a wand that's going inside of me.

"Alright, this will feel a little cool but shouldn't be too uncomfortable," Jessica says as she reaches under the paper to press the small stick into my vagina. Her eyes look at me as she slides it in. "That okay?"

I nod, even though having it in there feels...squicky.

Then I look back at Ben, who is still standing just inside the door.

I reach my hand out.

"Come here. You should see it."

The apprehension on his face stays the same, but he moves forward and stands like a tree next to my chair, his hand coming to rest on my shoulder.

Instantly, I feel a lightening in my chest.

Jessica clicks around a few times on her computer with one hand, her other still holding the wand inside me.

The grainy screen suddenly fills with a large black space and...the shape of a baby.

My mouth drops open.

This is...completely different than my first ultrasound. I was at seven weeks and the sac was mostly empty except for a tiny little thing that looked like I'd swallowed a button.

Now...

This baby has a big head and a belly and legs.

She moves the wand slightly, shifting the picture, and I can see a little arm.

"Baby looks great," Jessica says. "Gimme just a second, and..." She clicks a few buttons with her free hand and then I hear it. The heartbeat.

A rapid thump, thump, thump that has me placing a hand over my mouth and tears filling my eyes.

Something pivotal within me shifts and slides into place as I watch the tiny body on the screen, listen to the fast rhythm of its heart beating.

I need to get back into therapy, talk out my shit with someone, make sure every ounce of joy I feel in this moment is the primary feeling I get every time I look at my child.

But in this moment, it doesn't matter to me how this baby was created. It doesn't matter to me that the choice wasn't mine. It doesn't even matter to me if I have to do it alone.

What matters is that the little heart beating on the screen is mine. My baby. My future. My sweet love.

And I will do everything in my power to make sure that little thing grows up with the best life it can possibly have.

A hand slips into mine, and I glance up, seeing Ben look down at me with awe in his face.

"That's amazing," he whispers, looking back at the screen,

leaning forward to get a better look.

I still wonder if he really understands what he's signed himself up for by asking me to marry him.

But if that joy and wonder in his eyes is any indication of the kind of father he will be?

I squeeze his hand back, and he turns to smile at me.

This.

This is what was missing the first time I did this.

Someone to share it with.

Someone who cares about what happens.

Someone who sees this as an important moment.

Ben gets it.

I can see it on his face.

In that goofy smile he seems to save just for me.

I close my eyes for just a second and let a few thankful tears fall.

Because I knew Ben meant it when he told me I didn't have to be alone anymore.

But now I actually believe it's true.

Hermosa Beach is a beautiful place to live, but a good 50 to 60% of the homes remain unrenovated and in their original condition, which makes them look a little shabby and beaten down. Of the ones that *are* renovated, most do not attempt to change the exterior.

My eyes flit over the white paneled siding of Ben's house, appreciating the delicate finishes that have clearly been made in the past few years.

This masterpiece...if I had to wager a guess, I'd bet money Ben did a complete teardown and rebuild. Or he had an incredibly skilled contractor. Either way, I'm impressed.

"You've already been here," he says as I wander around taking in the front of his home.

"Yeah, but it was dark and I was throwing up in your bushes. I wasn't exactly paying attention," I reply, laughter in my voice.

I feel like I'm on cloud nine.

Things between me and Ben feel...different somehow, like the sex and the ultrasound have bonded us in a special way we didn't have before. I may have had a little mental breakdown after the sex, but I mean...come on. It was still amazing up until that point.

Obviously, there's a tiny voice within me that's saying I shouldn't get too emotionally wrapped up in how I feel right now. But, it's rare for me to feel this good, so I'm gonna hold on to it with both hands.

"Alright, well this time I'll give you a full tour that includes more than just the bushes and the toilet."

I stick my tongue out at him as he unlocks his front door and we walk in.

It's much larger on the inside than I was expecting, much more open and airy, though also a little more sterile.

From the outside, the property looks like it's built for a family. It looks welcoming and warm with potted plants and a well-maintained yard, which is hard to do near the beach.

But inside, it's high ceilings and white, white, white.

"You're familiar with the entry bath," Ben says, his eyes light and his tone teasing as he gestures to the place where I cleaned up after my time in the shrubbery. "Upstairs there are four bedrooms and three bathrooms. We can go up there in a minute, but downstairs there's an office over here," he continues, leading me down a short hall that opens into a spacious at-home office that's beautifully decorated and clearly not used at all. "This is the laundry and garage area," he adds, indicating the door across from the office.

"I don't know why, but I always pictured you living in some crazy mansion. Like Batman with an underground cave."

Ben laughs. "You know, that actually sounds horrible. I don't like caves."

I giggle and follow him back to the main area, where he shows me the kitchen and living room, which I saw last time I was here.

What I *hadn't* noticed were the floor-to-ceiling windows that look out into a beautiful backyard. It looks completely different in the light of day.

"Wow," I say, taking a look at the manicured space.

"Wanna see something cool?" he asks.

"Duh."

He laughs, then presses a button.

What I thought was a wall of windows begins to recede into the walls, leaving the living room open to the yard.

"The windows double as collapsible doors."

I cross my arms. "Well that's just super cool."

He laughs again. "Alright, so I don't live in a mansion, or a big compound like some of our families do. I wanted a normal house for…" He pauses, clears his throat. "I just wanted a normal *home*, so there isn't a driver or a pool or a wine room…although I *do* have a maid service and keep a wine cooler in the kitchen."

I shift on my feet. Ben assumes I'm used to all of those things.

I mean, technically I am, but I was living a very different life in Santa Barbara than what most people envision.

I had a job at an art store.

I never used the credit card my parents had in my name.

I drove a beat-up Honda Civic until it crapped out on me and then I rode the bus.

Maybe I had the comfort of knowing I could be taken care of if something crazy happened, and that's an assurance a lot of people don't have, but I didn't spend my college years being pampered.

For some reason, I want Ben to know that.

Maybe not today, since it will invite more questions than I feel prepared to answer right now.

But definitely at some point.

"You know what we should do tonight?"

Ben turns from where he's looking out at his yard.

"We should have a sleepover."

He grins, and I can feel it tickle the base of my spine. He might be a nerdy kind of guy, but damn if he doesn't know how to look at me in a way that hits me where it counts.

"I think I can get behind that."

We spend the next thirty minutes wandering through the upstairs bedrooms, discussing which one would be good for the baby.

Which feels crazy.

Talking about baby rooms.

The good thing about the house being incredibly bare is that everything is a blank canvas. There's room to make adjustments and changes and add decorations.

Because I'll be the woman of the house.

Something else that feels completely crazy.

And then Ben shows me his bedroom.

A large king bed. A dresser. A walk-in closet next to the master bath.

I step into the bathroom and smile at the large soaking tub.

"You're welcome to use it any time you want," he says.

I wrinkle my nose.

"I'm not supposed to take baths while I'm pregnant. It's not good for the baby for me to be in all that hot water."

"Maybe after, then?" he says, flicking off the light as both of us head back out to the landing and toward the stairs.

After.

There's this mental divide in my head that seems to be difficult to get past.

I can see myself moving in here. Getting things ready for the baby. Settling in and even coming back here with the baby once it's born.

But that after part is like a gray fog. I can't see anything past that—Ben with the baby, me running around chasing a toddler, or any other thing that's to come in the future.

And I don't know why.

A few hours later, I've stopped by my house for an overnight bag, showered, changed, and I'm preparing to return to Ben's for a movie, pizza, and sleeping over.

If I'm completely honest, my body is hoping for more sexy times even though my heart and mind aren't sure we can handle it.

"Remmy."

My brother's voice stops me in my tracks.

I turn and look over my shoulder, finding Dominic walking toward me from the kitchen.

"What's up?" I ask.

I love my oldest brother. I really do, but he acts like a second dad sometimes and it makes me want to, like...kick him in the shin. Which I know isn't very mature of me.

But Jesus, let me have some damn freedom. It's why I pushed so hard to move away for college. I couldn't imagine having my mom and dad *and* brother watching my every move.

Dominic eyes the bag in my hand. "Where are you off to?"

I hoist the bag a little higher on my shoulder.

"I'm staying over at Ben's tonight," I reply, making sure my shoulders are back and my chin is high. I don't even let my voice tip up at the end like I'm asking a question.

Because I don't need anyone's permission.

Besides, Dom knows I'm already pregnant. It's not like I can get *more* pregnant.

At that thought, I giggle.

He crosses his arms. "If you're going to continue to bounce around town with him and he's going to introduce you to his family as *his fiancée*"—my heart stops—"you better sit your butt down with mom and dad or they're gonna hear it from someone else first."

I swallow, though my throat suddenly feels like sandpaper.

"You're lucky they're out of town right now or this kind of *chisme* might have gotten back to them."

Gossip.

My parents have never been the types of people who find it important to stay up on town talk. It wouldn't be very Catholic of them to spread gossip, so my mom tries to steer clear of it.

But my brother is right.

They can't hear about it from someone else.

"Okay. I'll handle it."

"I'm not kidding, Remmy."

"Neither am I, Dominic."

His eyes narrow at me, and I let out a long sigh.

"You know, when we were younger, you spent a lot more time on my side. Now it feels like you're always trying to manage me, like I'm a dog that needs to be trained."

I see his nostrils flare but I ignore it.

"I miss the guy who used to read to me and watch movies with me on weekends and sneak me chocolate when mom wanted me to watch my weight. So it would be great if, at some point, I could have you back as my brother and not as my trainer."

Something comes over his face as his eyes widen, but I don't stop to give it a second thought before I head out to the garage.

Chapter Sixteen
BEN

When I bought this house several years ago, I was envisioning something specific for my life. I hired the best designers and contractors to make it perfect.

Now, it's just an empty façade.

A place where I shower and shave and sleep before leaving again.

It isn't a place I enjoy being.

Not because of what it was *supposed* to represent to me—a future, stability, happiness—but because of who I am now compared to who I used to be.

The man I was when I graduated from college was someone filled with hope, filled with plans and goals and a list of things to accomplish in life, steady in a belief that they were all achievable.

The man I am now struggles to find hope anywhere. Sits rooted in irritation and exhaustion and avoidance. Wonders what exactly the future holds other than more turmoil and betrayal.

The past few years have been...particularly rough for me.

Which is why today was so surprising.

Holding Remmy's hand as we both watched the ultrasound was nothing short of magical.

And it's been a long time since I've felt any kind of magic in my life.

I'm starting to wonder if maybe I should let this be what it is and just run with it.

Take this friendship with Remmy, this strange thing we seem to have stumbled upon, and just enjoy it for what it is.

I shake my head, wondering when this easygoing, lighthearted version of myself decided to come out to play.

It's been a long time since I've felt this carefree.

Thinking back, I don't know if I've *ever* been this carefree. I've always had something intense on my mind, a strong focus, a calculated perspective.

Today, I feel like maybe I should take a break from that and just...enjoy.

My phone rings, and my entire demeanor changes when I see the name on the screen.

Dad

This is what I've been waiting for, right? This was my big game, to try to weasel myself between him and what he wants because of what I have.

And now he's calling me, for the first time in a very long time.

"I'm back!"

I hit decline and set my phone face down on my desk, grinning at the sound of Remmy walking through my house.

This is what I need to focus on. Right here. Right now.

"Alright, so I got Oreos and vanilla ice cream and chocolate chip cookie dough so we can make pazookies. Plus a frozen pizza we can shove in the oven if we want, *and* I grabbed a few movies from the RedBox at the grocery store."

Her voice echoes through the house, filling it with something I didn't realize was missing.

Life.

When I come around the corner and find her standing in my kitchen, her feet bare and her hair damp, loaded up with bags she's trying to extricate her arms from and place on my counter, I actually feel my heart start beating in a different way.

"What's a pazookie?" I ask.

She turns to look at me with shock. "Are you *serious*?" she asks. "Have you never been to BJ's?"

I laugh. "I've *received* BJs, but I can't say I've ever been to one before. What is it?"

She fake gags. "Gross. Keep your blowie stories to yourself. I'm talking about the restaurant. They have them all over and they make these massive warm cookies and put ice cream on top."

Remmy hums happily and claps her hands together, looking off into the distance like she's remembering a long-lost love.

"They're the most delicious thing in the world, so get ready to have your socks knocked off."

I find myself walking forward, toward Remmy, where she bops around my kitchen trying to find the things she needs to make her pazookies.

Once I'm standing right next to her, she stops.

"Oh." She laughs. "Sorry, didn't realize you were right there."

She grins and my eyes zero in on her lips, on her mouth, on the happiness I didn't know *she* was capable of expressing any more than I was.

"Remember how I said we should just be friends and not do any physical stuff?" I say.

She laughs, but it cuts off when my hand comes up to her face, pushing some of her hair behind her shoulder.

Remmy nods. "I wasn't sure if you still felt that way after...the art gallery."

I shake my head. "I want to take it back."

She sighs. "That sounds awesome."

And then we launch at each other.

Our mouths open and our tongues tangle, my hands taking her face and stroking along the smooth skin.

I kiss her mouth and then her cheek and then down her neck, my lips feeling her pulse beating rapidly through her skin and the vibrations of her moan as I begin to suck on her pulse point.

"Ben," she whispers.

I groan, not wanting to stop and hoping her use of my name is in pleasure and not to get my attention.

"Ben, wait."

Pulling back, I look at her face, seeing the flush of her skin and wondering how far down it goes, remembering that the skin she hides away under her clothing is a slightly lighter color than the tan skin of her arms and legs.

"Yeah?"

"Don't..." She pauses, and for a second, I worry I've done something wrong. "Just...don't come inside me, okay?"

My shoulders sag. "No problem."

The relief is obvious in her face, and then she presses her lips back to mine, her hands beginning to roam along my body.

It feels so good when she traces her fingers under my shirt and up along my back, her hands still cool from holding tubs of ice cream and a frozen pizza.

"The ice cream," she says as I drop to my knees and tug down her little shorts and panties, letting them drop to the tile floor.

"Fuck the ice cream."

She giggles, but she goes quiet when I slip a hand between her legs and grip her ass, pulling her forward so my mouth is pressed against her pussy. I open wide, letting the taste of her flood my mouth, using my tongue to hit every nerve that I can.

One of Remmy's hands slaps down on the countertop to brace her body as she cries out in pleasure, the other digging into my hair as she shifts her weight to try to give me better access.

"Fuck, Rem," I say, tracing a hand up her thigh and across her body before slowing to rub her clit. "You are so wet. You been thinking about this a lot?"

She nods, her eyes closed and her breaths uneven.

I keep rubbing her, my tongue flicking at her opening.

"Tell me what you've been thinking about."

My words come out as a demand and I feel a shiver race through her, her eyes opening as she looks down at where I kneel before her. Her hips rotate against me as I lap at her.

"I've been thinking about you, naked and getting me off like this," she says, her voice breathy and fluttered. "Jerking yourself in a tight fist because you're so turned on."

I groan, sucking her clit into my mouth and pressing a finger into her center. Her fingers grip harder into my hair and I let her pull me in closer.

"And then once you get me off, you take me hard on the floor, and we both...mmmm...we both have bruises on our knees after," she rushes out, her words getting cut off when I slip in a second finger and start searching for that spot inside her that will make her tumble over and tremble.

I look up at her, continuing to suck and lick and play, making sure to catch her eyes. And then I stroke the spot that has her shouting out my name, her hands dropping from my head to my shoulders to give her better balance.

Her pussy spasms around my fingers several times before I feel her body go liquid and she begins to slump in my arms.

Pulling out my fingers, I help support her as she wraps her arms around my neck and lowers down so she's straddling me as I sit on my knees.

She pants out her breaths but I press my lips against hers anyway, making sure she tastes how good it is to have my mouth against her.

"Take your pants off," she whispers into my ear. "I want you to fuck me into the ground."

My dick, which was already a solid root in my pants, feels like it's growing even harder. I've never felt this kind of base need to rip someone apart and get inside them.

Remmy makes me feel that way. Makes me want to do the dirty things you hear about but never actually try.

I make quick work of tugging off my clothes as Remmy yanks off her top and bra and rolls off me to sprawl out on the tile next to me.

"Do you want to move to the living room?" I ask as I move to crawl over her. "This might hurt your back and..."

"I like it like that," she says, smiling as she yanks me to her.

I drop down so our bodies are pressed together, completely naked, my length resting where she waits warm and wet for me.

Looking her in the eyes, I shift slightly and rub myself against her sensitive bud, making her body convulse in my arms as a shiver runs through her.

"You like the hurt?" I ask.

Remmy bites her lips and closes her eyes, nodding her head as she moves her hips against mine.

"So much."

I pull back slightly, notching myself against her opening, and then I take her direction and thrust into her.

She cries out, her entire body locking up as her fingernails dig into my back.

But I don't stop. I ram into her over and over and over again, leaning down and taking one of her nipples into my mouth and sucking on it with brutality.

I feel like a different man with her today than I was at the art gallery. The man at Sheldon House was barely able to restrain himself, barely holding on to his orgasm before Remmy got hers.

Today, I'm *un*restrained. My body is so focused on hers, on giving her exactly what she wants, that I feel like I could give her anything, be anything.

She wants to be fucked into the floor? I'm on it.

She wants a little bit of pain? I'm there.

I didn't even know sex this aggressive could feel this good, but fuck me if I'm not willing to follow Remmy on whatever pathway she wants to lead me down.

"Yessss," she says, her body already beginning to fall over. "I'm...oh fuck, Ben. I'm coming."

"I know," I say, sweat dripping off my face at the exertion as I keep hitting that one spot inside her. My entire body feels primed and ready to let loose at the feel of her clenching around me.

But I don't want to come yet. I'm not ready for this to be over.

"And you're gonna come again."

Her eyes fly open and she watches me as I keep going. As I continue to work, to press in and draw out, our skin slapping and echoing through my house.

I don't know how long it goes on, how long it takes, but I know my back is screaming and my muscles are nearing exhaustion when I feel her digging her heels into my calves, when I feel her arms holding me tight as she begins to shout out another release.

At the feeling of it, I finally allow myself to focus on my own, hitting inside her a few more times before I pull out and begin to jerk myself.

Remmy watches, her body a sweaty, replete mass of bonelessness on the ground in front of me.

"Shit, Remmy. I'm right there...it's...yes."

I come, shooting along her chest and stomach, feeling the ripple throughout my entire body before I collapse to the side, my body unable to hold itself up any longer.

We both lie there, panting aggressive breaths, cool tile slick underneath us.

She shifts her body, turning to the side and wrapping her arm around my middle.

I take the hint and push my bicep under her head so she isn't sprawled just on the floor and we can snuggle up together.

We lie there for a minute, just doing nothing, until Remmy starts to giggle.

I look down at her, finding her eyes already looking up at me. "What's so funny?"

She shakes her head.

"Fuck the ice cream," she says, her voice dropping deep in imitation of what I said to her at the start of this.

And then she starts giggling again, the sound splitting my chest wide open and sewing it back together again.

I turn fully on my side and yank her close, moving her body slightly so I can bring her face up close to mine, and then I press my lips against hers, cutting her giggle off.

It feels so good like this, with her.

A loud boom from behind me startles us, and we both pull back. I spin my head around and see someone bolting in through the front door.

Remmy presses herself closer to me, hiding the front of her body along mine.

"What the fuck?" I yell, trying to move to cover Remmy but also to figure out what's going on.

"Get the fuck up and get your clothes on."

My entire body jolts at the sound of Wyatt's voice.

"I'm not looking. Just get up and get dressed. Right now."

"What the fuck is going on?" I say, standing and grabbing my boxers as Remmy tugs on her bra and slides to the side so she's protected from Wyatt's view by the kitchen island.

And then he says two words that rock the foundation of my world like I didn't think could ever happen again.

"It's Ivy."

Nobody has any answers for us.

The only thing I know is that my sister is in the hospital and we have all been relegated to a waiting room, desperate for knowledge about what's going on.

Paroxysmal Nocturnal Hemoglobinuria.

It's a big fancy crazy word that means my sister gets sick a lot. She's had PNH for a while. It makes it difficult for her to build up red blood cells, so something like a normal cold or small infection can knock her on her ass for months as her body tries to recover.

She's been on regular medication to manage her symptoms and sickness, but it requires that she goes in to see a doctor at the USC Medical Center every two weeks to have it administered since it involves an IV and several hours of monitoring.

Today, she's not at USC, though. She's at Roth Memorial, which means everyone we know is huddled in the waiting room...waiting.

For answers.

For prayers.

For anything that will make this feel like just a speed bump instead of a car crash.

She collapsed on the kitchen floor.

That's what Wyatt told me.

She had been complaining about being tired and not feeling well but promised it was normal, said it wasn't anything outside of the everyday, ordinary fatigue she has all the time.

And then she collapsed on the floor.

Hannah was with her.

The two of them have grown extremely close over the past few months, ever since she moved to town and gave my sister someone new to talk to. The times I've been around them, the pair like to go off into corners and giggle as they sign to each other.

At first, I was worried about an outsider infiltrating our family unit, as fucked up as it is, but I know Ivy's deafness has been a hindrance for her ability to interact with some of the people we know. When the two of them are together, Ivy's face is almost always plastered with smiles and happiness...and that's what started to matter the most.

Thank fuck Hannah was there with her today, that she had the foresight to add Ivy's medical information into her own phone weeks ago.

They rode in the ambulance together, held hands as Ivy went in and out of consciousness.

I haven't seen my sister in weeks.

And now we're here, sitting in the waiting room just hoping for something to go fucking right in Ivy's life.

For *once*.

Remmy is sitting next to me, holding my hand, regularly asking me if I want anything to drink or eat.

It's funny to me that the one person in this room I know the least is the one who is providing the most comfort to me, is focused entirely on me and making sure I'm okay.

I glance at my watch again. It's been over an hour and we still have no information.

No diagnosis or explanation.

We don't know if she'll live or die, or if she's already dead.

My entire body shudders at the thought.

There has just been *no* news.

And I don't necessarily think that means it's good news.

"How long has she been sick like this?" Remmy asks, her voice low as she leans into me, her thumb stroking the back of my hand, our fingers woven together in a way that provides a small but needed balm to my soul.

I sigh, wishing I had any answers for her. "It's really complicated," I say, looking into her eyes. "Truthfully, I just feel too exhausted to get into it right now, okay?"

She nods, understanding and compassion etched in her brow.

"You also don't even know half of what's going on."

Wyatt's jab comes from across the room.

I lift my eyes to connect with his and see him glaring at me, the anger and irritation brimming out of him enough to sense from where I sit fifteen feet away.

"You have something to say, Wyatt? Say it."

His eyes stay focused on me as he stands and takes a step in my direction.

"I have *lots* to fucking say. That's your sister in there and you've been nowhere near her fucking appointments and meetings with the doctors and regular medication sessions."

I grit my teeth.

"Instead, you've been too busy playing fucking house and pretending you could ever be a father to even care that your sister's health has been deteriorating while we wait for a fucking donor."

Any other conversation in the waiting room has come to a

standstill, all eyes and ears focused directly on us.

My eyes narrow but I don't react.

I wait.

I wait because that's my strength.

My brother is the hothead, the one with strong emotions. Sometimes, it serves him well. Other times—like now—it makes him look like a fucking asshole.

So.

I wait.

And I watch for the moment when I see he realizes what he's just done and said, wait for him to deal with his emotions and realize he's using this anger to deflect his fear.

He pants out a few breaths and brings his hands up, clasping the back of his head.

Wyatt bends at the waist, and I can see him visibly struggle to take in deep breaths. So I take a step closer. Then another. And another, until I'm right next to him as he crouches, trying to catch his breath.

I drop down next to him and wait for him to meet my eyes.

It takes him a minute, but eventually, he does.

"Feel better?" I ask, being careful not to let my irritation show in my tone of voice.

Wyatt shakes his head.

"That's because you're not mad at me. You're scared, and that's okay. We're all scared, but getting angry at me isn't going to change anything."

His eyes well up and he wraps his arms around me, leaning his body into mine. I drop a knee, bracing myself, and then wrap my arms around him, too.

We've always had a strained relationship. Not because we don't love each other, but because we didn't have the right boundaries.

As much as neither of us want to admit it, I was more of a parent to Wyatt than either of our parents ever were. So it makes sense to me that when he's scared or upset or angry, he takes it out on me.

He knows I'm the one who loves him the most. Knows I'm the one who will make sure things are okay for him. Knows he won't ever have to handle the bullshit life hands him on his own.

It's why he avoids me when he doesn't want me to know

what's going on in his life.

Why he hides things from me.

He knows I'll get involved and try to help.

And sometimes, he thinks he doesn't deserve it.

But in this moment, with Ivy in the hospital going through god knows what, we don't have the option to be stubborn.

We *have* to lean on each other to make sure we stay strong.

Chapter Seventeen
REMMY

I watch the two grown men embrace on the floor of the hospital waiting room, and my heart clenches.

It truly does.

Clearly, Ben and Wyatt are having a much needed, brotherly bonding moment that will hopefully allow them to be here for each other while Ivy struggles through whatever this is.

But I can't help but look around at the faces that are also watching me.

Half of the people in this room are here for Ivy.

Lucas, Lennon, Paige, Wyatt, Hannah, Ben. Ivy's dad and Krissa, her nanny Vicki and her mom.

There are a handful of other people here for their own reasons, too. A couple I don't recognize holding hands in the corner. A guy I think owns one of the bike rental places near the pier. A woman and little girl who were talking quietly to each other as she lay snuggled in the woman's arms.

Some of them are watching Ben and Wyatt.

But some of them are looking at me.

Their eyes narrowed, or squinted in confusion.

Because Wyatt just unofficially announced some things we'd been hoping to reveal on our own timeline.

Sure, the process of dating and presenting our engagement to the people we know has fallen a little off course.

But the pregnancy?

...pretending you could ever be a father...

Maybe these people didn't understand. Maybe they don't know...

Lucas knows already. I didn't know Wyatt knew, but I assume that means Hannah knows as well.

Vivian and Calvin Calloway are both staring at me. Neither of them seem to have any emotions on their faces, but that could just be because of plastic surgery on her part and the lack of a soul on his.

"I'm going to get some fresh air," I say out loud and to nobody in particular. I'm just desperate to get away from this feeling of being watched. "I'll be back."

And then I wander out of the waiting room and through the sliding doors that connect to the main lobby.

I push forward, trying to get outside, needing a chance to catch my breath and...

"Remmy."

I clench my eyes shut.

This isn't what I want. This isn't what I need.

Not from him.

So I keep walking, ignoring his voice until I get outside and can gulp in the salty sea air that allows me to feel like my lungs are expanding for the first time.

"Remmy."

"What?" I say, my tone tense.

I turn and look at Lucas, who stands in front of me looking just like he always has.

Like a man who cares about me more than I deserve.

"Are you okay?"

"No, I'm not fucking okay," I bite out, my hands clenching into fists at my sides. "But today isn't about me and my emotional problems, okay? Go back inside."

There's a pause and I keep my eyes glued to the ground. But I know he steps closer because his same old flip-flops that he's had for years come into my line of sight.

"You're not on the outside, Rem."

My head pops up, unsure if I heard him correctly. "What?"

"I said...you're not on the outside. I know you think you are, know you believe nobody wants you around and we're all plotting against you or hoping you fail or...any number of other horrible things. But, I just want you to know that's not the case."

I scoff and shake my head, wrapping my arms around myself when a chill ripples across my skin in the cool, damp air of a beachy evening.

"Thanks, Lucas, but you don't know what you're talking about. I've *always* been on the outside. Nobody wants to see me succeed or be happy. But they don't have to worry." I let out a humorless laugh, my voice dropping as I mumble to myself. "I'll end up pregnant and alone, just like I deserve."

Lucas takes another step forward, and I watch as he reaches out to place a hand on my shoulder, his thumb stroking my skin.

"You have to let that go, Remmy. Let it die. Let it be...the past. Whatever wrongs you think people are holding over your head? They're not. I know they're not, because I've talked to them about it. Everyone wants to move on and let go. Now it's just on you to decide if you want to make your way back into the group or keep choosing to live your life on the 'outside'."

He lifts a shoulder as his hand drops away from me.

"Just that simple?" I say, laughing again and feeling tears welling this time. "It's just that simple? Just make my way back?"

When I look at Lucas, I feel like I've been punched in the gut with how sincere he looks, with the compassion and concern and care in his eyes.

"Yeah. It's just that simple."

We stand there for a moment longer, both of us just staring at each other before my eyes drop to the ground again.

As much as I'd like to believe him, it *isn't* that simple. And it never will be.

I've seen and done things that will never be undone, that will never be forgiven—things I'm not even sure I want to forgive myself for.

So even if on the crazy off chance it is that simple for them, it isn't for me. Just because they're willing to welcome me back with open arms doesn't mean I deserve it.

And that would be more than enough to keep me away.

"I'll be honest though, Rem, sometimes I think you like it there, think you prefer it."

I grit my jaw but keep my eyes on the ground.

"Or maybe you think...you *deserve* it."

My eyes close and I will myself to hold in the tears that are starting to build up inside me, that familiar tingle and pinch around my nose letting me know I only have a few more moments of keeping it together before I can't hold on any longer.

"Maybe you don't remember, but you've bared your secrets to me, Remmy. I *know* you. I know who you are, and where you come from, and what you've been through."

He drops down slightly and puts his face in my line of sight.

"And I also know what you've overcome, and how you've tried so hard to regain the control you felt was stolen from you."

The first tear falls.

"One of the things I've always admired about you, from the time we were young and stupid, is that you've always been this strong, confident woman, no matter what bullshit came your way. Don't forget that part of you. You might not be for everyone, Remmy, but that doesn't mean you have to change who you are."

Suddenly, I'm enveloped in a hug, an embrace so warm and comforting it makes me want to snuggle into Lucas and try again.

I let out a long sigh.

"Thank you," I whisper, squeezing him tight and then taking a step back, out of his arms.

As much as I appreciate his kind words and care, as much as a part of me does truly miss the goodness Lucas brought to my life, I know we don't belong together. I know he belongs with Lennon, and I can't allow my desperate desire to be seen overshadow what I truly want or need.

Which might actually...be Ben.

Ben who is thoughtful and caring and promises me I'll never be alone.

Ben who has made my life so much better over the past few weeks.

And who is standing just a few feet away at the entry to the hospital.

"Ben," I say, giving him a shy smile and wiping away the handful of tears that have fallen, streaking my cheeks.

His brow is furrowed as he looks between me and Lucas.

"They're allowing family to go back to see Ivy," he says, his voice tense and his eyes tired.

I nod. "Do you want me to go get you anything? Or anything for Ivy?"

Instead of answering, he sticks out his hand. "I said they're allowing family in. I came to get you."

The pitter-patter in my chest that only Ben seems to elicit doubles in strength, and I have to work to hide my smile as I reach out and slip my hand into his.

I haven't seen Ivy since I've been back in Hermosa Beach.

Wait, no, that's not true.

I saw her at Lucas' 4th of July party, though I was focused on Lucas and she spent her time with Ben and Wyatt.

But other than that, I haven't seen her. Haven't interacted with her. Haven't tried to talk to her or learn about what's going on in her teenaged life.

And now, looking at her in the hospital bed, I really wish I had done all those things.

When we were younger, back in high school when Ivy was a toddler, I loved visiting the Calloway house. The majority of my time was spent with Lucas, and he and Wyatt were best friends, so I definitely spent some time there. I *loved* seeing Ivy wander around, her little feet slapping the floor, her giggle echoing through the house.

But I didn't really *know* her.

I never took the time to learn to talk to her, or to learn sign language.

Now, I sit in the corner as her family fills the room, and I've never wished more that I could understand what she's saying as her hands move sluggishly to talk to her mother.

Ben and Wyatt stand just behind her, watching, and then all together, all three of them laugh at something Ivy signs to them.

"It's not that hard to learn, you know."

I turn to Hannah, who is sitting on the couch next to me.

"I started learning because I wanted to be able to talk to my friend Melanie's daughter. It's not that hard, and I'm sure Ivy will love having a sister she can talk to."

Nodding, I turn to look back at them.

"I just wish I'd tried learning sooner."

"Don't we all," she says, a dash of wistfulness in her tone. "But if you spend your time learning instead of wasting time wishing you'd started earlier, you'll be shocked at what you can accomplish."

I grin. "You're one of those eternal optimist types, huh?"

Hannah shrugs. "I didn't used to be. I guess I just...learned to be more positive once I realized it's my choice to enjoy my life, whatever comes my way."

Then she drapes an arm across my shoulders, giving me a friendly smile that looks genuine and kind.

"I'm glad you're here, Remmy. For Ben. I know it means a lot to him."

I don't say anything in response, mostly because I don't know *what* to say. We sit together in silence for a few moments before she gets up and walks over to Wyatt, slipping a hand into his, her eyes focused on Ivy.

I allow myself to think about what she just said as I watch the Calloways interact with each other.

I love what she said because it's so true.

I'm the only one who can choose to enjoy my life.

I can't expect anyone to make me happy, or to change my circumstances so that I feel like I'm allowed to enjoy things.

Look at Ivy.

She's lived through a lot.

An illness as a kid that made her deaf. A blood disease that slows her down and makes it easy for her to get sick. Her parents' divorce and all the other Calloway drama. The emergence of a sister and brother she didn't know anything about.

And she's in a hospital bed right now.

But she's still smiling.

I don't know why we were kept waiting for so long or what's going on with her health, but Ivy passing out on the floor was apparently a side effect of her medication.

Her doctor, Dr. Lyons, who Ivy sees at USC Medical Center, drove in to talk to all of us.

Apparently her body is rejecting the medication she's on, isn't responding the way they'd hoped.

I don't know all the specifics, probably because I don't really understand what's wrong with her, but Ben and Wyatt and Vivian all looked...like ghosts when she told them.

They looked back and forth at each other like they just couldn't believe it.

I know they're worried. I can feel it.

Their fear is leaking across the room in a pool I can only hope Ivy can't see.

But kids are perceptive, and I wonder if she's just putting on a brave face for them.

I open a browser screen on my phone and try to search for the disease she has. I heard the doctor say it, but the words were so long I don't even know if I'm searching for the right thing.

The best way I can help Ben is to understand enough so that he doesn't have to answer my questions, and to stand by his side as he does everything he can to support her.

The couch dips to my right and my whole body tenses as Calvin Calloway sits too close for my comfort.

"It's good to see you, Remmy."

I try to give him a smile, but I know it falls flat. "If only it were under better circumstances." My eyes scan the room. "Where's Krissa?"

"Oh, she went home. She's feeling a bit tired and I don't want her to feel unwelcome in a room full of people who don't want her around."

The comment makes me uncomfortable, but I am far from fluent in the language of how the Calloways interact with each other.

Lucas told me once that Vivian and the kids take direction from Calvin by attending events as *one big happy family*, which is absolutely beyond me, but hey, whatever floats your boat.

"So tell me, how long have you and Ben been seeing each other?" he asks, leaning back in the couch and lifting one leg to rest it on the other.

I open my mouth to reply then realize Calvin has leaned even closer to me.

"And be honest," he whispers.

Something inside me turns cold, and when I turn to look at his face, I see something calculating behind his expression, something unfriendly that makes me uncomfortable.

My body freezes up and I try hard to get myself to relax.

This is just Ben's dad.

This is just Ben's dad.

Clearing my throat, I try to give a somewhat coherent response.

"Things are pretty new," I say, trying to stay vague.

"You know, I thought you were dating Lucas over there, for quite some time, if I'm not mistaken, though I don't normally keep up with the teenage gossip."

I let out an awkward laugh. "We're not teenagers, but I get your point." Then I gesture to Lucas, who stands at the foot of Ivy's bed. "But Lucas and Lennon have been something for a few years now."

He hums his acknowledgment, but his eyes don't follow my hand to focus on Lucas in the distance.

They stay on me.

"It just…all seems rather quick, and I'd hate for you and Ben to face something difficult that makes your relationship feel like you didn't know what you were getting yourself into."

I nod, trying to stay neutral but wishing desperately that Calvin would lean the other direction, or just get off the couch and go away.

"It has been fast," I say, and then from across the room, Ben catches my eye. Just like that, something settles in my chest. "But when you know, you know. Isn't that what they say?"

I watch as Ben rounds the bed and walks toward us, his eyes staying on mine until he's right in front of us.

Only then does he look at his father.

"Excuse us, dad. We'll be heading out."

Calvin stands, still wearing his suit from the day and looking completely unrumpled. Unlike most fathers who'd look like they're falling apart as they wait to get news on their sick daughters, Calvin looks like he doesn't have a care in the world.

Happy, even.

He places a hand on Ben's shoulder.

"Make sure you answer next time I call you, hmm? We have

something important to discuss."

And then he grins at me, the deceptive glint in his eye enough to make me wish I could sink into the couch to escape from him. He turns and strolls from the room, not acknowledging anybody else before he goes.

Not even his daughter, who's lying sick in the hospital bed.

Ben watches as his father leaves, but then he returns his attention to me.

He drops down so he's squatting in front of me, placing his hands on my knees.

"Are you ready to go?"

I shake my head. "Don't feel like you have to leave because of me. Stay as long as you want. I can stay too, or I can go. Just tell me what you need."

He stays where he rests in front of me, his eyes searching mine with a soft expression before he surprises me by leaning forward and placing a kiss on my lips.

Unlike our previous kisses, this one isn't lustful or needy. It isn't wrapped up in the hope that something sexual is coming down the line.

This kiss is intimate and affectionate, and it squeezes at my heart in the best kind of way.

"Ivy's good for now. Let's go home, get some food, and rest, and then we'll come back tomorrow."

I squeeze his hand. "If that's what you want."

We both stand and walk over to Ivy's bed, Ben slipping between her and their mother to lean over and kiss her forehead goodbye.

He signs something and she furrows her brow, looking over at me then back to Ben.

When she says something in response, everyone laughs.

"What's happening?" I ask, keeping a smile on my face.

"Ben said you're here with him," Hannah answers, "and Ivy asked if you and Lucas finally realized you don't belong together."

I laugh, looking at Ivy, who is now looking at me. "You're perceptive," I say out loud, watching her eyes dip to my mouth as she reads my lips. "It's good to see you, Ivy, though I wish you were feeling better."

She nods but doesn't say anything, and I take that as my cue to leave the family behind.

I wave my goodbyes, not wanting to draw anyone's attention, and then slip out the door, waiting for Ben to say his own goodbyes and join me.

As I stand in the hallway, my mind falls back to what Calvin said to me before Ben walked up to us, about me not knowing what I'm getting into.

It's left me feeling unsettled.

"Ready to go home?"

I grin at Ben when he comes out of the room, his expression tired but looking so much calmer than it did just a few hours ago.

I nod, feeling a lightness at the idea that I'm going home with him. "Ready."

And then he takes my hand in his and we head out.

Chapter Eighteen
REMMY

"Can we talk about the night at the art gallery?"

My question pops out of me as we sit at Ben's kitchen table, nibbling on Oreos as we wait for the oven temperature to rise so we can bake the pizza. I'm not normally one who wants to hash things out, but especially after Calvin's comments at the hospital, I have a few questions, and I'm hoping to get some answers.

Ben shifts in his seat. "You mean when we had sex and you fled the room like you found out I had leprosy?"

I purse my lips, realizing I walked right into that.

I was so focused on what happened earlier in the night, I forgot about what ended it—me clamming up and turning into a zombie after sex.

Ben can tell his response to my question has embarrassed me, so he reaches across the table and puts his hand on mine.

"I'm sorry. I didn't mean anything negative about you. I just know I felt like shit afterward and hated wondering if I'd done something wrong."

I nod.

"Okay," he continues, "how about this—how about I ask a question and then you ask a question. We can each ask..." He twists his hand from side to side. "How's three questions?"

"Why three?"

"Two doesn't seem like enough and four is too many."

I nod, grabbing another Oreo out of the blue and white package. Twisting it apart, I eye Ben.

"Can I go first?"

He raises an eyebrow but nods.

Well, shit. Now that I have the ability to ask three questions, cart blanche, I don't even know what to ask.

Thankfully, the oven chooses that moment to beep and Ben holds up a finger, slipping out of his chair to go over and put the pizza in.

I feel lucky that I have a few extra seconds to think, because now I have to decide what I want to ask.

But before I can really choose anything, Ben plops down in front of me.

"Okay, shoot."

Flustered, I ask the first thing that comes to mind.

"What was happening between you and Krissa in the hallway?"

I see Ben grit his teeth, and then he starts drumming his fingers against the wooden kitchen table.

"She was telling me I was using you to get over her."

My mouth drops open and I can't help my gasp. "Oh my god, did you guys used to be together?"

Ben lifts his hand and holds up one finger.

"Is that your second question?"

My shoulders droop, and I pick up my Oreo and shove it into my mouth whole in irritation.

"Your turn," I grumble.

Ben grins but turns contemplative. His elbows rest on the table and his hands are steepled together, his fingers pressed to his mouth as he thinks and watches me.

"Everything seemed good until the very end," he says, and I know he's referencing our frantic sex in the staff room at Sheldon House. "What changed that had you climbing off of me so upset?"

I hated how I responded, but mostly because I didn't know it would be something that would happen. Being in control of my body is...the most important thing to me, and having Ben see me fall apart like that made me feel horrible.

Sure, he's seen me cry and get angry.

But seeing me shutdown because of sex? That's a completely different type of vulnerability. Now he wants to know why, and I don't know what to tell him.

I pull my hair forward over my left shoulder and start braiding it, trying to figure out what to say, but the more time goes by, the more I realize I have to tell him the truth.

Not because he needs to know, but because *I* need him to know. I want him to know he didn't do anything wrong. For some reason, in this moment, that outpaces my desire to keep it to myself.

"When I was fifteen, I was raped," I say, careful to keep my eyes on my hair. "He drugged me so I couldn't fight back. He told me I was nothing, and then he came inside of me."

My eyes flit up to Ben and see him frozen in place, his gaze laser focused on me.

"He's the only one who has ever not worn a condom, so I didn't know I would react that way."

Ben sits back in his chair, one hand holding his chin and mouth, the other tucked under his arm. He looks like...well, to be honest, I don't know this expression from Ben. I don't know what's going on in his mind.

I can only hope he'll tell me.

"Fuck, Remmy, I'm sorry."

I shake my head. "It's not your fault."

"That doesn't mean I can't wish you hadn't gone through that." He leans forward and places his hand on mine on the table. "Thank you for telling me."

There's a fear I've learned sits in the minds of all rape victims: the fear of not being believed, of being seen as having deserved it, having been asking for it.

And no matter what we do, we have to accept and push past that fear with every person we decide to tell.

Every. Person.

Because your best friend might believe you, but your mom might not.

Your boyfriend might say you didn't deserve it, but his friends might feel differently.

An academic advisor might say *nobody* is asking for it, but a woman who sees you in a short skirt might say otherwise.

Everyone has an opinion.

Everyone thinks they have a right to tell you whether it really happened or not.

Sitting in front of Ben, seeing this wide-open expression, this complete willingness to be here in this moment with me…it takes down a layer of bricks I didn't realize I could remove from the wall I try to protect myself with.

I say the only thing that's on my mind.

"Thank you for believing me."

"Alright, time for next questions?" I ask, wiping my hands on a paper towel and pushing my plate away, leaving the uneaten crust.

"I get to go first this time."

I roll my eyes.

After our last questions, we took a break. Ate some ice cream before dinner and then wrapped up with the pizza.

"Alright, fine. I guess that's fair."

He grins at me and takes another bite of the pizza he has been cutting up with a fork and knife—which I told him was serial killer behavior—as he decides what he wants to ask.

"Why did you and Lucas really break up? And I don't want a glossed-over answer. I want the full story, from the beginning to the end."

I let my head fall forward and rest my eyes on the heels of my palms. "I don't want to talk about Lucas," I say, still reeling from our conversation outside the hospital.

Ben just sits silently and I lean backward, crossing my arms with a sigh.

"This definitely isn't a fun game of twenty questions, huh? Instead it's *let's ask every deep, emotionally draining question in the world.*"

Ben grins but continues to just watch me, and I groan,

knowing I should just get it all out there.

The honest version.

"Okay, if you want the beginning, I'll give you the beginning. When I first met Lucas, it was right after we moved to town and I was immediately smitten."

I reach out and play with the paper towel that's wadded up on my plate, thinking back to the moment I first saw him, when he was hanging out at school with Paige and Wyatt and Lennon—the perfect little foursome.

"Even then, I'm pretty sure his favorite person was Lennon. They were together a lot, but as we got older, he started spending more time with Wyatt and the other guys. Paige always made sure to include me in stuff with her and Lennon, until we moved to Colombia for a few months when I was fifteen."

I pause, wondering how detailed I want to be.

"I loved it there. I didn't realize it at the time, but my parents were going through a divorce conversation, so my mom wanted to spend time with her parents and siblings. She left and took me and Dominic with her. Mati stayed with my dad. It was amazing and I got to use my Spanish all the time at my grandfather's estate and whenever I went into the city. Medellín and Colombia became a part of my soul. I loved that summer."

I rip my paper towel in half.

"Until I was raped. After that, I wanted to go home. Thankfully, my parents figured things out and we left a few weeks later. Moved home, got resettled. But I wasn't the same, and something inside me knew it would change everything."

Ben sits completely still across from me, watching my every movement and listening to my every word with rapturous attention.

"Lucas and I started dating. We broke up and got back together a few times, usually because of me." I shake my head. "I didn't want to be responsible to anyone but myself, but Lucas was what I wanted, even if he wasn't what I needed. So I dated him because he was good and kind and caring and I loved him. But I slept with other boys because, to me, that meant I was in control of my body and could do with it whatever I wanted."

Sighing, I lean to the side and rest my head in my hand, wondering what on earth Ben could be thinking of me right now, how he sees me after finding out who I really am.

"We broke up when he found out I was cheating on him but got back together when I explained how I felt...when I told him the truth, about my rape and how I was having trouble managing the feelings in my body. So Lucas helped me manage it by having sex with me whenever I wanted it but never expecting it from me when I didn't."

Ben's lips tip up at that, and I can't help but smile, too.

"It sounds great from a guy's perspective, I'm sure, but Lucas wasn't a crazy sexual person. Maybe that was because we never really had the chemistry, or maybe it's because he just wasn't that guy, but sometimes, I know I pushed when I shouldn't have. Then I left for college and everything changed."

"You didn't have him around anymore."

I shake my head.

"I didn't. I did want him around, but it was unrealistic. The idea of not enjoying myself because my body belonged to someone else was just...too much at the time. I hadn't worked through anything, hadn't been to therapy or talked to anyone but Lucas about my past. I called him after I'd slept with a few guys and he came to see me at school and we talked about it. That's when we decided on an open relationship."

"Did Lucas ever want that?"

I shake my head again.

"Of course not. He's one of those crazy loyal, caring guys who could probably sleep with one woman his entire life and be set. But that's just not me. I want to do what I want to do with my own body. It doesn't belong to anyone but myself."

Ben nods, and I feel like he gets it. Even if he doesn't approve, he gets where I'm coming from. So I continue.

"After we opened the relationship, I had a short fucking spree until I cooled off. I realized the issue wasn't that I wanted to sleep with everyone, but that I didn't want to feel like my body was beholden to one other person. Unfortunately, the damage was done at my school and this bitch of an RA gave me that award because I slept with her boyfriend."

I wrinkle my nose.

"By the way, it is *so* fucked up that women attack other women when their boyfriends cheat. Like, it is *not* my fault that your man wanted to be with someone else. Why should I take all the blame?"

Ben chuckles under his breath.

"Anyway, when I started at my new school, my advisor suggested I talk to a therapist, so I went there and started to deal with some of the trauma I'd experienced from my rape. But then..."

I bite the inside of my cheek, my nose starting to sting with emotions and unshed tears.

"I slept with him. He was a good guy and I twisted things around until he wanted me, because talking about my problems made me feel horrible and I just wanted it to go away and the only coping mechanism I had was sex. I spiraled out again until I found a female therapist during my last year that helped me realize that by sleeping with everyone just because I could, I was still letting someone else control my body, just a different part—my mind, my heart, my emotions—and I didn't want that anymore. I wanted to be in control of things myself."

"Absolutely."

I get up from the table and go over to where I see a box of tissues in the living room, plucking out a few and returning to sit in front of Ben.

"I'd been working really hard on things but wanted to wait until I felt like I was really improving before I shared anything with Lucas. And the longer I waited, the more I felt him pulling away, and the more I wanted to pull away as well. We stopped talking, barely shared any information, saw each other rarely. For all intents and purposes, we weren't dating anymore."

"And then Lennon moved back."

I nod. "And then Lennon moved back. I could feel that everything was changing between us, but the stubborn part of me couldn't imagine letting him go when he'd been so wonderful to me and so loving. He was what I thought I wanted, so I held on even though I knew it wasn't right anymore."

I dab the tissue under my right eye, catching a single tear before it falls.

"I thought maybe if I let the two of them fizzle out, we could work after, but I was just kidding myself. Sometimes, it's easier to avoid and pretend than actually face the things that are going to rip you to shreds, you know? And Lucas and I breaking up wasn't something I was prepared for."

"So what made you decide to actually finally break up?" Ben asks, his head tilted to the side, his brow furrowed. Not judging, just watching.

"When I came back from our trip to Colombia in May and found out I was pregnant, I knew it wouldn't be fair to him to try to keep us together. Knowing Lucas, he would have tried to take responsibility for the kid. I returned to Hermosa to talk to him, and I knew...I could just feel it. What was going on with him and Lennon was serious, and I could never steal his entire life from him like that. I couldn't...be the person who made him feel obligated to help me. He'd already been that man for me enough times."

I see Ben's eyes moving rapidly across my face and then he sits up straight.

"You got pregnant on a trip to Colombia?"

I swallow awkwardly, feeling my throat begin to close in on itself, wondering if I can tell him the next part. I take in a deep breath and then let it out.

"The man who raped me when I was fifteen is the son of one of my grandfather's friends. Victor. He raped me again, but this time, he didn't even have to drug me. I was terrified and my entire body shut down. I told him no, but I didn't try to get away. I didn't fight. I just lay there, trying to be anywhere else but where I was."

I pause, my stomach turning over as I consider my next words.

"This baby was conceived because of a rape, and now I don't know how to feel because...not being able to fight him made me feel weak and worthless. But if I *had* fought him, I wouldn't be pregnant now."

I look up at Ben and wipe my tears away. Then my hands wrap protectively around my stomach

"Even though I never wanted to be pregnant, I can't imagine my life without this baby now, and I haven't even met it yet."

Chapter Nineteen
BEN

I've never understood those people who go to the movies and come out with wide eyes and their minds completely blown. When I was in high school, I went to see *Avatar* with my brother and a few of his friends. The cinematography was phenomenal, the creation of a new world absolutely breathtaking. We loved it.

But they talked about it for weeks. Every time I saw them around, it felt like they were focused on how 'mind-blowing' that movie was, and I just wanted to hit them over the head.

It didn't make sense to me.

That kind of thing doesn't happen to me. I'm not one for surprises or strange emotions because of something crazy and new.

It takes a lot for me to have my mind blown by something, probably because I'm an incredibly deliberate person. I think things through more than others, so I'm usually prepared.

Rarely am I surprised.

What Remmy is telling me has blown all of that out of the water and left me feeling destroyed and like I have to completely adjust the way I perceive the world.

"He raped you again?" I ask, my voice growing tense and hard, the anger I feel at whoever this guy is building rapidly.

She nods, her eyes glazing over. "I decided to go riding and he cornered me in the stables at my grandfather's house."

"Oh my god, Remmy."

She keeps shaking her head.

"I keep thinking it's my fault. I mean, who gets raped by the same guy twice?"

I'm out of my chair and walking around the table before I can even think about it, moving her chair so she's facing out and I can kneel in front of her.

"Remmy, you are *not* to blame. Do you understand me?" I say, trying to convince her with my voice, with my body, with the way I put my face near hers. "That fucking asshole took what did not belong to him. No means no. You shouldn't have to fight in order to get him to listen to you."

She nods, the tears falling harder from her eyes.

Remmy always seemed like this larger-than-life woman to me, even when she was in high school, like nothing could ever break her or beat her or trip her up.

Strong and resilient, all the time.

Getting to know her lately, I'm seeing more of her underbelly, her soft spots, her weak spots, the emotions that seem to be rolling through her all the time.

It makes me wonder how much of her attitude in life was the armor she had to put on every day to protect herself.

Now I want to look back at every single conversation we've ever had and scrutinize each breath and look and word, from her and from me, because the last thing I want to do is bring up something dark from her past.

I place my hands on her stomach, on the tiny little bump that's starting to show in her thirteenth week.

"And I just want to make sure I say this out loud so you never, ever, *ever* have to worry."

Her eyes flit up to mine.

"This baby might not have been a part of your plan for your life, and it may not have been conceived with love…but you bet your fucking tits it's going to *be* loved. By you, and by me, every single day."

Remmy covers her face with her hands and starts sobbing—or at least that's what I think until she pulls her hands away and I see that she's both sobbing *and* laughing.

"Bet your fucking tits?" she asks, and I smile, feeling thankful that she was able to find some levity in this very heavy moment.

Her hands rest on my shoulders then rise up to my face, her thumbs stroking softly along my cheekbones.

"You know, with every day that passes by, I feel luckier and luckier that we decided to do whatever this is. Normally, I don't want to be helped, but for some reason, I was okay with accepting help from you."

My stomach twists at her words. Because it's true—I did want to help her—but I wasn't completely selfless.

I lift a hand and wrap it around her wrist, allowing myself to enjoy the feeling of her touch, of her soft, cool skin as she shows me affection.

"Thank you for being what I need right now," she continues. "I hope whatever I am to you, I can be what you need as well."

I squeeze her wrist, the feelings I feel for her beginning to boil over from my heart and into my chest where I used to have an empty cavity, a vacant space.

But she helps fill that void.

I rise up, unable to stop myself, and press my lips to hers. It's soft, the pressure of our mouths together feeling like the comfort of a blanket during a storm.

My mouth opens against hers and she slips her hands off of my face, wrapping them around my neck, bringing her body flush against mine. I let my hands drop to her hips, lifting her out of her seat and coming to a standing position.

"I want to carry you up to bed, but I don't want to risk dropping you on the stairs," I say after pulling my lips away.

She grins against my mouth, kissing me again once, twice. "Mr. Calloway, are you calling me fat?"

I chuckle, letting my hands rove to her ass and giving it a squeeze. "Never, but I do love this thick backside of yours, for sure."

Remmy giggles, dropping her legs down so her feet touch the floor. Then she takes my hand in hers and leads me toward the stairs.

When we get to my room, she crawls into the bed still fully clothed and I flick off the lights, following in her wake.

Lying there, I put my arms around her, and by some unspoken agreement, we just allow ourselves to fall asleep wrapped up in each other.

I wake in the night, my eyes glancing to the clock sitting on my nightstand.

It's after three in the morning and I feel oddly awake.

When I look at Remmy, I see she's awake too, her eyes watching me.

"Do you think we're going to work?" she whispers, inching closer to me so we're pressed together. "That we can have a happy life together even though everything is a lie?"

In that moment, it feels like the world slows down and I start to notice everything.

I can feel the breeze from my open patio door leading out to the slight view of the ocean, the softness of the sheets beneath me. I can smell the salt in the sea mixing with the air fresheners Ivy made me get because she said boys are stinky.

And I see Remmy, lying on my bed, her long, sexy body stretched out next to me.

"Not everything is a lie," I answer, my hand coming out to wrap around her and snuggle her up against me. Then I take her hand in mine and bring it down to where my dick is growing hard between my thighs.

She grips me and I moan.

"Not everything is a lie," I repeat. "The way you make my body feel isn't a lie."

Remmy strokes along my shaft then slips her hand beneath my clothes, taking me in her hand, the feeling of her warm palm against me sending a jolt through my body.

"But that's just physical," she whispers, her lips pressing against my neck, and she begins to suck and bite at the skin. "I *know* I can make your body feel good. I'm talking about your mind, your soul, your…"

She trails off.

Your heart.

That had to have been what she was going to say next.

"Give it time," I say, then I sigh as she gives me a particularly delicious squeeze. "We're going to make it work. I know it."

Remmy pulls her hand out of my pants and tugs her shirt off, leaving her in the same bra she was wearing earlier today when we had sex on the kitchen floor.

But now it's after three in the morning, and our late-afternoon romp downstairs feels like a million years ago. It feels like a different time, like we were different people—not only on our own, but to each other.

I don't know why, but she's not just the woman who is supposed to help me anymore. She's Remmy, an absolute goddess I can't seem to get enough of, a woman who has been so strong and has come out stronger on the other side of a life that continued to beat her up and throw her down to the mat.

Maybe that's why. Maybe she's different to me now because I'm getting a better picture of who *I* am, too—or at least who I want to be.

And who I want to be is a man who could never be the reason she gets taken advantage of again.

We strip our clothes off slowly, enjoying this new closeness, this new intimacy that neither of us were expecting.

I hold her near me as I drink from her mouth and pleasure her with my fingers, loving the sounds of her soft cries and pleas for more.

"I want you inside me," she says, a phrase I've heard from her before. "I want you so deep I don't know where I end and you begin."

We shift on the bed, and she flips over so she's on her stomach, rising to her hands and knees.

My eyes fall to the tattoo running up and down the length of her spine, text in a swoopy cursive that I can't read.

"Like this," Remmy says, drawing my eyes back to her ass as she sticks it out toward me and bows her body.

I grin, moving up behind her and rubbing my dick along her center, groaning when I feel the slickness.

"Soft or hard?" I ask.

She looks at me over her shoulder, a wicked smirk on her face. "I always want it hard."

Chuckling, I notch myself against her opening and slam into her so hard it lifts her legs off the bed.

Her hands grip the bedding and she drops her face into the pillows, her shouts muffled by the fabric.

I feel like a machine as I pump into her, as I fill her over and over, as I try to give to her everything I can in this moment. I can't solve all the things that have given her problems over the years when it comes to sex, but I can be sure she enjoys what we're doing now, certain she feels like she's in control, positive she's wrung out and exhausted and sated at the end.

"I want to see your face," I say without stopping.

Remmy pushes up so she's on just her knees, bringing her back against my chest, my motions stuttering for a second as I adjust to the new position.

I wrap my arms around her from behind and grip her breasts, loving the feeling when she brings her hands up and around my neck to play in my hair.

"Kiss me," she says, tilting her face up to mine.

I dip down and press my lips to hers, sucking on her tongue and nibbling on her lips.

"Ben, it feels so good," she says, pulling back and taking my hands into hers.

She leads one to her breast and the other to her clit then moves her own hands to reach back and grip my ass as I continue to slide in and out of her.

I follow her directions, pinching her nipples and gripping her breasts, loving the feeling of their soft plumpness filling my hand. All the while, I stroke her down below, adjusting our position just slightly so her legs are spread wider and I have better access to flick and caress her clit.

"I love this," she whispers. "It's never felt like this before."

I feel the same way, but I can't seem to verbalize anything in response, my entire being focused entirely on getting her to where she wants to be, to that blissful place that can take you to the peak.

"I'm there, Ben. Fuck, I'm right…there."

Two more pumps and I feel her clench, her entire body bending forward as she grips the bedding and groans out her pleasure.

I pull out and begin to stroke my dick, chasing the orgasm that's just a few seconds away.

Pulsing in my palm, I let out a long sigh, relishing the relief of finally reaching that height, that place of paradise and ecstasy that makes me feel like a king.

I slump to the side, falling down onto the bed next to Remmy, my eyes closing briefly as I come down, my heartbeat going crazy.

She rolls to the side and looks at me, her eyes soft and dewy.

Then she snuggles in beside me, wrapping her arm around my chest and pressing her face into my sweaty skin.

And with her wrapped up next to me, I can't help but hear that tiny voice in the back of my mind that asks how long it will be until the other shoe drops.

"What does your tattoo say?"

"Hmm?" Remmy's eyes flutter open where she's lying at my side.

She's gloriously naked, lying on her front, all that tan smooth skin of her back bared to the room with nothing but a sheet covering her below the waist.

When we crawled under the covers earlier, she told me she'd read you're not supposed to sleep on your stomach later in pregnancy, so she's taking advantage while she still can.

Part of me wishes she'd lie on her back so I could see her gorgeous breasts, but I also like this view, all her thick hair in a messy tendril, scattered along that smooth skin, twisting in my sheets.

"Your tattoo," I say again. "What does it say?"

Remmy's eyes close again and she tucks the pillow in closer to her face.

"*Convierte tus heridas en lugares donde la luz puede entrar en tu alma.*"

"Damn, you sound sexy when you speak Spanish."

She giggles, the sound muffled slightly.

"What does it mean?"

"Turn your wounds into places where light can enter your

soul." Remmy pauses, her eyes opening again to look into mine. "I got it during my senior year, after going through the therapy that started to really help me sort through my issues."

I don't know what to say in response, my mind unable to drift to anything positive or encouraging to say, though I don't necessarily think that's what she needs from me.

My hand reaches out and I trace it up and down her spine, provoking a shiver I watch ripple through her body.

And then I rise onto my hip and lean forward, bending over her body, placing my lips at the base of the tattoo, which runs from her tailbone all the way up to her neck.

Kiss after kiss I place on the tattoo, on her wounds. Wishing there was something I could do to take them from her, to heal them over, but knowing I can't.

When I finally make it to the top, I realize Remmy is breathing heavily, her breaths coming out hard and awkward.

"What's wrong?" I ask, suddenly worried I've crossed a line or a boundary I didn't know was there.

Remmy shakes her head and then turns. Toward me, not away—a good sign.

"I just don't know how you manage to take the things that make me feel the most worthless and instead make me feel beautiful and powerful and strong."

I grin at her. "It's easy to do when there's a lot of amazing raw material to work with."

She smiles and then rises up slightly, scooting onto her side and giving me a little peek of the goods before she adjusts the sheet and grabs a pillow to snuggle up to.

"Let's talk about something else," she says, no longer looking like she's about to doze off and tucking her face into the pillow she's holding so I can only see her eyes. "I never got to ask my second question."

I groan, my upper body falling back to the mattress. "You sure you don't want to talk about something else?"

Her eyes twinkle and I know she's smiling, which is confirmed when she lifts her chin and tucks the pillow in under her neck.

"Alright, fine. What's your second question?"

"You were vague earlier about you and Krissa, about what she said to you in the hallway."

I shift so I'm also on my side and rest my elbow against the bed, propping my head up with my hand.

"What really happened between you and her?"

Sighing, I stare at the span of sheet between us, wishing she'd gone the easy route and asked me about Ivy or my mom or something else—anything but my dad and my ex.

But after she revealed so much earlier, there's no way I can pussyfoot around this. I have to be open about what happened.

"Krissa and I started dating when I came home from graduate school," I start, thinking back to the day I first saw her. "I was twenty-three and she was celebrating her eighteenth birthday, which didn't feel like a crazy age difference at the time. I was in the process of buying the failing restaurant that would eventually become Bennie's, and she was working at a temp agency and had been struggling to get placed. We hit it off and I helped her get a job as a receptionist at my dad's office while his usual assistant, Pauline, was on maternity leave. We dated for about a year and she was practically living with me at the time."

"Here?"

I nod. "I always wanted a family, even though I rarely dated or made the time for something that important, so I bought the house hoping it would become a place for me to grow into. Then one day, I went to his office for a meeting and found him fucking her on his desk."

Remmy winces. There was a time when telling this story would have made me want to wince, too, the memory a pretty shitty one to recall. But today, it feels like a long-ago life, a different version of me, and the emotional connection I had to that moment has been severed.

I had thought I loved Krissa, but in reality, we were very different people. My hurt at her betrayal was more about my ego than it was about her.

"She acted like it was true love with him, like what she was doing with me was just fucking around. Told me she would *of course* choose my very successful father over me. So I went home and dumped all her stuff on the lawn."

She giggles. "I shouldn't be laughing because I'm sure that was horrible, but it sounds like a movie."

I roll my eyes. "It felt like a movie. She came to me in tears a few weeks later, trying to apologize, asking for forgiveness, but I knew it was just because she realized my dad might be the better mark financially but was less likely to marry her. She tried to come back to me because she realized she'd screwed up her own plan to be taken care of and be handed a big, rich life. Thankfully for her," I add, sarcasm evident in my tone, "it all worked out just fine in the end."

Remmy pokes my arm.

"Clearly not if she's coming up to you in dark hallways trying to show you her boobies."

"She was *not* trying to show me her boobies."

"Um, she was *absolutely* trying to show you her boobies. That's just Homewrecker 101, and I know because I've been in her shoes."

My brow furrows. "What do you mean?"

She sighs. "The boyfriend—my RA's boyfriend…I wanted his attention so I shoved my tits in his face."

"Didn't you tell me you had no idea he was dating someone?"

Remmy pauses. "Well…yeah, but—"

"No buts. You didn't intentionally go after someone who was taken."

"Technically, neither did Krissa. Weren't your parents already divorced?"

"Yes, but she was dating *me* at the time."

Remmy waves her hand around and then points at herself.

"Did you not hear my entire story about me cheating on Lucas *multiple* times?" she asks.

Something thick and ugly crawls through my chest at the thought.

"That's different," I argue.

"Why? Because I'd been raped and I was using my sexuality to be in charge of my body? Sure, that makes it different for *me*, but that doesn't make it different for Lucas—the guy I was cheating on. He didn't deserve that, not at all, and I don't deserve to be forgiven for it just because my life was hard."

Her voice is strong, and it makes me admire her even more.

Maybe I shouldn't.

Maybe I should look at her situation and think to myself, *The last thing I need to do is get involved with someone who has cheated when I struggle with trusting women.*

But I can't.

Remmy feels different.

Maybe I'm wrong. Maybe she isn't different and I'm setting myself up for another colossal fall.

I guess that's the risk you take when you're falling in love, right? You're...

My throat closes up.

Wait.

What the fuck did I just...?

"Hey, I wasn't trying to freak you out. I told you I went to therapy to deal with a lot of that. I don't want to be that person, okay?"

But I feel frozen.

Did I just...

Did I just admit to myself that I'm falling in love with her?

Oblivious to my internal dialogue, Remmy shifts closer to me on the bed, shoving her pillow out of the way so her warm body is pressed up against mine with only the sheet between us.

"The last thing I want is to equate myself to Krissa, who has clearly set her sights as high as getting to the position of trophy wife. But, I am trying to be honest about myself and my past and...I can't ignore the similarities."

I force myself to focus on our conversation, trying to shove the four-letter word out of my mind and return to now.

"So what ended up happening?" she prods, her fingers coming up and stroking along my bare chest, playing with the light smattering of short hair.

I clear my throat and try to refocus.

Krissa and my dad.

"I didn't take her back," I say, clearing my throat and working hard to bring my scattered thoughts back to center. "Of course I didn't. But, when my dad *did* decide to marry her just a few months later, I got really angry and did something I shouldn't have."

Remmy edges closer to make sure our eyes meet, and I can see a hint of humor in their depths.

"You mean Mr. Perfect Benjamin Calloway did something bad? I'm on the edge of my seat and can't wait to hear all about it."

Her ability to lighten things has me fighting a grin, but it does eventually fall away when I muster up the courage to tell her about one of the most shameful things I've ever done.

"I started an affair with a married woman, the wife of the yacht club owner."

Remmy's eyes widen, but other than that I don't see any disgust on her face at my absolutely horrible actions.

"My dad was supposed to be buying the property from Larry, but he'd been waffling. He and his wife had been having problems, so I took advantage and used Nancy then made sure we were found out just in time for him to reject my dad's deal."

I sigh, scrubbing a hand across my jaw.

"It wasn't one of my finer moments in life, and I may have pushed it overboard by planting some information about me being some sort of gigolo for married housewives around the South Bay to make the domino effect even bigger."

"Didn't you worry about what people would think of *you*?" she asks, surprise still evident on her face. "I mean, part of me can understand the anger at your dad and desire to get even, but I can't imagine having to deal with the repercussions of all the gossip, especially if you were just building your business."

I nod. "That's the part I didn't factor in. I'd planned this...'revenge' but didn't realize I was hurting myself as well. Or maybe I realized it, but I just didn't care."

"It makes sense why things are so intense between you." She pauses. "And the weird comment he made to me tonight."

My entire body tenses. "What comment?"

"When we were at the hospital, he said something like *you have no idea what you're getting yourself into*. It really irritated me, but it makes sense if there's lots of drama between the two of you. He's probably just stirring the pot."

My head bobs in agreement, but inside I'm reeling.

My dad wasn't calling earlier to tell me about Ivy. He was calling to talk to me about Remmy. I can feel it in my bones.

If my new strategy to bring him down has rattled him enough that he's dropping hints to Remmy, I must have finally found his Achilles heel.

"I'm glad that's all behind you," she says. "Glad we're both moving beyond the past and trying to focus on happiness now."

I nod, my stomach turning over at my unspoken lie.

Because I *haven't* moved on.

It *isn't* behind me.

This very relationship is *because* of my desire to wreak havoc in my father's life, my desperate need to inflict on him the ultimate pain that I can think of.

As Remmy snuggles into me, mumbling something about waiting to ask our last questions, I wonder if—this time around—I'll be fully prepared to take on the consequences of my own actions.

Chapter Twenty
BEN

I take the following day off as well, though this time I take a legitimate sick day so I can go to the hospital and be with Wyatt and my mother.

"Thanks for coming," Wyatt says, extending his hand to me when I walk into Ivy's hospital room.

I know it's his way of apologizing. He's never been particularly good at it, but it's more than a lot of people are capable of doing, so I don't treat it lightly, sticking my hand into his.

And then I go in for the kill, tugging him in for a brief hug I know he never would have asked for but certainly needs.

"Thanks for inviting me," I say, my words soft.

We both know he's invited me to these things before, to Ivy's earlier diagnostic meetings and difficult conversations with Dr. Lyons. In the past, I avoided them.

I can say it was because I wasn't welcome all I want—and technically, it's the truth—but the truer truth is that I was somewhat embarrassed about the reason my mother didn't want me around.

She told me, in the wake of the scandal with Larry Belton's wife, that I was no longer welcome at Calloway functions, said I could consider myself excommunicated from the family.

I made a joke—*excommunicado, like John Wick*—which she didn't find amusing. We have very different senses of humor.

And then she told me what an embarrassment I was, and that if I didn't care about my own reputation, I should at least care about Ivy's.

That's what made me pull back, pull away. I didn't want to create any more drama or problems for my little sister, who was already going through so much.

But now, I'm not allowing that to dictate my actions anymore.

My mom doesn't want me to come to fundraisers and events they host? That's fine.

However, there's no way she's keeping me away from my sister, especially when she's sick and lying in a hospital bed, looking like she's been smacked over the head.

"The bruising is new," I comment, observing the way her skin has turned blue in certain spots. "Is that normal? Is that just something I don't understand?"

Wyatt sighs, keeping his voice low so he doesn't wake Ivy, who needs all the sleep she can get while her body tries to fight off whatever this infection is. "It's something we don't understand either."

When Dr. Lyons walks in, I can tell by the look on her face that she doesn't have great news.

"Should we..." I only ask half of the question, pointing to Ivy.

But Dr. Lyons shakes her head. "Let her sleep. If she wakes, I'll start over, but for now, the best thing she can be doing for her body is resting."

My mom steps forward, her short stature seeming even smaller today, her face riddled with nerves.

"Tell us what's going on, please," she says, and my heart breaks at the worry in her voice.

She's been an imperfect mother, without a doubt, but what I would *never* doubt is the fact that she loves her children.

"As I suspected and told you last night, Ivy's body is resisting the medication."

"Do you know why?" Wyatt asks. "When we talked about it a few months ago, it seemed like you were optimistic."

The doctor nods. "I was. There have been many patients who have had wonderful experiences with the eculizumab or even an off-brand synthetic, but for some reason, Ivy's body has begun to reject it. The medication's job is to decrease the destruction of red blood cells, which you all know is what PNH does to the body. But, there are a huge number of potential side effects, and unfortunately, it seems like Ivy is experiencing some of those."

She opens up her folder, flips through to a page, and begins reading.

"Her white blood cell count is down, she has a cold, she's begun reporting numbness and blurred vision during her IV appointments and extended weakness in her legs"—she flips the paperwork closed—"and that doesn't include the things that are caused by the PNH itself. The fainting, the increased risk of sickness, depression, lower appetite—has Ivy been still experiencing most of those? She didn't fill out her paperwork properly at her last appointment."

"I'm...I'm not sure," Wyatt says, looking to mom.

"She's been experiencing a lot of that," she says, "but she made it clear that she didn't want to talk about it because it was just normal for her."

Dr. Lyons nods, and something dark climbs into my throat at the expression on her face.

"I'm going to be frank. I know I've said in the past that the bone marrow transplant is Ivy's best option at living a normal life." She pauses. "We're getting to the point where it may be her only option, period. She's starting to exhibit symptoms patients experience in the months before their body can no longer fight off the infections and complications any longer."

We stand there, frozen, all of us unable to truly process what she's telling us.

That Ivy will die if we don't find a donor.

"It may be classless of me to say this, but if there was ever going to be a time when you could use your family's name and connections or your financial weight to move things around, this is it."

We spend a bit longer talking about what will be happening next, a plan for Ivy's recovery from her current infection, before Dr.

Lyons leaves us, likely heading back to her own hospital.

"I'm going to call your father," my mom says, leaving the room, the aroma of her favorite perfume swallowed immediately by the scent of antiseptic and other hospital smells that make me sick.

"He doesn't deserve to fucking know what's going on," Wyatt grumbles, leaning forward in his chair and taking Ivy's hand in his, watching her where she lies, blissfully asleep and not having to deal with her body's weakness for a few hours.

Our dad never really bonded with Ivy when she was born. We assume it was because he was already out the door on our mom, and because he had a good idea that she wasn't his biologically.

Their relationship has always been a strained, constant set of bumps in the road, with him rarely being a part of her life.

Which is why it was so weird that he was here yesterday, and with Krissa.

"Do you know why he was here last night?" I ask, unable to keep out the uncomfortable idea that he may have used his daughter's hospital stay as an opportunity to talk to me or Remmy.

Wyatt shrugs. "Not sure. It was kind of weird, though, especially since he came with the child bride."

I roll my eyes.

Wyatt loves to refer to Krissa as the child bride. Obviously there is a massive age gap between them, but I feel like that should be the least of our problems with her.

With them.

I take a seat in the chair my mom left empty on the other side of Ivy's bed, crossing my arms and leaning back, just watching her where she reclines, multiple lines connected to her body.

When my mom first told us we were going to have a baby sister, I wasn't that excited about it. I liked my life just fine as it was, didn't need anything new or crazy to disrupt the order I craved.

It wasn't until I saw her for the first time in the hospital that I fell in love with her.

She was so tiny, a little pink ball of wrinkles, like a Shar-Pei, and I instantly knew it would be our job to love and protect her, to do everything we could to make her life amazing.

Now I'm getting a sense of déjà vu. She's snuggled in a hospital bed, looking so tiny and desperately needing to be taken care of.

And I don't know if there's anything I can do.

Wyatt told me about their shot-in-the-dark idea to get Hannah to be a donor, and how it didn't pan out. About the aggressive search they've been doing to find a match somewhere in the world and how they've turned up no results.

The only thing I can think, over and over in my mind is, what else can we do?

Seriously.

What else can we do?

Because I'll do it.

I don't care what it costs or who I have to talk to or schmooze or…it doesn't matter.

But I don't know where to start.

"We're going to figure this out."

Wyatt says it like a statement, but when I look up at him, I see the question in his eyes.

He's not saying it.

He's asking me.

Just like he used to when we were kids and Ivy was getting sick. Or our parents were getting divorced. Or something else in our lives was going wrong.

He'd look to me and ask me if it was going to be okay.

If we were going to figure it out.

And as much as I want to agree with him, as much as I want to look him in the eyes and tell him yes of *course* we're going to figure this out, I just can't this morning.

Not when I'm looking at Ivy in this bed, feeling lost and confused and not knowing where to begin when trying to look for answers.

So I look Wyatt in the eyes and I say the only thing I can say that is the absolute truth.

"We're sure as hell going to try."

I stay at the hospital for a while longer, only leaving when I've been assured that Wyatt and my mom are sticking around.

The nervous energy is thrumming through my veins, and I

need to get to the gym to burn some of it off. Then, maybe I can head back and bring Ivy some non-hospital food.

I spend an hour at Jim's, pushing my body as hard as I can to max out my physical limits. Shower, change, and swing by the house to grab a photo book I have from when Ivy was a lot smaller.

It was actually a gift I gave to her for her birthday—her fifth or sixth, I think—but she was too young to appreciate it at the time, so my mom told me to hang on to it and give it to her when she was older.

Today could be a great day to go through it together.

When my phone rings, I yank it out of my pocket, not looking at the screen as I go through the books I have in my study, trying to find the specific one I want to bring with me.

"This is Ben."

"Hello, Benjamin. I'm surprised you answered."

My focus instantly drops away from the shelves and I spin where I'm standing, as if I could turn around and look my dad in the face.

"You know, there are a lot of things I'd love to use to strangle you right now," I say, my anger beginning to bubble up, "but that would mean I'd have to spend time looking at you while I did it, and I'd rather not."

He laughs.

The motherfucker's daughter is in the hospital, and he's laughing that his son wants to strangle him.

"You know, Ben, I have to be honest with you, I don't understand all this animosity between us."

"That's bullshit. Even if I didn't loathe the very sight of you because you're a selfish asshole, I'd still want to spit in your face because you're incapable of taking even a fucking moment of your day to spend with your daughter who is in the hospital."

"She's not my daughter and we all know it," he says, his words coming out with a sigh, as if he's exhausted at the very idea.

"Then what were you doing there last night, huh? And don't fucking lie to me."

There's a pause, and I wonder if he hung up or if I accidentally did. But then I hear him moving around, possibly the sound of a door closing.

"I have to say, Ben, I know you're angry at me because of what happened with Krissa, but...Remmy Wallace? That's the big play you've been banking on?"

I grit my teeth, my anger continuing to grow until it feels like it's going to suffocate me.

"If you think marrying Remmy Wallace is going to get you *anything* from Bob, you're sorely mistaken."

"If I remember correctly, going after Nancy Belton sure did sort things out for me for a short while," I reply.

Even though I know it's a mistake to bring up what happened between my dad and Larry, I'm feeling taunted, and it's too easy of a hit between the eyes for me to pass up.

My dad hums in acknowledgment.

"Yes, you were able to block the sale of the Hermosa Beach Yacht Club. Commendable, truly." He pauses. "But was it really a battle well won? I seem to recall the wake of that scandal, and it did quite the number on your life, didn't it?"

My hands clench into fists at my sides.

He's a master manipulator, my father, a man capable of some absolutely horrible things.

Like earlier this summer when he threatened to drag Hannah's name through the mud if Wyatt didn't help him at some sort of ceremony.

Honestly, I think I have it in me to be as ruthless and calculating as he is—maybe even more so. I could absolutely decimate him, rip him into tiny shreds.

But I have to remind myself of the ways my dad and I are different.

He thinks he's this formidable opponent because he doesn't have any weak spots.

What that really means is that he has nothing to lose.

And he has nothing to lose because he's completely ruined his relationships with his entire family.

Wyatt and I are able to be jerked around because we value our relationships, our family, our lovers more than we value winning.

And maybe that *does* make my dad bigger and better and stronger.

But it doesn't make him happier.

It doesn't satisfy his soul.

Suddenly, everything clicks together and makes sense in a way I didn't realize it could, in a way I couldn't have planned for even if I'd been working my hardest.

"You know, dad...it did do a number on my life," I start, pausing for a moment and taking a deep breath. I know I'm making the right choice, but sometimes, you just need to take a second to fortify your mind if you're going to take a giant leap. "And that's why I won't be doing anything like that again."

He laughs, something long and deep and riddled with anger. "Sure you won't."

"I get that you assume my relationship with Remmy is about how I can get to you, and honestly, at one point, that was true. I knew getting her to marry me would be the greatest way for me to bring you to your knees, especially since Wallace Media owns more than half of Calloway Corporation."

At *that* statement, I hear nothing but silence.

"You didn't think I knew that? That you stumbled through some bad business deals over the years and needed some saving?" I scoff. "The fact that you were able to get an honorable guy like Robert Wallace to help you out and keep it on the down-low still astounds me, but it isn't my problem. Not anymore. So consider this my notice. I'm waving the white flag. I'm not trying to come after you."

"You're so full of shit. I don't know what you're playing here, but I'll figure it out eventually. Don't kid yourself thinking you can pretend to bail and I'll just close my eyes."

I shake my head and let out a sigh.

"It's sad, don't you think? That this is what matters to you most? That your entire life is about getting what you want and winning at all costs? I'm starting to realize...that's just not enough for me."

He doesn't say anything else, so I decide to wrap it up. I have more important things to do today, anyway.

"Look, I gotta go. Ivy's in the hospital, and that's where my priority is. I'll see you around."

And then I hang up, grab the photo book off my shelf, and head back out the door, deciding not to give my father's fucked-up games another thought.

Chapter Twenty One
REMMY

I don't think I've ever seen Dominic sit so still before. His eyes are narrowed and focused entirely too surely on me, his hands frozen mid-motion—the left holding a flopped-over section of today's newspaper, a habit he picked up when we were living on my grandfather's *finca* in Colombia and didn't have access to the internet; the right delicately looped around the handle of a coffee mug that was, only seconds ago, moving toward his mouth.

My oldest brother isn't thinking about taking a sip of his coffee anymore, though. That black tar he drinks down by the barrel every day hovers in the air in front of him, almost forgotten as he watches me.

Maybe this was a mistake.

He clears his throat, the first sign that he isn't a wax figurine in at least a solid minute. He reaches out and sets his cup back on the saucer then uses both hands to slowly and methodically fold his newspaper in half.

Drawing his attention away from his morning coffee and the news? Yes, this was definitely a mistake.

He clears his throat again, and then he reaches up to adjust his tie. It would almost seem like a nervous gesture to someone who didn't know him.

But I *do* know him, and it is *not* a nervous gesture.

"Would you mind...repeating yourself?" he finally says, his eyes still focused on my face like floodlights.

Surely he's searching for answers, some kind of indicator that he's misunderstanding me.

But I know what I said, and I'm not taking it back.

He half-smiles, half-grimaces—the only way he knows how to put someone at ease, though I don't think he's ever understood how much more terrifying it is than just his blank stare.

"Because it sounds like you just said..." He trails off.

I run my hands into my hair at the base of my neck and pull the still damp heft of tendrils over one shoulder, focusing my attention on putting my thick and unruly mane into a braid and hoping to alleviate my nerves.

Spoiler alert: it isn't working.

I continue the slow, methodical steps of braiding my hair, only daring to look up at Dominic once, giving him what I hope looks like a genuine smile, and then I repeat the words I said to him just a few moments ago.

"I'm going to move in with Ben."

When I left his house earlier this morning, kissing him softly on the lips and murmuring goodbye before the sun had even risen, there was a pang inside of me that I wasn't expecting. I realized as I sat in the back of the hired car I'd called to take me the short few blocks home that I didn't want to leave Ben's.

I want to take him up on the offer to move in with him—now. That way we can figure each other out a little more and move things forward.

Get ready for our life together.

Get ready for the baby.

And when I got home and saw that Dominic was awake and sitting out on the front patio, sipping his coffee and reading the paper, I decided he would be the first person I'd tell.

A part of me that hasn't lived at home in years felt like slinking into the house without attracting his attention.

But the other part of me that has experienced freedom and independence over the past same number of years said *fuck that shit* and strolled boldly across the patio with my head high and shoulders back.

Now that I've told him, I have two completely new sets of emotions rolling through me. One says I should take it back and sprint away to hide in my room, and the other sights in relief that I was able to get it out and wants to run upstairs to pack a bag.

My brother leans back in his chair, his elbows resting on the arm rests and his fingers twisting together over his chest as he studies me.

I know poking the bear won't lead to anything good. So I wait, sitting across from him while his eyes, sharp with knowledge and wisdom, attempt to bore holes through my body.

He nods once. "That's what I thought you said." His hand comes up to scrub at his chin, smooth from the barber's shave he gets once a week before leaving for the office. Then he reaches out and picks up his coffee cup to take a sip.

Once he settles it into the saucer once more and leans back, I feel my body brace for impact.

"I think it's a great idea."

My shoulders fall, and I feel confusion flood my system. "Seriously?"

Dominic laughs, a rare thing for him and something I so miss.

"Of course." His eyes soften, and a warm, soothing sensation coats the insides of my body, covering my nerves and calming my jitters. "This is the man who is planning to act as the father to your baby when it isn't his, am I right?"

I nod. "Yeah." My voice is thick.

"Then why should you not be next to him, where he can take care of you and support you in whatever comes next?"

Shifting in my seat, my mind races trying to understand why *this* is the time my brother decides to blow my mind.

"You look confused."

"I *am* confused," I reply.

"Why?"

"Because you're flipping the script. You were telling me before that he was *interesting* because he was willing to be the father, and you're supposed to tell me only easy women move in with a man before they get married. How many times have we been told a man doesn't buy a cow if you give the milk away for free?"

"I've been watching you with him for weeks. I might not think he's the right guy for you, might think he has more to prove if he wants the chance to be, but *you* are the one who makes that choice in the end. *You* are the one who will have to live with your choice."

And then Dominic leans forward and focuses his attention on me with a ferocity I haven't seen from him in a long time.

"And I want to be clear about something. You are not a cow," he says firmly through gritted teeth. "And you're not for sale. Your value has nothing to do with sex."

It feels like I've been slammed in the chest with a cannonball as everything within me shifts and flexes at Dom's declaration. It's like I've been staring at words on a page for so long, and he's come along and pulled it out of my hands, flipping it over so I can read what I once was trying to understand upside down.

I swallow awkwardly as I assess my brother, the man I snapped at last night and begged to be my brother again. I feel so thankful for his opinion right now, his empowerment, his choice to return my agency to me.

Maybe that's the part of growing up I've been struggling with the most—balancing my own independence with the expectations my family has for me.

I want to value my parents' opinions and live up to what they want for me, but I also want them to believe in me and support me as I flounder around figuring out what I want for *myself.*

"Will you help me tell mom and dad?" I ask, my voice a whisper.

As brave as I was feeling when I got home, I know it will feel different trying to tell my parents.

Dom reaches out and puts his hand over mine.

"I love you, Remmy, and I support you always. But that's a battle you have to fight on your own."

I have every intention of telling my parents. I really do. But the cowardly part of me believes it will be easier to do so if I've already moved in with Ben.

That way I'm letting them know what I'm doing, not asking for their permission.

I pull out just the primarily important things: a suitcase full of clothes, my makeup and hair care toiletries, and a handful of photos from my bookshelf.

The picture of me and Lucas stays behind.

When I finally get to Ben's, it's nearing sundown, the entire day having passed me by as I packed and wandered around my childhood home, reminiscing about memories from forever ago as I went from room to room.

My hope is that now I'll get to make new memories in these rooms, with Ben and the baby.

My hand comes up to rest on my stomach, an emotional wave coming over me at the thought.

We walked through his house together a while back, discussing options for which room would be the nursery and whether or not I want my own room.

That was before the sex, before the intimacy I have felt with him over the past few days, the closeness I've never felt with another man before, not even Lucas.

I was indecisive then. Now, I know I want to share a room with Ben, want to wake up next to him in the mornings and fall asleep with his arms around me after we've sated each other's needs.

Letting out a sigh, I head to the balcony and open the sliding glass door, wishing I'd gotten here earlier so I could enjoy the phenomenal ocean view from his bedroom's vantage point, my first night at his place as a person who lives here.

I step outside and rest my hands on the cool, damp metal of the railing, closing my eyes and allowing myself a moment to myself. It's a chance to take a calming breath and inhale the ocean breeze, to listen to the sound of the waves clapping against the shoreline.

Ben doesn't have an oceanfront property like some of our other friends own. Instead, he sits toward the back of town, his property raised slightly so it has a view even if it doesn't have direct access.

I was actually surprised the first time I visited a few weeks ago.

I want to laugh to myself.

It's crazy when I think about how little time has passed since Ben first proposed this crazy idea. It's hardly been a month and I'm already moving in and trying to get settled, really settled.

Dominic looked a bit skeptical when he pulled up out front earlier this evening. I could see it in his face.

"This is where he lives?" he said, eyeing the two-story family home with fascination, like the idea of living in anything other than a beachfront mansion was a strange concept he might have heard of once but never experienced.

"It's a family home," I replied, rolling my eyes.

Even though I wanted to gag at my brother's elitist attitude, I somewhat understood where he was coming from.

Most people we know don't live in homes like this one. Hermosa Beach has multi-million dollar mansions, surfer cottages, and tons of apartment buildings. What it doesn't have is traditional single-family homes on a decent-sized lot with a yard and a white picket fence.

Even in Colombia, my family owns a penthouse apartment in the richest area of Medellín, and two *fincas* outside of the city with hundreds of acres.

In this town, if someone has the money, they'll spend it expanding the square footage of their house. If they don't have the money, they'll live in an apartment or one of the shitty cottages that have been 'upgraded'—and I use that term very loosely—by people who think they know how to gut a home.

People don't waste money on yard spaces, on beautiful exterior refurbishments like potted plants and picket fences. Truth be told, I didn't used to think Ben seemed like the guy who would choose any of that shit in the first place.

While he wasn't a man who crossed my mind often before the day of the pier-to-pier swim, I can honestly say if I'd been asked, I would have bet he lived in a massive, ostentatious, Calloway-esque property with a racquetball court or a sauna or something boujee like that.

Not in a house that looks like the Cleavers live in it.

But now, knowing Ben as well as I do—or as well as I *think* I do—it makes complete sense.

He bought the house that represents the life he wants. He wants the family, the happy home.

And I hope to give it to him.

Dominic gave me a look that fell somewhere between disbelief and amusement as I stared up at the house from the street, knowing I was making the right choice but feeling nerves all the same. "Scoot, *hermanita*," he'd finally said. "I have a meeting to get to."

"At 8pm? Is this meeting in a hotel room?"

He just glared at me as I giggled and climbed out of his car, then he put his car in park to help me get my massive suitcase from the car to the door.

He kissed me on the forehead and said exactly the words I needed to hear.

"If he ever fucks up, just let me know and I'll come kill him."

I smiled and waved as my brother drove off to his own lady of the night.

Now, standing on the patio that gives me a direct view of the beach, even if it is a few blocks away, I begin to think about a way to make the inside look as much like a family home as the outside.

Because this *does* look like a family home, like something bought with the intention of filling it with people, a spouse and kids.

But it certainly doesn't *feel* like a family home, at least not on the inside.

Even Ben's bedroom...as beautiful as it is, it was definitely designed by someone who was trying to create a show-stopping space, not someone trying to set up a comfortable room with the owner's personality and life in mind.

I want to change that for Ben, want to fill his home with the same kind of warmth I want to bring to his heart and his mind.

Make it a place we both feel safe and happy.

Rugs. Throw blankets. A dog bed. Family pictures, posed as they may be.

Ben might be a neat and ordered kind of guy—everything has its place, everything put away until needed, beauty over function—but everything is going to change for both of us. I think our home should reflect that.

Of course that idea makes me want to shit my pants when I

hear Ben walking through the front door.

He freezes when he sees me sitting at the kitchen counter, eating a bowl of cereal.

"Hey."

I grin.

"Hey yourself."

He looks at his watch, probably seeing that it's a little after eight.

"Were we supposed to do something tonight?"

I shake my head. "Not together, but I did something tonight."

He doesn't say anything, just patiently waits for me to say whatever it is I want to say.

That's something I really appreciate about Ben.

His patience.

I slip off the stool at the counter and take him by the hand, pulling him through the house and up the stairs, enjoying his light chuckling.

But it cuts off when we walk into his bedroom.

When he sees my empty suitcase in the corner, he eyes me curiously before taking the lead and moving over to the walk-in closet, flipping on the light and finding clothes that belong to me hanging on the right.

Ben turns to look at me.

"You moved in?" he asks, his voice quiet.

I nod. "I hope that's okay?"

He doesn't say anything, and I have a brief moment of panic where I wonder if I really fucked up by overstepping. He might have given me a key and asked me to move in, but I never agreed and told him a date.

I just showed up.

But my panic dissipates when I see the disbelief on his face, like he couldn't have imagined anything more perfect to come home to. He rushes at me and wraps me up in his arms.

"Welcome home, Remmy."

Chapter Twenty-Two
BEN

When I first spoke with Remmy about this whole marriage thing, I envisioned us being friendly roommates with a child, two people helping each other out.

I never envisioned long nights of sex all over the house, or sitting in our underwear on my balcony with coffee in the mornings, decaf for her and regular for me, talking about the day. I didn't ever imagine she would want to come with me to the gym or visit me at work or that I'd start to regulate my hours at Bennie's so I could get home faster, sooner, be at her side more often.

I find myself laughing more. Smiling more. Enjoying my days more.

She goes with me to visit my sister every day as Ivy slowly recovers from the infection and cold that caused her to faint.

What feels crazy to me is that as soon as we stopped trying to put on a show for everyone else about this relationship, our horrible attempt at trying to convince people we were dating, that's the exact time when people started asking us what's going on.

The news of Remmy's pregnancy doesn't seem to have spread after Wyatt's allusion to it during his anger-fueled tirade in the hospital waiting room, which is great news for her since she isn't ready to tell her parents yet.

But people *know* we're together now.

For sure.

Which is why it isn't surprising when Remmy tells me she needs to plan a day to go home and talk to her parents about us moving in together.

What *is* surprising is the Sunday morning a few days after she brought her stuff over when Remmy and I wake up to an aggressive pounding at the front door.

"Remington!"

My tired eyes widen when I hear an older female voice calling up to us through the open doorway leading out to my second-floor balcony.

"*Remington Wallace, ven acá ya mismo!*"

Remmy flies out of bed, pulling on a pair of boxers and a long-sleeved shirt before she books it out of the room, her feet thundering down the stairs before I can even lug my body out of bed.

I'm pulling on a pair of track pants and reaching for a shirt when I hear the upset voice of who I can only guess is Mrs. Wallace as she enters the house and begins shouting at Remmy, her words echoing through the entry and volleying up to me.

"...had to hear it from Sonya Mitchell that my only daughter has *moved in* with Ben Calloway. I told her she had to be mistaken, said *my* daughter would never, ever make such a stupid choice when she knows what it would do to her mother, and then she told me a few years ago, Ben was involved in some...some *scandal* involving Larry Belton's wife and prostituting himself to other rich women in the community."

I wince, realizing just how hard that decision is going to bite me on the ass now that I actually have something I want—some*one* I want—and am desperate to keep.

"I return from our trip to Hartford and find that your bags have been packed and things are missing from your room and you're...here...wearing his underwear and answering the door at seven in the morning."

"Mom, I can explain, if you'd—"

"I don't need you to explain. I need you to march your butt upstairs and get your things. The car is waiting out front."

There's a pause, both from the two of them downstairs and from me where I stand frozen on the landing, wondering if I should go down and have Remmy's back or if I should let her fight this battle on her own.

She's never complained much about her parents apart from her fear that they'd kick her out if they found out she was pregnant without a husband. She didn't have anything negative to say other than that they're kind of traditional.

In fact, most of her stories about her family are positive. Great brothers, loving mom, present dad. Apart from the near divorce when she was in high school, they seem like they love and care about each other.

So I don't know if I should be supporting her in a decision to stay here by vocalizing my perspective or by letting her learn to vocalize it herself.

Ultimately, I don't have to decide.

"No."

"Excuse me?"

"I said no. I'm not packing my things and coming home. My things belong here. *This* is my home."

Something hard thumps in my chest at her words, my awe at her continuing to grow the more I see her coming into herself.

"This isn't your home. This is a brothel, the home of a...a..."

"A what...a rapscallion? A scoundrel?"

I want to laugh at Remmy's choice of words but manage to hold it back.

"A man who is only after one thing from you, Remington."

"For your information, Ben is not after sex from me," she says.

I hear her mother gasp, and I want to jump down the stairs and say that's not entirely accurate.

"Well, that's not true. He does want sex from me, but he also wants more than that. We belong together."

"Remington, you are *so* naïve. Men only want one thing from you and it rests between your thighs. Why on earth would a man ever buy the cow if he can—"

"*I am not a fucking cow!*" she screams.

I take that as my cue to go downstairs. There is no way I'm

letting her get any more riled up, whether it's her mother or not.

When I take my first steps down, I see that Remmy has her back to me and Mariana is standing just inside the door, eyes wide at Remmy's outburst, her hand against her chest.

"My worth to a man has nothing to do with what's between my legs," she continues. "And maybe *some* men only want one thing from a woman, but Ben is not *some guy*. He's the man I'm going to marry."

Mariana's eyes meet mine as I drop down to the bottom of the stairs and come to a stop just behind Remmy. Quietly, I press up against her just slightly so she can feel my strength, feel that I'm here with her. I slip my hand into hers as I take a look at her face, a pang of sadness weaving through me at the tears building up in her eyes.

"Clearly, you've been away from us for too long," Mariana says, looking ruffled but trying to contain it. "You've let men like Ben corrupt you, take things from you that you can't get back. Come home so we can—"

"Corrupt me?" Remmy asks, though I know she heard her mother just fine. "Let's talk for a second about things being taken from me that I'll never get back, shall we?"

Remmy steps forward, not getting much closer to her mother but putting some space between us. I take the cue, stepping back. She's strong enough to handle this on her own.

"Let's talk about the time you took me to visit our grandfather, and Victor *raped me* when I was fifteen years old."

Mariana's face pales.

"Let's talk about the dozens and dozens of men I've slept with to try to get rid of that feeling I still don't know how to manage, the feeling of someone else stealing control of my body. Or how about the fact that when we went back to visit your father, Victor raped me *again*."

My body feels like a live wire as I watch her go to bat for herself, as she stands in her own skin and demands to be listened to and taken seriously.

"Ben is the best of the men I've ever been with or seen, because he is willing to take the broken and battered and beaten-up parts of me and help me hold them together so I don't shatter *every fucking day*."

"Remington that is…quite the…accusation against Victor. He

is the son of one of your grandfather's closest friends, and you should be careful that—"

"I'm going to stop you right there," I say, my voice deep, my tone hard. "You have *one job* when your daughter summons up the courage to tell you she was raped. *One*, and that's to believe her. Period."

Stepping forward, I put my body between Remmy and her mother.

"Clearly, Remmy has no interest in going anywhere with you today, so I am going to kindly show you to the door. She will reach out to you when she's ready to talk."

Her face is still pale and she looks rattled down to her very bones, but Mariana takes my direction when I open the front door and stand next to it, waiting for her to leave.

She walks through and then turns around to look at Remmy, who is standing tall and brave and fierce even through the tears that track down her cheeks.

And then she turns and heads out to the black car that's waiting for her in the driveway.

I slam the door and dart for Remmy, who is already dropping down to her knees, her body racked with sobs, her emotions too much to handle.

"I'm so proud of you," I whisper. "So proud."

"She didn't believe me," she cries, her body shaking. "She didn't...she..."

"I know, honey. I know. I'm sorry."

I hold her in my arms, cradling her to my chest, wishing I could do anything to make her not feel so hurt.

It feels like my lot in life right now is to watch the women I love go through things I can't help them with.

All I can do is hold her and be here for her.

So that's exactly what I do.

When I settle Remmy into the couch and set up a Netflix marathon for her, I know I'm not the guy who can help her through this. As much as I want to be, I'm just not.

So I slip off when she falls back to sleep, her body shot from her adrenaline rush, and make a phone call.

It's nearing sunset when there's finally a knock on the door.

I climb out from where I was sitting behind Remmy on the couch, her body snuggled up against my chest, both of us under a blanket.

As emotional as she is, it was a wonderful way to spend the day, with her in my arms.

But I know what's behind that door will be helpful for her in a way I can't be.

When I open it, I grin at the short, pixie-haired brunette who is the spitting image of my friend Mark.

"Hi Josslyn," I say, pulling the door open wider. "I'm Ben."

She smiles and gives me a hug then breezes past me without saying a word.

I hear a gasp in the living room, and as I peek around the corner, I watch as Remmy flies off the couch and races toward Josslyn, the two women embracing tightly.

"Oh my god, how are you here?" Remmy asks.

"Ben called me."

I see Remmy's eyes rise to meet mine from across the room. The gratitude shining out from her can be seen and felt all the way across the room, and it makes me feel amazing, even if that's not why I made the call.

"I'm gonna head over to the hospital, spend some time with Wyatt and Ivy," I say. "You guys hang out. Josslyn, there are a couple of guest rooms—feel free to pick."

She looks back at me and nods.

Remmy lets go of Josslyn and walks over to me, taking me into a hug as well.

"Thank you," she whispers before placing a kiss on my lips.

"I hope this helps with whatever you need right now."

I wave goodbye, grabbing a jacket as I head out into the cool night air of early September in Hermosa Beach.

Before I close the door, I hear the two start talking.

"Damn, girl—he's fucking hot."

I smile to myself as I hear Remmy's giggle, knowing she's going to be okay, and then I head off to see Ivy.

She smiles through tired eyes when I walk in the door, sitting up in the bed.

I didn't know you were coming tonight, she signs, her hands moving a bit more sluggishly than usual.

I had a craving for blueberry muffins and thought I'd see if you were in the mood, too.

Her eyes widen and her smile grows.

Oh my god, I love blueberry muffins.

I laugh, nodding in acknowledgment as I cross the room, dropping the grocery store bag off my wrist and onto the empty space near her feet on the hospital bed.

I glance around as she rips open the plastic in search of the half-dozen baked treats that are waiting for her, noticing that the room looks completely empty.

Where are mom and Wyatt?

She shrugs, both of her hands occupied as she begins pulling the paper wrapper off the bottom.

Most people love the muffin top. Ivy likes the muffin butt.

She cracks up when I say that.

I take a seat in the chair next to her bed, pulling out my own muffin, both of us eating and watching a cartoon with subtitles on the TV.

I'm surprised my mom and Wyatt aren't here. I thought we'd talked about a rotation so Ivy doesn't have to be alone.

Did they say anything about being here or going somewhere?

Ivy watches my hands but then returns her attention to her muffin, and I instantly realize something's wrong.

Shifting in my seat, I rest my arms on her bed next to her legs, taking one of her hands into mine to block her from continuing to use her muffin as an excuse not to talk to me.

Talk to me.

A moment passes before she finally realizes I'm not playing

around, and her hands rise even if her expression stays neutral.

I told them I don't want them here anymore.

My brow furrows.

Why would you do that? If I were in the hospital, I wouldn't want to be here alone and bored out of my mind. You're watching cartoons, for god's sake.

She giggles, but it's small and fades away quickly.

I just feel bad that I'm sick again, *and that they had to reschedule everything* again. *Wyatt and Hannah were supposed to go on some trip and they had to change the whole thing.*

But they want to be here for you because they love you.

I see her hands clench momentarily before she continues.

I know, but it sucks being the reason they can't just live normal lives. I get sick all the time, and it's such a burden to...

I put my hands on hers, stopping her midsentence.

"No." I say it as she watches me, her eyes dropping to my lips to read what I'm saying. "You are *never* a burden. *Ever.*"

Letting go of her hands, I continue signing.

All of us want to be here with you because you are one of the most important people in the world to us. Wouldn't you want to climb into this bed and snuggle with me if I were sick and you were scared for me?

A beat passes before she nods.

Alright. Eat your muffin, no more bullshit, and I'm gonna find us something better to watch than this.

She giggles at my language then pulls her muffin closer and starts picking at it again.

I grab the remote and flip through, feeling thankful when I find a channel with one of those home renovation shows. Ivy loves those, and it's great for her because she doesn't usually have to read the subtitles to see what's going on.

Once that's done, I settle back in my chair, grab my phone, and tap out a message to my brother.

Me: Where are you guys?

Only a few moments pass before I see the little bubbles pop up.

My brother might not be in the room right now, but I know wherever he is, his focus is still on Ivy.

It doesn't surprise me that his response is almost instantaneous. And when his message pops up on my phone, I laugh quietly to myself.

Wyatt: Cafeteria. You here?

Me: Yeah. In Ivy's room. She said she kicked your asses out.

Wyatt: I think she needed some space. Mom went home. I'm staying the night tonight.

Me: You guys have been handling this for the most part. I can stay tonight.

Wyatt: You sure? Hannah was going to come by and hang out for a while, too. It's not like I was handling things alone.

I grin.

It is completely unsurprising that Hannah was planning to come and help keep Ivy company tonight.

But I know they could probably use some relaxing time, just the two of them, especially if they were originally planning for this week to be a trip to London.

Me: I'm sure. I'm here tonight.

I wait for Wyatt's response but nothing comes through, so I close my phone and settle back in my chair.

Catching Ivy's eye, I give her the update.

I'm gonna stay here tonight.

She smiles at me, and I know I'm not only doing right by my brother, but also my sister, my baby sister who I need to make sure I'm spending more time with.

Really?

I nod, reaching out and squeezing her foot through the hospital blanket.

It's been too long since I've gotten you all to myself, I add. *Tonight is gonna be just you and me. Date night.*

Ivy grins and snuggles more into her bed, twisting to the side and watching me with hope in her eyes.

Seeing it there makes me happy, because I want *her* to be happy.

She deserves it. If any one of us deserve to be happy, it's Ivy.

"Knock, knock."

I turn my head and look to the door, my eyebrows rising when I see Logan Becker with a clipboard and a long white jacket.

"Hey, Logan." I stand, crossing the room and giving his hand a shake. "Good to see you."

"You too." His eyes flit to Ivy, who I realize is slowly starting to doze off.

"So much for our crazy party tonight," I joke, gesturing to my sister before returning my attention to Logan. "You on rounds or something? Is that what it's called?"

He gives me an easy smile. "Yeah, I'm on tonight. Checking in on the champions all over the east wing." Then he crosses his arms and nods his head in Ivy's direction. "I heard she was here. I don't know why I didn't make the connection that she's your sister, though. I saw on her chart she's dealing with PNH?"

Nodding, I turn so we're both facing away from her, thankful in this moment that her deafness will prevent her from hearing what I'm about to say. Habit has me lowering my voice.

"Gotta be honest, Logan…we're terrified. Dr. Lyons said she needs a bone marrow transplant but she's already in the system and there aren't any matches."

"No siblings that can provide it?"

I shake my head. "Wyatt and I were adopted, and we're not even close to a match. She has two half-siblings, but Dr. Lyons said they're not a match either. So we just have to, what—sit and wait and hope a miracle happens?"

When Logan doesn't respond, I look over and see him lost in thought, stroking his face.

"I might know a guy," is all he says.

I laugh, remembering my own *I know a guy* moment with Remmy just a short while ago.

"You sound like you're trying to get me a stolen car stereo. What does *I might know a guy* mean in the medical world?"

He grins but keeps his eyes on Ivy.

"There's this doctor at the hospital I used to work at in Seattle. He's been gathering patients for a trial with PNH. There's a chance Ivy could be a perfect candidate."

"Are you serious?"

He nods. "They're testing out using bone marrow from partial matches instead of identical matches. So, parents, siblings, half-siblings and cousins with partially matched marrow—"

"Oh my god," I whisper. "Logan, we have to get into that trial. Tell me what we need to do and I'll do it—whatever we have to pay."

Logan puts a hand on my shoulder. "You don't have to pay to be a part of a trial. That's not legal. I'll call him tomorrow and get more details."

A sense of urgency is thrumming through my veins.

"Ben, I always encourage patients and their families to hold on to hope, always, but don't get too hyped up just yet, okay? I don't want you to rest all your hopes on this just for me to come back to you in a few days saying she isn't eligible for some reason."

I grit my teeth but nod in understanding.

"I get it. I do."

We both stand in silence for a second and watch Ivy sleeping. I don't give a fuck what Logan says to me about hopes. I will rest all of my hope on anything that could possibly help her.

Even if I'm left devastated at the end.

Chapter Twenty Three
REMMY

"So what you're saying is that you've found an amazing guy, stood up for yourself, and made choices about your future that you're happy with."

Josslyn looks at me with an eyebrow raised.

"You make it sound like everything is going wonderfully," I reply, tucking myself into the pillow I'm holding to my chest. "And it's not. *Clearly* it's not."

She scoffs.

"Girl, everything is all about perspective. Trust me on this one. Okay, sure, some of the shit you're dealing with is heavy. *Heavy*," she stresses, drawing out the word. "But that doesn't mean you can't see the positives crawling out from among that steaming pile of negative shit."

I make a face. "What a visual."

Josslyn laughs, that deep, full-body laugh that first drew me to her in the first place.

I might seem happier now, but I've never been a very smiley, laughy kind of person. When I first started college and Josslyn was assigned as my roommate, I thought clearly the administrators had made a mistake.

There was no way her carefree, can-do, ass-shaking attitude was going to be a good match for me. I was in a dark place, and I could just feel that Josslyn's light was going to poke holes in my black balloon of unhappiness and self-doubt.

Luckily, she won me over. I say luckily, but I really mean lucky for me. I still wonder why she wants to be friends with my negative, pessimistic ass, but I don't ask questions. I just say a thankful prayer that we stumbled upon each other and that she saw something in me that made her want to stick around.

We're snuggled into bed in one of the upstairs guest rooms. The minute Josslyn and I were alone, she told me it was Snuggles and Struggles Time then led me upstairs.

I've spent several hours vomiting up everything that's been going on over the past few months. We had a lot to catch up on as we haven't talked since I left for my trip to Colombia in May and she moved to Colorado to use her business degree by helping her sister manage the family weed farm.

I told her about the rape. About the pregnancy. About the breakup with Lucas. About Ben's insane proposal. About how we've been bonding, both emotionally and physically. About what Lucas said to me at the hospital. And about the blowup with my mom today.

The entire time she's been watching me enraptured, telling me my life is crazier than a telenovela. Which is true. I grew up watching those with my mother, and the shit that happens in them? Nothing compared to my life right now.

"You get what I'm saying though, right?" she continues.

I roll my eyes and flop down on my back, covering my face with the pillow.

"Everyone has shit. Yes, yours has been...I'll admit, crazier than most, but there are still good things that can come out of those. It's just harder for you to be able to see the positives *while* you're going through the hard stuff."

She yanks the pillow off my face.

"Like when you dropped out and fell off the face of the earth for three months. In all that time, you never would have been able to identify anything positive that might have come from it—but look where it led you," she says, slapping my arm. "You went to Alta Mesa and got this dope-ass degree you never would have considered, and you actually have ideas now on what you want to do with your life. All because some complete bitch was a complete bitch."

I puff out some laughter through my nose but refuse to smile. That might be true, and I might feel thankful that I found Alta Mesa and the inspirational support of Melody Cohen—but that doesn't change how I feel, doesn't change how exhausted I am because of how hard it is to push through shit like this over and over and over again.

It just feels like I can't catch a break.

"I think you need to go back to therapy," she adds, snuggling into her own pillow, her eyes still on me.

I groan.

"I don't want to go back to therapy. I already did it."

This elicits a snort from Josslyn.

"Hate to break it to you, sister, but that's not how therapy works. You don't go, fix all your problems, and then never use it again. I honestly believe everyone should have a therapist all the fucking time. The point is to continually work through things. It's ongoing. And with the second rape, and the pregnancy, and all these big changes in your life…I mean, it just sounds like something that could be really helpful, especially since you acknowledge that it was helpful in college."

We sit in silence for a few minutes.

That's another thing I love about Josslyn. Most of the outgoing people I know feel a constant need to fill time with the sound of their own voice. Josslyn is comfortable with silence, with there being nothing.

Because sometimes, being together is important, but there isn't always something to say.

She gets that.

She gets me.

And it's one of the many reasons I love her.

Eventually, we both start to doze in and out, Josslyn's soft snore an indicator that we'll need to pick this conversation up tomorrow.

She must be exhausted. She said Ben called her on my phone

and then had her on a plane within a few hours.

I grin, thinking about him taking the time to try to figure out what I need in the wake of the conversation with my mom. We don't know each other well enough for him to truly get me, and yet he was still able to get me connected with Josslyn, and in record time.

Glancing at the clock, I realize it's nearing midnight and I don't know if Ben's staying out to give us time or if he's still at the hospital.

When I look at my phone, I see a missed text from him from a few hours ago. Must have been while I was wallowing.

Ben: I'm gonna stay with Ivy tonight, give my mom and Wyatt a break. You and Josslyn doing okay?

I smile. It's a weird thing to realize you're on someone's mind. When Lucas and I were dating long distance, we rarely sent each other messages. If I'm honest, it's because I wasn't thinking about him. I was busy with my own life and my own things.

Here's Ben, very consumed with what's going on with his sister, and he still has me on his mind.

It feels good.

Not because I need him to prioritize me over his sick sister, but because I love that I'm in his thoughts.

Love that he wants us to stay connected.

Me: Things are good. Thank you for calling her. It's been exactly what I needed.

And it has been.

"I'm gonna go sleep in my room, okay?" I whisper to Josslyn, knowing she can't hear me but not wanting to leave without saying anything.

Halfway to Ben's bedroom, I realize I called it *my room*, and I let out a little snort. Clearly I'm getting comfortable here.

I switch off the hall light and close the bedroom door then crawl into Ben's bed, sighing when his familiar scent wafts up from his sheets as I drop my body down.

If he can't be here tonight because he needs to be with his sister, enveloping my body in his sheets is a nice second option to have.

I'm reaching out to the nightstand to click the lamp off when my phone dings again.

Ben: Sleep well, beautiful. You're amazing and strong and brave, and I'll see you in the morning.

Setting my phone back down, I tuck my pillow in close, breathing in deeply and feeling very lucky.

For tonight, I'm able to fall asleep without wondering for even a moment whether I deserve it.

I wake up when I feel a body wrapping itself around me, tensing for a split second of panic until I hear Ben's groggy voice.

"Coming home to you in bed is like some kind of drug," he says, snuggling up against me from head to toes, his arms sliding around my middle and his face nuzzling into my head. "God, I love the way you smell," he continues. "It's that cucumber shit you use, and it's just..."

I hear him inhale and then let out a long sigh.

"How was the hospital?" I ask, wishing there were some way I could look at his face but stay in this same position.

He pulls me tighter. "I slept like shit."

I laugh, twisting in his hold so we're face to face.

He opens his eyes, a lazy smile overtaking his features. His hands come up and hold my face.

"You're so beautiful," he says, then he leans in and places a kiss on my lips.

I snort. "I look like shit."

He hums his disagreement, his eyes narrowing even through his exhaustion.

"I *do*. I never washed off my makeup the other night and then I cried all day yesterday and last night. You're seeing me on day three of unwashed stank."

Ben giggles and kisses me again.

"I love your stank."

He tucks me into his chest, and I take that as my cue to be quiet. Clearly he's exhausted. I've only slept in a hospital one time in my life, the night Mati broke his arm when we were in elementary school. I slept fine, but little kids can sleep in arm chairs with no problems, and I'm assuming that was the only option for Ben last night.

I snuggle with Ben for a little while, holding him close and just enjoying his nearness, until I open my eyes and realize it's after nine.

I give him a little poke and he wakes, cracking one eye to look at me.

"I'm gonna shower and go get breakfast with Josslyn," I say. "Do you want us to bring you anything?"

He shakes his head and turns, stuffing his face into his very fluffy pillows.

I kiss the center of his back then push out of bed, wandering out of the room and over to the guest room.

After I knock lightly, I open the door a tiny bit.

"Morning."

Josslyn's muffled voice comes at me from under her blankets where she's cocooned herself.

"Brunch?"

She flings back the covers and starfishes on the queen-sized mattress.

"You know I'm all about brunchy goodness!"

It takes us about an hour to get ready, each of us taking a shower and spending time to put on our makeup. I don't even try with my hair, though, opting for my signature side braid and a headband.

"Mary's is my favorite," I tell her as we pull into a parking space around the corner from the best breakfast spot in Hermosa. "When I was in high school, our group used to meet here every Monday. We used to call it Monday Mournings and we'd mourn the end of the weekend."

"Ha! That's clever," she replies, both of us climbing out of the car and walking to the front.

"Woah, why is it so busy?" she asks as we come around the corner and find a horde of people outside Mary's. "Aren't weekdays supposed to be slow at the beach?"

I roll my eyes. "Not during the last holiday of the summer."

Her face scrunches up. "What kind of holiday is on a Monda... Oooooh." She points at me, realization dawning. "It's Labor Day."

Nodding, I maneuver through the crowd, leading Josslyn toward the hostess stand. Back in high school, we used to have a reserved table every week, holiday or not. That would be great today.

When I reach the front, I smile at the hostess.

"Wallace. There are two of us. And can we sit outside?"

She nods and writes down our information. "Should be about an hour."

My nose scrunches, but I nod, turning to face Josslyn.

"Remmy!"

At the sound of my name being called, I look over to the patio, my eyes widening when I see it was Lucas.

He's at a table with Lennon.

And Paige.

And Wyatt and Hannah.

Rebecka. Aaron. Ji-Eun. Otto.

I swallow awkwardly, wondering why he would call out to me like that, drawing all the attention my way.

"Is that them?" she asks, her voice quiet.

I nod, not feeling like I have the ability to speak.

My eyes scan the table, noting some eyes looking at me and some not.

"You should at least go say hi, even if it's awkward," she says, and I feel her hand give me a small nudge.

In my mind, I picture a parent trying to scooch her child forward toward potential friends, and it makes this weird noise bubble up in my throat.

"Was that a laugh?" Josslyn asks.

"Kinda."

I take a deep breath and decide to suck it up.

I don't have to spend time with people who don't like me, but I also can't assume people don't like me before they're given a chance to even *talk* to me. If I remember my last night with this group correctly—my first night back in town when I returned to Hermosa in early July—everything was fine.

Everyone was friendly and kind and asking questions about my life in Santa Barbara.

Except for Paige.

Paige who is looking right at me from her end of the table, her expression unreadable.

I shake out my wrists and then walk over, smiling through my nerves.

"Monday Mournings are still a thing, huh?" I say as I reach the table. "After all these years."

"Brunch and booze?" Aaron says, a shit-eating grin on his face. "You couldn't pay me to give it up."

I laugh, feeling the knot in my chest loosen just slightly at Aaron's ridiculous response.

"Everyone, this is my friend Josslyn. She was my roommate freshman year of college and my closest friend in Santa Barbara."

Josslyn waves, smiling her face off.

"Ahhhh, so *this* is who you replaced us with," Rebecka jokes. "I see how it is. And now you bring her here to flaunt her, to rub it in our faces. Thanks a lot."

Titters rise up from around the table.

"Why don't you guys join us?" Lucas says. "We just got here a few minutes ago. We haven't even put our orders in yet."

A part of me wants to say yes, wants to sit down and chat. But I don't know if it's sincere, or if it's just Lucas being...

"We ordered bottomless mimosas."

My eyes fly to Paige's, and I can't hide my surprise.

Her expression is neutral, but I can see a softness in her eyes. Something that looks a bit like...grace.

I clear my throat, looking around at the group, seeing open expressions.

They may not be my best friends anymore, but I don't know if they ever were. I don't think I was ever in a place where I could really have a best friend other than Lucas, who I clung to.

The people sitting here now are years older, years wiser, weathered by some of the bullshit that happens in the world and, for whatever reason, they seem open to welcoming me back.

"You know, today I'm hanging out with Josslyn. She flew into town to surprise me and I want to focus on her, but..." I pause. "Maybe I could come next week." I clear my throat, my eyes flitting around the table. "With Ben."

Wyatt leans forward, his hand still wrapped around Hannah's, and looks me in the eyes.

"Sounds perfect. We'll see you next week."

Chapter Twenty Four
REMMY

"It was so great to see you," I say, wrapping my arms around Josslyn and squeezing her tight. "I just wish you could have stayed longer."

"Yeah, I know—I'm pretty awesome. But three days is really all I can handle with you and the man looking at each other with smoldering eyes all the time."

We both laugh and I step back, slipping back to Ben's side.

"Next time, we'll come visit you," he says, his arm around my shoulders.

I get a flash, a picture in my mind of the two of us and a baby flying out to visit Josslyn in Colorado.

The grin that overtakes my face is massive. All-consuming. And I snuggle into Ben as Josslyn climbs into the back seat of the car he hired to take her back to the airport.

"She's great," he says.

"She is."

I wave as it drives off then turn and take Ben by the hand.

"Speaking of great," I say, "you wanna know what's great?"

He grins, following me inside. "Hmmm?"

"Shower sex."

His eyebrows rise. "I'm gonna say I was not expecting that to be what came out of your mouth, but I'm totally okay with the very dramatic subject change."

I laugh, giggling as I race into the house.

This playfulness with Ben is different than I'm used to. Obviously, everything will be somewhat new with my only relationship comparison being Lucas.

We were kids. We never had the freedom to be playful with our sexuality. With Ben, I feel like I can be open about it, open and willing and so, so, *so* turned on.

Like now, as he catches my hand and pulls me so I'm up against the wall at the bottom of the stairs.

He presses his lips against mine, and I open for him, the taste of him exploding on my tongue as our mouths twist and writhe against each other.

"Before the shower," he says, pulling back and touching his forehead to mine. "I have something I want to show you."

"It can't wait until after?" I say, my voice breathy and needy.

He groans, dropping his hands to my waist and pressing his lips back to mine. I feel his fingers twitch and I wrap my arms around his neck, thinking I've won.

"No, it can't wait," he says, surprising me, and then he pulls back and takes me by the hand, leading me through the kitchen and living room, over to the hallway that leads to the garage and his office.

He stops suddenly, spinning to look at me with a wariness in his eyes.

"We can change anything you don't like," he says. "Just remember that, and the fact that this was worked on only at night when you were sleeping."

My brow furrows.

"What are you..."

But before I can continue, Ben opens the door to the laundry room.

Only it isn't the laundry room. I mean, it is, because the laundry room is inside the garage...but the garage isn't just a garage anymore.

It's...

"An art studio."

My hand drops his and I raise both to my face, covering my mouth as my eyes flit around the room, taking everything in.

He's removed anything to do with a garage, though I honestly don't know what was in here before.

Now, it's filled with sturdy, beautiful wooden shelves, matching tables, a massive easel, a drafting desk, and more supplies than we carried in the entire art store I worked at in Santa Barbara.

I step down into the room, the polished concrete floor cool on my feet, spinning around and getting closer to examine everything.

My eyes snag on what's propped up in the corner.

"I had Dominic bring them by," he says.

Moving to the side, I reach out and begin to flip through my canvases. I left most of them in a small storage unit when I left Santa Barbara, knowing I'd have a lot to explain to my parents if I came home from the school I was supposed to be attending for a business degree with over 200 canvases created at a completely different college.

But I did bring a few home. I've thought a few times about going back to collect them, along with some of my other items. After the confrontation with my mom a few days ago, though...I don't want to go home.

Knowing Ben contacted Dom and he brought them over...

I turn to Ben. "Why would you do this?" I ask.

"Why wouldn't I?"

I pause at that, looking around.

"Isn't that what relationships are supposed to be? You're supposed to think about what would make the other person happy. And if we're really doing this—getting *married*—I can't imagine missing an opportunity to make you smile."

I move toward him quickly, taking the two steps out of the garage—no, the art studio—and barreling into Ben's body.

I'm overwhelmed with emotion. He seems to make me feel that way a lot.

I press my lips against his, feeling a need rising up, an urge to show him how he makes me feel.

We kiss and we kiss as I move slowly forward, pushing Ben

backward and through the door of his study. My hands roam, tickling up his sides and lifting his shirt, a brief shiver racking his body as he raises his arms to let me take it off of him.

Once I feel the carpet under my feet, I begin kissing my way down him, across his firm chest and abs. I drop to my knees, my hands going to the button of his jeans, popping it open and pulling down the zipper.

"You don't have to blow me to say thank you," he says, his eyes glued to me, his breaths coming out in pants.

I tug his boxers and jeans down in one go, freeing his shaft, my hand gripping it hard and giving it a firm stroke.

"I know I don't have to," I reply, and then I slide him into my mouth all at once. No teasing. No taunting. Just wet heat I know will drive him fucking crazy.

His head falls back and his eyes close.

I pull him out then lower my mouth to suck on his balls while I pump him.

He sucks in a sharp breath through his teeth, his hands going to my hair, gripping me as he slowly begins to rock his hips.

"I don't have to," I say again, trailing my tongue along his length. "I'm doing it because I *want* to."

I stroke him firmly, lifting my hand to play with his sac, to twist and tug as I thrust my hand up and down, my hand slick from my spit.

"Because I *need* to."

"Need to what?" he asks, looking down at me, dazed and half out of his mind.

"Need to feel you come down my throat."

He lets out a tortured moan, his eyes slamming shut like he can't handle it as I suck him back into my mouth, adding pressure with my tongue and gripping his ass with my fingernails.

He comes within minutes, his hands tight in my hair, his hips pumping against my face.

I swallow him down, making sure I work him all the way through it until I see him jolt a little bit from sensitivity.

"Fuck."

It's all he says as he slumps slightly, dropping down into his desk chair bare-bottomed.

Grinning, I stand, loving the look of absolutely sated exhaustion on his face.

I step over to him and press a kiss to his forehead, and then his nose, and then his lips. Before I can pull away, his hand comes up and holds the back of my head, his mouth opening, his tongue coming out to twist with mine.

"Is that what I taste like?" he asks me.

I giggle, realizing this might be the first time a guy has ever asked me something like that.

He pulls me back down and continues to kiss me, lifting me up so I'm straddling him on his desk chair.

"We're gonna break the chair," I say, not wanting to move as he kisses my neck and sucks on my skin.

"We're not."

"It doesn't feel sturdy."

He keeps kissing me, his hands holding my face and then working down to my hips before sliding between my legs.

I let out something between a moan and a squeak when his fingers shift my shorts to the side and rub against my center.

"How long have you been this wet for me?" he asks, sliding a single digit inside. "Since you proposed shower sex?"

I shake my head.

"Earlier?"

I shake it again.

"When?"

"I'm always this wet for you. When I think about you, when I'm near you, when I wish you were inside me. I'm...oh my god."

My words get cut off as he slides in a second finger then hooks them to the side, finding that spongy place inside me that makes me feel like all my bones are melting out of my body, leaving me in a puddle of emotions and pleasure.

"Guess what, Remmy?"

I shift my hips, rocking against his hand, not responding.

"I *need* something, too."

My head falls forward, my eyes closed, and I suck on his neck as he continues to finger me, his other hand shifting under my shirt and lightly stroking my nipple through my bra.

"What do you need?" I ask, wanting nothing more than for him to keep doing exactly what he's doing.

But then his mouth comes to my ear and I hear him whisper.

"To fuck you so hard you can't breathe."

Before I have a chance to register what's happening, he's

pulled out his fingers and swung me around so I'm lying on the carpeted floor, his hands removing my clothing with swift ease.

One minute he's yanking my bottoms off, and the next he's inside me, stretching me, holding my wrists in a vice as he rams into me over and over again.

I never knew I needed it like this, swift and hard and angry.

I'm sure if I talked to a therapist about it, there'd be a reason, but for now, I'm just enjoying what continues to be the best sex of my life. With Ben. It feels so good and leaves me breathless.

He pounds into me with relentless energy until my entire body seizes, every muscle clamping down as I pulse with my orgasm then all releasing in one swoop that has me lying on the floor like a rag doll as Ben finishes, pulling out and shooting on my stomach.

"Holy. Fuck," he says, panting and gasping then falling to the floor next to me.

"What is it...with you...and wanting to...fuck me on the floor," I ask, trying to catch my breath.

He laughs. "No idea. I've never had sex outside of a bed before you, so...it's definitely different for me, too."

I grin, liking the idea that we're both experiencing new things together, things that are new for *both* of us. I didn't know if I'd ever be able to have something like that with a man. I never knew it was something that *mattered* to me.

But now that I'm experiencing it, I cherish it.

Ben grabs his boxers and wipes off my stomach, and then the two of us slowly get up and make our way upstairs.

"We still didn't have shower sex," I say, eliciting a deep belly laugh from Ben.

He wraps his arm around my shoulders as we enter the bedroom, yanking me in and pressing a kiss to my lips.

"Good thing we've got plenty of time for that."

The following morning, Ben kisses me goodbye and heads to the restaurant. He told me he has a lot of catching up to do with all the time he's been taking off recently, and I shooed him out the door, assuring him that I understand.

And I do.

Doesn't mean I don't miss having him all to myself.

I spend a little bit of time in my new art studio, examining the materials Ben bought for me, pleased to see he's either done his research or hired someone who did theirs.

Yanking out a blank canvas, I get it set up on the easel and pull out all the paints I want to use.

But before I can start, my stomach grumbles.

At seventeen weeks, my little pooch of a tummy is starting to be a bit more visible, and my hunger has definitely returned in full force.

"Let's go feed you," I say out loud, looking down at my belly button. "Otherwise you're going to be a monster."

I giggle to myself, walking into the kitchen and filling the electric kettle with water so I can make some tea. I'm imagining the delicious bowl of cereal I plan to make when the doorbell rings.

The hairs on the back of my neck stand up, and I turn, wondering who could be stopping by.

For a split second, I wonder if it's my mom, and before I can think better of it, I race over to the door and fling it open.

To say I was sorely mistaken is an understatement.

"Miss Wallace. How lovely to see you."

I purse my lips when I see who's standing there.

"Mr. Calloway. Ben's at work."

"I'm not here to see Ben, actually. I'm here to see you."

I clutch the door, feeling nervous and uncomfortable and feeling guilty about feeling that way.

The guy might be a slime-ball, but he's not going to hurt me, right? He's Ben's dad.

I take a deep breath and let it out, trying to calm my nerves.

"Do you want to come in?"

He grins, looking like a shark who has just captured his prey.

"Thank you. This shouldn't take too long."

I step to the side, opening the door for him and then closing it behind him.

"Can you just give me a second?" I ask, rounding the corner to the kitchen. "I need to turn off the kettle."

"Take your time," he calls after me.

I click it off and grab my phone, shooting off a message to Ben to let him know his dad is here. Everything might be fine, but I've watched enough serial killer documentaries to know that sometimes, you just need to let someone else know when a creepy guy comes to your house.

"You said you wanted to talk to me?" I say, finishing up preparing my cup of tea as Calvin walks into the kitchen.

His eyes wander around the space, probably taking in the stark white interiors.

"To be frank, Miss Wallace, I'm here to ask you what I can give you that will make you end this clearly fake relationship with my son."

I nearly drop my cup. "I'm sorry...what?"

He grins and takes a step toward me.

"We both know whatever is going on between the two of you isn't genuine. There aren't real feelings and emotions. Love isn't a part of the picture. I don't know what my son promised you in order for you to agree to this little game you're playing, but I can promise you my wealth and connections *far* exceed his, and I can almost guarantee I can double whatever he's offered you."

I inhale deeply through my nose, feeling lost and confused and...angry.

I feel angry that Calvin is here trying to buy me, trying to control and manipulate me.

"I don't know what you think," I finally reply, "but the way I feel about your son is genuine. He isn't offering me anything."

Calvin laughs, the sound irritating my insides.

"We both know that's a lie. At the very *least* he's offering you a port in the storm."

I shake my head. "I don't understand what that means, but—"

"It means he's giving you a place to go to hide your *pregnancy* from a family that might be...less than receptive, isn't that right?"

My head tilts back and I square my shoulders.

"Listen up, Mr. Calloway. I don't care what you have to say anymore. You have no right to come in here and make crazy accusations about your son."

He cocks his head to the side, assessing me.

"You know, Miss Wallace, I might have misjudged this situation entirely."

"Great. Let's just call it a day and you can go."

"No, no, no. That's not what I mean. What I mean is I assumed you both came into this from the same vantage point, thought you both understood what you were doing. But what it sounds like to me is that my son has wrapped you around his little finger...and that *you* have fallen in love with him."

My nostrils flare.

"I'm going to say right now that none of this is your business."

Calvin grins at me, looking far too pleased with himself. Then he claps his hands together.

"Alright, well, it looks like I don't have to give you anything in order to get you to end your relationship with my son."

I nod. "Correct. There isn't anything you can give me that will make me not want to be with him. Period."

He tucks his hands in his pockets. "Nothing tangible—absolutely. Although..." He lifts one hand and points in the air, as if he's just had a thought. "I do think there is some *information* you could receive that might change your mind."

I cross my arms.

"Did you know your father owns 51% of Calloway Corporation?"

My angry expression shifts, smoothing out as I finally open my ears and listen to what he's saying.

He nods. "It's true. I don't own the majority share in my own company. A few bad investments—it happens, but I didn't have the assets to dig myself out, and your father...good man that he is...saw an opportunity to save a corporation that would leave thousands of people without jobs if it declared bankruptcy."

My arms fall, my mind tracking back through everything I've ever heard my dad say to me about work over the years. Did he ever mention something like this?

Not that he shares much with me, but...I feel like this is big. This is *really* big. How could this not be public knowledge?

"He kept it a secret as a favor to me, not wanting to worry shareholders or employees. And because he's a good man." He pauses. "Of course, my *son* has been aware of this for quite some time, though I'm not sure how he found out. Regardless, he's been looking for ways to get revenge against me for...well, for some mistakes that were made in the past."

"You mean Krissa," I interject, my irritation with Calvin continuing to grow the longer he talks.

His eyebrows rise. "So he told you! I thought that was something he was hoping to keep a secret—well, as much of a secret as can be had in Hermosa. What is it you kids call it? The gossip machine? There wasn't a lot out there about me and Krissa and Ben, thanks to another large scandal in town going on at the time with the city council, but I wouldn't expect you to remember or care about that since you were away at college at the time."

Gritting my teeth, I move to pass Calvin, hoping I can get him to the door and shove him out on his ass. I don't want to hear any more from him.

Not about him or Ben or Krissa or my dad. None of it.

But he grabs my arm, halting me before I can get by.

"Do I need to spell it out for you, you stupid cow? He only wants to marry you because having you as his wife means he controls your father. Got it? He doesn't care about you at all. All he cares about is getting access to your dad so he can hurt *me*." He pauses and my stomach rolls. "Although if the rumors are true, I'm sure he's heard fucking you wouldn't be a hardship."

"Get the hell out of my house."

My head whips to the side, finding Ben standing in the doorway. My heart sags when I see him, my personal safety more of a concern at the moment than whatever shit Calvin is spewing in my direction.

Calvin drops my arm immediately, giving me a cold smile, then turns and heads for the door. When he comes up next to his son, I can see Ben clenching and unclenching his fists.

"Good to see you, Ben. I'm sure we'll be…talking soon."

It's the last thing he says before he strolls out, whistling something terrifying as he goes.

Ben charges into the room, slamming the door behind him, and before I can even blink, his arms are around me.

"Oh my god, Remmy, I'm so sorry. If I'd known he was coming over…fuck, I'm so sorry."

His embrace is warm, his hold strong, and it would be so easy to snuggle into his arms and just push everything Calvin said to the side.

I want to. I really want to.

Because I was happy. I was *happy*.

I press my face into his chest.

I knew it was too good to be true.

Chapter Twenty Five
BEN

It's been a long time since I've driven that fast. Three days after I got my driver's license, I gave in to some peer pressure and tried to race my new car against Mark Jessup's down PCH.

I got pulled over, got a speeding ticket, and my mom told me I was grounded for two weeks and took away my license for a month. Of course, one of the only times I get in trouble, my mom is ready to roll out the punishments.

Today, though, I wouldn't have stopped for any police lights as I blew through a stoplight and got home in record time.

And when I walked through that front door and found my father with his hands on Remmy?

I about fucking lost it.

He's lucky all I did was shout at him to get the out. I might not be a violent man, but the feelings that raced through my veins in that moment were enough to scare even myself.

My focus was on Remmy, though.

I needed her in my arms, had to make sure she was okay.

The panic inside me is throbbing uncontrollably at the words my dad said as I walked in.

He doesn't care about you at all. All he cares about is getting access to your dad so he can hurt me.

I hate that he told her, because I'm sure it was surprising, but at the same time, I'm thankful. This means there aren't any secrets, no dark hidden corners or skeletons.

His last words, though...

I pull her in tighter against my chest as they roll through my mind.

Although if the rumors are true, I'm sure he's heard fucking you wouldn't be a hardship.

I've always known my dad is a heartless, chauvinistic, pigheaded asshole—but I never thought it would be something that would come into play for anyone other than my brother and me, maybe people he works with.

Those words to Remmy...that was his attempt to take her out at the knees, to hit her as hard as he could where he knew it would cut her the deepest.

Fuck him. *Fuck. Him.*

"God, I'm sorry it took me so long to get here," I say, pulling back and placing my hands on her face, as if by looking carefully enough at her I can be certain she's okay.

I press my lips to her forehead, willing my racing heart to calm, trying to let my irritation and anger go.

But then Remmy steps out of my arms and wraps her own around her waist. It makes her look small and unsure.

"Is it true?"

Her voice sounds wobbly, sad...wounded in a way I didn't know was possible.

"Was the point of you wanting to marry me because you wanted access to my father?"

"I'm...I mean...Remmy, we talked about this, our reasons, before we ever started—"

"You told me," she interrupts, her voice turning hard, her eyes narrowing, "your reasons were private, but that it was mostly to get your mother off your back about who you were dating." She scoffs. "How did I not see that was bullshit? You and your mother aren't even talking. Why would she care about who you're seeing? Or who you marry?"

"Remmy—"

"You used me."

"And *you* used *me*," I reply, my own voice rising, not understanding why she's so angry. "I might not have been entirely honest, but that was about keeping my plan a secret, not trying to keep it from you specifically."

"Bullshit. You manipulated me because you wanted something from me that you knew I wouldn't give you if you asked. So instead of being honest with me, you lied. You snuck around trying to mastermind some...*plan* you thought would allow you to take over your father's company."

My brow furrows. "What? No, I don't want my father's company. I just wanted—"

"What? What did you want? What was so important that you were willing to exploit my pregnancy to get what you wanted?"

I'm so startled by what she just said that my words get locked in my throat, in my mind, unable to be freed as she spins on her heels and bolts from the room, racing up the stairs.

All I can do is follow in her wake and hope once I get to where she is, she'll listen.

But when I get to the doorway of my bedroom, my stomach drops at what I find.

"What are you doing?"

"Packing."

I watch, frozen, as she lifts the clothes she's placed in my dresser and dumps them in her suitcase in one swoop. Then she heads into the closet, pulling out her dresses and other nice things.

I move in between her and the suitcase, blocking her ability to chuck her last bit of clothing in.

"Move, Ben."

"Don't do it, Remmy."

She tries to move around me, the hangers rattling where they hang in her arms, one or two falling out of their garments and landing on the carpeted floor with a muffled clatter.

"Ben..."

"We've talked about this," I interrupt, knowing if I don't do everything I can to convince her, she'll leave. "You've told me about how you solve your problems. You avoid. You cut and run because you hate confrontation, because it makes you feel scared and uncomfortable and weak."

She shakes her head but doesn't move, just keeping her eyes on the center of my chest.

"Don't do that this time," I say. "Don't give up so easily. Because this, what we have...it's special. It's important."

"Important because you want something from me," she says, but her voice doesn't sound as sure anymore.

Shaking my head, I step closer. "That's not fair—at all. I would *never*..." I pause, trying to get my words right, feeling like everything I've tried to plan and prepare for is falling through my fingers. "Remmy, when this started, I thought we were both just two people in fucked-up situations trying to figure out how to solve our problems. If I'd thought for any reason that we'd be here now, that I'd feel...like *this* about you, I would have done this all differently. I can't go back and change it, though. All I can do is move forward from here and try to do the best thing I can for you, for the baby...for us."

"Why?" she says, tears slowly tracking down her face. "Why do you want to do the best for us?"

I step into her and take her face in my hands again, wiping the tears away and wishing I could do more.

"Because I love you," I say, knowing it's the only thing I can say to convince her my feelings are genuine and not just based on her last name. This is my Hail Mary, at best, and I have to hope and pray and wish that it will be enough. "I've been in love with you. With your wild hair and your obsession with Oreos and the ridiculous way you seem to get paint everywhere on your body even when you're fully clothed."

More tears fall, her eyes wide.

"I am *lost* in you, in this terrifyingly beautiful love. And I would give my everything to follow you deeper into the unknown."

Her eyes drop to my lips, and I take that as my cue, pressing mine to hers.

I hear a clatter of plastic as she drops the clothes completely, her hands rising and coming around my neck. My hands drop to her hips and I lift her so her legs can wrap around my waist.

"You really love me?" she says, pulling back to look me in the eyes. "You're not just saying it because..."

"There are plenty of things I might lie to you about," I say, and her face falls. "Whether or not I like a hat you want to wear.

Whether or not your ass is getting bigger because of the pregnancy."

She gives me a tiny smile when she realizes what I'm saying.

"I might tell you I love the idea of moving or putting a pool in the backyard."

She giggles, and my heart soars.

"But I will never, ever, *ever* be lying to you when I tell you I love you."

She rests her forehead against mine. "Good, because I'm in love with you, too."

I let out a long, relieved breath, not having even realized I was waiting for her to tell me she felt the same. Now that she has, I'm overwhelmed by the rush of emotions flooding my body.

This, between us, the realness of it...wasn't anything I ever expected to happen. I assumed what Krissa did to me was going to be enough to keep me from falling for anyone ever again, thought my ability to trust was going to be forever shattered and beyond repair.

Now, I can feel in my bones that that's not true.

What I felt for Krissa wasn't love in the first place, and it certainly didn't hold a candle to what I feel now, for Remmy.

No. What I felt for Krissa was something else entirely.

I think I was in love with being what she wanted, with being the object of her desire and affection. How I felt about her was directly correlated to how she made me feel, which makes sense when I consider my life spent away from women and partying. It was new and exciting and surprising.

But it wasn't timeless.

What I used to believe was love was actually a superficial attempt at finding something meaningful.

Now that I've found the depth of love I feel for Remmy, I can't imagine ever wanting to wade in shallow waters again.

"So, this isn't fake anymore, huh?" she asks, her eyes still tinged with pink from her earlier tears but her mood much higher and happier than before.

I lift my hand and stroke the side of her face, tucking some of her loose hair behind her ears. "No. It's not fake."

"Do you think...it would be crazy if we made it really real?"

My eyes fly to hers and I pull back slightly to get a look at her face.

"What?"

"I mean, why don't we just...go. Go to Vegas or the courthouse or something and make it official. Just you and me. Forever, today, tomorrow—right now."

I chuckle and pull her closer to me so we're snuggled closer together on my bed—*our* bed. Then I kiss the crown of her head where her big bun of messy hair is sticking up and wild.

"I love that idea, but let's still give it a little more time."

"Why?"

"As bad as things are now, I know you love your mom and your family. You'll want them to be there, even if you feel angry now."

She sighs, her breath warm against me, heating me through my shirt.

"And to be honest, I'll want my family there, too."

Her head flies back, her eyes wide.

"I mean my mom, you little nutball," I say, rolling my eyes. "My dad will *definitely* not be invited."

Remmy nods, returning to her earlier position, her head resting against my chest.

But then there's a long pause of silence, and I can tell she has something to say.

"Spit it out. I can hear you thinking."

"How did things get so bad?" she asks, her fingers coming out and tracing along the seam of my shirt. "Was it really the way you told me before? About you and Krissa?"

Shifting us around, I prop myself up on my elbow so I can look her in the face.

"What I told you about my relationship with Krissa and how things happened with my dad...that was all true. The only thing I left out was that I've been trying to come up with a way to knock him down a peg or five. When you started telling me about your own situation, I just instantly jumped to the potential solution."

"Which was?"

"My hope was that by marrying you, I'd simply be a constant

threat to my dad," I say, hating the way it sounds. "It wasn't about taking over his company or getting him kicked out or anything like that. It was simply about making him believe he was no longer the master manipulator and *I* was the one controlling the puppet strings."

Remmy nods, her eyes assessing.

"The thing you have to realize about my dad is that he's spent my entire life teaching me that winning and being in control is the most important thing, that nothing else matters. So when it finally came time to try to knock him on his ass, the only thing I could think of was figuring out how to take away his control, or at least convince him he wasn't top dog anymore."

"Why is he like that?"

I shrug, having thought about it plenty myself. The hours I've spent wondering what force propelled my dad to become so aggressively controlling, so maniacal...ultimately, all that wondering was a waste.

If a man doesn't see anything wrong with his behavior, it doesn't matter what made him that way in the first place. He's never gonna change.

"I don't know what made him the way he is," I answer. "I just know *now* that the last thing I want is to be like him. What kills me the most, though, is that by focusing on him, I threw all my own goals out the window, all my desires and dreams for the future. My plans to build up a culinary empire...I lit them all on fire by staying here and managing Bennie's."

Remmy's brow furrows and she sits up.

"You did *not* throw your life away," she says, her voice strong and firm.

I grin at her, appreciating the sentiment even if I don't entirely agree.

"Thank you, but it's hard not to think about it that way when I consider the fact that I let anger guide my decisions. My plan was to build up Bennie's for the first year and train a manager, and then move on to the next project. But instead, I let myself get distracted by the most cliché thing in the world—revenge."

Remmy stays silent for a moment before speaking, and the minute she opens her mouth, I know she's going to say something important.

"When I dropped out after first semester freshman year, I had a really dark time. My thoughts were trying to convince me that ending things was a better option than staying around for the pain I was going through."

I squeeze her hand, my chest *aching* for her, for what she went through.

"Thankfully, Josslyn was there for me, and eventually I found a therapist to help me work through why I'd had those thoughts in the first place. I realized I felt guilty about those few days, about the emotions I'd felt, wondering why I was so weak that my mind couldn't seem to manage life just like everyone else was."

Her hand reaches out and touches my chest, right over where my heart beats steadily for her.

"But in therapy, I learned to *forgive* that version of myself, for everything she'd been through that made her feel like that was the only choice. I learned to forgive her, and embrace her, and love her, to thank her for the hard work she did to crawl out of that hole in the ground so I can be this version of me today. I think that's what you need to do, too. If you only focus on the potential life you think you threw away, you'll never truly be able to enjoy the life you're building now. You have to forgive that man, the man who sacrificed his dreams for revenge, who was clearly in a lot of pain and scrambled to find a way to manage it the only way he knew how."

I place my hand over hers on my chest, overwhelmed by her words, by the way she sees things so differently than I do, and yet so clearly.

Because truly, this might be the first time I've been able to reflect on the past few years and actually acknowledge the points she's making.

I *was* in pain.

I *was* scared.

I *was* angry and overwhelmed and lost.

And I did what I thought was best at the time.

It's okay to admit that the choice I made was the wrong one. Right?

Admit it was wrong, and then be better *today*. Choose better *today*. Refocus my energy on something more positive *today*.

"Josslyn suggested I try going back to therapy, and I'm thinking it's a good idea," Remmy says, regaining my attention. "Maybe you should consider it, too?"

I nod, knowing she's right but still feeling too overwhelmed to respond, my mind brimming over from everything Remmy just said.

"You okay?"

"Yeah," I say, my voice low. "Yeah, I am."

We go back to a comfortable silence, our bodies still snuggled together, both of us enjoying each other's company and basking in the simplicity of what our love means.

"You sure you don't wanna run off to Vegas?" Remmy whispers, eliciting a chuckle from me. "I'm totally cool with wearing something off the rack. It doesn't even have to be white, you know?"

This girl.

"You deserve a real wedding, Remmy," I reply. "Something you get to think about and plan and be proud of, not some hasty thing we've rushed to put together. We're not a secret, and we're not temporary. Let's take our time."

I can *feel* her roll her eyes.

"Why do you have to be so logical?"

"I'm just built that way. I guess you could say it's one of my many superpowers."

She pulls back and looks at me, her eyes light and full of mischief.

"Do you like super*heroes*?" she asks.

I clear my throat. "I mean, I'm a little confused about the change in subject, but yes. As you like to point out frequently, I'm a bit of a nerd. I am very connected to the Marvel Universe."

Remmy beams at me. "We should totally roleplay in superhero costumes."

I snort. "Is everything about sex with you?"

Her smile never wavers. "Duh. Have you not heard about my reputation? Even your dad has heard of me."

Narrowing my eyes, I flip her around so she's lying on her back.

"Pulling my dad into this conversation is too far."

She giggles and tugs me down so I'm hovering over her, my face inches from hers.

Then she licks her lips and bites her bottom one.

"You know, I could get used to this."

"What?"

"Playful sex. Silly sex. It's never been like this before, fun and ridiculous and goofy and…"

"You think we have *goofy* sex?" I ask, knowing I'm baiting her.

She rolls her eyes, her hands rubbing up and down my shoulders and biceps.

"I think we have *great* sex. I'm just saying it's different. With you it's so different from how it's ever been before."

"I think it's pretty great, too."

Remmy swats my arm. "Well, duh. You were practically a virgin before me—of course it's going to be amazing. Sheesh, there's so much for me to teach you."

I sigh, dropping my head.

She takes my cheeks in her hands and lifts my face back up so I'm looking into her eyes—her beautiful fucking eyes that I know I'm never going to get enough of.

"You know I'm joking, right?"

I nod. "Of course I do." I pause. "Besides, the only thing you were faking was our relationship, because I know it definitely wasn't the orgasms."

She bursts into laughter and I raise my fist in the air, knowing I've won this round.

"Oh my god, I love you."

I grin at her. "I love you, too."

I give her a long, hard kiss, the kind I'll get to give her every day for the rest of our lives, and I hope she feels it as deeply as I do.

Chapter Twenty Six
BEN

"You're sure?" I ask as I park the car. "Because if you change your mind, I can take us home right now."

Remmy grins at me. "I'm sure. I've actually been looking forward to today."

"You have not."

Her smile falls. "Okay, maybe I'm petrified, but hey…" She pauses as I laugh. "At least I'm trying, right?"

I nod, taking her hand in mine and kissing her knuckles.

We both get out, each of us in jeans and casual tops, and we walk down the road toward our brunch destination.

Mary's.

She told me about the Monday Mournings invitation. I know Wyatt's been doing this shit since he was in high school, but I've never been invited or wanted to attend.

Hell, even now I don't want to attend, but it seems important to Remmy, to spend time with the people she was friends with when she was younger, to see if they are people she wants to continue friendships with now as she starts to rebuild a life for herself here.

When we walk up to the entrance, we bypass the hostess, Remmy leading the way as we walk hand in hand over to the long table in the corner of the outside patio.

We're not the last ones to arrive, but we're not the first either. Lucas and Lennon are already here, and so are Paige and Hannah.

"Hey," Remmy says, her voice soft as she comes to a stop next to an empty chair. "We're still good to join in this morning, yeah?"

There's a pause, a silence for a moment that makes me wonder if I need to get Remmy out of here as quickly as possible.

But then I hear it, from the far side of the table.

From Paige.

"Absolutely. We're glad you're here."

Remmy bites her lips nervously, nodding before taking a seat one over from Hannah, leaving a spot open for Wyatt. I take my spot next to hers.

"Where's Wyatt?" I ask.

"He's coming. He just said he wanted to swing by and drop off something for Ivy first."

I nod. I've been much more firm about being on the steady rotation for Ivy at the hospital over the past few days. It gives me a chance to chat with Logan, who said he's gotten in touch with his buddy at Seattle Children's and is waiting for a packet to get delivered full of tests and other paperwork Ivy will need to complete before they can know if she's a good fit for the trial.

I haven't mentioned any of it to my family yet, mostly because I want to manage their emotions like Logan said we should. I know my hopes are set on this trial, but I don't want to disappoint Ivy if it doesn't pan out.

"I'm gonna swing by today and drop off some flowers for her," Paige pipes in. "Maybe play some card games or something."

"That's an awesome idea."

"Do you think your mom would have a problem with me going?" Lucas asks. "I know she's had some opinions about..."

"No. You should absolutely visit. Spending time with Ivy and helping to keep her upbeat and happy is the priority, not anything my mom has said about"—I wave my hand—"anything. You're her brother, too, and she needs all the love she can get."

He gives me a small smile then returns his eyes to the menu.

"He's just parking," Hannah says, looking at her phone then up at me. "Wyatt, I mean."

I nod. "Hey, weren't you guys supposed to go on a trip?" I ask, realizing I never heard about the week in London that had to be rescheduled because of Ivy's hospital stay.

Hannah grins at me.

"We're leaving in a few days. Wyatt said he was going to talk to you about time with Ivy to make sure…"

"Whatever it is, I'm there," I interrupt. "You guys deserve a trip, and I love my sister. I'll handle it."

It's hard not to feel good when Hannah beams at me, her smile radiating across the table like the sun.

"Will you be back for the fundraiser?" Lennon asks, drawing all of our attention to where she sits quietly next to Lucas.

"Oh I'm pretty sure that's the plan. We're only supposed to be gone for a week."

Lennon's relief is obvious, her shoulders dropping and her smile reappearing.

When her eyes connect with mine, she explains.

"Events like these fundraisers are *always* filled with friends of my mother's, and it will be helpful for me to have some of my own friends there so I have people to look at when I'm doing my speech." She shudders. "I hate standing up at the front."

Lucas drapes his arm across her shoulders. "Why don't you practice it for everyone?"

Her cheeks blush. "Maybe later."

Wyatt chooses that moment to drop into a seat next to mine, giving me a grin that says he's exhausted.

"Give me the dates you'll be gone," I say before he even has a chance to bring it up. "I'll make sure Ivy's taken care of."

He squeezes my shoulder, a familiar sign of affection from him when he's unable to express his gratitude.

Over the next fifteen minutes, the conversation ebbs and flows as more of my brother's friends join us, a handful of people I recognize but whose names I couldn't come up with even though I've been introduced to them in the past.

Whenever I look at Remmy, she has this odd look on her face. For a little while, I worry about it.

Until she turns and looks at me, smiling.

"You okay?" I ask.

She nods, her eyes returning to look out over the group of people at the table with us.

"It's just a weird feeling, you know?"

"What is?"

"I never thought I'd have anything like this again—a group of friends." Then she places her hand in mine. "It's just an idea I'm adjusting to."

I lift her hand and kiss the knuckles, knowing in that moment that I need to get her a ring, something I didn't do the first time around.

"New can be good," I say. "Relationships can be good. There is a lot of good still coming your way in life, Remmy. Don't doubt that."

She grins at me. "I'm trying not to."

I want to tell her it's the same for me, want to say that before her, I didn't know what my life would become, if I'd live it alone or end up finding somebody to share it with.

Now, I know exactly what my life is going to bring me.

Smiling. Laughter. Happiness.

And so much love I can hardly stand it.

But I can't tell her any of that. Not yet, at least.

Before I can say any of that, I have a few stops to make.

Remmy is putting her love and trust in me, and I'm going to give my everything to make sure I never stop deserving it.

Even though I've interacted with the man a handful of times in my life, I still feel like I'm meeting someone new for the first time when I'm walked into his office at Wallace Media.

Robert Wallace is a force to be reckoned with, absolutely, but he isn't my dad's peer in the business world anymore.

He's my girlfriend's father.

Or my fiancée's father.

Either way, he's the protective dad of the woman I want to spend the rest of my life with, and it's hard to see him as anything other than that as I approach him.

Robert has a massive smile on his face and rounds his desk to shake my hand before motioning to two arm chairs facing each other in the corner.

"Come, sit with me. I was just about to take a break for some coffee this morning."

At that very moment, the door to his office opens again and a young man pushes in a coffee cart, coming to a halt a few feet away from where Mr. Wallace and I take a seat.

He shifts in his chair, his long legs stretching out in front of him as he adjusts his jacket and tie.

"Andrew, I'll have my usual. Ben, anything for you?"

I smile. "I try to stay away from caffeine as much as possible."

"I have a pot of decaf," Andrew says.

"That would be great. Black, please."

He begins preparing our drinks, and my attention shifts back to Remmy's father.

To the reason I'm here.

"So tell me, Ben, what can I help you with today?" he asks, folding his hands so they settle across his stomach, his position lazy and comfortable.

Clearly a man in charge.

"I'll get straight to the point, Mr. Wallace—"

"Bob."

I lift the corners of my lips. "Bob, I'd like to ask Remmy to marry me, and she's hinted to me—well, told me bluntly, actually—that it's important to her that I ask you for your blessing. So," I finish, spreading my hands, "that's why I'm here."

The smile on Bob's face drops a bit, but he sits in silence, just watching me.

It unnerves me slightly.

I've always liked Bob. From the things I hear about him, he's an honest man, a hard worker, the type of guy who believes his company should be ethical from top to bottom. In essence, he's the complete opposite of my father.

But the way he's assessing me now? That's not the businessman. He's shifted his view of me just as I did with him.

I'm no longer a peer's son or another business owner in town.

I'm the man with a shitty reputation who wants to marry his baby girl.

A coffee appears on the small table that sits between us. I sit forward, picking up the cup and lifting it to my lips, blowing softly before taking a sip.

It scalds my tongue, like coffee is supposed to do, and I take another sip.

"Mariana told me you two were...*seeing* each other, but I didn't realize things had gotten so serious."

Bob accepts his own coffee from Andrew, using the spoon that rests on the saucer to mix whatever is inside the cup.

I nod. "To be completely honest, Bob, everything between us happened rather quickly. But, I can assure you that how I feel about your daughter is *very* serious."

He shifts in his chair, leaning to the side a little and resting his chin in his hand.

"My wife likes to avoid town gossip, you know," he says, slowly stirring his coffee. "It's her Catholic upbringing, all that stuff about proverbs and slander. I don't always subscribe to the same ideas she does. In business, you have to know who you're dealing with, so choosing not to pay attention to the things being said about the people I work with would be foolish. So, for the sake of honesty, I'll be honest with you as well." His gaze turns firm, his eyes narrowing. "I've heard a few things about you that make me wonder what kind of man you are, Ben, and it makes me question if you'd be the right person to marry Remmy, if you'd do right by her and the baby."

My eyebrows rise and Bob's face slips back into something easy as he lets out a small chuckle.

"Oh, yes, I know about the pregnancy. I know *most* of the things about my kids that they think they're hiding from me. I have a pregnant daughter who changed schools and got an art degree, a gay son with a boyfriend who works as a bartender at The Wave, and another son who busts his ass working for me even though he wishes he could lead guided treks through the mountains."

I'm shocked at Bob's words but work hard to control my facial expressions.

"Mariana and I look at the world a little bit differently. She has some...fairly specific ideas of what she thinks will make our kids happy. Her background guides her views on morality and decision-making, but..."

Bob pauses, then leans over and grabs a picture off a shelf to his left. When he hands it to me, I see a picture of a very young

Mariana and Bob holding a very, very tiny baby.

"That was Jasmine."

My eyes fly up.

"She was our firstborn. Spent three months in the NICU fighting for her life after being born too early." He shakes his head. "We never got to take her home from the hospital."

I feel my chest tighten as I listen to him speak, my own emotions welling up as I imagine how scary that must have been at the beginning, how heartbreaking at the end.

"Like I said, Mariana and I look at the world differently. She has specific ideas about how to make sure our kids live their best lives. She thinks she knows what's best for them." He shrugs, his eyes looking off to the side, something wistful coming over his face as he thinks over whatever brief memories he has of his first-born daughter. "If I learned anything from losing Jasmine all those years ago, it's that we have to appreciate every moment with our kids, even if we disagree with their choices. All I want is for them to be healthy and happy, whatever that looks like."

I take one more sip of my decaf and settle the small mug into the saucer that still sits on the table. Then I rest my elbows on my knees, leaning forward, prepared to pitch myself as the best thing for Remmy's happiness.

But Bob lifts a hand, keeping me silent.

"Having said that, I don't necessarily think you would make my daughter happy. As such, I can't give you my permission to marry her—not until you prove a few things to me."

I nod, realizing that, as friendly and kind as Bob can be, he's still a man who is used to getting his way, and that means I might piss him off.

Because I have no intention of listening to him.

"You know, Bob, I can respect that. Completely. But I'm not here asking for your permission. I have every intention of marrying Remmy, regardless of whether or not you approve. I love her, and she isn't a piece of property that needs to be given to me by anyone other than herself."

Bob's eyes narrow and I see a tick in his jaw, but he remains silent, just watching me.

"I came here to ask for your *blessing* because I know it means something to Remmy. Even in the face of worrying that her parents would kick her out of her home and banish her from the family if they found out she was pregnant, she still values your voice and support in her life, still wants to know you stand behind the decisions she's making for her future."

At that, those hard eyes soften, and I watch as the father replaces the businessman in the chair across from mine.

"I am going to work my ass off to be an amazing husband to Remmy, and a much better father to this baby than my dad ever was to me. I would love to have your blessing on our marriage because what makes Remmy happy is what makes *me* happy." I pause. "But I also know I can make her happy with*out* your blessing. All due respect, sir, but I don't intend on letting anyone's opinions get in the way of giving her everything she wants."

"You think you can give her what she wants?" he asks me, his voice easy and smooth as he sits forward and rests his arms on his knees, mirroring me and linking his fingers together. "What is that exactly?"

I smile, imagining Remmy at her happiest, that brilliant smile shooting out of her like it can't be contained.

"An art studio in my garage so she can paint her emotions. A home where she feels happy and safe. A husband who cherishes her every step. A partner who will love this baby just as much as she does. A supporter who encourages her dreams. A man who treats her with care and respect. A friend who makes her laugh." I shrug. "I might be someone who has made a lot of mistakes in my life, but I can give her those things."

There's an extended pause where Bob just sits across from me, unmoving, unblinking.

Until he blinks rapidly, over and over again.

And that's when I realize what I'm seeing.

Bob Wallace is fighting back glassiness in his eyes.

"You know, Ben, maybe you *are* the right person for my daughter," he says, sitting back in his seat and putting his chin up, a move that reminds me so much of Remmy when she's trying to be brave and sure even when she's not.

"I *know* I am."

At that, he grins.

And then he stands.

I follow suit, pushing out of my chair and stepping toward Bob as he extends his hand to me.

"You have my blessing, son."

I squeeze his hand.

He squeezes mine right back.

"Thank you, sir," I say. "I'm happy to hear it."

He nods his head and I take it as the dismissal it is, turning to head for the door.

"Oh, and Ben?" Bob calls after me.

When I turn to look back, he has a serious expression on his face.

"I know there was...an incident between my wife and Remmy a little bit ago at your house, and..." He pauses, thinking things over. "Can you just make sure Remmy knows no matter what, both of us love her and she's *always* welcome to come home?"

I grin, happy to know reconciliation between Remmy and her mom is a lot nearer than I had anticipated.

"Will do. But with all due respect, sir, her home is with me."

Bob chuckles lightly. "I guess it is."

Chapter Twenty Seven
BEN

Everything.

That's what Ben makes me feel when he looks at me.

Once, there was a man who told me I was nothing. For too long, I allowed that man to control my life, even though he wasn't anywhere near me.

I won't allow that any longer.

The painting on my canvas is a reflection of what I feel today. Content.

Usually, I paint when my emotions are too big and I don't have any true outlet. For so long, my emotions were a jumbled mess full of big, scary things I could never fully work through or understand.

So I just assumed my aesthetic was dark. Angry. Murky sadness displayed in images of storms and closed doors.

I didn't realize I was even...*capable* of painting something like this.

It's a similar picture to the storm painting I was working on for a few weeks before I angrily bathed the canvas in broad black strokes from my brush.

A beach. The shoreline with clouds in the distance.

But the previous image was all dark blue water with white caps from raging wind, blacks and grays filling the sky with a distant storm.

This image is serene water with lapping waves and pebbled sand, pale blue skies with patchy clouds just barely hiding the sun, beams of light in reds and oranges and yellows shooting out from behind them.

The palettes are completely different, the emotions they evoke nowhere near the same.

One is violent and angry and fearful.

The other calm, peaceful, hopeful.

I'd love to show this to Melody at some point and see what she thinks, see if she would still encourage me to go to graduate school knowing my talent is swayed so severely by emotions.

And honestly, I'm okay with knowing that.

I'm fine with accepting that what made me talented as an artist was the darkness that made me feel worthless and out of control. The world is filled with tortured artists, right?

But I would choose how I feel now over artistic talent any day.

"That's so beautiful."

My head turns at the sound of Ben's voice, and I can't help but bite my lip at the sight before me.

He stands on the top step at the entrance to the art studio, leaning against the door frame, wearing nothing but a pair of sweatpants. His feet are bare, as is his chest.

I left him wearing slightly less than that when I crawled out of bed at six this morning, overwhelmed with emotion and needing to let it out somehow.

Spinning my chair fully around, I stand, stretching out my back, my arms lifting over my head.

"It's not even close to done yet, and I'm not sure I like it."

Ben drops down the three steps and comes over to where I stand, wrapping his arms around me from behind and resting his chin on my shoulder, our faces side by side as he assesses my work from a closer vantage point.

"What don't you like about it?"

I let out a long sigh, not really sure how to answer that. "I don't know. It's just...different."

"Different, how?"

I place a kiss on his cheek and then step out of his embrace, walking over to the corner where my favorite canvases are neatly organized. Pulling out three, I lean them against the wall so they can all be seen.

"See?"

"See what? More examples of how talented you are?"

A little thrill rolls through me at knowing how much he likes my work, but I shove it aside.

"They're completely different. You don't see a theme?"

"Of course I see a theme," he responds. "They're darker. Moodier."

"Better."

He scoffs. "No, not better. I might not be an artist, so I will never be able to look at artwork and say what other people can or should value in a painting. Trust me, my mother was beyond irritated at my commentary when we went to a few art galleries together when I was a child."

I can't help but giggle at the image that conjures, a young Ben at a gallery pointing at things and being loud with Wyatt.

"But Remmy, you're incredibly talented. Sure, you spent your college years working within one kind of theme, probably because that was the lens through which you viewed the world."

He walks over to the painting I started this morning, his eyes bright as he motions to it.

"This painting? It's gorgeous. It makes me feel calm and happy. Maybe that's your new shift, you know? It's just a little rebranding. Companies do it all the time."

Rebranding.

Huh.

I never thought about it like that.

"Your art is a reflection of who you are," he continues. "If you're trying to see the world and your life differently, it only makes sense that your focus would shift, that you might adjust your lens. It doesn't mean you're losing your *talent*."

I grin, appreciating the time he's taking to be encouraging and supportive.

"I love you."

He smiles back at me.

"I love you, too."

Ben places a kiss on my lips, his hands framing my face, and I can't help but wrap my arms around him, enjoying the feel of his body pressed against mine.

"I'm taking you on a date tonight," he says. "So be ready at five for a bike ride."

We pedal down The Strand at a leisurely pace on our date night, enjoying the late afternoon sun and cool breeze. It's a Friday evening a little bit before sunset, so a lot of people are out and about, strolling, running, skateboarding, rollerblading, walking their dogs.

It's been a long time since I've ridden a bike, so I mistakenly wore a dress I had to tie together between my legs so it doesn't fly up and show my lady business, or get stuck in the gears.

"They're doing the volleyball tournament coming up soon," Ben tells me as we get closer to the pier, his attention focused in the distance, where construction workers are beginning to set up structured bleachers around a sand court.

"I completely forgot about that. I used to love coming down here with Mati and Dom when we were kids."

My brothers, tasked with watching me since I was only a kid and they were a few years older—still kids, but hey, that's parent logic sometimes—wanted to watch the athletes jumping around in the two-piece swimsuits beach volleyball women wear.

Well, Dom wanted to watch. Mati just went along with it.

"One time, we were seated in the bleachers and they weren't paying attention, so I snuck all the way down to sand level. I was actually sitting next to the coaches, watching the game." I chuckle thinking about it. "I don't know if I realized I wasn't supposed to be there or not, but I definitely found out for sure later."

"What happened?"

"A friend of my mom's was watching it on TV and saw me sitting there by myself, called her up to laugh about it. My brothers got in so much trouble for letting me wander off."

Ben laughs. "That's funny. I've actually never watched one of the matches before. We should go to one together this year."

Grinning, I reach my hand out to him, our bikes side by side for a second, and take his hand in mine.

I love letting my mind think about the future now. For a lot of my life, the future was a topic or concept I avoided at all costs. It required that I make choices I didn't want to make.

It feels different now. I'm *excited* about thinking on future things, all the experiences I get to have with Ben for the first time as we learn more about each other.

Like today. Earlier, he told me about his love for cycling and how he does it nearly five or six days a week. I didn't know that before, and now, there are decades ahead of us where I'll get to learn about all the things that make Ben tick.

Eventually, we make it to the pier, both of us shoving our bikes into a rack and locking them together.

Ben looks at his watch and I take a second to untie my dress. "Wanna walk down to the end? Our reservation isn't for a little bit."

I nod and he takes my hand in his, the two of us strolling down the length of the wooden pier.

"I haven't been out here in a long time," I say, taking a deep breath in. "It's amazing how being down here completely changes how the ocean smells. It's like...more powerful. More full."

"Completely. There's nothing like the smell of the beach."

"Do you enjoy living in Hermosa?" I ask, realizing I've never heard him say anything about it. "You don't seem like a beach guy, and you originally planned on leaving."

Ben shrugs. "I don't *not* enjoy it. Sure, I might have been happier somewhere else at one point or another. I really did enjoy moving away for college, but I don't know if I have ever really pictured myself living anywhere else." His head turns to the side. "What about you? Are you going to be happy being here?"

I take a second to think about my answer before I respond, feeling like, for me, it's a little bit more loaded.

When I moved away to college, I picked somewhere far enough for independence and freedom, but close enough to still come home regularly if I wanted to. I chose a place with enough similarities that I didn't feel like I was in a completely different world

It's along the coast, so the landscape is very similar: the same kinds of palm trees; same coastline; same bits of brown, dehydrated mountains in the distance.

But there's a feeling here I can't really describe that makes being back in Hermosa Beach feel unlike anything else. Maybe it's a certain smell, or just the rush of memories. I can't really place it.

All I know is that I spent years running away—from the people, from the expectations—years that I wasted, clearly.

Because even through the uncertainty and emotional ups and downs I've experienced since being back here, I still think about it as coming *home*, as being back where I belong.

"Yeah," I finally say, keeping my answer short and sweet, a smile creeping onto my face. "I'm really glad I'm here, with you and back near my family, even though things aren't perfect. It's home."

Ben tugs me closer at my answer, wrapping his arm around my shoulders, our long strides matching step by step until we finally make it to the end.

Piers in the South Bay are deceptively long. Once you get to the end and you're standing on what feels like the edge of the world, the ocean looks even bigger and more intimidating than it does when you're along the shore.

He stands behind me for a few minutes, his arms wrapped around my front, his hands resting softly against my lower stomach in a gesture of love for this unborn baby that has my heart melting into a puddle.

"What time's our reservation?" I ask. "Do we have time to watch the sunset?"

I see his hand rise in front of me as he looks at his watch.

"It's 6:45 and our reservation is for 7:00. Let's walk back."

"Bummer," I say, spinning around wrapping my arms around his middle. "Nothing sounds better than just standing here with you."

He snuggles me closer, ignoring his own suggestion about walking back, giving us a few minutes to just enjoy the sun as it drops in the distance, the handful of clouds giving just enough coverage to paint the sky in oranges and pinks.

"You know, I had a plan for this," he says.

"Mmhhmmmm." My mumbled acknowledgment is hummed quietly as I continue to stare off into the distance.

Ben pulls back slightly, drawing my eyes up to his.

"I had a whole plan, a dinner reservation and candles and soft music."

My brow furrows.

"Huh?"

And then he steps back even farther...before dropping down on one knee in front of me.

"Remington Wallace," he begins, and I can't help it when my hands fly to my mouth, my eyes wide. "Tonight I had a plan for how I was going to do this, because I like plans. I like when I have things laid out so they make sense for me. But, I'm starting to see that sometimes, scrapping the plan and going with something completely different can be the best thing in the world. When you came into my life, just a short while ago...I thought I had a plan then, too, thought I'd mapped things out perfectly. I'm going to be honest—you blew it to shreds."

I let out a soft laugh.

"But I've never been happier, choosing to leave behind 'the plan' and instead welcome something new and beautiful and better than I ever could have imagined into my life."

He reaches out for one of my hands and I quickly place my left palm in his.

"I never could have planned for you, for the type of happiness you bring to my life, for the way it makes me feel to make *you* happy. God, that smile is my favorite thing in the world."

When I smile at him, he points at my face.

"That smile, right there. Remmy, I want to spend the rest of my life making you smile like that, loving you with everything I have."

And then his hand drops to my stomach, the heat from his palm warming something inside of me.

"That goes for this little baby, too. I can't wait to be their dad, to make sure they know how loved they are, give them the best chance at being happy and healthy and so overwhelmed with love that we embarrass them to death."

I giggle, but it fades off quickly as he continues, my soul overflowing with love and gratitude for this man who has completely overtaken my heart.

"Remmy," he continues, his hand dropping to his pocket and emerging with a tiny blue box. "I want you to be my wife on this unplanned, unmapped life, on this crazy journey into the unknown. I can't imagine anyone else standing at my side. We were both lost when we started this thing together, but every day that I'm with you, I feel found. If you spend your life with me, I will never let you get lost again. I will spend *my* life searching for you in every moment, in every blessing, in every piece of happiness."

He opens the box, revealing a beautiful ring, a princess cut diamond sitting on a white gold band. Simple and elegant and gorgeous.

"So, I'm going to ask you my third question," he says, and my heart pings at the reference to our previous conversations. "And it's the most important one. Will you marry me?"

At his final words, I drop down on my knees in front of him, bringing my face level with his.

"Nothing in the world would make me happier than to be at your side. Yes, I'll marry you."

He grins, taking the ring out of the box and slipping it onto my finger.

I examine it for a second, something shifting in my mind before I look back at him, at the man I'm going to spend the rest of my life with.

Ben leans forward and presses his lips to mine in a soft kiss, something delicious and slow and sweet.

When we talked about the future before, I couldn't ever see it, could never imagine what it would truly look like for the two of us to be together, married, with a child.

Now, as he wraps his arms around me and I hear the distant applause of some of the other people watching the sunset on the pier, I can see it.

That future.

The two of us, together. Doing all the crazy shit that happens in life.

Chasing after a toddler.

Going on trips.

Making breakfast together on the weekends.

Spending Christmas with our families.

I'm going to give my everything to Ben when I become his wife, and in return, I'm going to be getting more.

So, so, *so* much more.

REMMY

"You look beautiful," Ben says for at least the third time so far this evening.

He looked a little bowled over when I came down the stairs in a sweeping gown with a deep V and a small train. It was the exact reaction I'd been hoping for.

"I know I decided to go with a maternity dress, but I didn't realize just how *maternity* it was," I reply, adjusting the fabric around my middle.

At twenty weeks, it's not realistic for me to smuggle my tummy around anymore, so I decided it was time to lean into it. Celebrate it. Stop keeping it a secret.

But that doesn't stop me from being self-conscious about the way my body is changing, growing larger every day.

Ben grabs my hand then replaces it with his own, his palm flat on my stomach where our son or daughter continues to float around, nestled safe and warm inside of me.

"You look *perfect*."

I look up at the man who makes me feel like a beauty queen even on the days when I feel like a swollen hippo.

"*You* look perfect," I reply. "I look like I'm smuggling a watermelon full of snacks into a movie theatre."

"I don't...know how to respond to that?" he says, his voice tilting up at the end in confusion.

I giggle. "Don't worry about it." Then I lift up on my toes and press a kiss to his lips. "I'm here and I'll get through the night even though these shoes are killing me. They really should tell you not to wear heels when you're pregnant."

"It makes you look like a badass, though," he says, a mischievous gleam in his eye.

It's weird. I always assumed my body in its best shape was what men wanted, which is why I've been getting nervous as my stomach has continued to grow, wondering how Ben will respond to my changing form.

But the sex has been *amazing*, especially since I'm at the part of pregnancy where I'm pretty much only one of two things: nauseous or horny.

Ben is always quick to help with either.

"Oh my gosh, Remmy, you look *gorgeous*."

We turn to where Hannah and Wyatt are approaching us, both also dressed in black tie.

"Thank you. So do you," I reply, taking in Hannah's long, pale pink dress with a hint of the roaring twenties.

"I'm assuming if you're wearing that, you're sharing the pregnancy?" she asks, her eyes twinkling as they glance to my baby bump.

I rest my hand on it and nod. "Yep. It's just one of those things. I can only hide away for so long, you know?"

Hannah laughs. "You look like you're absolutely glowing. Did I hear correctly that some congratulations are in order?"

I bite my lip and nod, sticking my hand out for Hannah to see my ring.

Ben's proposal was...absolutely perfect, and when Hannah asks about it, I give her the bare bones: that he proposed on the pier at sunset.

I don't dive into it too deeply.

There's something important to me about keeping that

moment to myself, knowing it was shared between just the two of us.

It was beautiful, and I love that it was *real*. If he'd tried to do something like that back when we first decided to pretend to get married, it would have been horrible.

But his proposal was everything I didn't even know I could dream of.

Afterward, we walked hand in hand back to Bennie's. Turned out, he'd reserved the entire rooftop, organizing music and candles so he could propose in the spot where he technically first proposed the idea of marriage.

He told me he'd wanted to do it over, but it ended up beyond perfect at the pier.

At dinner that night, he told me about his conversation with my dad. I was shocked. I can't believe he got *my* dad to give us his blessing. I actually cried, mostly about my dad, but also a little bit about my mom.

My mom is stubborn, just like me, and she is a conflict avoider, just like me. I definitely come by it honestly. Now, there's a baby I'm making public knowledge, along with the engagement.

It's hard to know there's a rift between us right now, and there's a lot we will need to work through. It will take one of us being willing to take the first step if we want to mend things. I'm not there yet, but I'm hoping to get there soon.

I know we will be able to reconcile things between us. I just have to give it some time.

Hannah sees someone in the distance and steps off to the side, which is when Ben steps closer to Wyatt and lowers his voice.

"How was London?" he asks. "Everything go okay?"

I look to Wyatt and watch him let out a long sigh as he rubs his stubble, he and Ben looking so much alike in this moment. Then he shoves a grin on his face as if nothing is wrong, though I could clearly see the opposite.

"I'll tell you about it later," he finally replies, patting Ben on the bicep twice before giving me a small wave and heading off in the direction Hannah just went.

Ben glances at me, his eyebrows raised.

"Well then," he says. "Let's go find our table."

I follow him through the crowd, my hand in his as we move toward table twelve.

When Lennon brought up the fundraising gala she's in charge of at brunch last week, Ben piped in to ask if it was too late to RSVP. Apparently he got an invitation and wanted us to attend.

It's been a long time since I've been to a large society function filled with politicians and big money families, and it took me a few days to get to a mental point where I felt prepared for it.

But tonight, even with this growing bump, I feel excited to be back in town for the first time.

I love Hermosa Beach. I always have. And staying away because of my emotions and fears and sadness...it always felt like a tragedy, like I was giving up on something important to me.

So being back, being out on the town with my fiancé on my arm...it feels good.

It feels right.

Ben pulls out my chair and I take a seat, assessing the other faces around the table.

"Have I met you before?" I ask, looking to a gentleman sitting across from me.

"Remmy, this is Dr. Logan Becker. You met him briefly at your prenatal appointment. He's also the doctor who's helping me get things with Ivy situated."

My eyes widen. "Oh my gosh, that's right. I've heard so much about what's going on with Ivy and the clinical trial—thank you for all your work on this. I mean, I'm assuming you'd do it for any patient, but as someone who cares for Ivy, thank you."

He grins. "I'm glad I've been able to get her connected."

Ben has been spending a lot of time at the hospital with Ivy. Dr. Lyons is hopeful that she'll be able to go home soon, but there isn't a specific date, and they won't release her into home care yet for a bunch of different medical reasons that I don't understand.

I can't imagine being thirteen and just cooped up in a hospital bed all the time, so I make sure to go by with Ben when he visits her. I'm still nervous about going alone, just because I don't know sign language, but I'm working on it—one of those online courses.

That's my life right now: sign language, hospital visits, and painting in the studio as often as I can.

I haven't decided officially what I want to do with my life just yet. Melody thinks I should go into art therapy, and that's a real consideration.

But I also want to focus on this little swimmie once I give

birth, so I'm allowing myself the chance to be patient and decide later.

"Hey fam."

Paige's voice cuts through my thoughts as she takes a seat next to Ben at the table.

"I was sitting with Lucas, but I thought I'd come over here and check out this crazy-ass ring I've been hearing about," she says, her eyes bright.

It feels like another olive branch, another opportunity to mend bridges and fix fences, for us to move past our past and find calmness in our future.

I'm not sure I'll ever be actual friends with Paige, but I can still appreciate what she's doing.

I stick my hand across Ben so she can give it a looksee.

"You two are engaged?" Logan asks.

"We are," Ben replies, a big smile on his face. "We haven't set a date yet, but it will be sometime after the baby comes."

Logan nods, his eyes straying to Paige for a second before returning to me.

"Congratulations."

Before anything else can be said, a voice comes out over the loudspeaker, and we all turn our heads to the front, where Lennon stands with a smile on her face.

"Welcome everyone!" she says, her voice calm and collected as she surveys the large crowd. You'd never know how nervous she is. "It has been an absolute honor to coordinate the celebration of the 50th anniversary of the Bernard J. Roth Preparatory Academy!"

A polite smattering of applause echoes throughout the courtyard.

Lennon launches into her welcome speech, which sounds almost exactly like the one she tested out on us two weeks ago at brunch, with a few minor changes.

It's beautifully written and does a great job of touching on history and contemporary moments in time.

But I can't help but tune her out as I turn to look at Ben.

"I love you, future Mrs. Calloway," he whispers, winking at me.

I grin back at him. "I love you too, future Mr. Wallace."

He rolls his eyes. "That's not how it works."

"You could be a Wallace. It would be very feminist of you."

"Would it make you happy?" he asks, leaning forward, his face inches from mine. "I'll do it if it makes you happy."

I wrap my arms around his neck, my eyes taking in the beautiful face of the man who loves me.

"*You* make me happy."

"And I'm going to keep making you happy for as long as I'm alive."

"You better."

And then he presses his lips against mine.

More stories will be coming in the Hermosa Beach series in Spring 2021!

Acknowledgments
FROM THE AUTHOR

If anyone had asked me a few years ago if I thought I'd be writing my seventh book right now, I'd say they were absolutely crazy. And yet here we are!

This book has been an absolute passion project from the very beginning, and there are several people who supported me through the process who deserve my undying gratitude.

My husband, **Danny** - always my first and foremost. Your unyielding support and love and belief in me... your willingness to beta edit... the constant chocolate supply you keep for me when I'm in the writing cave... you truly are the best husband in the world. My own romance hero. As I've said before, it is because of you that I believe happy endings exist. Thank you for giving me *your* everything.

To my family - **mom, dad** and **sister**. Even though you don't read my books (understandable considering the level of sexiness within these pages) your belief in my abilities and your constant encouragement is always appreciated. Thank you for being my cheerleaders!

To my sweet **J-Crew** and to **The Jillybeans** – I wouldn't be able to get through a release without your support, your feedback, your desire for the next book. Thank you for surrounding this book and raising it up to the eyes of the masses.

My editor, **Caitlin** - thank you for helping polish this baby up. I was so proud of how much less I used the word 'that' this time around, and I hope you were, too! Your work is exceptional, and I'm so thankful to have you as a part of my release process.

The amazing **Becca** - who knew that our past together in Evanston would circle around to you 'working' for me again?! Your guidance to make sure my characters accurately reflect people tied to Colombia and Medellín is so appreciated. Your touches helped their experiences and reactions feel authentic and true. I love you to death, and hope to visit you in Colombia... soon!!!

And to some of the amazing women that live life with me on this fantastic island - **Cam, Jess, Kristy, Melissa, MaryLou, Dawn**, and **my Bunco ladies**... thank you for every opportunity you've taken to give me wine, ask questions, go on walks, ask more questions, and basically give me not only a place to talk about what's going on in my #authorlife, but also a myriad of chances to step away from it when I need to. All of you are incredibly important parts of my life.

To the **bloggers** and **readers** who have been reviewing this title, and every other title - the people who keep coming back for more. I write for you. It's *because* of you that I'm able to have a career. So *thank you.* Truly. From the bottom of my heart.

Lots of love, and smooches,
Jillian

About the Author

JILLIAN LIOTA

Jillian Liota is a southern California native currently live in Kailua, Hawaii. She is married to her best friend, has a three-legged pup with endless energy, and acts as a servant to two very temperamental cats. When she isn't writing, she is traveling, reading a good book, or watching Harry Potter.

Always.

To connect with Jillian:

Join her Reader Group
Sign up for her Newsletter
Rate her on Goodreads
Visit her on Facebook

Check out her Website
Send her an Email
Stalk her on Instagram
Add her on Amazon

More Titles
FROM JILLIAN

The Keeper Series
The Keeper
Keep Away

The Like You Series
Like You Mean It
Like You Want It

Hermosa Beach Series
Promise Me Nothing
Be Your Anything
Give My Everything

Cedar Point Series
The Trouble with Wanting
The Opposite of Falling

All books are available on Amazon, Kindle Unlimited, and for sale through www.jillianliota.com

Made in the USA
Las Vegas, NV
28 December 2021

39694651R00182